MW01069127

PAPYRUS

Also by John Oehler

Ex Libris

Tepui

Aphrodesia

PAPYRUS

John Oehler

CreateSpace

This is a work of fiction. Names, characters, places, and incidents either are the product of the author's imagination or are used fictitiously, and any resemblance to persons, living or dead, businesses, companies, events, or locales is entirely coincidental.

Copyright © 2013 by John Oehler
All rights reserved.

The AMAZON BREAKTHROUGH NOVEL AWARD logo is a trademark of Amazon.com, Inc. or its affiliates.

Cover design by Dorothy Oehler

ISBN-13: 9781479221639

PRINTED IN THE UNITED STATES OF AMERICA

Dedicated to my wife, Dorothy

ACKNOWLEDGMENTS

The main events in this story take place in 1983. Thanks to Conoco Inc., I made many trips to Egypt in that and preceding years, and all the locations I describe are faithful to that time. Except perhaps for the Hotel Princess Cleopatra, which may have been gone by then but where my wife and I stayed during a ten-day sojourn on our honeymoon in 1968.

The ancestries of Tiye and Tutankhamun have been debated off-and-on for many years. In my shelves of books and articles, the best treatment by far, in my opinion, is *Tutankhamen* by Christiane Desroches-Noblecourt (New York Graphic Society, 1963). I want to thank her for her scholarly but highly readable work which, despite other opinions and so-called evidence to the contrary, has stood the test of time.

Dr. Alexander Badawy, at UCLA in 1966, taught the first two courses I took in Egyptology and turned me on to the significance of Queen Tiye. I'm sorry he did not live to see *Papyrus* published.

I thank my long-time friend, Nick Harris, who gave my first completed manuscript of *Papyrus* to his mother, then a vice president at Bantam. And I thank her for her initially crushing but sage reply, "Tell him to take a course in creative writing."

In early versions of this story, David was the hero. It was Robyn Conley, an author and book doctor, who pointed out what should have been obvious to me, namely that this is Rika's story. Thanks to her insight, I rewrote everything from Chapter 1 to the end and, I think, made it a much richer story.

Don Peck, former chief pilot for Conoco Inc., explained to me how a Gulfstream G4 is flown, from take-off to landing, as well as the aircraft's in-flight capabilities. What I learned from him now occupies a whole chapter in *Papyrus*.

Claire Brunavs of *Jane's* (the military intelligence publisher) found the perfect landmine for my story's needs, the Soviet-made MON-100. She sent me the description from *Jane's Mines and Mine Clearance* along with a photograph and cut-away diagram. This is how Rika knows so much about them.

Rick McLemore, an instructor in mixed martial arts, taught me the moves that Rika makes in hand-to-hand combat situations.

Dr. Joy Dobson gave me valuable advice on medical matters portrayed in the story. She, my brother Bill, Douglas Yazell, and Dorothy Stevenson also gave me thoughtful reviews of the manuscript.

Papyrus was my first novel. It went through countless rewrites over many years as my writing skills evolved. For tremendous help in refining the story I sincerely thank my former and current critique partners: Chris Rogers, Stacey Keith, Marcia Gerhardt, Marty Braniff, Jack Thomas, Rick Nelson (now sadly deceased), Bill Stevenson, Vanessa Leggett, and Rebecca Nolan.

Most of all, I am eternally grateful for my wife, Dorothy, the woman I married in Kathmandu more than forty years ago and who continues to be the best thing that ever happened to me.

PAPYRUS

EIGHTEENTH DYNASTY

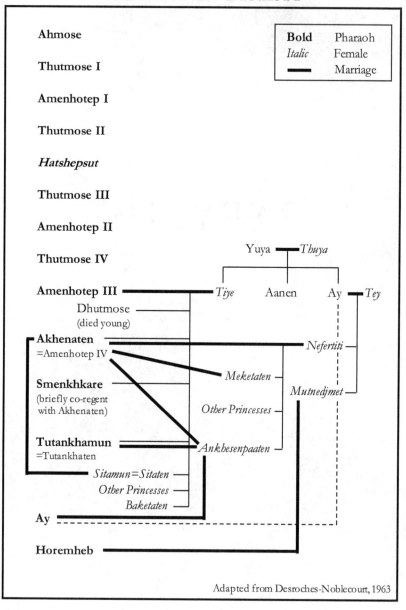

Adapted from Desroches-Noblecourt, 1963

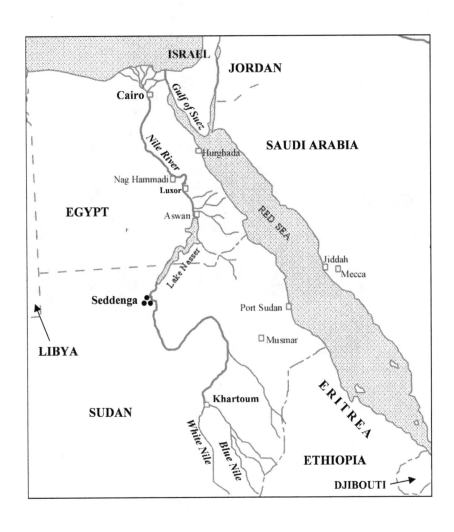

Prologue

Eighteenth Dynasty

From her palace in the City of the Globe, Queen Tiye summoned her elder brother, Ay, to inform him of her decision. She received him at midday in the water garden, dismissing her youngest child, the boy whose coronation name would be Tutankhamun.

"I am guided by the divine light of Aten," she said when they were alone. A desert breeze riffled the ponds, and Aten's face reflected in a thousand sparkling smiles upon the lotus flowers, the papyrus stalks, the red colonnade surrounding her tranquility. "My tomb shall be in Nubia, at a secret location in the land of our fathers."

Trembling, Ay knelt before her.

She knew his fear but did not share it. For the Sun Globe steered her course. "When my time is come, you will bury me in a bath of restorative oils. It will be done while the breath of life is still in me."

Ay raised his face, eyes pleading.

Gently she laid a hand on his shoulder. "Beloved brother, I have spoken."

Chapter 1

1977

As daylight broke above Eritrea's eastern peaks, Rika Teferi wrestled the steering wheel of a Zil stake-bed truck and scanned the sky for MiGs. This was the most dangerous time of day, low sun angle, long shadows easily spotted from the air. She and her squad should have laid up under cover half an hour ago. But they were so proud of their catch that they'd voted to press on. Now they were almost home.

Bouncing over rocks, she led the small convoy of captured Ethiopian military vehicles along a dry riverbed flanked by gray limestone cliffs. The truck's cab stank of cheap cigarettes, and the muscles in her arms ached with fatigue. But soon she'd be able to bed down in her own little corner of the caves.

To signal the sentries who no doubt had her in their sights, she held her sniper rifle out the window, shaking it triumphantly in the cold mountain air. A kilometer farther on, she trundled up onto the bank, halted under a patch of thorn trees, and hit her horn.

Like a dam bursting, the cliff face erupted, pouring out village members from a dozen camouflaged openings. With whoops and cheers, men and women swarmed over the two Zils. Children banged the sides of the armored personnel carrier and clambered up to dance on the prize trophy, a Soviet-built T-55 tank.

"Rika," Alem shouted. Out of the melee, her younger brother

surfaced at her window, sporting the perpetual grin that endeared him to everyone, especially the teenage girls. The week-old wound where a bullet had grazed his neck still showed pink against his ebony skin. "We also got a Zil. And ten cases of rocket-propelled grenades."

"Excellent." Captured arms were the lifeblood of Eritrea's battle against enslavement.

"But a tank!" Alem stepped back to look it over, then opened her door. "How many soldiers?"

"One. And six wounded." She hated taking a life. Her stomach for it had never developed after the first time when, at age ten in their old village, she'd had to use a wood-splitting hatchet to stop an Ethiopian soldier about to dash little Alem's head against a boulder. Now a sharpshooter, she usually aimed for the thigh or shoulder where destroyed bones guaranteed permanent retirement from battle, thanks to the miserable medical care most Ethiopians received.

Climbing down from the cab, she saw a ragged girl, maybe six years old, poking her finger into the shiny bullet holes that snaked across the truck's door and driver's-side mirror. As always, when they had to move vehicles in daylight, the exterior mirrors—even if shattered like this one—were folded in to prevent reflections that might attract Ethiopian MiGs.

"Stand back, watch your hands," she told the child before slamming the door.

"Come on, they're calling for you." Alem pulled Rika into the crowd around the tank, where her second-in-command stood in the driver's hatch telling their story.

Cries of "Well done" and "Good job" swelled Rika's heart. So too did the beaming face of Faven, the pretty subordinate she'd been training to be a marksman and who last night had lamed her first Ethiopian.

Now a young man renowned for his poetry climbed up to stand among the children atop the tank. Eyes blazing, he launched into a proclamation of imminent victory over the Soviet puppets in Addis Ababa. Faven gazed at him with undisguised adoration.

But they'd already been out here too long. The sun was climbing, warming the crisp African air and threatening them with exposure to the enemy.

Though their narrow canyon was well-protected from Ethiopian ground troops, it remained vulnerable to air attack. So rebel forces here, as elsewhere in the highlands, lived their daylight hours in subterranean towns hewn from rock.

Cutting off the poet, Rika shouted, "Let's continue this inside."

She and the other drivers returned to their vehicles. Starting her engine, she glanced up at the crystalline sky. Another beautiful day—to be spent underground.

It was then she noticed the little girl studying herself in a triangular piece of glass. It matched a chunk missing from the Zil's mirror, probably dislodged when Rika slammed the door. *Oh, no.* The girl sat on a rock, her back to the sun. How long had she been sitting like that?

With a chill, Rika searched the sky for aircraft. Clear. She hopped down from the cab and jogged to the child. "No, you can't use that out here."

"It's mine." The girl clutched it to her chest. "I found it."

"Take it inside." Rika turned the girl toward the caves.

As the child scampered off, someone yelled, "MiGs!"

Rika looked up to see two specks aligned with the riverbed and diving fast. *The mirror.* In a sprint, she caught the girl, snatched her in her arms, and dashed for the nearest entrance. "Run to your classroom."

Pushing past others who were crowding into the caves, Rika rushed back to the Zil. No time to move it now. She heard the tank's engine turn over and saw black diesel smoke billow up from its exhaust vent. Faven shouted at a crying boy trying to crawl down from the turret. Rika vaulted onto the tank, grabbed the boy, and handed him down. "Quick! Get him inside."

The turret started rotating. Downstream, the MiGs leveled out barely two hundred meters above the ground. A strafing run, she thought, until she saw the bombs hanging under each wing. *No!* People were still scrambling for the caves.

She ducked under the tank's 100-millimeter cannon as it rose toward the oncoming jets. A million-to-one chance, if it was even loaded. But she knew the turret-mounted machinegun was loaded.

She climbed up behind the machinegun, swung it around, and ratcheted back the cocking arm. With the gunner's hatch closed, she had to slide her legs along either side of the stubby gun mount and lie on her back.

Gripping both handles, she picked a spot several hundred meters in front of the MiGs and opened fire, spraying back and forth in their flight path. The heavy gun rattled in her hands, spewing hot brass out the top as it sucked the ammo belt in one side and flopped it out the other at ten rounds per second.

One MiG leapt upward to the right, its wings rocking erratically. The pilot ejected. But in that same moment, the second MiG released its bombs.

For a heartbeat, Rika couldn't tear her eyes away. Like two fat sharks, the bombs came at her, undulating slightly as they closed for the kill.

Sheer terror broke the spell. She pushed out from under the machinegun, rolled off the lee side of the tank, and dived between the treads of the armored personnel carrier.

Rifle shots. Rika twisted around to see Faven tracking the MiG on full automatic as the last villagers veered around her. "No, Faven! Run!"

With a deafening roar, the bomb-dropper streaked past. An instant later the ground shook. From the point of impact, flaming napalm arced out in a tidal wave of liquid fire, flooding earth and sky.

Instinctively, Rika covered her head. Between the steel treads, she felt the searing heat and smelled the sickening sweetness of jellified gasoline. She gulped a lungful of air against the threat of asphyxiation.

Then she heard the screams.

#

In the quiet efficiency of their underground hospital, where survivors barely moaned, those first screams still rang in Rika's ears.

Forced out of the operating room by two nurses wearing white facemasks, she watched stubbornly through a window in the double doors, willing herself not to cry. Her khaki shorts and shirt were stiff with dried blood from victims she'd helped carry. The three who might yet live lay on canvas-draped wooden tables as doctors peeled away charred skin and applied salve under bright lights powered by a generator droning somewhere in the distance.

Faven was not among them. What remained of her lay in a different room, with the four others who had burned to death. Her name meant "light," but her blackened body had only been recognizable by the rifle still clutched in one hand.

Eight casualties. Wracked with guilt, Rika slunk back through cold, brick-lined corridors to the cubbyhole that served as her room. For the next few hours, she sat on her cot, head in hands, the stink of incinerated flesh clinging to her. Had Faven tried to emulate her? Would the eager understudy have done something so foolish if she, Rika, had not fired on the MiGs with a lowly machinegun?

Five dead, three horribly disfigured. And the blame lay not in her slamming the Zil's door and dislodging the piece of mirror, or the little girl's sitting with her back to the sun. Both of those were accidents. The root cause lay in her own leadership. None of this would have happened if she'd waited until next evening to bring her squad home. It didn't matter that they'd voted. She was in charge, and she should have known better.

Alem called to her through the curtain covering her doorway, then stepped inside with a plate of freshly fried injera pancakes, the sourdough staple of Eritrean meals. "Have you eaten anything?"

Not since yesterday evening. But the rich, yeasty aroma she normally loved brought a knot to her throat. She waved away his offering.

"I have a plan," he said, setting the enameled metal plate on the floor.

She eyed him guardedly. No longer the pudgy little boy who loved being tickled, Alem had become a rebel's rebel. He often infuriated his commanders by striking out on unauthorized missions with a few of his friends. But tales of his daredevil exploits delighted the children, and she'd seen more than one elder nod approval.

"Their forward airbase." With a wicked grin, Alem knelt in

front of her. "It would take us only a week to get there. The MiGs never fly at night. Two of my friends are expert with rocket-propelled grenades, and you and I can pick off anyone who tries to save the planes. In ten minutes we can destroy the entire squadron."

Worse than reckless, Alem's plan verged on suicidal. She was about to reject it outright and forbid him to go when redemption flashed in her mind.

She sat up straight, her pulse quickening. If successful, the strike could deal a crippling blow to enemy morale. It would show the generals in Addis Ababa that their most expensive equipment was vulnerable. It might even be enough to bring them to the negotiating table. If that were the outcome—and she helped achieve it—she could stand at the foot of the five new graves and feel something akin to peace.

Faven's face came to her in a mist. *Do it for us.*

Rika gripped Alem's shoulders. "We'll do it."

Adrenalin surged through her. She pictured the hated jets exploding on the tarmac, soldiers dropping under the unerring fire of her German sniper rifle.

"Rika." Grim-faced, their elder brother, Efrem, towered in her doorway. "Come with me."

Efrem, head of the family since their father had died under Ethiopian interrogation, was a senior commander in the Eritrean People's Liberation Army. His orders were obeyed.

Expecting a humiliating reprimand from her superiors for not hiding the captured vehicles until nightfall, she stood, tucked her bloodstained shirt into her shorts, and followed Efrem to the operational command center.

At a steel table surrounded by wall maps sat two gray-haired members of the Politburo. And her mother.

A shiver swept up Rika's back. Was she in deeper trouble than she'd thought?

"Sit down," one of the parliamentarians said, gesturing with the stump where his right hand had once been. Rika didn't know his name but did know he was Party chief in a town about fifty kilometers away. When she'd seated herself on the folding chair facing them, he leaned forward. "We have taken a decision.

Tomorrow you will leave Eritrea."

Her muscles tensed. How was this possible? No one had ever been banished from—

"We have enrolled you in the spring term at University College in London."

"What?" She jumped up. Efrem put a hand on her shoulder, but she slapped it away. "That's insane. I won't go."

The man with one hand sat back. "This is not a request. You are not free to refuse. It's an assignment, to prepare you for a higher purpose."

Confused now, as well as shocked, she turned to her mother.

Once beautiful, her mother had become as haggard and thin as most other Eritreans, thanks to Ethiopian confiscation of food relief. She was blacker than Rika, without the admixture of Italian blood that came from Rika's paternal grandfather. Head draped in a green shawl, her mother nodded stoically.

Rika threw up her hands. "I don't understand."

"Sit," the man with one hand told her. When she complied, he said, "This is an honor. You and six others have been selected to obtain university degrees. In preparation for forming the nucleus of a new government that will rule Eritrea once we gain our freedom."

It took several seconds for her to digest this. The war had been going on for sixteen years, the first shot fired on the day she turned five. So far as she was aware, they were no closer to independence now than back then. "Have there been victories I don't know about?"

"No." The second Politburo member, a paunchy fellow she knew only as The Professor, rubbed bloodshot eyes behind his thick glasses. "But we *will* win. And when we do, we will not have a government run by military officers. It will be run by trained intellectuals. If you succeed in your studies, you will be one of them."

"Minister of Culture," Efrem said from behind her.

"Culture? What do I know about culture? I'm a fighter."

"That has not gone unnoticed, especially today." For a moment, the man with the stump looked wistful, as though he'd really prefer to keep her here, in the field. Then his eyes hardened.

"But you are capable of more."

"You have uncommon intelligence," her mother said. "Rare aptitude. And you have read every book we have on African history, from the pharaohs up to this genocide we face today."

"So what?" Rika demanded.

Her mother bestowed a sympathetic smile. "History is vital. When we win, we will leave our caves and rebuild our country. The foundation of any worthy society is an appreciation of its heritage. It will be your job, my daughter, to bring that knowledge to our people. To give them pride in something other than armed victory." She paused, then added, "If it is any consolation, I am leaving, also. To bolster our aid efforts in Oslo."

That, Rika could understand. Her mother, although too old to fight, had a preacher's way with words. And Scandinavians were major contributors of medical supplies to Eritrea's cause.

But she, Rika, was not too old. As a warrior, she was in her prime. Yet no matter how rationally Rika pleaded, her mother and the one-handed man took turns in a maddeningly logical, double-barreled assault that destroyed her every argument.

Close to tears, she tried appealing to her mother's heart. "Don't my wishes matter?"

"From each according to his ability," Efrem recited.

Rika whirled on him. "Ability? Where was your consideration of my ability when you promoted a less capable *man* to squad leader before me? Twice!"

"That was different."

Bastard. She turned again to her mother. "I won't do it. I couldn't stand to be away for four years."

"At least six." The Professor scraped back his chair and stood, weighing in with a frown that said he'd had enough. "Once you have achieved your baccalaureate, you will proceed to a doctorate, preferably in another European country to gain broader exposure."

Her fingers went cold.

"Only doctoral degrees are globally respected," he said. "For the new government to be accepted among the community of nations, respect will be essential."

She felt like an insect being sucked dry by spiders.

"We must all make sacrifices," her mother said.

"But this—"

"This," hissed the man with the stump, "is far less of a sacrifice than eight other people made today."

Chapter 2

Six Years Later – 1983

Something was wrong. Sliding the papyrus aside, Rika stood from her desk, the only surface she'd bothered to clean in this tiny office on the second floor of the Cairo Museum. Crowded with wooden cabinets, dusty crates, and glass-fronted bookcases, the office smelled of mouse droppings and old paper, more like an attic storeroom in some English country school than a workplace for serious research. But at least she had one large window. If only it would illuminate the deeper meaning of this document on which she'd staked her future.

She stretched to relieve the tension in her back. Honking traffic outside her window, usually background noise, suddenly grated like biting into tinfoil. Why couldn't Egyptians drive without honking?

And why did Tiye's writing seem so utterly banal?

The Sorbonne would never grant a doctorate for a mere translation of third-rate literature. If that's all she could tease out of this papyrus, she'd have only two choices: find another thesis topic, or quit. The former meant at least two more years of homesickness, made worse by having to work on a subject not nearly so dear to her heart as Queen Tiye. The latter meant she would return to Eritrea a failure, one more casualty of the never-ending war for nationhood. Both meant defeat.

A knock interrupted her thoughts. Probably the tea boy on his three o'clock rounds. He'd let himself in.

She ran a finger over the margin of the baffling document. A foot wide, two feet long, and as smooth as vellum, Queen Tiye's last and longest papyrus was unadorned with the colorful figures common to most royal papyruses. Even the Sun Globe at the top, with its hand-tipped rays blessing the text, was penned entirely in black, like the columns of hieroglyphs below. From this style alone, she felt it could not have been recorded by a court scribe. Yet it was addressed to Tiye's youngest son, King Tutankhamun.

In Paris, she'd come across a 1936 translation. Inept, in her view, but sufficiently intriguing to convince her the flowery language was allegorical and, in studying the original, she would find justification of her passion for the queen, proof of her contention that Tiye, a black African of humble origin, had given birth to one of the greatest revolutions in history.

But even in her own translation, too many passages seemed pointless, almost contrived. Glancing at her stack of notes, she felt, surely, Tiye's final message to her last son had to be more profound than a mixture of poetry and standard praise formulas.

The knock came again. She turned. Obviously not the tea boy. And none of the museum staff ever called on her, a lowly graduate student. Curious, she crossed to the door and opened it.

A European man blinked, then grinned. No, not European. American, to judge from the full cut of his sport coat and his typically American, perfect teeth. A head taller than she, he was handsome in a rugged sort of way, with sun-streaked hair and brown eyes that looked pleased at what they saw.

"May I help you?" she asked, mildly flattered by his reaction.

His hand went to his neck, as if to adjust a tie, although he wasn't wearing one. "I was looking for something, and one of the guards sent me here."

A guard would. They knew if they disturbed any member of the regular staff, they'd get their heads bitten off. But she was temporary, a foreigner, and a woman. Opening the door a little wider, she shifted her weight to the other foot. "What are you looking for?"

"The Narmer Palette."

Interesting. Not a usual item on the tourist agenda, which

seemed to entail a headlong dash through the Tutankhamun exhibits and little else. She felt half-inclined to simply give directions. But a break would be welcome. She'd reached an impasse with the papyrus, and only forty-five minutes remained until the closing bell. Besides, Narmer's Palette was one of her favorite pieces, a landmark in African history. "Come with me."

At a brisk pace, she led him down the Grand Staircase to the main floor. Skirting the Great Hall with its monumental statuary, she took a side corridor, passing two dimly lit display rooms before turning into a third, where she stopped at the tall glass case in the center. There, among a jumble of minor pieces, stood a slate tablet the size and shape of a small arm-shield. She swallowed her disappointment at how little regard the museum seemed to have for some of its finest treasures. "Here it is."

He scrutinized it through the glass, then walked around to peer at the other side. "It's more impressive than its photos."

"You've studied it?"

"Only in a history class. I understand it symbolizes the first union of Upper and Lower Egypt." Turning to her, he smiled and extended his hand. "I'm David Chamberlain."

"Rika Teferi." His grip was cool and firm, his calluses as hard as hers had been in Eritrea. The kind of hands that could be strong and gentle at the same time. Summoning her best English, she said, "Yes, it records Narmer's victory over the kingdom in the Nile Delta. But that's not the main reason it's important. Its greatest significance is that it marks the beginning of the god-kings. Narmer's claim that Pharaoh was a god formed the basis of a political system so powerful it lasted almost three thousand years."

David Chamberlain let out a low whistle, then furrowed his brow. "But the Sun King, that pot-bellied fellow out there in the main hall, he didn't claim to be a god, did he?"

"Akhenaten?" She narrowed her eyes, surprised a tourist would know such a thing. Perhaps he wasn't a tourist. If not, then what? "You must have paid close attention in your history class, Mr. Chamberlain."

"Please, call me David."

Yes, American. First names already. "You're right. Akhenaten's reign was a short break in the tradition. But it was the closest Egypt ever came to utopia."

"Utopia?" He arched an eyebrow as if disputing her assertion.

Rika rose to full height. "More utopian than most countries today. Under him, class boundaries disappeared. Human rights flourished. Government became more open. Official documents were written in the spoken language, instead of the old courtly formulas. Even art was more honest, as you saw in Akhenaten's statue. What did you say ... 'pot-bellied?' Effeminate is a better word, with his wide hips and narrow shoulders. No other pharaoh dared to have himself portrayed so truthfully. Or to create such a free society."

"A visionary," David said, the challenge now gone from his face.

"Not him. His mother, Queen Tiye, was the revolution's architect. At least that's what *I* believe." A belief still based on circumstantial evidence—no thanks to the papyrus—and on what disparagers in Paris belittled as wishful thinking. "I may be the only person who thinks so."

David stepped closer. "Is that what you're working on, here at the museum?"

"Trying to." She caught a whiff of male perspiration, unnervingly provocative after months of social drought. "It's my research for a doctorate at the Sorbonne."

"You sound like it isn't going well."

The understatement brought a sour taste to her mouth. She should wrap this up and quit for the day. But his look of concern seemed to tap a need inside her, the need to talk to someone who cared, even if his care was superficial.

"It's more difficult than I expected. I came to Cairo four weeks ago, thinking Tiye's last papyrus would be the key, especially since she wrote it to Tutankhamun." Rika lowered her eyes to the Narmer Palette, buried among lesser artifacts like the wisdom she'd hoped to find within the inconsequential prose. "Now I'm not so sure."

"You're working on a message to Tutankhamun?"

"He was Tiye's son. The one who became pharaoh after Akhenaten. The papyrus was found in his tomb."

"That's fantastic!"

She couldn't help smiling. Nobody in France, and certainly no one here, had ever acted so excited about her work. Was he really interested, or just chatting her up as a prelude to asking for a date? The intensity in his eyes suggested the latter. But that might not be all bad. On impulse she asked, "Would you like to see it?"

"The papyrus? I'd love to."

With a new lightness in her step, Rika led him out of the room and down the corridor. "I think Tiye is the most underrated woman in history."

"How do you prove such a thing?" He strode beside her, his heel falls echoing off the stone walls. "I don't mean to pry, but I'm a scientist, and I have some experience promoting contentious ideas."

She stopped. "What kind of scientist?"

"Remote sensing. Gaining information about the earth with various airborne sensors. I'm here to fly a survey for an oil company. I got in this morning, and when my meetings finished early, I decided to come here." He brushed aside a lock of hair that had fallen across his forehead. "I've always loved archaeology."

Briefly she wondered if there might be oil in Eritrea. So far as she knew, no one had ever looked. But then who would take the risk with a war going on?

"Anyhow," David continued, "if I have my way, we'll be using a technology that took me two years to get people to accept."

"That's how long I've been working on *my* theory." Ever since her studies of Eritrean history took her back to ancient Egypt, its commerce with black Africa, and the African commoner who married Pharaoh and revolutionized an empire.

Feeling encouraged by David's triumph through persistence, maybe even a faint bond, she took him back up the stairs and into her office. The papyrus lay on her desk, her notes to one side, a cup and saucer from the tea boy on the other. That boy. How many times—

"Jesus," David said. "They let you just leave it out like that?"

She almost laughed. "The staff works with artifacts every day."

He shook his head, then leaned forward. "It's beautiful."

"Here, let me move this out of the way." She reached in front of him for the teacup.

"I'll get it." His hand shot out, bumping hers into the cup. The cup upended in a clatter of china on china.

"Oh, no!" She snatched up the papyrus by its two top corners. A puddle of tea ran down, turning to rivulets dripping onto her desk. "Quick, get something to wipe it."

Frantically he searched the desk drawers, then tried brushing the papyrus with his sleeve. "Lay it down so I can get it better."

"No! There's tea everywhere."

Shoving away the cup and saucer, he mopped his sleeve over the desktop. "Lay it down now." As she did, he yanked his shirtfront out of his trousers and pressed it into the wettest areas, crowding her aside as he blotted. Then he stood there, speechless.

Rika pushed him away and bent to examine the precious document. Near the bottom she stopped. So did her breathing. Five characters smeared. No, six. A wave of nausea swept over her.

"How bad is it?" he asked.

"Ruined." Along with her life. She braced herself against the desk.

"Rika, I'm so sorry."

All her work, the years away from home, her one great chance to earn the respect of everyone who mattered, devastated by a single careless act. Not to mention the papyrus. Its smudged hieroglyphs stared up at her like the bewildered faces of wrongfully punished children. Then a tiny red W caught her eye. Red? The characters were black. Jerking open a desk drawer, she pulled out her magnifying glass. "Oh, my god."

"What is it?"

"Look at this snake," she said, handing him the glass.

He leaned down. "It's different on the right. Zigzag, instead of undulating. Like a symbol for mountains."

"Not mountains. It means water."

The closing bell rang. Fifteen minutes.

"And this bird," he said. "The smeared side looks more like a shepherd's staff."

She grabbed back the glass. "It does." But were they just mistakes, errors the scribe made and later corrected? She looked again. No, the overwritten characters were next to each other, in different columns. Too much of a coincidence. And they were dark red and much finer than the black ones.

Hardly able to believe it, she sank into her chair. "There's writing under the writing."

Chapter 3

Almost to herself, Rika muttered, "What am I going to do? If I tell Dr. Ragheb, I'll have to admit I've damaged it." Deportation would be the best she could hope for. More likely she'd end up in an Egyptian jail. Her throat knotted at the memory of an Ethiopian jail she'd once liberated, its Eritrean inmates reduced to slobbering zombies.

"Who's Dr. Ragheb?"

"The museum director. Thank God he's not in today." She glanced at the connecting doorway to Ragheb's office, then stood and paced to uncoil the tension wringing her stomach. "I could try to restore the characters. And act like nothing happened."

David stepped into her path. "That's crazy. Don't you want to know what it says? Why would somebody hide something if it weren't important? Especially a queen. It could be a tremendous discovery."

"I know, I know. But we'd have to destroy all the writing on top." Unconscionable. In her mind's eye, the opportunity of a lifetime fled before the looming shadow of doom. "The only thing I can do is try to restore the characters and hope no one ever notices. The thought of it makes me sick."

"Wait a minute." He took hold of her shoulders. "What if the scanners on my airplane could look through the upper layer and see the writing underneath?"

"Scanners?"

"Instruments aimed at the ground through a window in the belly of the fuselage. We could use them just like they do with old paintings. There's no damage at all." His grip tightened. "Rika, the plane is parked at the airport right now."

Was it possible? "But how would we—"

Someone knocked.

Rika whipped around and froze. The door handle was already turning.

"Where can we hide this?" David said behind her.

She barely heard him for the hammering heartbeat in her ears.

The door opened a few inches. And the face of the tea boy appeared. "You are finished?" he asked in Arabic.

Rika stared at him, fixated for some reason on a brown smudge below the twelve-year-old's left eye.

"I take your cup now?" he tried again.

In a rush, her senses returned. "Yes. Here, I'll get it for you." She turned to see David, arms crossed, buttocks propped nonchalantly against her desk where his sport coat covered the papyrus. Good thing one of them had been thinking. With shaky fingers, she retrieved the cup and saucer, held them in both hands to keep them from rattling, and gave them to the boy. *"Shukran,"* she said. Thank you.

When the door closed again, David let out his breath in one long whoosh. "Jesus H. Christ."

Rika leaned against the door, her mouth as dry as the dusty cabinets. If this were Eritrea, and the tea boy had been an Ethiopian soldier, she'd be dead. She was losing her edge.

And her priorities. In a few minutes, the guards would begin their rounds. "We have to get the papyrus out of here."

"So you agree to take it to the airplane?"

"If we can. But even if we can't, I have to take it someplace to restore the writing. Someplace private, where I can concentrate."

"How about my room? I'm right across the street. In the Nile Hilton."

"Fine. But first we have to get it out of the museum."

David lifted the papyrus. "It's too stiff to roll up tightly. What if you carried it out, wrapped as a parcel?"

"The guards would check it." She'd never seen them stop any

of the regular staff, but they occasionally puffed up their chests with her. "They even check my book bag sometimes."

The closing bell rang again. Five minutes.

"I've got it." David unbuttoned his shirt.

"What are you doing?"

"Hold this." He handed her his shirt, then wrapped the papyrus around his back, under his arms. "Now help me on with the shirt." He pressed the ends of the papyrus to his chest with one hand and slipped the other through his shirtsleeve, then switched hands to repeat the procedure. Straightening, he tucked the shirt back into his trousers. "How's that?"

"It still shows." For a second, she worried about his body oil staining the papyrus. She'd just have to live with it.

David put on his jacket, buttoned it, and squared his shoulders.

"That's good," she told him. "I can't see anything."

"Then we better get going before I lose my nerve."

Rika bit her lip. She was about to entrust Tiye's papyrus—and her own fate—to a total stranger, a stranger willing to steal from a museum. But she had no other choice. "You go first. It's best if we're not seen together. I'll clean up here and meet you in your room. What's the number?"

"Seven-twenty."

She pulled open her door. "Go."

#

Approaching the entrance, David felt naked. What the hell had he gotten himself into? Letting his passion for discovery derail common sense, then jumping in like Prince Valiant to take all the risk. Sweat ran down his sides. His tongue tasted like he'd been licking an old tire.

Several guards, obviously waiting to lock up, stood with bored expressions in the ticket-window foyer between the main doors and the exterior iron gates.

Not knowing what to do with his eyes, David first looked at the guards, then away. Then, thinking averted eyes might be suspicious, he focused on a guard's shirt button, counting the steps it would take to reach those gates.

He was ten feet from the foyer when a voice behind him said, "One minute, sir."

David's heart almost exploded. Was it him the voice was calling? Should he look back, or keep walking?

"Sir." The voice was louder.

David wanted to run.

The guards by the entrance seemed suddenly more interested.

"Sir!"

As casually as he could, David stopped and turned. It was another guard, gaunt as the Grim Reaper, emerging from the crypt-like gloom of the Great Hall and coming straight toward him. David swallowed hard, his mind scrambling for excuses.

The man stopped, not three feet away, and put two fingers to his lips.

"You," David blurted, now recognizing the fellow who had shown him to Rika's office. With an involuntary laugh, David thrust out his arm to shake hands.

The guard gave him a limp paw and let him pump it. Then he pressed his fingers to his lips again.

Cigarette. The man wanted a cigarette. "I don't smoke anymore," David said. "But I'll bring some next time."

No response.

"Tomorrow I bring cigarettes, okay? Tomorrow cigarettes."

One of the guards at the gate spoke out, evidently translating David's words. The others laughed.

"Okay?" David asked, nodding stupidly.

The man shrugged.

"Good. Then I'll be going now, okay? And thank you." He carried on toward the doors, saying, "Thank you," also to the other guards as he passed them.

When he reached the steps outside, he heard them laugh again. Seconds later, the heavy gates clanged shut.

#

Rika found room 720 and knocked.

When she'd left the museum, she'd seen no hint of unusual

activity, so David must have made it. In reality, the guards rarely questioned a tourist, except for random harassment, and they would have thought twice about stopping a tall, well-dressed man whose self-assured bearing suggested influential connections.

His door cracked open. David shot glances up and down the hall, then pulled her inside. He was shirtless and held a half-empty glass of what looked like whiskey. The papyrus lay on his bed. "I think I've just used up eight of my nine lives."

"Nine lives?"

He related some fable about reincarnated cats, then told her his experience with the guards.

"You did well," she said, shuddering at what might have happened if he'd bolted. Staying cool under fire took nerve.

"Want a Scotch?" he asked.

She crossed the room and looked down at the ancient document, a priceless artifact from the tomb of Tutankhamun, lying there on a Hilton bedspread. He came to stand beside her, his muscular torso so close she could feel his body heat. Stepping away, she dropped her book bag on a chair. "A Scotch would be good."

As he poured, she looked out his window at the pyramids across the Nile, faint triangles in a yellow haze of air pollution from the Soviet brick factory and millions of cars. Below her, five lines of traffic packed a three-lane street. She pictured the Egyptian obelisk in London, the so-called Cleopatra's Needle, decaying to illegibility thanks to vehicle exhaust. "We must return the papyrus tomorrow."

"I've been thinking about that." He handed her a drink, then plopped down on the couch where his tea-stained sport coat lay wadded in a heap.

Too agitated to sit, she stayed by the window, wishing she could open it to relieve the piney stink of institutional air freshener.

"I'm supposed to go to the airport at four-thirty in the morning," he said. "We can go together and use the scanners then. But we won't have much time. A bunch of officials are coming at six."

Rika's grip tightened on her glass. The ice cubes clinked. "What kind of officials?"

"An oil-company executive and some ministry guys. We're giving them a demonstration flight. But if I can get an idea tonight of which techniques are most likely to work on the papyrus, then we should be able to do it in less than an hour."

"David! I can't possibly translate the text in one hour."

"You don't have to," he said with a wave of his glass. "Whatever we see, I'll get a photograph of it, and you can work from that."

She considered this for a moment. "All we do at the airport is snap a picture?"

"Essentially. And you'll have plenty of time to take the papyrus back to the museum. The same way I got it out, and at the same time you usually go, so everything looks normal. I'll have to stay with the officials, but you can use my room to get ready."

"I'll use my own," she said firmly. "The museum gives me a room in the Princess Cleopatra. It's across the square."

David's eyes lit up. "We're neighbors."

And staying that way. Despite any visceral attraction she might feel, she had no room in her life for someone whose bungling had jeopardized everything she'd worked for these past six years. Although—she looked down at her glass—if she were honest with herself, she shared some blame for spilling the tea. Still, the sooner this was over, the better. At least tomorrow was Friday, the beginning of the Muslim weekend, so she shouldn't have to worry about the museum staff being there. Except the guards.

"In the meantime," David said, pushing himself up from the couch, "we have less than twelve hours to figure out if there's some kind of difference my scanners can detect between the two layers of writing."

"And repair the damaged characters." Had he lost sight of their most urgent need?

David walked to the bed and knelt in front of the papyrus. "How did they make black ink in ancient Egypt?"

"Usually it was charcoal mixed in water."

"Makes sense. That's why hot tea smeared it. Both are water-based."

With the cold fire of whiskey stinging her throat, Rika crossed to an armchair and sat. The glass dribbled condensation in her lap.

Americans and their ice-clogged drinks.

"So, elemental carbon. Infrared should do it."

"What are you mumbling?" she said to his back.

"The carbon will absorb heat and give us a negative image we can subtract." His head bent closer to the papyrus. "What about this lower layer that didn't smear? Could they have used a fat or an oil?"

"Possibly. Tiye was devoted to natural oils. She believed in their healing powers and had them brought to her from all over the world."

"A red oil. That's perfect."

"Why?"

Standing, he turned to face her. "Organic pigments have conjugated bonds that respond to ultraviolet. So, we should be able to see the lower layer without much interference from the upper one."

"Truly?" She had no idea what a conjugated bond was, but it didn't matter.

David flashed a heroic grin. "Now all you have to do is repair the writing."

"That," she told him, "is not so easy." And more Scotch wouldn't help. She set her half-empty glass in a porcelain ashtray on the end table beside her.

"Why not? Can't you write hieroglyphs?"

"Of course I can. But I have no experience making ink from charcoal. And no calamus to write with."

"Calamus?"

"The reeds they used for pens."

Over the next quarter hour, David came up with a slew of ideas. Eventually they settled on India ink and Scripto pen points.

"There's a shop that sells school supplies not far from here," she remembered aloud.

They found it three streets away, bought the things she needed, and headed back, David pausing to hand some money to a leper huddled in a doorway.

"Most people wouldn't go near that man," she said as they crossed the street.

"Most people are wrong."

So David Chamberlain had at least one redeeming trait, besides discipline in adversity. And a quick mind. And maybe ... *Enough.* They had work ahead of them.

In the Hilton, she stopped at the souvenir shop. "I need one of those tourist papyruses. To practice on before I do the restoration."

Inspecting the ones with the most unpainted space, she held them up so they were backlit and searched for uniformity and seamlessness of the pounded strips of plant stem. The quality was good, for tourist souvenirs, although none came close to a royal papyrus, made from only the stems' soft core. She finally selected a painting of the Sphinx.

In his room, they cleared the built-in desk and placed table lamps on each side of her work area. They'd just laid out the papyruses and her writing supplies, when the phone rang.

With a frown, David picked it up. "Blue. You're in the bar? Ah, look, man, I'd love to, but jet lag—"

Rika grasped his arm. This was a godsend.

"Hold on a sec, Blue. There's someone at the door." David set the phone down and motioned her toward the bathroom. "What?" he whispered.

"Please go."

"But—"

"Just for a few hours. It will help me concentrate if I'm alone." The restoration had to be perfect, and she wasn't sure she could do it.

Chapter 4

Alone in the rising elevator, David could still see Rika's eyes—like fire trapped in black opal. The feel of her shoulders lingered in his palms. And despite the high-pitched wail of Egyptian Muzak pouring from the overhead speaker, he could hear her voice, a strange mixture of British and French accents spoken softly but with authority.

A few hours, she'd said. In a few hours it would be dinnertime. He'd take her out. Her choice of restaurants. With the Prince Valiant ordeal now mercifully over, he was in a mood to celebrate. Once she'd fixed the papyrus, Rika would be, too.

The doors opened, and David turned into the Hilton's rooftop lounge. Tall windows on three sides looked out on a city already twinkling at dusk. The bar itself ran down the center, forty feet of gleaming wood, complete with brass foot rail. About a dozen customers, all western men in business suits, perched on barstools, their needs seen to by a hefty Egyptian in white shirtsleeves. A small sea of tables and chairs surrounded the bar, and upholstered booths rimmed the windows.

In this urbane setting, Blue was hard to miss. The red-bearded giant, clad in rumpled desert khakis, half-filled the nearest corner booth. A Queensland native, Blue had "Outback" stamped all over him. But beneath the burly surface lay reflexes quick enough to win the Stanford badminton championship two years running and a brain that could literally "read the record in the rocks."

Next to Blue sat a blond fellow about twenty-five who looked bright-eyed and freshly scrubbed. He wore slacks and polo shirt, and a small silver ring in one ear.

David slid into the empty space where an unattended beer bottle waited. "I see you already ordered."

Blue introduced the blond fellow as Kai Pedersen, a Norwegian new hire. "Pinched him from Statoil a few months back. He's been out on a seismic job down by Suez." Blue drained what was left in his bottle and flagged down a waiter to bring more. "Kai's a rock climber, so I figured you two had something in common."

David now recognized the earring as a miniature carabiner, the ring that snaps through the eye of a piton for running rope. Cute, but rather affected.

Kai leaned forward with a look of admiration. "Blue says you did El Capitan."

"Years ago, and just barely." The Yosemite landmark, a Grade VI ascent by almost any route, was David's toughest climb ever. He'd almost slipped to his death, but no one knew that except him. "I don't think I could do it now."

That last comment brought a faint smile to Kai's face, as though it pleased him to believe David was in decline. Sitting back, Kai said, "I found some good places near the Gulf. Big jumbles of fault blocks. The highest are only about fifty meters, but they're technically difficult. If you have a free day, I could take you."

"Thanks, I'll keep it in mind." David might have had fun showing this kid what technical climbing was all about, but he hoped to spend his spare time with Rika. He took a swig of beer, creamier than he'd expected with a slight cereal flavor. "Pretty good brew."

"Stella Export, mate. The only Gypo grog they don't filter through a horse."

Blue would know. The guy lived on beer and Vegemite, or seemed to when he and David shared an apartment at Stanford. In the nine years since then, they'd stayed in touch and gotten together a few times. Blue, who'd spent most of his professional life in Africa, was now a senior geologist with SEECO, Suez Energy Exploration Company, the company that had contracted David's employer to fly a confidential survey.

"*Ja takk.*" Kai gawked past David's shoulder as if he'd just spotted the Playmate of the Year.

Turning, David saw an Egyptian couple, impeccably dressed in eveningwear, glide into the room. The woman reminded him of Sophia Loren. The man was handsome enough to deserve her.

"Look at those tits," Kai whispered.

Too big, was David's opinion, although he liked the fragrance of jasmine that trailed after her. Take in the dress a little, and Rika would look great in it.

Blue frowned at Kai. "Off limits, son. Stick to expats."

"One can dream."

"You'll get warts. Didn't your mum tell you?"

As the couple made their way to a distant booth, the waiter Blue had flagged down appeared with three fresh bottles.

Blue waited for him to leave, then said to Kai, "Davey used to build bombs."

Not build, design. And how kind of you to bring it up. So far as David was concerned, the biggest bomb in all of Oak Ridge had been his marriage.

"Now he's all aflutter," Blue continued, "about some new wonderfulness he's bringing to Mother SEECO." With a glance over his shoulder, he lowered his voice. "Ground-penetrating radar."

Kai, apparently recovered from his fantasies with Miss Loren, narrowed his eyes. "I read about that. *Time* magazine, last year. The Space Shuttle found old branches of the Nile, right?"

"You sure you want to talk about that here?" David asked Blue. This would be the technology's first commercial test, and SEECO's VP for exploration wanted to keep it secret until he decided whether to use it on the full survey. Convincing him was the whole idea behind tomorrow's demonstration flight—and the key to making or breaking David's career.

"Kai's one of us, now," Blue said. "But keep it brief."

David snuck a peek at his watch. Only thirty minutes since he'd left Rika. It felt like an hour. The bar was starting to fill up, more businessmen whose rowdy laughter and disheveled suits spoke of a welcome end to a long day.

Angling himself toward Kai, David tried to avoid looking at the silly earring. "I lobbied NASA for two years before they finally flew my instrument on that Shuttle. And it worked perfectly. That photo in *Time* doesn't do it justice."

"And the winner is ..." Blue made a rolling motion with his hand that meant move it along.

"Hopefully you," David said. "SEECO's trying to locate ancient river deltas that could be oil reservoirs in the Gulf of Suez, using an MSS. A multi-spectral scanner."

Kai nodded.

"Unfortunately, even Digital Image can't guarantee the MSS will do that. And ours is the best there is. But ground-penetrating radar is ideally suited for your needs."

"Our wet dreams come true," Blue interjected.

"If you want this fast, then kindly shut up." David faked a scowl before turning back to Kai. "Radar is absorbed by moisture. But in extremely arid environments, like the Egyptian desert, it can penetrate the ground until it hits an anomaly, like bedrock. Since big rivers cut down into bedrock, the radar sees where they ran, even though the rivers themselves are long gone and covered over."

"So," Kai said, "we find the river beds and trace them to their deltas in the Gulf?"

"You got it. The deltas you're looking for were made fifteen million years ago by branches of the ancestral Nile. We find the largest of those branches, and they should lead us directly to the biggest potential reservoirs offshore."

"Smart."

"Bloody brilliant," Blue told him. "And if you breathe a word—"

Shouting erupted at the bar. A stool fell over, and patrons stepped back as two men in loosened ties squared off. The darker one cursed in Italian, the other in English. With pleading eyes, the burly bartender implored them to calm down. When they ignored him, he slid their bottles and drink glasses out of reach, then retreated a pace.

Not much of a bouncer.

The two hotheads circled each other to mixed mutterings of caution, rebuke, and encouragement from the bystanders.

"Shit." Blue hauled himself out of the booth. Balling his fists, he strode up to the bar like a Viking bent on pillage. Suddenly it was quiet. The two adversaries gaped as Blue stepped between them, dwarfing both. Whatever Blue said, David couldn't hear. But the Italian finally snatched up his jacket and stomped out. The other glared a second longer, then sat down on his stool.

David saw a look of relief on Miss Loren, as she released her escort's hand.

Returning to their booth, Blue wedged into the space he'd left. "Disgraceful the way some children act when their mums let 'em out."

"I'm surprised the bartender didn't step in," David said. "He's big enough."

"Egyptians are too polite."

Their waiter came up with three new bottles of Stella Export, ice chips still clinging to their sides. "Compliments of the house, sir."

"Crikey, mate, you don't have to do that."

"Please," the waiter said.

Blue thanked the man, then knocked back half of his bottle. "So, where were we?"

"We were marveling," David quipped, "at the lengths you'll go to for a free beer."

"Me mission in life, sport. That and sheilas."

When Kai looked confused, David said, "Girls."

"Oh." Kai smirked. "I've heard."

David checked his watch again. Not quite an hour since he'd left Rika. He wasn't sure he could wait "a few hours." Denver to Cairo was a long flight, and despite the recent excitement, jet lag and alcohol were dragging him down. Imagining dinner with Rika helped. Imagining a kiss afterwards helped even more. He took several deep breaths to oxygenate his blood and heard Kai finishing a sentence.

"... but the army never showed up."

"They never do, lad."

"What are you talking about?" David asked.

"Landmines." Blue polished off his bottle and pushed it aside. "The coastal areas are littered with them. Some going back to World War Two."

Kai burped, then explained, "They're a big problem for seismic surveys. We have to run a mine clearance crew before we can go in. When they find them, we store them in a roped-off area and call the army to dispose of them."

"And the army can't be bothered," Blue chimed in. "But you gotta call 'em anyway. Sometimes it's best to just run a herd of sheep through the area."

David frowned.

"Hey, sport, better them than us."

"You need better technology." David turned to Kai. "Did you find any mines this time?"

"Twelve, all Soviet. And two of them were huge. The crew cut the trip wires and taped the electrical contacts, but that didn't help me sleep much easier." Kai contemplated his fingernails for a moment. "Some things are better in Norway."

"Not the pay," Blue said.

"Speaking of pay." Kai nudged toward Blue to let him out of the booth. "I assume you're picking up our bill. I have to finish my report."

"Blue-eyed Arab."

As Kai left, the waiter cleared the empties, then deposited two full bottles on their table.

When Blue slid one toward David, David pushed it back. "I've still got most of this one." And a looming headache.

"Suit yourself." Blue chugged about a third of the itinerant bottle before unsnapping the leather cover over his watch face. "Gotta shove off soon, myself. Big darts tournament tonight. You need a lift to the airport tomorrow?"

"SEECO rented me a Budget car and driver. And another one for the crew."

Oh, shit. He'd almost forgotten the crew. David made a mental note to call their rooms tonight and confirm that the flight plan was filed and preparations were on schedule. They'd be leaving the hotel even earlier than he and Rika tomorrow morning.

"Word of advice," Blue said. "Treat your driver right, and he'll do just about anything for you. Tipping's fine, but the best thing would be some genuine Yank clothing. Especially Levi's or Adidas sneakers. They're worth gold here."

"So happens I brought both." David thought a second. "But the kid dresses straight out of *GQ*."

Blue squinted. "A kid?"

"Well, he says he's twenty-three, but he looks like he just got out of high school."

"Don't tell me. Is his name Hagazy?"

"Yeah. How did you know?"

Blue burst out laughing.

"What's wrong?" David asked, suddenly wary.

"Nothing, squire. Hagazy's a good lad. Had him myself, before I got my license. And he'll love the Levi's." Blue emptied his current bottle and picked up the last one. "By the way, he's nineteen."

"Oh, great."

"Not to worry. He's given a few passengers heart attacks, maybe, but never had an accident. At least that I know of."

David could believe the heart attacks. Hagazy's driving style reminded him of himself when he opened up his Porsche on back roads in the Rockies.

"And I'm pretty sure he's not a stoolie. But keep your nose clean, anyway."

David snapped to attention. "Stoolie?"

"Didn't anyone tell you? The Budget franchise here is owned by the head of the Secret Police."

#

Approaching his room, David took more oxygenating breaths. What he really needed was half an hour of rope climbing in the gym. And some Listerine. His mouth, to use an expression of Blue's, tasted like the bottom of a birdcage.

Plus he definitely was not "keeping his nose clean." He'd have to play things very carefully with Hagazy, especially tomorrow morning when the papyrus would be right there in the car.

"It's me," he called as he inserted the key. The room smelled of the sharply pungent perspiration he associated with black athletes. Rika looked haggard. "Finished?"

"Not yet."

Stepping up behind her, he saw that she'd cleaned the smudges and repaired all but one hieroglyph, which was totally red. "What happened?"

"The upper character was so ruined I had to remove it. Now I have to draw it again, completely by myself." She wiped her forehead with the back of her wrist. "It can't be too small or too big. And it must be in a line with the others, and not inclined to the left or right."

"Can I help?"

She shook her head. Beside her, the painting of the Sphinx looked like a symphony score of practice strokes.

"I'll sit over here." He dropped into an armchair and gazed at Rika's profile as she dipped her pen. Without doubt, she was the most intriguing woman he'd ever met. He had no idea where she came from. Her skin was dark olive-brown, her hair a helmet of sable curls, both of which suggested African ancestry. But her face had the high cheekbones and delicate lines of a fashion model from India.

She wore stylish jeans and a white cotton blouse. As she hunched over to touch pen to papyrus, the blouse tightened across her back, and he could tell she wasn't wearing a bra. Bold in a Muslim country.

Before fantasy stirred him too far, he shifted his eyes. Her leather sandals lay next to the couch, one crossed upside down over the other. He noticed now that she'd planted her feet flat on the carpet, presumably to stabilize herself as she worked. In a TV program he'd once seen, a master engraver planted his feet that same way while cutting plates for the twenty-dollar bill. As she lowered the pen again, he found himself holding his breath in a sympathetic effort to steady her hand.

The same hand that had bumped into his and spilled the tea. Obviously she thought it was the other way around, he bumping her, but only an idiot would raise that issue now. Besides, when the dust settled, when they'd imaged the hidden text and returned the papyrus to the museum, she'd look back on today as a blessing in disguise.

Could the shared experience develop into something stronger? Rika lit his fire like no other woman he'd ever met. The second she opened her office door, he'd felt dumbstruck, as if clouds had parted to reveal an angel.

Unfortunately, she seemed not to share his feelings. Given time, he might sway her. But his work here would end in just a few days.

"Why did you sigh?" she asked.

"Huh? I didn't know I had."

"Well, I'm finished. Would you care to have a look?"

Quickly he crossed to where she was sitting. Although he knew by now exactly which characters had been damaged, he was hard-pressed to pick them out. "You should have been a counterfeiter."

"I'm glad it's over." With a long groan, she stretched her arms and arched her back.

It was a moment he couldn't resist. Moving behind her, he placed his hands on her shoulders and gently massaged the muscles.

"Oooh. That feels good."

In the mirror, he saw her eyes close. With only a heartbeat of hesitation, he bent down and kissed her neck.

Rika's eyes popped open. For several seconds, she stared at him in the mirror. Then she stood. "I should leave."

Shit, he'd blown it.

She stepped around him, picked up a sandal, and slipped it on.

"Wait a second. I was going to take you to dinner."

"I don't feel like going out." She slid on the other sandal.

"Then we'll order room service." He opened a desk drawer and pulled out the menu.

But as he tried to hand it to her, Rika shouldered her book bag. "Another time, perhaps. I'll see you in the morning, four-thirty outside my hotel."

Damn. He couldn't let the night end on such a sour note. "Let me walk you back."

She opened the door. "I know the way."

Chapter 5

Eighteenth Dynasty

Queen Tiye woke to the urgent whisper of a servant girl. "Divine Mother, we approach Semna."

"Cover the windows and inform Princess Baketaten."

When the girl had draped the cabin's windows and left, Tiye stepped onto the deck of the royal barge. In the gray light of pre-dawn, low fog hugged the river. Its vapor coated her skin with a cool sheen as she listened to the rhythmic dipping of a hundred oars on the vessels fore and aft. Upstream, soldiers on the scout boat extinguished the torches by which they had steered through the night. Beyond them, in the faint distance of the far bend, the twin fortresses of Semna rose ghostlike through the mist. Flanking the Nile, they marked Egypt's southern frontier, its border with the black kingdom of Nubia.

Tiye's fingers tingled with anticipation. Almost there.

Movement atop the stone fortifications told her soldiers were manning their posts. Quickly she retreated to her cabin, for her presence on this voyage was a closely guarded secret. Only those on board and a select few in the Egyptian capitals knew, their tongues silenced by oaths of loyalty. All others believed the barge carried Princess Baketaten on a pilgrimage to the homeland of her mother.

Even fewer knew the true purpose of the expedition. Tiye, dowager empress of Egypt and a deity in her own land, was going home to be buried alive.

#

Two days the royal barge and its attendant vessels lay moored at Semna's docks. Local officials hosted ceremonies in honor of Baketaten. Laborers, with much shouting and thumping, replenished the flotilla's provisions. Craftsmen repaired sails, replaced broken oars.

Tiye remained secluded, her isolation relieved only by visits from her elder brother, Ay, when he could disengage himself from his responsibilities as Baketaten's guardian. On those occasions, Ay's hand recorded passages of her final message to Tutankhaten. His memory supplemented hers as they reminisced with joy and sadness over their long lives together.

On the morning of the third day, the princess and her retinue reboarded the royal barge. Rowers on the towing boat eased the barge into the current. The other vessels, carrying soldiers, servants, kitchens, and the queen's personal cargoes, took up their positions. At a sign from the scout boat, the expedition resumed its journey south.

Once past Semna, Ay undraped Tiye's windows, and she gazed out at the passing scene. A rising heron caught her eye, graceful and white against the dark foliage along the bank. "Strange," she mused, "the country here looks no different from Egypt. Yet I always feel a difference. Do you feel it, also?"

"Always I do."

Like her, Ay had been born in Nubia and had spent his life at court in the capitals of Egypt. He had become the highest official in Akhenaten's government, holding such titles as Commander of the King's Horse, Personal Scribe to the King, and Royal Fanbearer. Yet while he had served her son well, Tiye loved him most for his wise counsel and his steadfast devotion to the true faith. She had chosen him as principal tutor to Tutankhaten and trusted him above all others as a confidant and advisor.

"I am happy to be in Nubia again. And I shall be happy to rest here, at last." She turned to Ay. "Let us continue the message to my son."

Upon a censer from which the sweetness of frankincense rose in wisps, he placed a silver dish containing beads of palm resin. As the resin melted, he stirred in ground madder root. In this, he dipped the end of a reed calamus. Then he poised his hand and waited.

Tiye had composed her thoughts and now spoke slowly and with deliberation. "Know, my precious son, that these words emanate from the glorious Aten. Life flows in the fluids of the body, as the flowing Nile brings life to Egypt. To be reborn, the fluids must never be allowed to run dry. One must be buried in a bath of restorative oils, and burial must precede death. In this way, the flow of life never ceases, but proceeds at an invisibly slow pace until full restoration is attained and the buried one reawakens.

"Shun the counsel of those who would have you accept the traditional methods, for they deprive the body of its essential organs and fluids.

"Follow only the procedures I have caused to be written. By them shall you find renewed life through the centuries. It is Aten's will that you, among all pharaohs, shall again rule in this world, and that I, as I counseled your divine father and his seed before you, shall again counsel you in the life to come.

"And having ruled again and accomplished good and mighty deeds, then, as the end of your days nears, shall you once more follow these procedures. And once more shall you rest, and once more breathe the breath of life. So shall you live through eternity. For the glorious light of Aten must always shine on the face of men, and you and I are His elected preservers. Prepare now for these things, and do not waver from the path I have shown you. You will know your time, as I know mine."

Although wrinkled with age, Ay's hand was steady, the tiny characters artistically formed. When he finished recording her words, he laid the papyrus on a low table and weighted it with small gold disks to keep it flat until the ink dried.

In the evening, as he had done on previous nights, he would cover the dried characters with new, larger characters drawn in an ink of charcoal and water. These larger characters formed a poetic text he was composing, in which Tiye praised Tutankhamun and honored him in the name of Aten. In this way, her true message was hidden, to be revealed only when Tutankhamun followed the instructions that his sister, Baketaten, would deliver after their mother's burial.

Chapter 6

At 4:25 a.m., Rika padded down the narrow stairs of her hotel. On the ground floor, the elevator stood open, exposing a tray of dirty dishes and the smelly remains of a half-eaten fish. The lobby, lit only by a parchment-shaded lamp on the front desk, appeared deserted—four armchairs and a rack of tourist brochures. But soft snoring behind the counter told her a night clerk was "on duty." Sticking to the path worn in the carpet, she moved silently toward the front doors.

A gravelly voice halted her. "Something is wrong, Madame?"

She turned to see a middle-aged man in wrinkled shirt and gray stubble, his hands clutching the countertop. Watchman's radar, she thought, the same subconscious vigilance that woke dozing sentries in Eritrea. Smiling, she said, "No, everything is fine," and continued toward the doors.

"One moment." He crabbed to the end of the counter. "You would not depart without paying your bill?"

"What?" She felt like telling him to go sit on an anthill. "The museum pays my bills. Check your records. Room two-ten."

He blinked as though she'd spat in his face.

Damn. Why had she taken offense at a man just doing his job? Must be nerves. The papyrus, and everything about it, had her insides in a knot. She stepped to the counter. "You were wise to ask."

He responded by scratching his armpit.

Having apparently mollified the fellow, Rika walked to the glass doors and peered out into darkness. No sign of David. He should have been here by now. She pushed through to wait outside.

The cool night air reminded her of Eritrea. She would miss the BBC broadcast of African news this morning, but they rarely reported on Eritrea, anyway. The war had gone on too long to be of much interest to the so-called international community.

A truck loaded with cotton bales rumbled past, the only activity she could see. The museum to her right was dark, an economy measure since the decline of tourism following Sadat's assassination. But across the square in front of her, floodlights still lit the Hilton.

Where was David?

He'd show up. He saw himself as the gallant knight saving the damsel. And he seemed to expect her to swoon in his arms.

That kiss. Did all white men view black women as easy conquests? She couldn't count the number of British and French men who'd evidently thought so. But she chose as her needs required, and unrealistic notions of long-term romance never entered her head.

Except with Jean-Luc. She shuddered at the memory. He alone had wormed his way into her heart—before breaking it with his insistence that she was too aggressive, too "hung up" on Eritrea, and should learn to wash laundry and clean their shabby apartment while he continued his studies. Bloody bastard. Feeling soiled by the experience, she rubbed her hands down the coarse denim of her jeans.

A white Peugeot braked to a halt at the curb. David jumped out of the back, dressed in a blue blazer, gray slacks, and red tie. "Sorry I'm late. Come on."

Jolted from her musings, she climbed into the rear seat. David hopped in beside her, slammed the door, and the car shot off like a mortar shell.

"Rika, this is Hagazy. He works for the rental-car agency."

Hagazy flashed a grin over his shoulder. He reminded her of what British magazines called a "teen heartthrob," with his brilliant teeth, slicked-back hair, and a silver-colored suit that had to be Italian. In Italian style, he rounded Tahrir Square on squealing tires.

She grasped the armrest. "Do we have to go so fast?"

"Hagazy, slow down."

"Much better to go fast, sir. Slow drivers make accidents." He swung around an army truck. "You see? That slow lorry can make an accident. Other people must always go around him."

"Slow down!" David reached into the front passenger seat, then sat back holding two Styrofoam cups with plastic covers. He handed her one. "Coffee. Hope you don't mind it strong. It's all I could get this time of morning."

Her cup was only half-full. Then she sipped and realized why. Turkish. Thick, hot, and every bit as good as Eritrean. "Thank you. It's delicious."

"The way Hagazy drives, I figured any more than two demitasse apiece would end up in our laps."

Thoughtful. She sipped again and felt the powerful brew invigorate her body. "You have the … object?"

David pointed to the rear-window shelf.

Twisting in her seat, she saw a white plastic bag with the Hilton logo and the word "Laundry."

She also smelled his aftershave. Six years in Europe had accustomed her to the idea of male fragrances and taught her they reflect personality. To her, his leathery scent conveyed understated masculinity. A distraction she didn't need.

As she sat back, Hagazy swerved onto the Corniche El Nil, the broad highway bordering the Nile on its eastern bank. Pre-dawn traffic was light, mainly stake-bed trucks bringing produce to the city. On the outbound side, Hagazy floored it.

Suddenly she realized they were heading south. "The airport is north."

Hagazy glanced at her in his rear-view mirror. "Faster to go this way. By Salah Salem."

Picturing the route, she decided he was right, at this hour.

They passed the southern tip of Zamalik Island, home of the Cairo Sporting Club and the city's wealthiest residents. Just ahead lay Roda Island. Between them, the Nile shimmered like black silk. Along its near shore, moored feluccas bobbed gently, sailing boats unchanged in design since the age of pharaohs.

"Rika."

She turned to see David's lips compressed in a hard line of resolve.

"I want to apologize," he said. "I didn't mean to offend you last night."

She assumed he meant the kiss. At least he was being gentlemanly about it, which called for a civil reply. "We were both tired."

With a curse, Hagazy veered around a horse-drawn cart loaded with oil drums. "Stupid villagers. They should not go on highway." A minute later, he turned left onto Salah Salem Avenue, running alongside the massive stone arches of the 14th-Century aqueduct wall that now divided Old Cairo from the modern city.

David rolled down his window a few inches, letting in a wash of cool air. "Could I ask where you're from?"

She couldn't help smiling. He was certainly treading lightly now. "Eritrea. Do you know where that is?"

"On the Red Sea."

"Very good." She took another sip of her coffee, cooler now. "I think most Americans have never heard of it."

"Eritrea's fighting a war with Ethiopia, aren't they?"

"We *have* been since nineteen sixty-one. It's the longest running war in African history."

He seemed to mull this for a moment. "What I'm not sure about is why they're fighting."

"Geography." Anyone who could read a map should know that. "Our coastline is a thousand kilometers long. Without us, Ethiopia is landlocked. We offered a corridor to the sea, but they'd rather kill us than negotiate."

On the hill ahead rose the Citadel, the medieval fortress housing Cairo's grandest mosque, where Egyptian presidents prostrated themselves before God and where Sadat's killers had holed up until the army cleaned them out. Violence and religion. They went together. Except in Eritrea, where both sides were Marxist.

David reached for her hand, then apparently thought better of it. "How did you get out?"

"Get out?" Her blood ignited. "You think I *wanted* to leave? I wanted to stay and fight."

"Whoa." He held up a palm.

Americans. What did they know? No one had ever invaded

their country, tried to enslave them, crush their culture. They were like big children, strong but naive. She sat back and looked out her window as Hagazy raced past the long, dark valley of the City of the Dead. His speed no longer disturbed her. The faster he drove, the sooner she'd be finished with this "scanner" business.

They zoomed through the northeastern suburbs of Cairo into Heliopolis, one of ancient Egypt's greatest cities, now thoroughly absorbed into the sprawl of apartment blocks and business towers oozing relentlessly out from the capital.

Maybe she'd overreacted. How could David comprehend her passion if he'd never stood with his back to the wall, trying to defend his people and his heritage from annihilation?

The buildings gave way to dark desert, scored by the four-lane divided highway that marked the final stretch to the airport.

"I'm not *trying* to make you angry." David now sat with his back against his door, giving her as much space as possible. Faint light from the dashboard picked out the cleft in his chin, the strong curves of his jaw and cheekbones. Wind blowing in through the partly opened window tousled his hair. "If you'd give me a chance, I'd like to be friends."

Friends. Was that possible? With a nod she said, "Fair enough."

David cracked a smile, which made her smile back.

Swallowing the last of the coffee he'd given her, she settled more comfortably in her seat. A hint of his aftershave drifted on the breeze from the window.

Hagazy hit the brakes and turned left into the airport. Skirting the half-empty parking lot, he pulled around to the military side, where he stopped at a red-and-white-striped barrier next to a kiosk.

A guard emerged. David rolled his window all the way down and handed the man a page of typescript on Egyptian letterhead, which Rika assumed to be his entry permit. The guard frowned at it, then motioned David to get out of the car.

But Hagazy leapt out, faced off with the man, and launched into a tirade.

She caught snatches of the gutter Arabic—how important David was, how much trouble the soldier would be in if he didn't allow them to pass. The guard's hand went to his pistol. She tensed.

But Hagazy stood his ground, stabbing his finger at the letterhead. Finally the guard retreated to his booth. Through its window, she saw him talking on a telephone. A minute later, the barrier rose.

Rika let out her breath.

"What did you say?" David asked Hagazy as they drove through.

"Stupid man. All soldier is stupid. They come from villages and can't read. Not even Arabic."

Hagazy's brazenness reminded Rika of her little brother, Alem.

They drove past a row of two-story concrete buildings, then onto the tarmac toward a white, twin-engine jet. And a jeep with two soldiers in combat fatigues.

"Park at the end of the wing and stay in the car," David told Hagazy. "We won't be long."

When the Peugeot halted, David nudged her to climb out on her side, away from the soldiers. Following behind her with the laundry bag, he waved to an athletic-looking man wearing a headset connected by cable to the aircraft's nose. A pilot, judging from the epaulets on his white, short-sleeved shirt.

Taking her hand, David said, "Watch your head," then drew her in a crouch to a spot under the fuselage between the wings. He placed a twenty-five-piastre Egyptian banknote on the tarmac. In the dead calm of pre-dawn, it stayed there.

"What are you doing?" she asked.

"You'll see." He led her out the other side, up the stairs, and into the plane, where he poked his head inside the cockpit. "How's it going, Jim?"

"A-okay." The deep voice came from a man in the pilot's seat. All Rika saw was a hairy arm with thick fingers pressing buttons in the cockpit's ceiling as he spoke. "We had some saber rattling at the guard shack, but otherwise no sweat. Forecast is for clear skies, winds ten to twenty out of the south. Should be a smooth ride for your honchos."

"They'll love you for it." David turned from the cockpit, took her elbow, and guided her into the main cabin.

Instead of having seats, the plane was filled with electronic instruments, some with open panels exposing multi-colored wiring, some sprouting black cables that snaked across the floor. A console with tape decks, video screens, and gadgets she didn't recognize ran almost the entire length of the cabin's left side. She'd never seen so much electronic gear crammed into one place, not even in the Ethiopian radar station her squad once overran and destroyed.

David called out, "Paul, you back there?"

A round head with receding black hair popped up from behind the far end of the console. The broad facial features looked Slavic.

"There you are. Paul, this lady is with the Cairo Museum. I've offered to analyze one of their documents for them. What's our instrument status?"

"So far, so good."

"Then how about getting the VIP cabin ready while I use the console?"

"You're the boss." Wiping his hands on a red cloth, Paul disappeared through an open doorway into a rear cabin.

David stepped past her and slipped into a metal chair that slid on runners down the length of the console. In dizzying succession, he flipped switches, pushed buttons, and turned knobs. The console lit up, status lights shining red, orange, or green. Needles kicked to life on what looked like voltage meters. Two video screens glowed pale blue. He peered at one of the screens, adjusted a dial that brought an image into focus, and sat back. "What do you think?"

Bending forward, she could clearly read, TWENTY-FIVE PIASTRES in block capitals and Central Bank of Egypt in cursive script. The banknote he'd laid on the ground. Impressive. "I didn't see the camera."

"One of six. Scanners, actually. Now we have to calibrate them." From the laundry bag he withdrew the tourist papyrus she'd used last night and a white candle like the one in her hotel room, for use in the event of power failure. He lit the candle, dripped some wax on her practice characters, then smeared the wax with his finger and handed her the papyrus. "Take this down and put it where the money is. The wax should be a good proxy for oil-based ink."

"Proxy?"

"Substitute. Look, we don't have much time. This is a two-person job, and I have to stay here. I'll explain everything later."

Rika bristled, not just at his authoritarian tone, but even more so at the implication that she didn't need to know what he was doing. "Explain it now."

With an audible breath, he swiveled to face her. "I have to adjust the instruments to distinguish the wax from your characters. That'll give me a starting point for imaging the hidden text through the water-based writing on Tiye's papyrus. If I don't get the power settings right, I could burn a hole in the papyrus."

"No!" She grabbed the laundry bag. "If there's any chance of that, I won't allow it."

"Oh, Christ."

"It's my head on the chopping stone."

David closed his eyes, then re-opened them. "I promise there won't be a problem, if you'll just do as I ask. Believe it or not, I'm an expert."

Probably he was. But she hated being at the mercy of something she didn't understand. Even the slightest hitch could—

"Rika, we're running out of time."

Clenching her jaw, she laid down the laundry bag, snatched up the tourist papyrus, and walked up the aisle.

She was halfway to the door when he said, "Keep your head out of the way. The scanners will be right above you."

Rika stomped down the stairs. Ducking under the fuselage, she saw that the Peugeot blocked the soldiers' view of her. She replaced the banknote with the papyrus, and looked up. Through a meter-square window in the aircraft's underbelly, an array of lenses eyed her. She scooted back and waited.

Five minutes later, David came down the stairs with the laundry bag and knelt beside her. "I can't see through the wax."

Damn. Like it or not, she was counting on him.

"But I think this'll work. I should have thought of it before." He brushed away the tourist papyrus and laid Tiye's in its place, face down.

"No! You'll scratch the writing." She reached for it, but he grabbed her wrist.

"Rika, it's just lying there. Don't slide it around, and it'll be fine." His grip on her loosened. "Trust me."

She scowled, frustrated that she had no other choice.

"Hold it by the corners to keep it flat. And don't worry if your hands feel a little warm for a second." With that, he was gone.

Warm? She eyed the lenses above her, wondering what kind of rays were going to come out of them. With a silent curse, she knelt low, stretched her arms out in front of her, and flattened the papyrus against the tarmac. To cheer herself, she thought of slamming a door in Mr. Chamberlain's face when this was all over.

"Friend of David's?" a man's voice asked.

Rika flinched.

"Sorry, I didn't mean to startle you." It was the fellow who'd been working at the jet's nose. Hands on knees, he smiled at her from under the wing, his blond hair and tanned face giving the impression of a German ski instructor. "I'm Chris Watson, the co-pilot."

She groped for a half-reasonable explanation. "We're making an experiment."

"Figured as much. David's always trying something new. Good luck."

As Chris Watson walked away, Rika slowly relaxed. For a moment, she thought her hands felt warmer, but it was probably just her blood flowing again. The beginnings of a cramp twinged in her right shoulder. How long did she have to hold this ungainly position?

David's magic probably wouldn't work, anyway. He was so damned sure of himself. But it wasn't his future at stake.

Across the runway, dawn broke as a pink streak in the graying sky. She heard distant vehicles shifting gears and smelled the familiar stink of diesel exhaust. Any minute now, the dignitaries would arrive. The soldiers in the Jeep would strut around, acting officious. If any of them saw the papyrus—

"Got it." David brandished a big manila envelope as if it were a trophy.

"Truly?" She pushed up into a squat, wary of disappointment but dying to see what he had.

He handed her the envelope, then slid Tiye's papyrus into the laundry bag. "There're five Polaroids. One of the whole thing and an enlargement of each quadrant. You can look at them in the car."

"No. I need to see them now." Extracting the 8 x 10-inch

photographs, she angled them toward the brightening dawn. The hieroglyphs showed white against a dark gray background.

"I had to invert the image because I was viewing the writing through the back of the papyrus."

Rika hardly heard him. She had found the enlargement of the papyrus' upper left quadrant. The opening statement read, *My beloved Tutankhaten, just ruler of the two kingdoms, fearless defender of the true faith, may the glorious light of Aten shine upon you through all of your days.*

Tutankh*aten*. She could hardly believe it. "Image of Aten." No one but Tiye would have called him that. The name was forbidden, changed to "Image of Amun" upon his coronation to appease the Amun priests and achieve political stability. "This is wonderful."

With a grin, David took her hand. "Come on. We have to get you out of here."

At the car, he opened the rear door, leaned in, and told Hagazy to take her to the Princess Cleopatra. Then he turned to face her. "Would you have dinner with me tonight? About six?"

Rika nodded. Who else but David could she talk to about this amazing discovery?

#

Sitting lotus-style on the bed in her small hotel room, Rika pored over the photos, consulting her reference books and jotting notes. This was not a typical text. Aside from the standard formulas—praises to Aten and so on—most of it dealt with a strange form of burial. And there were many words she didn't recognize.

In no time at all, her watch read 8:45. The museum would open in fifteen minutes. Quickly she unbuttoned the denim shirt she'd worn to the airport, then bent at the waist and wrapped the papyrus across her bare back. In this posture, without another pair of hands to help, getting the shirt back on and tucked into her jeans was like twisting through a contortionist's hoop. She winced as the brittle edge of the papyrus bit into her nipples, one of the few times she wished she owned a bra. In Eritrea, few could afford such frivolities, and women weren't overly shy about their breasts.

Straightening at last, she glanced in the mirror. No good. Because she was shorter than David, the papyrus rose higher on her back, making a sharp, unnatural curve at her shoulder blades. In front, it rode halfway up her breasts. A shawl would help, but she didn't have one.

Her windbreaker. She yanked it from a hanger in the closet, draped it over her shoulders, and tied the arms around her neck, letting the ends hang freely down her chest. Not perfect, but she was out of time.

Trying to look normal while keeping her upper body rigid, Rika walked into the museum at 9:05, waved at the guards, and went directly up to her office. Inside, she opened the document cabinet and slid out the papyrus's holder. Made of insecticidal cedar wood, it consisted of two trelliswork lath frames hinged together like book covers. She laid it open on her desk, then untied her windbreaker, dropped it on her chair, and unbuttoned her shirt. Bending at the waist, she peeled off her shirt to remove the papyrus without snagging it. She placed the papyrus in its holder, and was reaching for her shirt when the inner office door opened.

She turned with a start, clutching the shirt to her naked chest.

The museum director gaped.

Chapter 7

For what seemed an eternity, neither Rika nor Dr. Ragheb spoke. Her heart hammered. She felt perspiration breaking out all over her. Which gave her an idea. "You startled me," she said. "I feel feverish and was trying to cool myself. I didn't expect anyone else to be here on a Friday."

Her boss, an intense man in his early fifties who always reminded her of a gaunt Omar Sharif, scanned the room with suspicious eyes, then walked up and put a hand to her forehead.

Knowing it must feel cold from perspiration, she said, "I'm getting a chill now."

Ragheb's frown softened to a soulful gaze. "Perhaps I can help." His hand drifted down to rest on her bare shoulder.

Rika stepped back. "It would help me most to get dressed."

She waited for him to leave, but he stayed put. Rather than risk a scene, she turned away to put her shirt back on. As she slipped her arms through the sleeves, she felt his eyes all over her. In a glass-fronted bookcase, she saw his reflection, neck craning while she did up the buttons. When she turned back, he'd found something to pick at on his shirt cuff.

"It might be a touch of malaria," he offered. "I could send for some quinine tablets."

"Thank you, but I don't like to take medicine. I think I'll just try to keep working and hope it will pass."

He glanced at the papyrus.

Rika held her breath, praying to gods she didn't believe in that he wouldn't look too closely.

"This can wait," he said at last. "Go back to your room and get some sleep."

The suggestion struck her as a windfall. She feigned reluctance but allowed him to persuade her.

Pointing to the papyrus, he said, "I'll put it away for you."

"No. I can—"

"I insist," he told her gently. "Now go. And be sure to drink plenty of tea."

Rika left her office and descended the Grand Staircase, her body suddenly trembling. Was it just a coincidence that he came in when he did, or did he suspect something? And if he hadn't suspected before, did her poorly concealed panic make him suspect something now? She missed a step and almost stumbled. Glancing back, she saw no one coming after her. Her heart rate began to settle.

Maybe she'd pulled it off.

#

That afternoon, Rika sat on her bed, nested in a clutter of books, papers, and the precious photos, her mind so immersed in the Eighteenth Dynasty that she almost didn't hear the knock on her door. Four-thirty. Too early for David.

"Who is it?" she called in Arabic, thinking it might be the maid.

Dr. Ragheb answered.

Oh, no. "Just a minute, please."

Frantically she pushed the books under the bed and tossed the covers over everything else. She stripped, threw her clothes in the closet, and pulled on a thin robe, clutching it at the neck and affecting what she hoped was an air of illness. After a deep breath, she opened the door.

Ragheb stood there—with flowers. "To hasten your recovery."

"My goodness, you didn't have to do that."

"I wanted to." He wore the same tan slacks and white shirt he'd had on that morning. But the shirt collar, previously open, was now buttoned at his throat. And he'd slicked back his hair, using something that smelled of lavender and looked oily to the touch.

Rika accepted the bouquet with trepidation. This was totally outside Arab custom. To merely call on an unmarried woman, unannounced and without chaperones, was forbidden in Islamic culture. Switching to formal Arabic, she said, "That is most kind of you."

"How are you feeling? You look much better."

"I do feel better. I'm planning to go back to work tomorrow."

He produced a small paper packet. "I also brought you some tea. It's very good for the stomach."

"You shouldn't have, but thank you. I'll make some now, to help me sleep."

Instead of taking the hint, he looked past her into the room.

Her gut tightened. He expected her to invite him in. It would have been unpardonably forward to actually say so. In older times, or in less "westernized" countries, even the implication would have cost him his life at the hands of the girl's brothers or uncles. But times had changed, she was a woman alone, and her position at the museum was in his hands.

Clutching her robe to her neck, she acquiesced. "Would you care to come in? For a minute."

"Thank you."

As he walked past her, Rika closed the door, but only halfway.

He declined her offer of the one chair in the room, crossing instead to the window where he gazed out in the direction of the museum to his right. "I apologize if I've appeared not to take much interest in your work." He turned to face her. "Actually, I am quite interested. How is it going?"

His words surprised her. As a scholar, he would know that the prime criterion for achieving a doctorate was a demonstrated ability to conduct independent research. Perhaps distancing himself from her work was his way of ensuring she could honestly claim it as her own. She felt an urge to tell him about the hidden writing, but decided to proceed cautiously. "It's going well."

"Queen Tiye was certainly a notable figure in the Eighteenth Dynasty," he allowed. "Not as notable as Queen Hatshepsut, of course, but still a distinguished woman."

Rika retreated mentally. No real change from the opinion he'd voiced when she first arrived—that Tiye was a minor personage, hardly deserving of academic attention, except possibly from a student. Feeling foolish that she'd let her hopes rise, Rika sat down on the edge of her bed. "I think her last papyrus is very significant. I'm looking forward to resuming my analysis of it."

"And when you've finished it, what then?"

"Hopefully, what I learn will meet the standards of the university and will qualify me for a doctorate."

"No, I mean after that. I assume you will receive your degree. But afterwards, would you consider returning to Cairo? I could secure a full-time staff position for you at the museum. There are many other worthy projects you could work on." His dark eyes grew more penetrating. "We might even collaborate."

Slimy tentacles seemed to slither up her legs. She smoothed the robe over her thighs, wishing the silky fabric were thick terrycloth. If she gave a positive response, he could interpret it as romantic encouragement. But rejecting such a coveted offer would be an insult that might spoil his evaluation of her to the doctoral committee. "I'll have to consider all my options at the time."

"Of course you will. But coming back to Cairo could be a wise decision." His gaze lingered on her, as if the weight of it would impress his words into her mind. Then he smiled. "And now, I have taken enough of your time. You should rest. I will see you tomorrow."

Relieved, Rika slid off the bed and stood. As she did, the covers slid with her, exposing a photograph.

"What's this?" he asked, picking it up.

Ice water flooded her veins. It was one of the enlargements of the secret writing. Fighting the urge to grab it, she said, "Just a papyrus. In the Louvre."

"There's Tiye's cartouche." He looked more closely. "But whose is this?"

Forcing her hand to move slowly, Rika reached out and took the photo. The cartouche in question was Princess Baketaten's. "I'm not sure. I'm just using this for comparative purposes." She tossed it back on her bed, face down.

"I don't think I've seen that papyrus before."

"As I said, it's in the Louvre."

He peered at her skeptically. "I've been through their entire collection. I don't recall it."

"But there are so many. And this is only a minor one."

Ragheb's eyes dug into her. But Rika forced a look of innocence, determined to maintain the standoff.

The silence dragged on. A rivulet of sweat ran down her side.

"I suppose you're right," he said at last. "In any case, the most important thing is that you regain your health." He pinched his lips, looked slowly around her room, then walked to the door and pulled it open. "I'll see you tomorrow."

#

Shortly before six in the evening, David strode into the Hilton, charged with optimism after the VIP demonstration flight and picturing an equally happy night on the town with Rika. He'd screwed up by moving too fast, but recovered his ground with the photos of the papyrus. Now he just needed to watch out for that short fuse of hers. Give her some room, go at her pace to wherever that led. He stopped cold when she sprang up from a chair in the lobby.

"I have to talk to you," she said, clutching her canvas book bag to her chest.

"What's wrong?"

"I can't tell you here. Can we go to your room?"

Alarmed, he walked her to the elevators, resisting a protective urge to put his arm around her.

In his room, Rika turned the wooden desk chair to face him and sat with the book bag in her lap. "Dr. Ragheb caught me."

David's fists balled in reflex. But she was free. So it couldn't have been too bad. His hands relaxed a little.

She described a harrowing encounter with the museum director in her office then an even scarier one in her hotel room, ending with, "I don't think he believed me about the photograph."

Not good. Stretching his fingers, David walked to the window and leaned back against the sill. The immediate problem was what to do if the director asked to see that photo again. "Could you find a picture of a papyrus in the Louvre? I could photograph it for you, and you could substitute it for the one he saw."

She shook her head. "There aren't any. Not with both Tiye's and Baketaten's cartouches."

"Cartouches?"

"A cartouche is an oval that encloses a person's name." Suddenly she sat up straight, the book bag sliding from her lap. "There *is* a papyrus in Vienna with Tiye's and Tutankhamun's names." Then her shoulders dropped. "But it doesn't have Baketaten's. And it's only a fragment."

Fragment? "I've got it." David pushed off the sill and squatted in front of her. "You find me a picture of the papyrus in Vienna. I'll photograph it, then we rip that photo into pieces. You tell your boss the maid accidentally threw out the photo he saw, and a few pieces were all you could find in the trash. You show him some bits from our torn-up Vienna photo. They have Tiye's name but not enough other writing to tell where the original really came from."

Rika's eyes widened, gorgeous, black as obsidian, their fire sparking like flashes of light off golden glitter. She grasped his head and kissed his mouth, a hard kiss that lasted only a second before she pushed him back to arm's length. "David, I can't thank you enough."

Half-stunned, he stared at her. She tasted like no other woman he'd ever known. "That kiss was pretty good thanks."

She looked aside, as if shy or regretful. He couldn't tell which. Then she leaned forward again.

He moistened his lips to receive her. But all she did was pick up the book bag she had dropped. Was she going to leave? He stood. "How about a drink? Or better yet, pick a restaurant. Hagazy's waiting downstairs to take us."

"I'd rather walk somewhere." She stood, also. "After everything that's happened today, I can't sit still. And I have to tell you about the wonderful things I've found."

A walk sounded perfect. David pulled off his tie and dropped it on the couch. "Let's go."

"Ah, I know. We can go to the pyramids."

"You mean the Sound and Light show?" David had hoped to see it before he left. "But isn't it closed on Friday nights?"

She grinned. "That's why we should go."

Chapter 8

As they pulled away from the Hilton, Rika rolled up her window against the growl of evening traffic and tried not to fidget. She couldn't wait to share her discoveries with David, but not in the car. Hagazy understood English too well. She felt like a racehorse, previously penned at the starting gate by research going nowhere, and now released into full gallop. Already she could see the finish line—her doctoral diploma, her return to Eritrea, her brother Efrem's dour face beaming with pride. Her younger brother, Alem, swinging her around in his arms.

Hagazy accelerated onto Tahrir Bridge, past the imperial lions flanking its bridgehead, and out over the dark Nile.

Would David appreciate what she'd found? She hoped so. She needed someone—and he was the only person she could talk to—to understand how momentous her discoveries were and to share her excitement.

David yawned. "Sorry, it's been a long day." He shrugged out of his blazer and folded it on the seat between them. Except for the front, his white shirt looked slept in. "But the demo went great."

Demo? "Oh, your demonstration for the officials."

"They loved everything. Especially the ground-penetrating radar. The two military guys had lots of questions about it." He rolled his shirtsleeves up to his elbows. "Hagazy, turn on the air conditioning."

Leaning forward, Rika closed the vent on her side. Artificially chilled air gave her sniffles.

David aimed his vent directly into his face. "Tomorrow

SEECO signs the contract, and we're off and running."

"Then both of us have had a good day." She waited expectantly but got only silence as they sped past the Opera House on the southern end of Zamalik Island, crossed a second bridge to the west bank of the Nile, and turned south on embassy row. A drip ran down Rika's nostril. She wiped it away with the back of her finger. Damned air conditioning.

"Soon," David said, touching her hand.

"Soon?"

He cut his eyes to Hagazy, then back to her. "Just hold on a few minutes. I *am* interested."

She squeezed his hand, adding perceptiveness to the plus side of his ledger. Then she sneezed.

"You okay?" he asked.

"Maybe we don't need the cold air."

"Hagazy, turn it off."

At the big roundabout of Giza Square, they slipped in behind a bus wheezing diesel fumes. Seconds later, horns blared as Hagazy cut across two lanes and escaped onto a broad thoroughfare. They sped past the garish marquees of Giza's nightclub district—well-patronized, even on the Muslim Sabbath—then turned down a narrow road beside an irrigation canal, uphill on a street lined with closed curio shops, and left into the parking lot facing the Sphinx. The lot was empty, the tourist center dark.

Leaving her book bag on the back seat, Rika climbed out into a balmy night on the Giza Plateau. Her head cleared. Her vision sharpened. Below, the Nile Valley sparkled like a necklace of diamonds. Beautiful, but nothing compared to this spot—the very edge of the vast Sahara. Here you could see the stars, hear the whisper of a breeze that had journeyed halfway across the continent. She could almost taste the spices from distant cooking pots.

A half-moon hung low across the Nile, bathing the Sphinx and pyramids in a soft glow. She scanned the plateau. "We must be careful. There are guards who are supposed to chase away visitors at night."

David told Hagazy to wait for them out of sight.

As Hagazy drove off, she felt herself unwind. "I love this

place. I come here every Friday night."

"I can see why." He looked around. "So what do you do? Walk among the pyramids?"

"Walk among them, sit among them. Once I climbed the biggest one." She pointed to the pyramid of Cheops. "It's illegal, but worth the risk."

His eyes lit up. "Let's do it tonight."

"I don't think so. It's more the sort of thing one does alone, for solitude." *Or with a lover.* For a moment, temptation tugged at her. But she needed to talk, to open a relief valve on the discoveries pent up inside her. "I'll take you to another place just as good. But watch out for scorpions."

She walked to the edge of the parking lot, stepped over the low stone barrier, and guided him down a shallow ravine and up the other side. On legs grateful for the exercise, she climbed a gentle slope, picking her way around piles of rocky debris and the ruins of small buildings made of limestone block, until she emerged into the cleared area between the forepaws of the Sphinx.

She heard an intake of breath and turned to see David gazing upward, his mouth open. Precisely her reaction the first night she'd come here.

"It's awesome," he said.

"Supposedly the face of Cheops. But according to legend, it's Horus himself."

"Horus?"

"The god of the Egyptian throne. Come, I'll show you." She led him toward the Sphinx's chest and the thick stone tablet, twice the height of a man, that stood in front of it. "This is called the Dream Stele. It was written by Thutmose the Fourth, the father of Tiye's husband. It says that, when Thutmose was a young prince and outcast by his father, he was hunting one day and fell asleep on this spot. He had a dream that Horus spoke to him. Horus was suffocating under the sand, and if the prince would unearth him, Horus would make him Pharaoh. The prince excavated the sand, found the Sphinx, and the god made good on his word."

"You can read all that?" David asked.

Rika laughed. "Not in this light. But that's what the hieroglyphs say. The amazing thing is that the Sphinx was already a thousand years old when Thutmose uncovered it. It's twice the age of the Parthenon."

David let out a low whistle. "Makes the Greeks and Romans sound like an epiphenomenon."

"A what?"

"Something minor that happened after a more important thing."

So he did understand. "That's why I come here. To feel the past and help me know the minds of the people who did great things in African history." She grasped David's hands. "And Tiye was definitely one of those people. Now I can prove it, thanks to the photos."

He beamed at her. "Glad I could help."

Beads of sweat trickled down his temples, and suddenly she realized it was hot in here from daytime heat stored in the Sphinx, whose legs and chest enclosed them on three sides. Recalling the air conditioning, she knew David must be uncomfortable.

"Let's go back where it's cooler," she said. "By the front of the feet."

As they neared the paws, a breeze picked up, carrying the mineral scents of sand and limestone, scents Tiye would have known very well.

"There's so much to tell you." Pointing to a block of limestone that was part of one toe, she motioned him to sit. "The best thing is, I can show beyond doubt that the new religion was Tiye's concept."

"Congratulations. You said before it was just a theory."

"Before, I only had the timing." Anxious not to swamp him with too many details, she summarized just the main points. "For thousands of years, Egyptians worshipped a pantheon of gods, with Amun at the top. Then along comes Tiye. She marries Pharaoh, and suddenly he begins worshipping Aten, the sun god. This new religion flowers under their first son, Akhenaten. It even continues in a minor way under Tutankhamun. Only when Tutankhamun and Tiye both die does Aten fall back into obscurity. To me, that couldn't be a coincidence."

"I'd call it strong evidence." He leaned forward, elbows on knees, moonglow trapped among the blond streaks in his hair.

"Especially the part about Tiye's husband worshipping Aten *before* Akhenaten became Pharaoh."

"Exactly!" She wanted to hug him for being so attuned to her thinking. "And the papyrus confirms it. Tiye says the new religion was revealed to her. That's what she calls it, a 'revelation.' I think you and I would call it 'inspiration.' Or maybe it was just a scheme. But it matches perfectly with her being a commoner, wanting to see other commoners treated with dignity and equality."

David stood and took her hands. "So she taught it to Akhenaten. Probably from the time he was a boy."

"Which explains why he was so ... What's the word? Zealy?"

"Zealous."

"Yes. He cast out the priests and defaced their images of Amun. So when he died, the priests rebelled, and there was almost a religious civil war. But Tiye prevented it. She appeased the priests by changing Tutankh*aten*'s name to Tutankh*amun*. And for the Atenites, she had him marry the princess who was Akhenaten's daughter and last wife." Rika swelled with admiration at the brilliance of Tiye's strategy. "What the priests didn't know, what no one knew before I read it in the papyrus, was that Tutankhamun was supposed to bring back the religion of Aten. Only this time, unlike his brother, he was supposed to do it slowly, little by little."

"But he died too young."

She squeezed David's hands. "Isn't it wonderful how everything falls together?"

"You *brought* it together. It wouldn't have happened if you hadn't held on to your belief that the timing was significant."

A rush of pride swept through her. "There's more!" When she let go of his hands, he looked disappointed. But she was too energized to stand still. "Sit down."

As he resumed his seat on the limestone block, the breeze freshened. Flurries of dust stirred in the distance, but the lion's paws sheltered them.

She paced a few steps to her left, a few steps to the right. "The biggest surprise is that Tiye wasn't buried in Egypt. She was buried in Nubia."

David screwed up his face. "Why Nubia?"

"That's where she came from."

"I thought she was Egyptian."

"No." Rika realized she must not have told him. Either it hadn't come up, or she'd assumed it was common knowledge. "Tiye was Nubian, the daughter of two Amun priests. When she was twelve or thirteen, her parents were summoned to the Egyptian court to receive some sort of tribute. That's where she met Amenhotep the Third."

Pausing, Rika pictured the scene, a young black girl standing between her parents while the most powerful man on earth looked down at her from his throne.

"They fell in love, and he married her." Rika couldn't help grinning. "You can imagine the scandal."

"Because she was a child bride?"

"No, that happened all the time. The scandal was that she was a commoner. The priests were furious."

"I don't get it. Why should the priests care who he married?"

"Because it threatened their power." Reminding herself that David wasn't an Egyptologist, Rika explained, "The political power of the priests came from their claim that all royalty were descended from Amun. Pharaoh was a son of Amun, and when he impregnated a royal princess, Amun replaced him at the … critical moment. So it was actually Amun impregnating one of his own daughters. But with Tiye being a commoner, they could no longer claim this. And to make matters worse, her husband sent out decrees announcing that Tiye was his favorite wife and only queen, and his children by her were his only legitimate heirs."

"The priests must have choked."

"More than that. They actually plotted against her by trying to stir up a public outcry. But the people loved her. There were even cults that worshipped her."

"A living goddess."

"I wish I'd been there." Sometimes she could envisage Tiye's life so vividly it seemed like she *had* been there. And with each re-reading of the papyrus she learned even more. The only thing better … "Can you imagine what a treasure house of knowledge her tomb must be?"

David straightened. "You say that like it's never been found."

"It can't have been. That's what's so exciting. No one would ever think of looking for it in Nubia. In fact, if they think about it at all, they assume it was plundered because of the Elder Lady."

"You're losing me. Who's the Elder Lady?"

Someone who didn't matter anymore, which was another of Rika's amazing discoveries. David would love this. "That's the name given to the mummy of an unidentified woman who was found in a tomb with lots of mummies. The mummies were put there in ancient times by priests who collected them from tombs that had been robbed. Most people think the Elder Lady is Tiye."

"But you don't."

"I used to. They x-rayed her skull, and it looks like the skull of another mummy, Thuya, who was Tiye's mother. Then recently they analyzed the Elder Lady's hair and compared it to a lock of hair that was found in Tutankhamun's tomb, in a little wooden coffin with Tiye's name on it. The two matched exactly."

David frowned. "Sounds convincing to me."

"Not if Tiye was buried in Nubia. The priests never would have gone that far south to look for pillaged tombs. Besides,"—she leaned in for the clincher—"the Elder Lady died in her late forties. And I can prove from the papyrus that Tiye wrote it in her sixties."

"Then how do you explain the matching hair?"

Hair? David was supposed to leap with excitement at the news of Tiye's age, not press a point that was now irrelevant. With a flick of her wrist, Rika said, "I don't know. Maybe one of Tiye's daughters. She had four or five."

Sitting back, David rubbed his jaw line.

This close to him, she could hear the rasp of whiskers unshaven since morning. What was he thinking? His eyes seemed focused on the ground. Or rather, unfocused. She glanced at her sandals, covered in dust, then up at the moon, then back at him. No change. How long did it take to digest a few facts?

Finally he stirred, a nod as if to himself. He looked at her. "I can help you find it."

"Find what?"

"Tiye's tomb. Isn't that what you want?"

"Don't be silly." She wanted lots of things and so far had none of them. The least achievable would be Tiye's tomb.

"It's not silly." He stood and clasped her arms. "A tomb is

nothing more than an anomaly in the ground. And that's exactly what ground-penetrating radar is designed to detect."

"David, you're dreaming." The most fabulous dream an Egyptologist could have, but still a dream. She pulled herself away. "Do you have any idea what it takes to make an expedition? The logistics, the people, the money?"

"Let's find it first. Then we'll work on those things."

He'd never make a military planner. "You have to think of the end before the beginning. The end is in Nubia, which is in the Sudan. Their government is as hostile and corrupt as Ethiopia's."

He planted his hands on his hips. "Then what are you going to do with this incredible discovery? Keep it to yourself?"

She stared at him, the truth of his words seeping into her like poison. She'd known before that she couldn't tell Dr. Ragheb, but in her enthusiasm she'd failed to look beyond that. If she tried to publish her findings, even as a doctoral thesis, she would have to reveal the source, or no one would believe her. If she didn't publish her findings, she'd never get her degree. The bitter irony burned through her, almost too much to bear.

"Rika, this is a huge opportunity for you. And great publicity for GPR. There's a four-day gap before the airplane's next job. We could fly it to Sudan and—"

"Stop it!" *Americans. They think they can do anything.* "The Sudanese would shoot you down."

"We'll get permission first."

She turned away from the unintended cruelty of his persistence. Short of Eritrea's independence, nothing she could imagine would be as wonderful as finding Tiye's tomb. Touching the things Tiye held most dear. Not just knowing *about* the woman, but standing beside her, feeling her spirit. Rika shuddered.

But it was all fantasy. Her eyes fell on the Dream Stele, the story of the outcast prince who dug up the Sphinx and became king. A nice fairytale. Turning back to David, she said, "This is not a fairytale. Things won't happen just because we want them to."

"Can't we at least try?"

The breeze had died. Heat from the Sphinx stuck her shirt to her chest. She felt grungy, tired, and in no mood to prolong this conversation. "It's impossible."

David thrust his hands in his pockets. "Have it your way. I—"

"Quiet." Rika heard the soft crunch of footsteps. Quickly she pulled some piastres from her jeans pocket, placed them on the stone where David had been sitting, then dragged him behind a tall mound of rubble.

"A guard?" he whispered.

She touched her finger to his lips. With any luck, the guard would take the bribe and wander off, his honor unoffended as he hadn't actually *seen* any trespassers. It had worked for her once before. But just in case ... "Hold me."

"Gladly." He wrapped her in his arms, holding her firmly. More firmly than necessary for a charade. But was it just a charade? When she'd brought him out here, was the papyrus the only thing on her mind? Whether it was or not, his embrace soothed her, softened the impact of her dilemma with the papyrus. She closed her eyes. Their bodies fit perfectly. Molded to him, she felt his heart beating against her cheek, smelled the cotton of his shirt, the heady tang of his perspiration.

A cough shattered her reverie. It came from the direction of the Sphinx. She caught a whiff of cigarette smoke, then heard the crunch of footsteps again, receding.

She pushed out of David's arms and peeked around the pile of rubble to see a tall man walking away, his galabeyah, the traditional Egyptian robe, flapping at his ankles. Unless she were mistaken, he was the same man she'd bribed to climb Cheops. When he disappeared, she felt David's presence behind her.

He turned her toward him.

His eyes had changed. They burned with an intensity that stopped her breath. He drew her closer. Looking up at him, she felt his fingertips touch her face, trace her cheekbones. Their lips met, a kiss so tender it sent shivers up her back. Then he gripped her hair and kissed her hard. Deep inside an ember ignited.

Rika pulled his hands from her hair and stepped back.

He looked at her as if asking what was wrong.

She felt his disappointment, surely as much as he did. Her lips still tingled. But feelings more profound than arousal stirred inside her, feelings she needed time to sort out. Willing herself to cool down, she said, "We should go."

#

Closing the door of her hotel room, Rika felt depleted. They'd ridden back in silence. Not only had he dangled a dream that had no chance of succeeding, but without knowing it he'd also shown her she had failed. Six years away from home, for nothing. Mission not accomplished. Disgusted, she flopped down on the bed.

Someone knocked. David? Halfheartedly, she got up and opened the door.

"Efrem! I don't believe it." Rika threw her arms around her brother's neck. In their native Tigrinya, she said, "I'm so happy to see you. What are you doing here? How did you find me?"

"Mother told me." He held her at arm's length. "You look beautiful."

Beautiful? He'd never said *that* before. Must be the years of separation. She pulled him inside and closed the door.

He wore a dark brown Egyptian robe and Arab headdress. His cheeks had grown hollow, his eyes more ascetic. Guilt seized her for not sharing his hardships. "Sit down," she said, the only comfort she could offer.

He stayed standing. "How are your studies going?"

"I'll be finished in a few weeks," she lied. "Then back to Paris to complete the formalities for my degree, and I can come home."

"Excellent. We all miss you."

But something in his tone made her wary, an uncharacteristic sentimentality. "Efrem, why are you here? Is something wrong?"

He took hold of her shoulders.

"Efrem, what is it? What's happened?"

He opened his mouth, but no words came out.

"Efrem!"

He released her. "Alem has been killed."

"No!" Desperately she searched his eyes for some uncertainty, some sign of doubt. All she saw was the glint of moisture. "Tell me it's not true."

But she knew it was. Her baby brother had always been daring, and she'd often feared his luck could not hold. She pictured his face, his roguish grin. "How did it happen?"

"They captured him."

Her breath stopped. She sank to her knees. Capture meant only one thing. They tortured him.

Chapter 9

Rika woke from a tormented sleep, feeling guilty that she'd slept at all. Her sobbing must have exhausted her. But Alem never left her thoughts. His face had swum in and out of her dreams, now grinning, now staring up at her with the sightless eyes of the dead. She shuddered. His loss left a cold cavity in her chest, next to the void she still felt from their father's death.

"I brought you something," Efrem said.

She twisted in bed to see him rise from the armchair by her window. He still wore the Egyptian robe but had shed the headdress. In the gray light of dawn, his face looked haggard, lined with fatigue.

As he walked toward the bathroom, she noticed a limp. "Efrem, what's wrong with your leg?"

"Shrapnel."

She sat up straight. "How bad is it?"

"It does not stop me." He disappeared into the bathroom.

Damn this war. She slouched back against the headboard and, a minute later, smelled Eritrean mountain tea. He must be brewing it on the hot plate she kept by the sink. The familiar aroma brought a lump of nostalgia to her throat.

Returning with two glasses of tea and a chunk of hard cheese, he placed them on the table beside her bed. From a pocket in his robe, he pulled out a *beles*, the cactus pear so popular in the highlands.

She could barely hold back her tears. "Did you bring this all the way from home?"

He shrugged, peeled the fruit with a short dagger, and laid it next to the cheese.

"Efrem, I do love you." She had always loved him, despite the fact that he rarely gave her reason to. She could think of only two occasions. The time when she was six that he'd beaten up two village boys picking on her, and one morning a year later when he actually took her fishing.

Perhaps Efrem's aloofness was one reason she'd doted so much on her younger brother. That, and some protective instinct she'd always harbored. "Poor Alem."

"He has been avenged. I saw to it personally." Efrem spoke matter-of-factly, as if reporting on a routine military operation.

And suddenly it occurred to her that a hardened commander wouldn't come all this way just to tell her about a death in the family. "Efrem, why are you here?"

He limped to the window. "I am trying to obtain arms."

"What?" Rika tossed off the blanket, swung her feet to the floor, and sat on the edge of the bed. She was still wearing her jeans and shirt from last night. "Why didn't you tell me?"

"You were in no condition."

Pulling a pillow into her lap, she asked, "How is it going at home?"

"Badly. Our Kalashnikovs grow weary."

"But we capture more with every raid on the Ethiopians."

"That is the problem. We capture mostly small arms." He turned from the window and sat in her chair. "We need heavier weapons. Something to knock out MiGs and tanks. Humiliate the generals and force a political solution." He rubbed his eyes. "Otherwise, this war of attrition will go on for eternity. Or until we lose."

A chill crept through her. Never before had she heard such dire words from her invincible brother. She leapt to her feet. "I'm going back to fight."

His lips twitched, the closest he ever came to smiling. "You are brave. But we have thousands of brave fighters. Your job is here."

"Don't start with that rubbish. I'm more than just a good fighter, and you know it."

"That is exactly the point. You are more than a fighter, which is why you were chosen for this assignment."

"Damn you, Efrem!"

Another twitch of the lips. "I must learn not to anger you. One day you will be my superior."

She threw up her hands. He had their father's ability to disarm, verbally as well as physically. She sat on the arm of his chair, noticing now how deeply the worry lines creased his face. "Let me help you."

"No. I am talking to embassies, and with them, military status is important."

"Which embassies?"

He rubbed his eyes again. "I saw the Libyans yesterday."

"Efrem, they're despicable."

"We have tried almost everyone else. Anyhow, the Libyans turned me down. Today I will visit the Palestinian mission."

Rika shut her eyes against the very thought. Had they become that desperate? "Can't we just buy arms?"

"What shall we use for money?"

"The Norwegians. Can't mother help?" But even as she spoke, Rika knew the answer. While living in Europe, she'd visited Oslo twice. Their mother had established an excellent network, but most of the contributions were "humanitarian." Food, medical supplies.

As if deciding this conversation had become a waste of his time, Efrem pushed himself up and walked to the door. "I have things to do."

#

With every ounce of willpower he could muster, David left the VP's office at SEECO without slamming the door. He tramped down one flight of stairs, stomped along the hallway past dark rooms deserted on the weekend, and stormed into Blue's office. "Those cocksuckers!"

"Good morning to you, too." Blue swiveled on the stool at his light table. "Which cocksuckers, specifically? This place is full of them."

"Those goddamn colonels on my flight yesterday." David

shoved some papers off a wooden chair and plopped down. "Or the goddamn generals they report to."

Reaching under the tabletop, Blue doused the light shining up through the well logs he'd been working on. "Care to explain?"

"They scuttled the GPR. All those years of work. The perfect test case. And they get all hinky because it does exactly what I told them it would do."

"Which exactly was …?"

"Image things under the ground. Dammit, this is a major advance with all kinds of potential. Not just in the oil business." David got up from the chair and counted off on his fingers just some of the applications he'd thought of. "Underground utilities, engineering hazards like faults and incipient sinkholes. You could detect smugglers' tunnels under borders. Landmines. You know how many people are killed or maimed every year by forgotten landmines? Hell, you could have used GPR instead of those poor sheep. Police could use it to find buried bodies. And theoretically it'll penetrate ice. You could use it to measure the thickness of glaciers and ice caps, get indisputable data on global warming."

He dropped back in the chair. "All it needs is a kick-start. Something glamorous to make people sit up and take notice, fund additional R and D. And the generals flushed it."

Blue stroked his beard. "If I were guessing, I'd say you're another victim of the fundamentalists."

"Fundamentalists? What are you talking about? You think they cast some sort of spell?"

"Over the whole damn country." Blue pulled a thin cigar from his shirt pocket and lit up. "Long story short, a year and a half ago, when Sadat was gunned down by fundamentalists among his own soldiers, the politicians and military got nervous as ticks on dip day. Who could be trusted? Who couldn't? Did the threat come from outside, as well as inside?"

"What does that have to do with GPR?"

A chunk of ash fell on Blue's shirtfront, but he didn't seem to notice. "You're not putting yourself in the paranoid mindset. Think security. If you can see into the ground with GPR, then maybe you can see into buildings, read secret documents the fundamentalists would pay for."

Insane. "GPR can't see into buildings."

"So you say. But wily foreigner comes with new magic."

David thought back to the demo flight, the questions the colonels had asked. He must have made too many assumptions about their technical savvy, interpreted nods as comprehension. But he could fix that. "I'll explain it to them better."

Blue shook his head. "Too late, squire. You wouldn't get past the front door. Sorry to say, but in this country when the military speaks, mortals don't argue."

#

Rika gazed into her closet, sickened by the thought of her proud brother going cap-in-hand from one embassy to another and being turned away like a beggar at a rich man's feast. Not being able to help him was yet another sign of how far removed she'd become from her former life. When he'd left, an hour ago, he hadn't even told her if he would be back.

Pulling a fresh shirt off its hanger, she pondered her own plight with the papyrus. Like the war, it seemed to have no solution. And she shouldn't have gotten angry at David last night for pointing out her dilemma. He was only the messenger. But it felt like everything she wanted had become a mirage, receding before her no matter how fast she ran.

As she buttoned the shirt, the other thing David had said came back to mind: *I could help you find it.* Less than a mirage. A pipe dream. Yet she couldn't help thinking of Tiye's tomb as her Sphinx, calling to her from beneath the sand, destined to remain buried for all eternity unless she woke and exhumed it.

What a trove of knowledge. The artifacts, the paintings, Tiye herself.

She shut the closet door, leaving the pipe dream inside. She had practical problems to attend to, not the least of which was finding a photo of that papyrus fragment in Vienna so David could copy it in case Dr. Ragheb asked more questions.

Efrem hadn't given up on his mission, and she wouldn't give up on hers.

#

In a spare office at SEECO, where Paul Rackowski had set up their ground station, David peered at the lines of data coming in from ten thousand feet. A standard survey, without ground-penetrating radar.

Paul, the electrical engineer who'd stopped checking his beloved equipment so David could image the papyrus, had almost cried when David told him to leave the GPR turned off. But by that time, David had lost interest in the job, and Paul's Polish expletives fell on uncaring ears.

Now, as the aircraft's flight lines crept across one of his two screens, David felt deadened by the boring familiarity of the room where he sat. He could be in Jakarta or London or Timbuktu, the ground station was always the same. Lights off, window blinds closed to enhance clarity on his monitors. Air conditioning set on "Max Cold" to compensate for the heat pouring out of all the electronic equipment. To his left stood a five-foot-tall metal rack filled with array processors. To his right, a twin rack holding transmitters, receivers, controllers, decoders. Right of that, four eighty-pound uninterruptible power supplies. Status lights blinked red and green. The UPSs clicked on and off with every fluctuation in Cairo's line current. Instrument cooling fans hummed—he'd once counted twelve of them in the backs of the various devices.

Clients went ga-ga. But to him, it felt like being submerged in a sensory deprivation chamber. Or being entombed.

Tomb. Tiye's tomb, and its potential glory, flashed into his mind in exquisite detail that he recognized as a compilation of all the Egyptian treasure he'd seen in museums. Rika had scoffed, but if he could find it, the news would make worldwide headlines. Just the kick-start GPR needed. In interviews, he could tout the whole range of GPR's capabilities. Especially its applications to oil exploration, where the big money was. Lots of oil companies worked in lots of desert nations. Grab their attention, and they'd come to him. Forget Egypt and its paranoid generals.

The perfect solution. Maybe his only solution. If Digital Image didn't start realizing a return on the expensive investment he'd rammed down their throat, he'd be out of a job. His broader visions for GPR would languish until some other bright spark tumbled to them independently.

Swiveling his chair, he stared at the wall. All he had to do was strike a deal with the Sudanese. He locates the tomb, they provide the manpower and equipment, and jointly they open it. The Sudanese get a tourist attraction, Rika gets to study all the stuff they find, and he gets to grandstand GPR. Plus, he and Rika would have more time together.

Everybody wins.

But he had to act fast. The SEECO job would finish in two days. He snatched up the phone and dialed Rika's office. "Would you have dinner with me tonight? There's something important I want to discuss."

#

When David arrived at Rika's hotel, she was waiting in front, her book bag over her shoulder, the low sun bathing her milk-chocolate skin. A goddess. He hopped out of the Peugeot, armed with a reservation at the Meridien Hotel for a candlelit table overlooking the Nile. "You look great."

She smiled, then extracted a thin volume from her bag and handed it to him. "This is the book with the photo of that papyrus fragment in Venice."

"I'll get you a copy tomorrow morning." He turned toward the open rear door of the Peugeot. "Ready to go?"

"There's a good kebab restaurant not far from here. I thought you might like to try it."

Kebabs? He'd set his heart on champagne, fine French cuisine, a romantic atmosphere that would make her receptive to considering his plan and maybe to a longer evening together.

"It's one of my favorite places," she said. "We can walk there in twenty minutes."

Well if that's what she wanted, then that's what they'd do. "Okay." He put the book in the car's rear seat and dismissed Hagazy for the night.

Rika set off down a busy thoroughfare, then led him into a warren of side streets that got narrower and grimier as they went.

They braided their way past deliverymen balancing bolts of cloth on their heads, workmen lugging tires, bicyclers jangling their bells. David switched his wallet to a front trouser pocket and kept his hand around it.

He walked beside her through a short alley to a one-lane road where honking cars crawled behind a splendid Arabian hitched to a wagonload of stinking garbage. Motor scooters used the sidewalk to get around. Ahead, a blacksmith pounded iron on a big anvil. A mechanic squatted on the engine under the yawning hood of a dusty Rolls Royce. High above, laborers balanced barefoot on bamboo scaffolding, laying bricks in the orange glow of the setting sun.

On the opposite side of the road, two young men walked hand-in-hand, an Arab custom with no romantic implications. But it raised an image of Rika and himself strolling home after dinner. He edged closer to her, letting his arm occasionally brush against hers.

Another turn brought them to a quieter street where butchers tended carcasses hung on display and men in galabeyahs sipped coffee around tiny tables on the sidewalk. Aromas of wood smoke and roasting meat reminded him of those perfect mornings in the mountains when you emerged from your tent to smell bacon frying on the fire.

Rika stopped. "Here we are."

They stood in front of a bead-curtained doorway flanked by windows with Arabic script painted across them. No view of the Nile, but this could work. Small, intimate. And they seemed to be the only foreigners, which would create a psychological bond.

She looked at him expectantly.

"I like it," he said.

A screech pierced the air.

David froze.

It came again, like a child being tortured. The men sipping coffee took no notice.

Rika grasped his hand. "Come inside."

Just up the road, an aproned man was strapping a monkey into some kind of harness under a wooden table where two men sat with forks in hand.

"Please," Rika said, tugging David's arm. "You don't want to see this."

The monkey was now firmly secured, flailing and screaming, the crown of its head projecting through a hole in the center of the table. The guy who'd strapped it there pulled out a large knife and laid its edge along the top of the table.

Rika yanked David inside. As she dragged him toward the rear of the restaurant, a long wail followed them.

David stopped her. "Did they just do what I think they did?"

"It's an ancient delicacy."

Eating the brain of a live monkey? Out of all the bad shit he'd seen in Third World countries, that ranked among the cruelest. He wanted to cold-cock the bastards.

"We can go someplace else," Rika offered softly.

He wasn't sure if the distress in her eyes came from shared revulsion at the atrocity or from the thought that she'd ruined their evening by inadvertently exposing him to it. In either case, he wanted to comfort her. "Let's find a table here."

Some of the tension lifted from her face. "There's one."

He followed her to the back corner and a white metal table no larger than a serving platter. Private, or at least as private as they could get. When they'd seated themselves, he looked around. The long, skinny restaurant, with a single row of tables on each side, was full of men, some of whom must have been staring at them, for they now turned back to their food. Near the front, a big fellow in a sweat-soaked T-shirt tended the grille beside a dowdy woman wearing a headscarf and skewering chunks of meat. As he watched, the woman wiped her hands on a towel and came up to them.

"I recommend the mutton," Rika said.

"Fine. What would you like to drink?" He was thinking beer, to cut the mutton's grease.

"They only have tea."

Then tea it was. He wasn't going to spoil her improving mood with complaints about the menu. When Rika had given the woman their orders, he leaned forward, spreading his hands on the table. "I want to talk to you about Tiye's tomb. Remember what you said last night about the problem with flying into Sudan?"

"Not just a problem. Suicide."

"Maybe not."

"David!"

"I'm just hypothesizing."

The woman returned with two glasses of reddish liquid. To buy time for the atmosphere to defuse, David took a sip. It tasted like mint and smelled like hibiscus. Pretty good, actually.

He focused again on Rika. "Purely as a matter of interest, is there any way to narrow down where in Sudan Tiye's tomb might be? I mean, it's a big country."

Rika seemed to relax a little. "Most tombs are on the west bank of the Nile, facing the rising sun. Why do you ask?"

"Curiosity." That information alone narrowed the search area tremendously. No way could he fly grid lines over the whole country. Still, the Nile was a long river. "Would it be in the north or the south?"

The woman arrived with two plates of kebabs. As she set them down, she said something to Rika.

Rika smiled. When the woman left, Rika told him, "She thinks you're handsome."

"And I think you're beautiful."

She smiled again, a slightly bashful smile that made him want to tilt her chin and kiss her. With her fingers, she slid a piece of meat off its skewer and put it in her mouth.

Those luscious lips.

"Aren't you going to try them?" she asked.

"Try them?" *I'd love to try them.*

"Your kebabs."

Oh. He looked for utensils, saw none, and used his fingers as she had done. The kebab was delicious. Seasoned with sesame, honey, and lemon. Not greasy, at all, and perfect with the tea. "They're excellent."

"I'm glad you like them." She ate another. "About Tiye's tomb, it's probably in the north. There were cults that worshipped her. Her husband built temples for them, which are all north of Khartoum. And the papyrus says her tomb was built by workers from one of those cults. There's even a name of their village. But I can't find it on a map."

He dropped his skewer. "Why didn't you tell me that before?"

"Why should I?" She wiped her lips with a knuckle.

"Because it could mean the difference between success and failure." *Okay, spring it.* He lowered his voice. "Look, here's what I'm thinking. We tell the Sudanese what you've found. and we get them to—"

"Never!"

He jerked back, shocked at her outburst.

"The Sudanese are criminals," she spat. "Fanatics."

"But if they knew about the tomb—"

"They don't care about tombs. All they care about is exterminating non-Muslims in the south."

"We could make them a deal."

"Deal?" She bored into him with her eyes. "I'll tell you what would happen with your deal. They'd go along with it until you opened the tomb. Then they'd sell everything inside to line their own pockets and finance more genocide. And before you could leave the country, they'd kill you."

#

Rika trudged up the stairs to her hotel room. How could David be so out-of-touch with reality? She wouldn't care, except that his harping on Tiye's tomb stabbed her with pangs of hopeless longing.

She unlocked her door, wishing for nothing more than a hot bath and a quiet night alone. But as she swung the door open, she saw a dark form behind it. She tensed to strike.

"No," her brother said.

"Efrem!" She switched on the light. "You frightened me. Why are you hiding?"

"I was not sure it was you."

"Who else would it be?"

Efrem pointed past her. "Earlier, it was him."

On the floor, protruding from the far side of her bed, was a pair of trousered legs. "Who is he?" she asked.

"No identification."

"Is he dead?"

"Just unconscious."

She dropped her book bag on the bed and walked around to look at the man's face. Egyptian probably, in his late thirties, with close-cropped hair and the build of a hippo. He wore a rumpled gray suit and heavy brown shoes, well-scuffed. "I've never seen him before. What happened?"

Efrem came to stand beside her. "I was waiting for you, when I heard someone fumbling with the lock. The noise went on too long to be a key, so I stood behind the door. This fellow came in and started rummaging through your things. When he saw me, I jumped him."

"A thief."

"Undoubtedly. But you are not rich."

"Still, I'm living in this hotel like a tourist."

"Perhaps." Efrem's frown said he wasn't sure it was that simple. "All right, you had better help me get rid of him."

As they would with a fallen comrade, they raised the man to his knees, then Rika held him from behind while they both lifted until Efrem could squat and flop the man over his shoulder.

Efrem stood with a grunt. "He eats too much."

Rika checked the hallway, then stood watch at the landing while Efrem carried the man to the rear stairs. Ducking around them, she led the way down until they reached the service area at the bottom. She heard kitchen noises in the distance but nothing close by. Moving to the deliveries door, she opened it a crack to see a loading dock and alley hemmed in by the hotel's exterior walls. Rubbish cans and cardboard boxes lined one side of the alley, all dark but for light filtering in from the street beyond.

"Clear." She opened the door wider.

Efrem stepped past her. "I am going to follow this guy when he wakes up."

"I'll go with you." She'd never worked with her brother before. She wanted to help, to show him she could.

"No," he told her. "Go back to your room."

#

In the third-floor study of his apartment above a gold-dealer's shop in the Khan el Khalili souk, Major Hosni Hassam sat back in his armchair, shutting out the tempting aromas of a late dinner his wife had prepared after putting their children to bed. He did not appreciate having his evenings interrupted, but Corporal Malik had pounded at his door and now stood shame-faced and empty-handed with a very curious tale.

What should have been a simple theft from a cheap hotel room had turned into something disturbingly different.

Snatch some photographs, no problem. As chief of Domestic Branch of the Egyptian State Security Service, Hassam considered it an easy favor to grant Dr. Ragheb, a brother officer from the glory days in Nasser's 13th Battalion. But then Malik, a former carnival wrestler with a cloudy eye, had been knocked unconscious and dumped in an alley.

More troublesome was the assailant—a black man with a bad leg, if Hassam could believe Malik's account. Yesterday Diplomatic Branch had reported a black man with a limp visiting the Libyan embassy. And just this morning they'd tried to follow a man of the same description when he left the Palestinian legation.

Normally, Hassam regarded the daily reports of Diplomatic Branch as pompous attempts at self-promotion. But if their black man and this black assailant were the same person, it was a different story, a story that soured Hassam's stomach.

"You can go," he told Malik.

As the door closed, Hassam stood from his chair, walked to the window overlooking the souk, and lit a cigarette. The smells of his wife's cooking no longer tempted him.

Chapter 10

"Efrem." Startled to wakefulness by the sight of him in the armchair, Rika pushed herself up against her pillow. In the darkness, only his profile showed against a dim glow coming through her window. The luminous hands of her watch read 5:35. "I didn't hear you come in."

"I would be disappointed if you had."

True, he could move as silently as a snake. But before she'd left Eritrea, Rika could *hear* a snake, even one slithering over rock.

"Your visitor," he said, "went to a house in the gold district of the souk. He stayed there about an hour, then I followed him to a shabby apartment building, which must be where he lives because he was still there three hours ago."

"So he works for a gold dealer. He *was* just a thief."

"Whatever he is, I can find him again. If necessary."

Rika doubted it would be. Thieves went for easy marks. After the beating he got last night, that thief wouldn't be back. Leaving the lights off, she scooped up the jeans and shirt she'd worn yesterday and carried them into the bathroom. "Do you want tea?" she called through the closed door.

"Please."

She set the kettle heating and returned to sit on the edge of her bed.

"Speaking of strangers," he said, "who is that man you ate dinner with last night?"

"David? He's a friend. Why?"

"You were also with him the night before. He brought you

back here. Quite late."

"Efrem." She stood. "Are you spying on me?"

He eyed her calmly, as impassive as an interrogator. "I am just concerned. You know as well as I do that affairs between black women and white men always end badly for the woman."

For a second, Rika's pique stole her tongue. What arrogant gall. The kettle whistled, but she ignored it. Through teeth barely unclenched, she informed him, "I am perfectly capable of handling my personal life."

He looked past her. "Shall I get the kettle?"

"No, get stuffed." She spun on her heel, stalked into the bathroom, and yanked the kettle off the hotplate. Did women ever stop being little girls to their parents and brothers?

To calm down, she took her time making the tea. Of course she'd thought about a deeper relationship with David, and under less stressful circumstances, she might have let it happen. But nothing in her life was going well right now. The papyrus, her thesis, that godforsaken war that continued to devastate the people and the land she loved. "Efrem, did you have any luck with the Palestinians?"

She carried their glasses of tea into the bedroom to see him shaking his head. "If one is not Muslim ..."

"Or Christian, or Jewish." She knew the litany. Godless Marxists was how the west viewed them. And the Soviet pigs were no better, supporting them against Haile Selassie, then flicking them away like snot on their fingers when Ethiopian Marxists came to power.

She thought back to small French cafes where students held earnest political discussions long into the night. It was all crap. In reality, governments couldn't care less about the liberation of subjugated people, unless they could gain something from it. "Isn't there *something* we could bargain with?"

He gazed at his tea. "Our only assets are location and coastline. They are not like gold we could sell and then find some more."

Gold. Rika sat on the bed, regarding her brother as pieces came together in her mind. If Tiye's tomb were half as good as Tutankhamun's, the artifacts could bring millions. Hundreds of millions. Eritrea could buy weapons beyond Efrem's wildest dreams, with plenty of money left over to rebuild their ravaged society.

She recalled the Englishman, Sir Geoffrey Brighton-Jones, who had approached her at the Louvre, willing to pay ten thousand pounds for a gold figurine in the museum's collection if she would "help it go missing." She'd thrown him out.

The thought of selling artifacts was repulsive. But then again, golden statues and alabaster vases were mere trinkets. The real value lay in the knowledge gleaned from documents, wall paintings, the mummy itself.

Rika gnawed her lip. Could she bring herself to pillage for the sake of money?

Can you stand by and watch Eritrea perish?

Her tea, untouched and now tepid, had a dull film on its surface. She set the glass on her nightstand.

"Efrem, I may have an idea. But I need to think about it first." All those reasons she'd told David about why it wouldn't work were still valid. And if she gave Efrem a plan half-cooked, he'd think she'd gone fuzzy-brained in her years away from home. Which she probably had. "I'll tell you tonight."

"I will not see you tonight." He levered himself out of the chair and placed his glass next to hers. "In fact, I may not see you again before I leave Cairo."

"Why not?"

"I have stayed with you too long. The Secret Police have noticed me, and I do not want to draw them to you."

"Secret Police? What happened?"

"It seems they keep an eye on some of the embassies I have visited." He laid a checkered cloth over his head and fitted the woven headband in place, completing his Arab costume.

She wondered where he'd stay, but a city this size had a thousand places. More important was how to contact him if her idea stood up to deeper scrutiny. A chalk mark, a broken branch. Maybe a flag. But not in her window here. The maid might take it down. "Efrem, when I want to speak to you, I'll hang a small Egyptian flag in the window of my office at the museum. It's on the second floor, next to—"

"I know where your office is." He kissed her forehead. "I must go. I will look for your flag." His eyes and tone of voice said he was humoring his little sister.

Rika almost slammed the door.

She stripped and stepped into the shower. As the hot stream soothed her temper, she released the brakes she'd applied to David's arguments. Northern Sudan, like most of Egypt, was largely uninhabited except along the Nile. Efrem and a squad of his men could slip in easily through the desert, provide the equipment and manpower necessary to breach the tomb's entrance, and truck away the contents. But only if the tomb were in some isolated spot where they could work unnoticed.

The critical factor was location.

#

In the mahogany-paneled conference room adjacent to the Head of Service's top-floor office, Major Hassam adopted a guileless face and waited for the right moment.

Only four men attended these morning briefings, the Head himself and the chiefs of his three operational branches: Domestic, Foreign, and Diplomatic. They sat in leather club chairs around one end of a long, burl-walnut table that smelled of beeswax and had cost more than Hassam made in a year. The Head, a rotund man who wore dark suits always buttoned at the belly, kept the room at arctic temperature with two window-mounted air conditioners that made bumping noises every few minutes as their compressors cycled on and off.

Hassam had already reported for Domestic Branch, citing new statistics that showed violent crimes were down from last year in both Cairo and Alexandria, which brought hearty congratulations from the Head.

Next was the chief of Foreign Branch, an ex-spy whose face bore the scars of childhood smallpox. He began with a reiteration that Yitzhak Shamir, Israel's new Prime Minister, had still not indicated whether he would honor the Camp David Accords, and ended with confirmation that Reagan was going to invade Grenada.

Last to report was the chief of Diplomatic Branch, a pointy-nosed weasel with slicked-back hair who decked himself out in tailored suits, European ties, and gold cufflinks in blatant imitation of the Head. Ass-lick.

Diplomatic Branch kept an eye on ranking foreigners, seeded their embassies with operatives in clerical roles, handled security for visiting dignitaries, and monitored immigration and emigration. The weasel's personal interests, according to Hassam's spies, lay in the sexual peccadilloes of ambassadors.

Hassam listened with half an ear to the usual snippets of trivia and the weasel's grandiose inflation of their significance. Then casually he said, "I gather the incident at the Libyan embassy was more serious than we were first led to believe."

The weasel glowered. "I was about to address that very issue."

Hassam knew he was lying. If he, Hassam, had not checked the records that morning, the "issue" would never have come up. It was too embarrassing. The charge read, "Assault Upon an Officer of the State."

"I was informed yesterday afternoon," the weasel said, "that this suspect did more than evade my men. He temporarily disabled them and broke the jaw of one."

The Head, who'd been a competent chief of Diplomatic Branch before his promotion last year, steepled manicured fingers beneath his double chin. "What information do you have beyond the physical facts that he is black and walks with a limp?"

"We suspect he's a citizen, sir. Probably of the criminal classes, endeavoring to emigrate in order to escape capture and prosecution."

Deftly done. The slippery bastard had turned the tables. By branding the black man as a citizen and criminal, he'd tossed the fellow into Hassam's own lap.

The weasel adjusted a silk handkerchief in his breast pocket, a foppish slap to Hassam's plaid sport coat and open-necked shirt. Hassam's neck was too thick to button his collar, his stature too squat and muscular for suits of fine cut. He chose instead to advertise his peasant origins with loose-fitting clothes, short-cropped hair, and plain talk. Behind his back, his subordinates called him "Bulldog," a nickname he did nothing to discourage.

Secretly, the bulldog was happy with what the weasel had just given him, for investigating the black man now fell officially within his purview. In the contest between tenacity and deception, the bulldog could be sneaky, too.

When the meeting was over, Hassam descended one flight of stairs to his own office. Half the size of the Head's office, it felt even smaller, most of its space filled with file cabinets, evidence boxes, and stacks of folders on the desk, table, and floor. A wall map of the city covered the regulation photograph of President Mubarak, but left Hassam's six commendation certificates clearly visible. In front of his desk, a four-by-six-foot rectangle of official green carpet marked his rank—a long way up from the two-by-three-foot piece he'd received on making lieutenant, but a long way down from the wall-to-wall carpeting in the office upstairs that *should* have been his.

Standing at his window, Hassam lit a cigarette and gazed at the grounds of Cairo University across the street. Some Nubian students chatted beneath a tree. Hassam flicked an ash toward his wastebasket. Egyptians of Nubian extraction were common enough and as untrustworthy as all the other blacks who darkened the planet. So, yes, the black criminal could be a citizen. But what was he doing in the girl's hotel room? With the lights off.

The girl—Frederika Teferi from France, Dr. Ragheb had told him—was noteworthy only for possessing the photographs Ragheb wanted. Had the black guy, for some reason, been guarding those photographs?

Hassam stubbed out his cigarette in the ashtray on his desk, then lit another and sat in his chair. A man with a limp. Cairo abounded with cripples of one sort or another. Some could probably overpower the prancing lackeys of Diplomatic Branch. But none Hassam knew of could come close to tackling Corporal Malik, the man he had sent to the girl's hotel room. That level of skill was not learned on the streets. It came from intensive training, the kind of training given to commandos and spies. And terrorists.

Which was why the Libyan connection pricked like a burr in his collar. How many times had that pig-eater, Gaddafi, threatened to overthrow Egypt? At least twice since Camp David incited cries for revenge in the Arab world. And although Hassam couldn't prove it, he still smelled Gaddafi's foul breath behind the fundamentalist fanatics who had machine-gunned President Sadat.

With a low growl, Hassam ground out his cigarette. Failure to anticipate and prevent the assassination had cost him his imminent promotion to Head of Service. And left him with a perpetual pain in his left shoulder that the idiot doctors called "psychosomatic."

But perhaps redemption was at hand. A black terrorist with links to Libya, dropped by chance into Hassam's own lap. The evidence, if you could call it that, was slim. Thin as threads. But he pictured his father at the loom, arthritic fingers turning strands of thread into stunning designs.

Weave the threads. Hassam lit another cigarette, withdrew a page of foolscap, and listed the leads he had so far. When he was done, he underlined the top two: Frederika Teferi, and her hotel room.

#

Leaning back in her desk chair, Rika rubbed the muscles of her neck. Five hours, and nothing to show for it. She swiveled to face the wooden cabinet where Tiye's papyrus stood in its latticework holder. *You want me to understand. I know you do.*

Dust motes danced in the afternoon light. In their random patterns, she couldn't help seeing the hieroglyphs she'd been peering at all day. Sa-djed-dju.

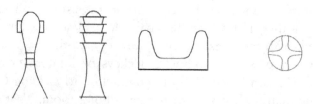

Their connotations were fairly clear. "Sa" meant safety or protection. It represented a life preserver made of papyrus and worn by people who worked in the swamps of the Nile delta. "Djed" meant stability, often in the sense of a long, peaceful reign. Originally a bundle of papyrus stalks, it acquired its enduring meaning because it resembled a vertebral column and came to be seen as the backbone of Osiris. "Dju" was the glyph for mountain.

"Safe and stable mountain" was Rika's best translation.

She could also read it as "mountain of safety and stability" or "mountain of protection and long, peaceful reign." In any case, the *newet*, the crossroads symbol beside the name, identified it as a town. And the text identified it as the home of Tiye's tomb builders. Tiye referred to them as, "faithful men of Sadjeddju."

But Rika still couldn't find the town, not even in the yellowed old maps she'd dredged up from the basement archives, maps going back to colonial days. Worse, according to modern maps, long stretches of the Nile valley where the tomb might be, or might have been, were now under cultivation. Out of bounds for working unnoticed.

Worst of all, what depressed her beyond words, was Lake Nasser. Created by the Aswan High Dam, Lake Nasser had drowned huge tracts of the Nile, including 170 kilometers of the river inside Sudan. Among the submerged monuments were the twin fortresses at Semna, the very gateway to ancient Nubia. If Tiye's tomb had suffered a similar fate, it was lost forever.

"Don't do this to me," she begged Tiye, immediately feeling foolish.

Standing, Rika slipped her two photos under a pile of notes in case Dr. Ragheb walked in. He'd flown to Alexandria that morning for some ceremony, but no telling if he might come by the museum when he returned.

Her stomach spoke, protesting a full day of neglect. A cup of tea would help and perhaps freshen her mind. After the accident with the papyrus, she'd told the tea boy to stop delivering to her office, that she would come to him. He'd be preparing now for his last rounds. She stepped into the corridor and ambled toward his cubicle.

Sadjeddju. Maybe the name had changed over the millennia. Certainly vowels were labile, consonants less so. Syllables came and went with the number of vowels.

An old man wandered out of his office and bumped into her. Rika apologized. He grunted, then shuffled past her, clutching a sheaf of papers and leaving behind an odor of musty wool. She continued toward the tea boy's cubicle.

Sadjeddju had three syllables, each a word in its own right, and each beginning with a consonant. So chances were good that any variation would also have three syllables. And while consonants could vary, initial consonants tended to be more stable. Sa-ja-ja. Sa-da-da.

Rika halted. She'd seen that.

Ahead of her, the tea boy wheeled his cart into the corridor, jangled it to a stop, and smiled. *"Shay?"* Tea?

She looked at him blankly. Sa-de-da. Sa-de-ga.

Saddenga!

She spun around and ran back to her office. There it was. Not Saddenga. Seddenga. How could she have missed it before? Seddenga was the known site of a temple built by Amenhotep III for the worship of Queen Tiye.

Charged with excitement, Rika snatched up her phone and dialed the number David had given her. "David, I know where to find Tiye's tomb."

Chapter 11

Eighteenth Dynasty

Twelve days farther south, the flotilla stopped. The lush farmlands of the north had given way to dryness, except for marshes along the Nile's banks and denser foliage on the few islands in the river. Such an island lay around the next bend. Its name was Sai, and Tiye wished to visit it in the company of her daughter only.

To Baketaten, she said, "Your grandfather's grandfather, the third immortal Thutmose, built a beautiful temple there." Then she divulged the real reason she hungered to see it and have her daughter see it. "It is also the place of my birth."

In peasant clothing, the women boarded one of the small attendant vessels in which two oarsmen took them to the island's northern tip. They walked inland alone. But as they approached the town it seemed strangely quiet. At the first outlying cluster of houses, Tiye found a dying man clutching his stomach in agony.

"Kafu," he moaned. "We are all cursed."

Tiye pulled Baketaten away. "Return to the boat. Say nothing of what you have seen or heard here, and do not turn back." Baketaten tried to protest, but the queen cut her off. "Do as I command. I will join you shortly."

Tiye knew about Kafu. It had been sent here before by evil spirits when she was a small child. Nearly everyone had perished. Her family had escaped only because her grandfather remembered the disease from his own youth and had warned them upon seeing the first signs.

Were she not the chosen of Aten, Tiye also would have fled. But Aten would protect her. When Baketaten was safely away, she proceeded.

At the edge of the town, she smelled the stench of burning flesh. Her heart wept, for it could mean only one thing. When she entered the main square, her fear was confirmed. Smoldering pyres of blackened skeletons littered the temple's steps.

Every Nubian and Egyptian knew that destruction of the worldly body would preclude any possibility of being whole in the next life. That the dead were being incinerated revealed the survivors' desperation to appease heathen spirits.

Wailing interrupted Tiye's mourning. She followed the sound to a nearby house and entered to find a mother rocking on the floor, cradling her baby. Tiye touched the infant, but it was lifeless, its skin covered with oozing blisters. The woman was delirious, keening incoherent prayers to deaf gods. A rivulet of blood running down from her ear confirmed Kafu.

Tiye closed the infant's eyes as tears welled in her own. She left the house and returned to the empty square. Save the putrid pall of dark smoke, the sky was as lifeless as the land. Even Nekhbet, the vulture, protectress of mothers and children, had abandoned it.

A gust of hot wind blew the stink of death in Tiye's face. She turned away, praying this was not an omen.

#

Two days later, bucking strong currents, the flotilla reached its destination. From the west bank of the Nile, an old wadi—dry riverbed—had been excavated to form a canal that led inland through a gap in the cliffs to an isolated valley. At the back of the valley, a low mesa projected toward them from the high plateau behind. Atop the plateau rose a pyramid-shaped peak.

As the procession of vessels turned into the canal, Tiye stood beside her brother at a window of her cabin. Her heart fluttered like a songbird in her chest, for what lay before her she had seen only in dreams.

"The site is well-chosen," Ay observed. "The first rays of Aten will pierce the gap to illuminate your resting place. The natural pyramid above will guard your safety."

"It pleases me well." Her eyes found the tomb's entrance, shadowed beneath a deep overhang cut into the mesa. There began her greatest journey.

The site swarmed with workers, all drawn from a cult that worshipped her in the nearby town of Sadjedju. Their devotion to the queen was the reason they had been chosen, and the reason she chose now to remain secluded.

But while the queen's presence could be kept secret, the arrival of a royal flotilla could not. The workmen would have known of its approach for days. They were cleaning the site in preparation and would not be disappointed to learn that the barge carried Princess Baketaten.

As at Semna, Tiye gave her youngest daughter explicit instructions. "Go with Ay. Assess my tomb's readiness, not only according to the chief architect, but also in the eyes of the funerary priests and of Senuset, my personal overseer."

Baketaten returned with good news. Construction was completed. Final touches were being placed on the paintings that covered the walls and ceilings. Tiye's sarcophagus was in place. The mechanism that would seal the tomb was ready, and the architect was confident that his elaborate devices were in perfect working condition.

Tiye could now give orders for her possessions to be transferred from the cargo boats to the tomb. Two days after that, at the moment selected by her astronomers, she would be sealed inside to begin her journey into the next life.

She retired for the evening and was wakened at dawn by a servant girl. "Divine Mother, they know you are here."

Tiye rose and peered through the covering over her window. On the bank, hundreds of laborers lay prostrate. Behind them, the canyon walls blazed fiery red in a glorious sunrise. She heard the confident footfalls of Ay striding along the deck.

He stepped inside, tall and resplendent in the leather corselet of an army general. "Divine Mother, a literate workman noticed your cartouche on one of the chests bearing your possessions. Word spread instantly. They hastened to finish their duties and have been waiting for you ever since."

Tiye had concealed herself so as not to disrupt their labors, for it was overridingly important that the tomb be completed by the astronomically determined date. But now that preparations were complete, she had no more need for secrecy.

When she stepped from the cabin—an old woman clad only in a white gown and simple headdress—the uproar was explosive. She waited a long time for it to subside, then addressed them. "Faithful men of Sadjedju, the glorious face of Aten shines upon you. In His light, you have created a resting place for me which surpasses all others. I am pleased."

Another roar erupted.

"From here I shall rise up into the dazzling presence of Aten. I shall extol to Him the faith and loyalty you have shown me. And then, at the appropriate time, I shall return and once again reign as your queen. I and my immortal son, King Tutankhamun, shall return together. Your days will be filled with prosperity and happiness. Until that time, I command you and your seed, through all generations, to protect this sanctuary of your Holy Mother."

A voice cried out, "Always!" And the vow was taken up as a chant by the assembled mass.

#

That night, Ay recorded Tiye's words with a heavy hand. When she finished, he laid the calamus aside. But he could not unshoulder the burden of knowing that, in only two days, he would see her for the last time.

Leaning back in her chair, she smiled peacefully. "The moment approaches, at last."

He lowered his head.

"Beloved friend and brother, this is a time of jubilation, not sorrow. Soon I shall touch the hand of Aten. My happiness could be no greater."

Ay's heart ached. What was his duty? To present for her deliberation, one last time, the risks of this terrible gamble, or to keep his own counsel and preserve her serenity?

He was about to speak when Baketaten begged leave to enter

the cabin. She bowed and excitedly recounted the fresh news. "Divine Mother, the chief architect informs me that the treasury is ready to be sealed. May I suggest that tonight would be an excellent time for you to view that chamber and the rest of the tomb."

"Go and make the arrangements," Tiye said. When they were alone again, she beamed at her brother. "Oh, Ay, my heart races."

Through her wrinkles, he glimpsed the young girl he had known so long ago. For the first time in many years he committed the unspeakable act of touching her. "My heart races also."

Chapter 12

Pumped with adrenalin, David spurred Hagazy to step on the gas. He'd told Rika he would pick her up at five, and it was already ten minutes after.

As the Nile sped past, muddy brown in the lowering sun, he blessed his luck at this fantastic turn of events: another shot at making a splash with GPR. Rika hadn't said what changed her mind, but had promised to tell him tonight. It almost didn't matter.

Hagazy swung off the Corniche and wove through rush-hour traffic to the square between the Hilton and the Princess Cleopatra.

When they rounded the last turn, David scanned the sidewalk in front of Rika's hotel, where she always waited for him. She wasn't there. For a second, he had that empty feeling of being stood up for the prom. But Rika wouldn't do that. Probably she was upstairs, still getting dressed for dinner.

Hagazy slid in to a stop.

"Wait here." David hopped out and strode through the front doors to the reception desk. "Can you phone Rika Teferi's room for me?"

The young man behind the desk dialed a number, then gave him the handset.

Rika answered on the fourth ring.

"Hi, it's me," he said.

"David, come up immediately. My room has been ransacked. The photos are gone."

His hands went cold.

"Something is wrong, sir?" the desk clerk asked.

So fucking wrong you can't imagine.

A minute later, David stood amid the chaos in her room. Clothes strewn, chair upended, mattress half on the floor. The mirror hung at a cockeyed angle. The closet stood empty but for one wire coat hanger. "Who could have done this?"

"Remember the visit from Dr. Ragheb?"

"You think your boss did it?"

"Not personally. But the photos are all that's missing. And he's the only other person who's seen them."

"Shit." David hoisted the mattress back onto her bed and sat on it.

"Whoever it was only got three of them. Two are in there." She pointed at her book bag on the floor by the closet. "The one of the whole papyrus and the enlargement with the tomb's location. I had them with me at the museum."

He perked up at this crumb of good news. "If Ragheb only has three-quarters of the text to translate, will he be able to tell it's from the same papyrus you're working on?"

"I think so. That's what scares me." Rika righted the armchair and sank into it. "They both claim to be Tiye's last message to Tutankhamun."

"Then he'll check the original."

"And probably find my restoration. It's not perfect." She closed her eyes. "I think I have to leave the country."

"What?"

"If he finds the damage, he may try to have me arrested."

No way. "We need to think about this before you do anything rash."

She looked at him dejectedly. "I've been thinking about it for the past hour."

"Just give me a minute." David stood and paced, stepping over black panties, a white camisole, a pair of jeans like the ones she was wearing. "What we need is time. He might *not* find your restoration. It looked damn good to me. So you don't want to do anything that might make him suspicious, like suddenly disappearing. You have to act innocent."

"I can't just go back to the museum."

"Yeah, I know. So, why wouldn't an innocent person show up for work?" David halted. "Because you're sick again. And you had to change hotels because your room was broken into and you don't feel safe here anymore."

Rika sat up straighter in the chair. "I'm listening."

The adrenalin was coming back. "You don't call him, because then he could question you on the phone. You send him a note. And you omit to mention the name of the new hotel. That way he can't come visit you."

"If he goes to the police, they could check all the hotels. I don't have any false papers to register with."

"What about my room?"

She glanced up at him, then shook her head. "If they investigate me, they'll find out about you."

Too bad. But unfortunately she was right. So some place that wasn't a hotel. "I've got it. You can stay with Blue."

"Who?"

"A friend of mine. A geologist at SEECO." He pulled her to her feet. "Rika, this'll work."

"Are you sure your friend would let me?"

The randy savior of expat women would welcome her with bedroom eyes. Gelding might be in order, but David would deal with that when the time came. "I'll call him right now."

As he turned toward her phone on the nightstand, she stopped him. "Don't use mine. The hotel might keep records."

"Good thinking. I'll call from my room. You pack your things, and I'll pick you up in …" Then it struck him. "No, I can't take you. We don't want any direct connection between you and Blue. A taxi."

"They might keep records, also."

Shit. David's mind churned. They were close. He could feel it in the tingling of his fingers. What they needed was an intermediate stop, something between here and Blue's place. "Okay, how's this? You take a taxi to another hotel. You're supposedly moving to one, anyway. Register in your own name, then go straight out the back door, and I'll pick you up there."

She stared at him a moment, then beamed. "That's good."

Her approval swelled his chest, until her smile faded.

"Which hotel?"

Some place that wasn't too nosy about its guests. "I'll find one and call you. Don't worry. It'll only take a second to tell you the name, and if you pick up on the first ring, no one will have a chance to listen in." He gave her a quick kiss and left.

With the tenderness of her lips still warm on his mouth, he had Hagazy zip him around the square to the Hilton. From a payphone in the lobby, he called Blue. "How's tonight to accept that invitation to your place?"

"So you haven't jilted me, after all. Crikey, mate, I was beginning to think you were scared of my cooking."

"I am. Don't cook." On the spur of the moment, David decided to say nothing about bringing a "guest." If Blue were in the habit of bringing girlfriends home, he might balk at having a third wheel in residence. He also decided against asking Blue for the name of a hotel. Although the Australian undoubtedly knew many love nests, David didn't want to put up with annoying innuendos. He had a better idea. "About eight?"

"I'll be here," Blue said and gave him the address.

Back outside, David found Hagazy chatting with some cab drivers. "Can you come up to my room for a minute?"

Over the past few days he'd grown to trust the boy. As they entered his room, David prepared to bet Rika's safety on the strength of that trust. "I want to talk to you about Rika."

Hagazy grinned. "You like very much. I think so."

Very much. David handed him the paper on which he'd jotted Blue's address. "I want to move her out of her hotel and take her to this place."

"Mr. Blue's house?"

Hagazy's immediate recognition surprised David until he recalled that the boy had been Blue's driver for a while. "Yes, but I want to take her there secretly. Can you help me?"

"Sure I help you. How we will do it?"

David explained the basics of what he had in mind. They tossed around several possibilities, and he settled on a scheme of Hagazy's. The kid was sharp.

Outside his window, stars already twinkled in the blackening sky. David wiped his palms on his trousers and called Rika.

#

Antsy at having to rely on such a hastily improvised escape plan, Rika checked out of the Princess Cleopatra and took a taxi through the evening crush to a 1920s-vintage hotel near the central train station. She paid cash for one night and went to her room, a rancid cell with a single bed, an armoire, one window nailed shut, and carpeting she wouldn't dare tread on barefoot. The caves of Eritrea were cleaner.

After mussing the bed, she ran water in the rust-streaked tub, then wiped it out with towels to make them look used. Good thing she didn't have to urinate—there was no toilet. She imagined earlier occupants with full bladders resorting to the sink, rather than trekking down the hall to the door labeled "WC."

The only luxury was an old tube radio beside the bed. She switched it on, checked the hallway, then lugged her suitcase down to a service entrance.

So far, she'd depended on herself. The next half of David's plan depended on him. Would he be there?

Emerging into a fetid alley littered with trash, she spotted the monumental statue of Rameses II and, just beyond, the lighted tower of the train station, a beacon against the night sky. Suitcase in one hand, book bag over her shoulder, she hiked around the square to the broad sidewalk in front of the terminal.

Loudspeakers squawked unintelligibly. Hawkers shouted their wares. Travelers hustling in and out sidestepped families who squatted among cardboard boxes, cloth-bound parcels, and ducks and chickens in wire cages. Clever of David to say he'd pick her up here. With her suitcase she fit right in.

Working her way toward the far end, she kept an eye out for his car among the taxis and buses picking up and dropping off passengers. A fat Arab woman bumped into her, muttered something, and kept going. A train whistle screeched. From somewhere came the smell of roasted peanuts.

Finally she spotted David, waving from the Peugeot as it edged behind a taxi and stopped at the curb. He jumped out, dressed as she was, in jeans and an open-necked shirt. "Only one suitcase?"

"That's all I brought to Cairo."

He heaved it in beside Hagazy and ushered her into the rear seat. Hagazy inched back into the flow.

"Everything go all right?" David asked.

"I think so." A flood of relief made her realize how apprehensive she must have been. "I signed my own name, like you said. The trail should lead there and stop."

"Perfect." He took a large, folded map from the rear window shelf and handed it to her. "Put this in your book bag, will you? It's an aeronautical chart. Do you have the letter to your boss?"

It felt good to let someone else take charge for a while. Rika fished the letter from her book bag and gave it to him.

Reaching over the front seat, David said, "Hagazy, I want you to have somebody—not you—take this to the museum tomorrow."

"No problem, sir."

David sat back and smiled at her, then slid his arm around her shoulder. "You're safe now."

With an internal smile of her own, she settled into his embrace. It, too, felt good.

Hagazy negotiated the square with the Rameses statue, then headed toward the Nile and turned south on the Corniche.

David's body heat warmed her, melting away the last of her reservations about his ability to come through in a pinch. In fact, over the past few days, every time she needed help, David had been there. She gazed out at the stars above an inky Nile, contemplating her sporadic love life. She'd never *belong* to any man. But with someone like David, she could imagine a long-term relationship.

"Tell me about this friend of yours," she said. "What kind of name is Blue?"

"Australian humor, because of his red hair. His real name is Rupert Ross." David glanced at Hagazy, then whispered in her ear, "I think Blue can help us. I want to level with him."

"Level?"

"Tell him everything."

Rika jerked away. "Not everything."

"Relax. I've thought about …" His eyes flicked again to Hagazy. "… what comes next. We could use a guy like Blue. He's spent years in Africa, and he's the best field geologist I know. Plus,

I trust him completely."

She squeezed her lips together. As in a covert military operation, the fewer people involved, the better. "I don't know."

"Just wait 'til you meet him. Okay?"

Hagazy turned off the Corniche el Nil into the densely treed suburb of Maadi. She'd never been here before, but knew it to be an enclave of rich expatriates. Freshly swept streets, tidy bungalows with tiled roofs and potted flowers, three-story villas behind high walls. Europe in Cairo, but not a soul out walking.

At one of the bungalows, Hagazy stopped. "Mr. Blue's house."

#

David had half-expected Blue to live in some facsimile of the frat wreck in *Animal House*, not a little white cottage with neatly trimmed lawn and shrubs. Company housing, obviously. Maybe SEECO was trying to domesticate him.

With a nod to Rika, David climbed out, retrieved her suitcase, then leaned back in and handed Hagazy a one-hundred-dollar bill. "You did a great job. Take the rest of the night off. I'll get Blue to drive me back."

Hagazy looked shocked. "I cannot. This is too much."

A twinge of embarrassment bit David. Money seemed like an ugly-American way to say thanks. But cash was all he had at the moment. Besides, he knew Hagazy supported his mother. To make the gift more palatable, he said, "Buy something nice for your mom. And tell her I'm glad she has you for a son."

Hagazy smiled humbly. "Thank you."

Feeling better, David picked up Rika's suitcase, walked her to Blue's front door, and knocked. Sounds of popular music came from inside.

"I like that song," she said.

David listened harder, but the volume dropped abruptly. "I didn't catch it."

" 'Africa,' by Toto. I especially like the line, 'I bless the rains down in Africa.' "

He knew the song, a big hit earlier in the year. But the line she liked had always reminded him of news photos of pathetic children with bloated bellies and flies on their lips. Had Rika experienced such things?

Blue opened the door. "Ey, cobber, 'owzigoin'?" Then his eyes widened. "Who's your lady friend?"

"Blue, this is Rika. Rika, Blue."

The huge Australian, barefoot, in cut-offs and a Grateful Dead T-shirt, stuck out his hand, enclosing hers like a ball in a catcher's mitt. "Pleased to meet you, ma'am." He cocked his head at the suitcase. "You folks planning to stay a while?"

"She is. Can we come in?"

"Of course." Blue stood aside, his eyes following Rika across the threshold.

"Don't even think about it," David whispered, as he carried her bag inside.

"Lucky you." Blue closed the door. "Have a seat folks. Can I get you a drink? I've got whiskey and beer, and there's probably a bottle of Gypo red lying around somewhere, if it hasn't gone off."

"A beer for me," David said.

Rika asked for the same.

"Then it's suds all around. Won't be two shakes."

As Blue strode off, David drew Rika to the couch, motioned her to sit, and sat next to her.

She scowled. "He didn't know I was coming."

"It's okay. He knows now."

"David."

"Don't worry." In the ensuing silence, he scanned Blue's living room. The furniture was all blond wood and Santa Fe pastels. Company-purchased, no doubt, from the people who supplied motel chains. The one standout was a burgundy La-Z-Boy recliner, served by an end table stacked with magazines, a box of cigars, and a brass ashtray. On the floor near the dining table stood a Revox reel-to-reel tape deck, an amplifier, and two Klipsch speakers. Nothing on the walls except a dartboard and a Felix-the-Cat clock with a pendulum tail. The minimalist existence of an expat bachelor.

Then he noticed something lumpy on the dining table, covered by a page of newspaper. He got up to investigate and found a big, Old-West style revolver with its cylinder out and a cotton cloth beside it that smelled of cleaning fluid.

"Black powder forty-four," Blue said. He padded into the room gripping three bottles of Stella Export by their necks. "I play with it out in the desert, near Bahariya Oasis."

Rika came to David's side. "I didn't think private firearms were legal here."

"Only black powder," Blue told her. "Takes so long to reload, the military reckons they're no threat. Pain to clean, though." He handed out the beers.

As David and Rika reseated themselves on the couch, Blue plopped down in the La-Z-Boy, which let out a hiss of air under his weight. "Cheers," he toasted. "So, how is it that I come to have a houseguest?"

"Someone trashed Rika's hotel room," David said. "I mean really tore it apart, like they were mad as hell. God only knows what would have happened if she'd been there."

"Strewth. I've never heard of such a thing in Cairo." Blue looked at Rika. "I'm sorry, love. Of course, you can stay here, long as you like. I've two spare rooms. You can have your pick."

"You're very kind," she said. Then she eyed David with an expression that asked, *Are you going to tell him the rest?*

"There's more." David swallowed a mouthful of beer and started at the beginning.

When he got to the theft, Blue sat bolt upright. "You stole a papyrus from the national museum?"

"We put it back."

"Holy Christ." Blue dug a cigar out of the box beside him, lit up, and proceeded to generate a stratus cloud during the rest of the story. At the end, he knocked off the ash and frowned. "Are you serious about this?"

"Dead serious." David had anticipated Blue's reaction and felt that commitment, resolutely declared, would create credibility.

"You think there might be a tomb somewhere in the general vicinity of these ruins in the Sudan. And you want to go down there and dig it up?"

"We need to fly over first, to be sure we can identify the exact location."

Blue narrowed his eyes. "The Sudanese gave you permission?"

"They will." David's earlier mental image of children famished by drought had given him an idea. "I'm going to offer them a groundwater survey, dirt cheap. Free if I have to."

"What, pray, does groundwater have to do with anything?"

"It's just an excuse to fly to Khartoum. Seddenga's on a direct line between here and there, only seventy nautical miles south of the border. So if we fly to Khartoum, we can turn on the scanners over Seddenga and process the data en route."

Pulling on his beard, Blue switched his eyes to Rika. "You go along with this?"

"Yes," she said firmly.

"I think we need more beers." Blue stubbed out his cigar and went into the kitchen.

David turned to Rika. "So?"

"He seems okay, if we really need him."

"I think we do."

Blue came back with three fresh bottles. "Okay, let's assume the Age of Miracles is not past, and you do find the thing. What then?"

"That's where you come in," David said. "We want you to join us."

"Me? Gee, thanks, mate. I'd just love to quit a well-paying job and go trotting off to the Sudan, where there's a bloody civil war in progress. But it's donkey's years since I last pillaged a Gypo tomb."

"We're not going to pillage," David told him. "Once we have the location as a bargaining chip, we're going to make a deal. Rika gets to study all the contents, but ownership stays with the Sudanese."

"No!" She moved away from him on the couch. "I told you what would happen if the Sudanese found out."

Suddenly confused, David said, "You just want to locate it?" That could be flashy enough publicity for GPR, but what did it give her?

"We're going to rescue the contents and take them out of Sudan. My brother will help. He can bring soldiers and equipment."

"Whoa." Where was this coming from? "You never said anything about doing it on our own. That's insane. We'd never get away with it."

"We have to."

Blue pushed up from his chair. "Sounds like you two have some things to work out. He extracted a handful of darts from the board, stepped back, and threw a bull's eye. "Let me know when you come to your senses."

"I need to sell the artifacts," Rika said, "to buy weapons for Eritrea."

Oh, man. So this was the reason she'd changed her mind about finding the tomb. David sat back, pinching his mouth. Obviously, she hadn't thought this through. But he couldn't just tell her that. He had to make her see it for herself.

Choosing his words carefully, he said, "Have you considered the risks? Getting into Sudan? Working secretly under the noses of what you say is a very hostile government?"

"Seddenga is in the desert, five hundred kilometers north of Khartoum and a hundred and fifty kilometers north of the closest town. No one will know we're there."

"What about getting out with a truckload of stolen artifacts?"

"If my brother can bring trucks in, he can get them out. Eritrea has a long border with Sudan."

"How would you sell them?" Blue asked, his arm poised to throw another dart.

"Yeah." David got up from the couch and took the dart from Blue's hand. Maybe with the two of them working on her, Rika would see the light. "Selling stolen treasure has to be a one-way road to life imprisonment."

"I know a man in England," she said.

"A fence?" David threw the dart and hit the wall. The woman he was falling for had contacts with a fence?

Without moving her head, she looked from him to Blue and back, as though considering whether to reveal a secret. "We can split the money."

Oh, Christ. A bribe. Had she gone completely over the edge?

"But you have to agree," she added, "that Eritrea gets at least ninety percent."

"Gotta map?" Blue said.

David's mouth fell open. What happened to the support? He thought they were both trying to dissuade her. Was Blue blinded by dollar signs?

Rika pulled several maps from her book bag.

After briefly checking them, Blue unfolded David's aeronautical chart. "Show me this place. Seduga?"

"Seddenga." Rika pointed.

"There's a road." Blue lowered himself onto the couch beside her. "Runs all the way down from the border."

Her eyes lit up. "I didn't see that. We could drive."

"Dirt track, according to the legend. But my Land Cruiser can handle it."

David couldn't believe what was happening. Somehow he had to gain control before this spiraled out of hand. Stall. Buy time for them both to sober up.

"Drive where?" he said, planting himself in front of the coffee table. "Seddenga's just ruins. You say the tomb builders lived there and the tomb must be nearby, but 'nearby' is still a damn big area. Until we fly over and actually pinpoint the location, you're just pissing in the wind."

Chapter 13

Major Hosni Hassam slipped the stolen photographs into a manila envelope, told his wife not to wait up for him, and left his apartment above the gold merchant's shop. In crepe-soled shoes, reliable and silent, he wound through the granite-paved passages of the Khan el Khalili souk. At this time of night, the ancient marketplace was mute and shuttered, catching its breath. Remnant smells of fish, perfume, and human sweat offered the only evidence that everything imaginable could be had here for a price.

He loved the souk. It was emblematic of Egypt itself, historic yet modern, a product of enterprise, a monument to freedom, vitality, and the splendor of the Egyptian spirit.

Alone, as he preferred, he navigated the dark streets, past carved storefronts, beneath stone archways engraved with Koranic inscriptions, to the shop of an antiquities dealer on his payroll. A window above glowed yellow. He pounded on the weather-beaten door.

The dealer's head appeared in the window. "Closed. Come back tomorr—" A coughing fit lopped off the last syllable.

"Open up," Hassam growled.

"Oh, it is you. One minute, please."

Lighting a cigarette, Hassam caught a movement to his left. A stray dog, skeletal and scabby, nosed down the alley in his direction. Hassam threw a stone at it. With a yelp, the cur bolted. *Parasite.*

Behind the door, a chain rattled, a latch scraped. The door swung open to the dealer's obsequious smile, his eyes squinting in the smoke of the perpetual cigarette between his lips. "*Abu*, come in."

Hassam smiled inwardly. *Abu*, meaning father, conveyed the deference he deserved.

The shop stank of dry rot and decades of dirt. Hassam threaded his way between trestle tables heaped with forgeries, junk, and an assortment of legal antiques from post-pharonic times. At the back, he swept aside a curtain and stepped into the man's inner sanctum. Here was the contraband, the illicit figurines and hacked-out bits of wall paintings brought to Cairo by the desert's latest generation of tomb robbers.

The dealer, wheezing like an old whore, pushed through to join him. "Shall I send for tea?"

"Not tonight." Hassam slid out the photographs from their envelope.

Fingers yellowed with nicotine accepted the prints, then spread them on a table.

In the man's stained hands and labored breathing, Hassam glimpsed his own future if he didn't quit smoking. He dropped his cigarette, ground it out with his shoe, and jabbed a thumb at the photos. "I need you to translate these. By morning."

"But *Abu*, that is not enough time."

"Seven o'clock." Hassam drilled his eyes into the man. "Do not disappoint me."

Like a patched old tire, the dealer deflated. "As you say."

Hassam left the shop with a lightness in his stride, buoyed by how readily men bent to his will. Returning to the gold district, he walked past his apartment to the narrow lane where he kept his car. The boy, Ishmael, sprawled on the front seat, dozing with the door open. As Hassam approached, Ishmael whipped out a knife.

"Good," Hassam said, nodding. Nobody could sleep with their ears open better than street kids. "Get out."

Ishmael, who protected the car from thieves and vandals, scuttled onto the pavement and stood at attention.

Hassam handed him some piastres. "I'll be back in a few hours."

Near the Citadel twenty minutes later, he turned off the main road and descended into a valley on the eastern outskirts of Cairo.

Despite a bright half-moon, the valley floor was dark, the town it cradled darker still. No lights shone from the windows, nor any in the streets.

He parked beside one of the few entrance gates in the high wall. There was no sound, no discernible movement. As if everyone were dead. Which most of them were.

This was one of the largest cemeteries ever built. Each house and every villa was a mausoleum, constructed by the wealthy as the final resting place of their earthly remains. Although it had no formal name, the place was known, and always had been known, as the City of the Dead.

Hassam's soft shoes crunched on brick chips and stone shards in the desert dirt. Many of the houses lay derelict, roofs collapsed, walls crumbling to rubble, their builders' descendants having long ago given up the tradition of gathering within to break bread, pay homage, and pray for the souls of the grandly departed. Whatever furniture the mourners might once have sat on was long gone, firewood for the desperate. Here and there, Hassam saw vain attempts at security—bricked-up doorways, windows barred or grated. Might as well shutter your mansion against the plague.

For although it was illegal, thousands of homeless had taken up residence in the crypts of the rich. It was a society totally closed to outsiders. And in its midst, like a viper in weeds, lurked the nerve center of Cairo's underworld.

A hundred meters inside the walls, Hassam detected the first signs of life. A flickering candle through a crack in a door, a female singer on a distant radio. The sweet smell of sugarcane boiling. The cry of a child.

He knew the place by heart and strode through its labyrinth of dusty streets fully aware that eyes watched him, but utterly confident of his own safety. Nobody here would dare accost a man in a sport coat who showed no fear and so obviously represented the law. Without doubt, the best part of his job was the power.

Near the center of the city, he stopped in front of a particularly grand villa, embellished with pillars, arched windows, and a dome atop the second story. No need to knock. The sentries would already have spotted him. Picturing a scramble of alarm inside, he smiled to himself and leaned against a brick wall to wait.

A few minutes later, the villa's door creaked open. Holding a kerosene lantern, a tall, hawk-faced man with a scar down his cheek glowered at him.

Hassam brushed past the man into an anteroom, then stood aside. Although he'd been here before and knew his way, he also knew the character with the scar to be a thief and a murderer. He had no intention of letting the guy walk behind him.

With Hassam following, scar-cheek climbed a limestone staircase to a landing where he rapped on a wooden door.

"Enter," came a gruff voice.

Scar-cheek pushed open the door and stepped back.

Inside, seated on an immense carpet, his bulk distributed over a pile of ornate pillows, was the person Hassam had come to see. Abdul Imbabi, Lord of Thieves.

"Peace be with you, Major Hassam."

"And with you peace." *And an eternity in Hell.*

Hassam gave the room a quick visual sweep, confirming they were alone, except for the dead interred in the walls of pink and white marble. In the dome overhead, faced with blue tile, patches of raw brick showed the real owners had not been here for years. From the top of the dome hung a teardrop chandelier of brass and colored glass that cast a garish but subdued light over the de facto owner.

Imbabi—bald, clean-shaven, and draped in a white satin galabeyah—gestured to a place at his right. "Please."

Hassam seated himself on the carpet, a Persian masterpiece he knew was once owned by King Farouk. As a sign of contempt, he kept his shoes on.

Apparently unslighted, Imbabi clapped his hands twice.

A boy about twelve, in dancer's pantaloons and embroidered vest, nancied in with a silver tray bearing a bottle of Chivas Regal and two crystal tumblers. Eyes lowered, he placed it between them and left, trailing a cloud of Chanel Number something.

"Will you take whiskey, Major?"

"If you will join me."

Imbabi's liver-colored lips thinned. "Ever cautious, eh?"

"As you, yourself."

"Here, I will pour, and you choose the glass you prefer."

Hassam selected the second glass, a piece of Baccarat that weighed about half a kilo. They each took a sip, but Hassam waited for his host to swallow first. In case.

"So tell me, Major … It *is* still 'Major'?"

"You would know if it were not."

A glint lit Imbabi's tiny eyes before they slitted. "What I do not know is why you have chosen to honor my house. Without invitation."

Setting his glass down, Hassam came straight to the point. "I am searching for a man."

"The one who disgraced your people at the Libyan embassy?"

Hassam wasn't surprised at the astute guess. "Not my people. But yes, that man. Do you know of him?"

"I might."

Hassam waited, knowing this would cost him. It always did.

"Such a man," Imbabi said, raising a finger, "could be very interesting, indeed, if he were the one I am thinking of. If I were you, I would be willing to give much to learn about him."

"How much would you be willing to give?"

"Surely for such a bird acquired, I would be willing to set other birds free."

"Which bird would you set free?"

"Oh, there would be several."

"For the man, perhaps. But for information only, I could conceive of only one bird returning to its roost. Which one would you think that might be?"

Imbabi scowled like a constipated tortoise, but soon salvaged his air of serenity. "I would have thought Ahmed Fathi."

"You want Fathi, instead of your nephew?"

Imbabi slammed his glass onto the tray, knocking over the bottle of whiskey. "My nephew is a pig! He can rot in your jail until the rats eat his filthy bones."

So, the once-rising relative was now less favored than the smuggler out of Alexandria. Hassam filed this news as he watched whiskey soak into a carpet worth more than he earned in five years. "If your information pleases me, then Fathi is yours."

"No, Major. Whether the information pleases you or not is no concern of mine. If you want it, then I must have your word that

Fathi will be released tomorrow. Otherwise, we are both wasting our time." Adjusting his robe, he settled back into the pillows.

Secretly pleased that the price was less than he'd expected, Hassam pinched his lips together as if struggling with indecision. Finally, he let out a breath through his nose and said, "Tomorrow morning, he's yours."

Imbabi peered into the backs of Hassam's eyes, then turned and clapped his hands. Instantly the boy reappeared. "More whiskey," Imbabi ordered.

As they waited in silence for the new bottle to be fetched, Hassam ran a finger over the carpet. Its threads felt as fine as the hairs on a woman's inner thigh. A treasure. Yet Imbabi seemed unfazed by the upended whiskey bottle or the dark stain spreading around it. Either he was faking apathy to flaunt his wealth, or he was such a pig that he didn't really care.

Hassam clenched his jaw. This was the parasite, the malignancy, he had to bargain with just to do his job. One day, he'd empty a clip into the bloodsucking bastard, then piss in his face.

The boy minced in with a fresh bottle, retrieved the spilled one, and hurried out.

Refilling his glass, Imbabi said, "The man you seek is a foreigner. A black man from the south, possibly Ethiopia or the Sudan. He walks with a limp."

"I know he walks with a limp. What else?"

"He moves in the night. What he does during the day I cannot say. Other than the incident at the embassy, of course."

"I don't need to learn from *you* what happened at the embassy."

Imbabi rolled the glass between his palms. "Did you know that was not the only time your men have been disgraced by him? Last night, when that walleyed corporal came to your house, he had been dumped among garbage cans by this very man."

"Useless!" Hassam got to his feet. "You tell me nothing I don't already know."

The door flew open. Scar-cheek and two others stood pistols in hand, apparently alerted by Hassam's outburst. At a flick of Imbabi's wrist, they retreated.

"There is more, Major."

"Then tell me now."

"This man seeks weapons."

"What?" He'd suspected a spy or a terrorist. Now the latter was confirmed.

"And not just rifles. He seeks rockets and armor-piercing bazookas."

"How do you know this?" Hassam demanded.

"He seeks them on the black market."

"From whom?"

Imbabi shrugged. "From those who might know how to procure them, I imagine. I, myself, have no knowledge of such things. But that is what I have been told."

Hassam's muscles tightened. The pain in his shoulder throbbed. "Was he successful?"

"I believe not."

"Why not?"

"Although I can only speculate about things of this nature, in which I, myself, would never become involved, I would suspect that the reason had to do with a shortage of funds."

Hassam glared down at the sanctimonious hippo. "Why would he try to buy arms if he had no money?"

"Ah, Major, the workings of such a mind are a mystery to me. Perhaps he thought he might find sympathizers to his cause."

"What cause?"

"That I cannot say. But there are many so-called liberation movements in the world today."

Hassam took a threatening step forward, lowered his voice, and spoke very slowly. "Is he in any way involved with any discontented group inside Egypt?"

"By the beard of the prophet, no!" Imbabi looked genuinely shocked. "If there had been any hint of that, you would not have had to come to me. Be assured, Major, I would have come to you."

"You are certain?"

"I have no knowledge of such a thing. On that you have my word."

Hassam studied the blubbery face for any sign of duplicity, but saw none. "Ask your people," he said finally. "I want to be sure. It will be worth your while."

"I shall."

"Now, what more can you tell me?"

"There is little." Imbabi oozed into his pillows again. "He has been seen at night, in the shadows by the museum. But no one sees him for long."

Hassam stepped back, ready to leave. "Learn more. And when you do, contact me at once."

"You may count on it, Major." Imbabi smiled but did not rise. "As always, I consider myself honor-bound to assist the authorities in whatever way I can."

#

With a troubled mind, Hassam returned to his car, steered up out of the valley, and headed for home. Although the streets were nearly empty, he drove at a camel's pace, rehashing Imbabi's words. *Rockets and bazookas.* The favored weapons of urban guerillas. *So-called liberation movements.* Always such movements sought to overthrow the "oppressors in power," the government. In the Middle East, the alleged oppression was usually seen as denial of religious rights, or at least the rallying cries were shouted in religious terms. And aside from the Arab-Israeli conflict, the liberation movements usually pitted Muslim against Muslim. Fundamentalist against government.

Hassam slammed his fist on the steering wheel. Khomeini's thugs ousting the Shah four years ago. Fundamentalists assassinating Sadat two years ago. And just last month, Nimieri proclaiming *Sharia* law in the Sudan.

He is from the south, possibly Ethiopia or the Sudan. Of course he would have no money. Ethiopia and Sudan were both bankrupt.

A honk jarred Hassam from his thoughts. A truck behind him. He eased to the right to let it pass and received a blast of diesel exhaust as thanks. Rolling up his window, he lit a cigarette to smother the stench.

Sudan made the most sense. *Sharia* distanced them from modern Arab states, but endeared them to Gaddafi, the whore-spawn behind Sadat's murder. Having failed in that attempt to destabilize Egypt, was Gaddafi trying again? The timing fit his fanatical impulsiveness—*Sharia* a month ago, and now a black, probably Sudanese, terrorist seeking arms locally. And checking in with the Libyan embassy.

Hassam stepped on the gas. He could not yet see the design. But he had the chilling sense that, once he grasped the threads and traced them back, he'd find a tapestry emblazoned with a single word. Revolution.

Chapter 14

Monday's first call to prayer woke Hosni Hassam instantly. He got up from his desk, rubbed the kink in his left shoulder, and opened the shutters. Sunlight had not yet touched the minaret of El Hussein mosque.

The smell of fresh coffee turned him toward the door.

His wife opened it a crack, peeked in, then barged through like a wet chicken, cackling chastisements for staying up all night. With protestations that he worked too hard, she placed a cup of coffee on his desk and fluttered off.

As peace returned, he heard a giggle at the door and saw the dark eyes of their eight-year-old daughter. "Leila."

She ran to his arms to be scooped up. "Ooh, you're all scratchy."

"You mean this?" He nuzzled her with his cheek.

"Don't," she begged, squirming in his arms. "It's awful."

"Do you think I should go and shave?"

"Yes."

"All right. But first tell me where your brother is."

"Asleep."

"Always asleep." Hassam dropped his voice to a conspiratorial whisper. "I'll make a bargain with you. I'll go shave if you promise to wake him mercilessly and tell him it's time to get ready for school. Will you do that?"

"Yes," she squealed, struggling to free herself from his arms.

He lowered her and chuckled as she scurried out of the room, all innocence and happiness.

Never would he allow that precious child to be cut and sewn, as his wife had been, "according to custom." He clenched his fists at the thought, slicing out the clitoris and stitching the labia together when the girl turned twelve. Pig-eating fundamentalists. Their barbaric practices and medieval fanaticism were a curse to humanity, a threat to the whole fabric of Egyptian society. If this limping black terrorist was part of a fundamentalist plot, Hassam would personally place a gun to the bastard's forehead, breathe Leila's name, and pull the trigger.

In the souk an hour later, Hassam gave some money to an old man selling tea from a brass urn on his back, then banged on the door of the antiquities dealer. The tea seller followed him inside to the dealer's back room, tipped two glasses of reddish brew, and left.

Tea in one hand, cigarette in the other, the bleary-eyed dealer sat back while Hassam read his translation.

Hassam frowned. A lot of praising and religious claptrap written to Tutankhamun by his mother, who was about to be buried in … "Nubia?"

"Queen Tiye was Nubian." The dealer stubbed out his cigarette, patted his pockets, and looked at Hassam hopefully.

Hassam tossed his pack of Marlboros on the table. "So she was black."

"Nubians are." The man coughed as he pinched off the filter of a Marlboro and lit up.

"What about this tomb of hers?"

"That is the strange part. An Egyptian tomb in Nubia. There are a few, of course, but they are all much later. Seven or eight hundred B.C." He picked some tobacco shreds off his lips, examined them as a schoolboy examines boogers, and flicked them away. "If I had the other photograph, I could tell you more."

Hassam stiffened. "What other photograph?"

"*Abu*, you gave me only three." The dealer arranged them in an "L" on the wooden table, then touched the bare space in the upper-right quadrant where another photo would have completed the rectangle. "There should be four."

"*Khara!*" Shit. Unable to read hieroglyphs, how could he have known? More important, what information did the missing photograph contain? Possibly key information, if the Teferi girl had kept it with her. Squeezing his lips together, Hassam slapped a wad of American dollars on the table, and stomped out.

A few minutes after eight, he parked at State Security Headquarters, a four-story Georgian edifice built of tan limestone during the English colonial occupation. The climb to his third-floor office winded him—damn cigarettes—but it also dulled his anger. He saw no possible link between a dead queen and a revolutionary plot, except one: Frederika Teferi. Both the photos and the black terrorist had been secreted in her room.

He summoned Malik, the corporal with the cloudy eye, and told him to go back to the girl's hotel and find the fourth photograph. "And while you're at it, arrest her."

#

In the darkened office that served as his ground station at SEECO, David tried to concentrate on processing data as it came in real-time from the aircraft's survey. But half his brain kept wandering back to Blue's house last night. Boiled down to its essence, Rika had asked him to risk his freedom, if not his life, to join her on a mission that was both hazardous and criminal. Was it a sign of her trust, or was she willing to endanger anyone, provided it served her cause? That she'd embraced Blue's participation suggested the latter.

And Blue, jumping in with both feet like Sir Lancelot to the rescue. David chafed at the admission that part of what drove him was fear of seeming less manly than the big Australian. But Blue had done one thing useful. Letting off David at the Hilton last night, he'd suggested that SEECO's Admin Manager, an Egyptian with wide connections, might be able to arrange a meeting at the Sudanese embassy. The suggestion had panned out. David's appointment was for one o'clock this afternoon.

A dropped line segment left a blank space on the latest image coming in. David brought up the matrix of corresponding numbers on the adjacent screen, found a faulty header code, and corrected it. Image repaired.

He leaned back to catch more of the cold flow from the air conditioner. On the plus side of all this, he'd grabbed the reins. He now knew Rika's real intentions and was in a position to stop her from doing something disastrous. Or help her. He'd tossed and turned most of the night, unable to shake that remotest of possibilities—that what Rika proposed might actually work.

#

Major Hassam slammed his hand on his desktop. "Where has she gone?"

"Unknown, sir. She took a taxi." Corporal Malik stood at something resembling parade rest. His gray suit, purchased a month ago and proudly worn every day since, wafted the underarm odor of boiled cabbage. "But the night clerk was still there, and he reported some very strange activities. Seems she's been seeing an American."

"What's strange about that?"

"For one thing, she's black, he's white. The other is, he once picked her up at four-thirty in the morning."

"Black? I thought she was French."

"She registered with a French passport."

French black. It was possible. Several African countries were former French colonies. If just dark, but not true black, she could be ethnic Algerian. Or Libyan. An agent of Gaddafi? "How black?"

"The night clerk just said 'black.' But I traced the American." Malik flipped open a small notebook. "His name is David Chamberlain. He's staying at the Nile Hilton. His room was reserved by an oil company called SEECO."

"Tear off that page and give it to me."

Complying, Malik said, "There's one more thing, sir. When the American picked her up, he came in a white Peugeot with a driver."

Hassam sat upright. Driver meant rental car. And the only car-rental agency in Cairo that used Peugeots was Budget, the agency owned by the Head of Service.

Malik's smirk said he'd already made the connection.

Leaning back in his chair, Hassam lit a cigarette. "Pull the records on Chamberlain's car."

With a nod, Malik headed for the door.

"Wait a minute." Hassam rose from his chair, took out a

twenty-piastre note, and handed it to the man. "Get your suit cleaned."

As Malik closed the door behind him, Hassam's private line rang.

"Hosni, I have a note here from Miss Teferi." Dr. Ragheb read it over the phone. "What, in God's name, happened?"

"Possibly my man was overzealous. But in any case, he found no photographs." The lie came easily. Old friend or not, Ragheb had no need to understand the crack he'd opened. He could, however, hold the wedge that would split that crack wide. Adopting his most amicable tone, Hassam said, "As to Miss Teferi's disappearance, perhaps I can be useful. I'll come to your office this afternoon."

"I don't understand."

"My friend, it's simple. With help from you, I can find her."

#

Entering the Garden City district of Cairo, with its mixture of Belle Époque mansions and modern high-rises, David reached inside his blazer to rub his armpits with his shirt. The salesman part of his job always turned on the spigots. It wasn't so bad after the first indication that a potential client might actually be interested. But before that, the uncertainty of whether he'd be laughed at, thrown out, or asked questions he couldn't answer made him sweat like a climber on frayed rope.

Hagazy pulled into a short driveway and stopped in front of a filigree of wrought iron. "Sudan embassy, sir."

Behind the gates stood a three-story mansion in white stone with French windows, balconies, and a balustrade across the top. Pretty rich for a country bankrupted by civil war.

Attaché case in hand, David walked to the gates and pressed the buzzer in a speaker box. Waiting, he noticed a video camera aimed down at him from one of the pillars flanking the gateway. He turned to face it, in case they wanted a good look.

The speaker squawked something he didn't catch.

"David Chamberlain," he said. "I have an appointment."

He also had an urgent need to pee. Why the hell hadn't he

thought of that before leaving SEECO? Probably because he was preoccupied with the "cautionary word" SEECO's Admin Manager had stopped by to give him after arranging the appointment. Did David know the U.S. had severed all relations with Sudan? When Black September terrorists killed the American Ambassador in Khartoum, the Sudanese tried them, found them guilty, and released them. "Not nice people," the manager opined. "And embassies are sovereign ground. Once you step inside, you're legally in the Sudan."

The right gate clicked open.

With a deep breath, David pushed through and closed it behind him. Only as he approached the front door did it occur to him that he should have told Hagazy to go for help if he wasn't out in an hour.

An Egyptian fellow in white livery showed him to a reception room off the main entry. "Wait here."

Faux pillars lined the walls beneath a twelve-foot ceiling carved in an oval starburst. The parquet floor, unevened by age and a bit creaky to walk on, gleamed from a recent application of a lemony polish David could still smell. The furnishings—couches, tables, chairs—looked like Mexican knock-offs of Danish modern. An eight-foot couch facing the front windows, also faced a gigantic photograph of a man David assumed was Sudan's president.

He wandered to a baby-grand piano in one corner. David hadn't played since junior high. He tapped middle C and heard a plunk closer to B-flat.

"You are a pianist, Mr. Chamberlain?"

David spun around. "Not really." Great, already off on an apologetic foot.

"I am the First Secretary." The man, slightly taller than David, had receding hair, a Hitler moustache, and a slight bulge under the left arm of his olive-green suit. With no move to shake hands, he gestured toward the long couch. "Take a seat."

Why there, David wondered, until the man selected a chair opposite, where backlighting from one of the windows made it hard to see his face.

At least sitting eased the pressure on David's bladder.

The First Secretary crossed his arms. "Let me begin by saying that, while our two governments do not always see eye-to-eye, the Democratic Republic of the Sudan has no quarrel with private citizens or companies of the United States."

David mouthed some gobbledygook, lauding the man's broad perspective in view of the increasing globalization of the world community, then broke into his sales pitch. He snapped open his attaché case, laid a color brochure on the coffee table between them, and paged through as he explained Digital Image's services. On a roll now, and in familiar territory, he showed examples of groundwater, vegetation, and minerals projects DI had completed.

Through it all, the First Secretary neither spoke nor moved. Face shadowed, he sat like an inquisitor listening impassively to a heretic's excuses.

David could get no read. His underarms dripped. His bladder ached. The lemony smell stung his nostrils, as if a whole bottle of polish had been rubbed into the floor between his feet.

In a flood of words he'd rehearsed before coming, David cast the bait. He cited UN forecasts of an impending drought in North Africa, recommended a groundwater survey in the region south of Lake Nasser, and concluded, "DI is prepared to offer a substantial discount if the Sudanese government can act quickly. Our aircraft is already in Egypt and has a short time slot available before its next job."

With no pretense of subtlety, the First Secretary leaned forward, forearms on knees, and asked, "What experience do you have in applying your techniques to military issues?"

Relieved that DI had a standard response to such questions, David recited, "We are not in the business of supporting military operations. However, Digital Image Corporation cannot control the ways our clients use their data."

A thin smile.

David rushed on. "I'd be pleased to take the plane to Khartoum for a demonstration. But it will have to be soon. If your government accepts my offer, I'll need two days to fly the survey, and the plane's booked up for the rest of the year after that."

The man stood. "Thank you for coming, Mr. Chamberlain. I may be in touch."

#

Major Hassam declined Ragheb's offer of tea. In the few moments it took to seat themselves on opposite sides of Ragheb's desk, Hassam assessed the big corner office. Low bookcases along the two walls with windows and high ones against the other two walls were filled with thick volumes and rows of journals, all perfectly aligned and dust-free. Atop the low cases, bathed in mid-afternoon sun, sat a line-up of alabaster vessels and stone figurines for which any dealer in the souk would have given both testicles. On Ragheb's polished desktop, an expensive fountain pen rested beside a sheet of letterhead he'd been writing on in miniscule Arabic script.

Meticulous, studious, trustworthy.

No wonder Nasser had chosen Ragheb as one of his personal secretaries.

Now, in starched shirt and wringing his hands, Ragheb said, "Hosni, I'm sorry I ever asked you to do this for me. I've made such a mess."

"Don't beat your own brow, my friend. Such things happen. But tell me, why *did* you ask?"

Ragheb lowered his eyes. "Vanity." He swallowed, Adam's apple bobbing, then looked again at Hassam. "It was a papyrus. A large one, in excellent condition. But I'd never seen it before, and I thought I'd read every major papyrus that's ever been found. When she wouldn't give me more than a glance, I felt insulted. My professional pride was offended, not to mention my intellectual curiosity."

Ragheb's shamed faced told Hassam the man spoke the truth. But while the photos appeared to be a dead end, a coincidence unrelated to any plot, that fact didn't exonerate the girl. "What was Miss Teferi working on, here at the museum?"

"By arrangement with the Sorbonne, she was studying a papyrus written by Queen Tiye." Ragheb shifted in his chair, an expensive, high-backed swivel chair like the Head of Service had. "That's what was curious about the photograph in her room. It mentioned Tiye, also."

Sorbonne. "So she's French?"

"Oh, I don't think so." Ragheb rubbed his chin. "Actually, I don't know. Her French has an odd accent. I assumed she was from Africa."

Hassam leaned forward. Now he was getting somewhere. "North Africa?"

"No, no. She's not Arab." Ragheb's eyes grew distant, as though he were picturing her. "Horn of Africa, I'd say. Maybe Djibouti, or somewhere near there."

Like the Sudan.

"She's quite beautiful," Ragheb murmured. Then he sat up straight, face blanched, with the trapped expression of a boy caught masturbating.

Interesting. Infatuation could be a powerful lever, if ever needed. Filing it in his memory, Hassam asked, "What else was she doing here, besides working on this papyrus?"

"Nothing," Ragheb said defensively. "Why?"

Hassam flipped up his palms. "I'd like to help you find her. Mend the damage I've caused you."

Ragheb's shoulders drooped. "Hosni, it's my fault."

"Perhaps if you showed me her office, I'd find a clue as to her whereabouts."

"You think so?"

"Can't hurt."

"It's right next door." Ragheb led the way through a side door into what looked like a storeroom. "That's her desk."

Hassam went through the drawers, finding nothing personal except a phone number on a scrap of paper, which he memorized at a glance.

"The papyrus she was working on is here." Ragheb opened a wooden cabinet, slid out a latticework contraption, and laid it open on her desk. "Not that it will do you any good."

Going through the motions, Hassam gave it a visual once-over, then did a double-take. There was a tiny V-shaped notch where a chip had broken out of the upper left corner. That same notch appeared in one of the three photos. "This is not the same papyrus as in the photograph you saw?"

"Not at all. This is basically poetry. Poor poetry, I might add. The one in the photograph had some instructions to Tutankhamun.

But Rika snatched it from me before I could tell what kind of instructions."

Rika? So Ragheb called Frederika Teferi by a pet name. With mock nonchalance, Hassam lifted an edge of the papyrus. Nothing written on the other side. He held it up to the light from the window. Nothing.

"What are you doing?" Ragheb asked.

"Just admiring it. I've never had one in my hands before." The writing in the photos had to be underneath the visible characters. How did Teferi discover it? And how in hell did she get pictures? Laying the papyrus on the desk, Hassam lowered his head to examine the hieroglyphs. A shine caught his eye. Four of the characters—no, six—were brighter than the others. His pulse quickened. Recent ink. "Has this papyrus been repaired?"

"Certainly not! We never alter an artifact. Why would you ask?"

"Just wondering." Hassam's skin prickled. Someone had altered it, most likely Teferi, and almost certainly to cover up her own removal of the surface characters. The only reason to remove them in the first place would be to confirm a suspicion that concealed writing existed. So the text itself, the hidden text, was important to her cause. Important enough that the photos were guarded in her room by the black terrorist. "Why was she studying this particular papyrus?"

Ragheb threw up his hands. "For her thesis. What does this have to do with finding her?"

"The more I know, the more I can help." He needed the full text, which meant he needed to take the papyrus to one of the labs at Headquarters. He picked it up. "I'd like to borrow this for a day or two."

"Impossible. I can't let anything out of the museum." Ragheb furrowed his brow. "Besides, why would you want it?"

"To have it photographed for the files. I promise not to harm it."

Ragheb stepped back, as if Hassam had blasphemed. "What files? What's got into you? This isn't a criminal matter. She's just a scared girl we're trying to help."

Scared for a reason I intend to discover. "One day. That's all I ask."

"Hosni, I cannot. Not even for you."

"I can get a police order."

Ragheb thrust out his chest. "It will have to come from ministerial level."

Bastard. Ragheb's rank matched his own, and the Ministry of Tourism, which supplied a large portion of Egypt's national income, wielded banker's power in the halls of government. Hassam wanted to flatten the sanctimonious bureaucrat.

But there might be a better way.

Chapter 15

Five-thirty, most of SEECO's staff gone home, and David was starting to see double. Typing at light speed, he crunched through the backlog of survey data that had come in while he was straining not to pee in his pants at the Sudanese embassy. Not only would he have to work until eight or nine tonight just to catch up, but there was still the summary interpretation to write. The air conditioning had shut off automatically at five, and his shirt, stiff with dried sweat from his session with the First Secretary, was rehydrating.

The phone rang. David snatched it up. "Rika?"

"What?" snapped the First Secretary.

"Excuse me, sir. I was expecting someone else."

"My government will accept your offer of a demonstration."

David gave himself a big thumbs up.

"However, Mr. Chamberlain, it will have to be either tomorrow or in two weeks time."

Uh, oh. "Sir, tomorrow is sooner than I was expecting." Even if he worked all night, he and Paul had to pack up the ground-station equipment. And the pilots were due at least one day of R and R. "May I ask if Wednesday wouldn't be just as good?"

"The Minister of Agriculture is leaving Wednesday afternoon for Brussels and will not return before a fortnight."

Shit. Okay, work all night, have Paul dismantle the ground station himself, tell the pilots R and R will have to wait. His whole crew would be angry, but he'd make it up to them somehow. "All right, I'll make preparations to fly down tomorrow morning."

"Excellent, Mr. Chamberlain. Now perhaps I might suggest that, if tomorrow is convenient, why not tonight?"

"Tonight?" No way in hell.

"I can arrange first class accommodation for you in Khartoum. You will meet with the Minister in the morning and conduct your demonstration in the afternoon."

"Sir, that's just not—"

"I know the Minister would be grateful." The First Secretary chose tactful words, but his tone was adamant. "It would allow him to spend time with his family on Wednesday, before leaving."

Damn. Caught in his own now-or-never snare. David checked his watch. The pilots were probably already in the bar, getting illegal. They'd have to drop everything. "Can I call you back in fifteen minutes?"

"Certainly, Mr. Chamberlain. But before we ring off, there is one more point. The Ambassador and I would like to join you on your flight."

God, no. That would ruin everything. "Sir, I don't think—"

"Perhaps I should stress, Mr. Chamberlain, that the Ambassador exerts considerable influence in Khartoum. He can be a powerful spokesman. On the other hand, without his presence I should think the proposed journey would be futile."

You slimy son of a bitch. How could he and Rika search for the tomb with two Sudanese breathing down their necks? Keep them in the VIP cabin. But there was nothing to do back there except look out the windows and drink, and nothing to see out the windows at night. Blue! Blue could drink with them, keep them occupied. "Okay, sir, let me see what I can do. I'll call you in fifteen minutes."

David hung up, dialed the Hilton, and asked for Jim Mitchell's room. No answer. He dialed again, requested the rooftop bar, and asked the bartender to page him.

A few moments later, he heard, "Mitchell."

"Jim, David. Are you and Chris drinking?"

"Bet your ass. Day's over and there's no flying tomorrow."

"How much have you had so far?"

No response.

"Jim?"

In a suspicious voice, Jim said, "We've just settled into our first beers. Why?"

"We have to fly to Khartoum tonight. I'll explain it all later, but how soon can we be ready to go?"

"God dammit."

"I'm sorry, but it's important."

"David, we just spent nine hours in the air. Give us a break. How 'bout we do it tomorrow?"

"We have to go tonight. Besides, it's a straight shot to Khartoum. Easy stuff."

"If it's so easy, why don't *you* fly it?"

"Jim, you're starting to piss me off."

"Then try this. We don't have clearance to enter Sudanese airspace. And everything's closed for the day."

"I'll get it. When can we fly?"

A long silence, followed by, "This better be worth it. Eight-thirty."

"Good man. And make sure the liquor cabinet is stocked. We'll have VIPs."

David hung up, dialed the Hilton again, and got Paul Rackowski out of the tub to explain the plane was going to Khartoum and he'd have to rig down the ground station on his own.

No objection from Paul. "Anything's better than one of your VIP demos."

Finally David called back the First Secretary. "Sir, I'm pleased to tell you that everything has been arranged. May I ask that you and the Ambassador meet me at the entrance to the airport at eight-fifteen."

"We shall be there."

"One last thing. The matter of obtaining clearance to enter Sudanese airspace on such short notice. I was wondering, would it expedite matters to cite the Ambassador's name?"

Measured breathing at the other end. Then, "Cite the name of General M'botou."

#

Twenty miles west of Cairo, on the road to Bahariya Oasis, Major Hassam stopped his car and scanned the terrain. Back to the east, the pyramids of Giza stood out on the horizon, three bright triangles lit by the last rays of the sun. In all other directions there was nothing but sand, the Western Desert, where foreign armies withered and only Arabs knew how to survive. The air was so pure you could read a book by starlight, the sand so clean even Bedouins could detect no smell.

Hassam pulled off the road onto some hardground between two sand hills, drove about fifty feet, then turned the car around, shut off the engine, and got out. An evening breeze barely whispered.

Leaning back against the hood of his car, he lit a cigarette. He should quit, let the desert air cleanse his lungs. But not yet. He needed the smoke to calm his nerves. For the sake of the nation, he was about to come closer than ever before to making a pact with Satan.

He slipped his notebook from his jacket pocket and tore off the page with the scribbles and sketches he'd made not one hundred feet from Ragheb's office. *2nd floor, west side. Small alcove off main corridor.* He'd sketched a plan view showing the alcove with a large stone sarcophagus at the front. Boxes denoted busts on pedestals around the three walls. He'd circled the box in the middle of the back wall. *Piece no. 32888. Unknown man from 12th Dynasty. Obscured from corridor by sarcophagus.* An arrow curved from the circle to another sketch, this one a front view depicting the pedestal and bust. He'd drawn a square beside the pedestal, just above floor level, and put a dot in each corner of the square. *18-inch grate. 4 screws. Vent to outside.*

Folding the paper, he shook his head. Incredible that the treasure house of his country should have such holes in its walls.

A red Fiat drew to a stop on the main road, then drove on. Scouts. They'd check the area farther west and wait there on lookout until the meeting ended.

Hassam pinched out the ash of his cigarette and deposited the butt in his car's ashtray. He would not pollute this pristine place, the eternal soul of Egypt, as sacred as the one law he considered absolutely inviolate—preserve the state.

If revolution did lurk in the shadows, he would crush it. Utterly and with his own hands. For the bright-faced innocence of his daughter, the gentle decency of his father. For Anwar Sadat.

Yes. For those things, he would engage the Deceiver himself.

A silver Mercedes with tinted windows stopped on the main road between the two sand hills. It waited a few moments, then reversed a short distance and pulled cautiously onto the hardground, coming to a halt ten feet from Hassam's car.

Hassam walked toward it, ignoring the two thugs in the front seat. When he reached the back door, a window glided down.

Embedded in the rear seat, like a giant nesting goose, Abdul Imbabi scowled at him. He wore a white galabeyah and black sunglasses, "This is highly irregular, Major."

"We are irregular people, you and I."

"Myself, I am a simple merchant. Unaccustomed to being summoned out to remote places in the night."

Taking some courage in the man's discomfort, Hassam said, "Relax, I have no tape recorder. I only want to speak with you about a small matter. Come, let us walk in the desert and enjoy the final moments of the day."

Hassam felt the eyes studying him from behind the dark glasses. Then Imbabi's bulk slowly shifted toward the door.

They walked to a low rise in the hardground from which they could look out over the desert through a depression in one of the long dunes.

Imbabi glanced back.

"Don't worry. Your bodyguards can still see you." Hassam removed his sport coat, held it in one hand, and lifted his arms out to the side. "You may now satisfy yourself that I am not recording this conversation."

"I trust you," Imbabi said, in a tone that clearly showed he did not.

"I insist. Because I will search you, also."

"Never!"

Hassam lowered his arms. Summoning his most ominous voice, he said, "This can either be very profitable for both of us, or extremely unpleasant for you. Do not imagine that I lack the means, both within and outside the law, of seeing you hanged." He paused for effect. "With heavy men, it is always messy. The head pops off and cracks open on the ground, like a melon."

Imbabi's hand flexed toward his throat.

"Now search me," Hassam growled.

"I will not."

"Then turn around and raise your own arms." Even more than Imbabi might, Hassam feared a record of this conversation. Blackmail at best, a firing squad at worst. He'd seen what a firing squad could do, and couldn't help imagining the horror of that final second as a storm of bullets slammed into his chest.

Very slowly Imbabi did as instructed.

Hassam's experienced fingers played rapidly over the man's robe, searching the repulsive folds of Imbabi's body for any evidence of a wire. They stopped at a pistol, felt its shape beneath the cloth—a nine-millimeter semi-automatic—and continued. Imbabi could never get to the gun before Hassam crippled him.

"We can talk now," Hassam said, putting his own coat back on. "I take it Ahmad Fathi has returned to you."

"I understand he is with his family."

"Then you know I am a man of my word."

"I never doubted it, Major."

"So I will come to the point." *And if you refuse, I'll have no choice but to kill you before you're halfway back to the road.* The rocket-propelled grenades in Hassam's trunk would see to that. "I want you to steal something for me from the national museum. In return, your thief can also take one item, just one, for you."

Imbabi's mouth fell open. "You ... you have thought of how to do such a thing?"

"Every detail." He watched Imbabi's body stir, an almost imperceptible squirming, like the beginnings of sexual arousal. Hassam, having bet his life on the man's overwhelming lust for the forbidden, heaved an inward sigh of relief. "I will show you in a minute. But first I will tell you that the thief must be small, preferably a boy."

Imbabi rubbed his jowls. "I may, perhaps, know of such a boy."

"And it would be convenient if he were to take a long journey afterwards."

"A very long journey."

"And the item for yourself must be small, as well."

"I accept that," Imbabi answered.

"Above all, you must never attempt to repeat what we are about to do. Not ever."

Imbabi pulled off his sunglasses. "I am not a fool, Major."

That, at least, was true. Parasite, son of a pig, but no fool. Now inextricably entwined in a dance with the devil, Hassam unfolded his sheet of notepaper. "You will see this only once. So memorize it well and listen closely to what I say."

#

Tracking the walls of Blue's sparsely furnished living room, Rika felt like a leopard trapped in a kraal. A whole day with nothing to do but fume over how badly she'd lost control of everything that mattered. Her freedom, her need to contact Efrem, her equal need to show him she wasn't just his little sister. Even finding Tiye's tomb was in the hands of others.

She walked to the sink in Blue's kitchen, ran a glass of water, drank half, and poured out the rest. She opened the refrigerator, then closed it and slouched back to the living room. A movement caught her eye. Blue was pulling into the driveway in his Toyota Land Cruiser. Eager for news, she started toward the back door, when the phone jangled. She wasn't supposed to be here, but if she waited for Blue, the caller could hang up. With a fugitive's wariness, she poised her hand over the receiver and lowered her voice to sound like a man. "Hullo?"

"Rika?"

"David." Relief swept over her. "Where are you?"

"About to leave the office and pick you up. We're flying to Khartoum in two hours."

"What? You can't ring up with no warning and just say—"

"It all happened faster than I expected. Is Blue there? Both of you need to pack overnight bags."

Blue walked in the back door and deposited a case of beer on the kitchen counter.

Waving him to come closer, she said, "David wants us to go to

Khartoum tonight."

"Huh?"

She held the phone so the two of them could listen. Like his house, Blue smelled of old cigar smoke. "We're both here now," she told David.

In a rush of words, he recounted a meeting at the Sudanese embassy and arrangements he'd made with the First Secretary. "Blue, you've gotta keep them liquored up in the rear cabin while Rika and I gather data. Rika, we'll say you're my assistant."

"That's insane. I don't know anything about what you do."

"We'll fake it."

"And the Sudan has *Sharia* now," she continued. "They won't take alcohol."

For a moment, David was silent. Then, "They're diplomats. Maybe they're exempt."

She strangled the phone. "You can't build a plan on maybes. And how are you going to get them past the sentry at the airport?"

"I'll have Hagazy say they're high-ranking Egyptian officials, and they'll just follow us through. Being black won't raise any eyebrows. I've seen lots of black people here, including one of the Egyptian colonels on my demo flight."

Covering the mouthpiece, Blue whispered, "He's bonkers."

"Rika," David said, "we have one shot to find Tiye's tomb, and this is it."

She closed her eyes. They'd be like unarmed hunters approaching a rhino. No support, no escape route if David's plan failed. It either worked or ended in catastrophe.

It had to work. She pulled the handset from Blue's grasp. "We'll be ready when you get here."

Chapter 16

Rika's anxiety burrowed deeper into her belly as Hagazy swung into the Cairo airport and stopped by some vacant parking spaces in a poorly lighted corner of the lot. Besides all the other ways this encounter with the Sudanese could go wrong, David now wanted to fly a "grid" over Seddenga—three parallel passes so they could "narrow the ground swath" and increase the resolution of their pictures. Neither she nor Blue had been able to dissuade him. The best she could do was make him promise not to try it if the Sudanese refused alcohol, or drank too little to dull their senses to the plane's changing course.

"Uh, oh," Blue muttered. Twisting around in the front seat, he pointed out David's window. "They've got CD plates."

Rika turned to see a black Mercedes approaching, its license number preceded by CD, for *Corps Diplomatique*. Idiots. No car that advertised its occupants as members of a foreign government would get into a restricted military zone without top-level permission. As it parked in a space behind them, she could think of only one solution. "Tell the Sudanese they have to ride with us."

Grim-faced, David nodded. "You better get in front with Blue. Hagazy, this is going to be a tougher sell than—"

"I'll talk to him," she said. "You convince the Sudanese."

As David walked to the Mercedes, Blue climbed out to let her squeeze in beside Hagazy. "I hope you know what you're doing, love."

So did she. Hagazy had said all Egyptian soldiers were stupid. Probably not, but there was one universal military truth. In Arabic she said to Hagazy, "Soldiers love to see politicians in distress. So when you tell the guard these men are Egyptian officials, say their big, fancy Mercedes broke down and make some comment under your breath like, 'Serves them right. Our rulers should learn how it feels when ordinary people—"

"Are packed into a bus like goats." Hagazy flashed a grin, his eyes dancing with mischief.

"Very good." Or at least good enough, if Hagazy's puckish attitude didn't irritate the guard. "Just don't overdo it."

David returned with the diplomats. He introduced the fat, black-suited one as the Ambassador, and the tall, sour-looking fellow with the Hitler moustache as First Secretary.

The latter gave Rika chills. It wasn't just the bulge under his left arm, obviously a pistol. It was the face. She'd seen that face on captured Ethiopian torturers. The hardened lines, twisted mouth, and most telling of all, the dead eyes. Like the eyes of a perch that has lain too long on the fishmonger's slab.

Almost certainly, "First Secretary" was a cover for Cairo station chief of the Sudanese intelligence service. She had to warn David. With this man on board, the grid was out of the question.

Assuming they got on board. First, they had to make it past the guard. And if that failed, run like cheetahs.

While David and the two diplomats wedged themselves into the back, she tilted toward Blue to keep her derriere off the gearshift and attempted to look dignified.

At the checkpoint, the sentry stepped from his kiosk, took one look at them, and dropped his hand to his holstered sidearm.

Hagazy hopped out with David's pass. Standing in front of the sentry, he inclined his head in what Rika took to be a conspiratorial whisper. She held her breath as the two conversed. The sentry shouldered around Hagazy, peered into the rear seat, then stood back and saluted. With a smirk, he returned the pass to Hagazy. As the barrier lifted, Rika let out her breath.

Two minutes later, they parked alongside David's jet. When everyone had uncoiled from the Peugeot, she leaned back in and said to Hagazy, "*You* are a hero."

He beamed, a brilliant full-toothed smile that reminded her of Alem.

Alem, who'd stretched his luck too far. She backed out of the car and looked at the gleaming white fuselage. They'd just used up a lot of luck for one night.

And the night was only beginning.

#

Riding high from getting through the checkpoint so easily, David ushered his guests past all the electronic gear into the VIP cabin at the rear of the aircraft. There were six leather seats, three along each side, the front pair facing aft. He led the Sudanese to the first forward-looking row, and waved Rika and Blue to the seats facing them. A conversational grouping. As the others made themselves comfortable, he pulled a bottle of Dom Perignon from the small refrigerator under the liquor bar and held it up, mentally crossing his fingers.

"By all means," the Ambassador said in a jovial voice that matched his corpulence.

David winked at Rika, who gave him a hard look for some reason he couldn't fathom. Everything was going perfectly. With his best salesman's smile, he popped the cork and poured four glasses. After handing them around, he placed the bottle in a holder next to Blue's seat. "There's more in the fridge." Receiving a nod, he turned to the Ambassador. "I have to go forward and check with the pilots, but I'll rejoin you right after take-off."

On the flight deck, where Jim Mitchell and Chris Watson sat amid a constellation of gauges, radar screens, and lighted buttons, he confirmed that the required clearances had been received. As Jim powered up the engines to a low roar, David strapped himself into the fold-down jump seat behind the pilots. Both literally and figuratively, they were rolling.

Once airborne, he showed his copy of the aeronautical chart to Jim and explained the mid-route maneuver he wanted to make. Each pass would be sixty nautical miles, between twenty and twenty-one degrees north latitude. Ten minutes per run.

"What's this all about?" Jim grumbled, his square jaw darkened with five o'clock shadow.

"Groundwater." David suppressed a twinge of guilt at his lie.

"And when you make the turns, bank as gently as possible. I mean really gentle. I don't want our passengers to feel a thing."

"Afraid they might wet their pants?"

"High-ranking diplomats, filling up on champagne. We don't want them to spill it."

"That'd be a tragedy."

"Yeah," said Chris, the co-pilot. "We'd have to clean up the cabin again."

David let them blow off steam a little longer, then returned to the VIP cabin.

A champagne bottle stood on the bar, presumably empty since a second rested in the holder beside Blue. The Australian made a surreptitious circle of his thumb and forefinger, signaling success so far. With an inward smile, David noted the desired effects. The Ambassador had unbuttoned his suit coat and was lounging contentedly, glass in hand, as though this were the luxury his status deserved. Even the First Secretary had relaxed his ramrod posture and now rested with one ankle on the other knee and his seat reclined a notch.

Only Rika seemed ill at ease, legs crossed, arms folded across her stomach. Just nerves or something more? He couldn't ask until he got her alone.

But first, he had to go through the charade of briefing the Ambassador on DI's capabilities. He did this using the same color brochure he'd shown the First Secretary. In the process, he credited several engineering advances to Miss Teferi's skill.

"I must say, Mr. Chamberlain, your company has excellent taste in engineers." The Ambassador's eyes glided over her, leaving a slime trail from her chest to the zipper in her jeans.

David's muscles tightened. So that was the reason for Rika's discomfort. A greasy sheen on the man's balding pate brought to mind Porky Pig roasting on a spit—after he, David, rammed in the skewer.

Blue, who must have detected a sign of loathing David couldn't hide, quickly offered another round of champagne. Ambassador Porky accepted in grand spirits. The First Secretary placed a hand over his own glass.

Anxious to get Rika out of there, David said, "Gentlemen, if you'll excuse us, there are some things Miss Teferi and I need to attend to. Because of the short notice, there hasn't been time to prepare the aircraft for our demonstration tomorrow. We need to do that before we land."

"Of course," the Ambassador said, his gaze on Rika. "But do not be too long."

As David and Rika left, she with her book bag, David heard Blue say, "Would Your Excellency care to hear about the revolution in Chad? I was there, and ... "

Closing the door, David hissed, "The Ambassador's a scumbag."

"Forget him. The other one's the problem. He's an intelligence officer, and he's armed. You can't do that grid you were talking about."

That explained her hard look before they'd even taken off. Intelligence officer made sense, even more so than his previous assumption of Military Attaché. But the guy had drunk at least one glass of champagne and should be somewhat mellowed out. "Don't worry. They'll never know. My pilots are as good as they get."

"Do it on the return trip," she said.

"What if they want to fly back with us?"

"They haven't said anything about that."

"But if they do, there's no way I can make the maneuver in daylight without their noticing. It needs to be now."

"David, it's too dangerous. If the First Secretary gets suspicious and finds out you're conducting unauthorized reconnaissance in his country, he could have us thrown in a Sudanese jail. And you, being an American, would probably end up in a tiger cage."

"Tiger cage?"

"An iron box, set in the ground, with just bars between you and the scorching sun. Too short to lie down in. Not tall enough to sit up. A strong man might last a month before they shovel out his roasted remains."

Sweet Jesus.

"The Sudanese use them," she continued. "Just like the Ethiopians and Somalis. It's a favored method for detaining enemies of the state."

"We're not enemies of the state."

Her eyes ground into him. "We are, if the First Secretary says we are."

A cold claw clamped David's gut, gripping tighter as the words of SEECO's Admin Manager came back. No U.S. Embassy in Khartoum. No diplomatic relations, at all, after Black September terrorists murdered the American ambassador and were set free.

With anguish on her face, Rika took his hands in hers. "I want to find this tomb more than anything. If you honestly think we have to make the grid now, then I will help you all I can. I just want you to understand what could happen if we get caught."

Christ. Before, she'd basically asked him to risk his life for her mission. Now she was saying she would risk *her* life on his judgment. The weight of responsibility felt like a physical mass, a giant medicine ball on his shoulders. If they didn't get the data, they'd never find the tomb, the critical element on which both of them had pinned their hopes. If they got caught trying to find it, the fates of five people on this airplane were in grave jeopardy.

It all came down to David's faith in the pilots. And in himself.

He squeezed her hands. "It'll work."

For a moment, she peered up at him, her lips rolled inward with doubt. Then she nodded. "Okay."

He knelt at the aft end of the console and unlocked the second chair that ran along the same track as the operator's. "Here."

Seating himself, he checked the navigation display. They were eight minutes north of the Sudanese border and twenty minutes away from their first pass, which would simply be a ten-minute continuation along their current flight path. That added up to thirty-eight minutes before the aircraft made its first turn. No matter what happened, they were safe until then.

He switched off the main cabin illumination, leaving only the dull red glow of the operating lights. In the reel-to-reel tape deck between his and Rika's monitors, he loaded the tape with the images of the papyrus, took three 8x10-inch Polaroids to replace the ones stolen from Rika's room, and gave them to her. Then he threaded in a new reel to record their runs.

Laughter sounded from inside the VIP cabin. Blue must be in top story-telling form.

David relaxed a little and let well-practiced routine take over. After opening the panel in the jet's belly, he switched on all the scanners and fine-tuned their outputs for the aircraft's altitude. Then he activated the resistivity coil embedded in the wings and fuselage and extended the gravimeter sonde out the aircraft's tail. With a final run through his mental checklist, he leaned back. "That's everything we've got."

"What should I do?" she asked, her fingers twisting the strap of the book bag in her lap.

"Nothing until we get the data. We'll use the aircraft's computers for image analysis, and that's where I'll need your help." He gave her what he hoped was a reassuring smile. "With any luck, we'll have the tomb's location before we touch down."

The navigational displays showed they were two minutes away from the first pass. He typed a series of commands. The tape drive turned slowly forward and stopped. "From here on, everything's automatic."

The door of the rear cabin opened, spearing a shaft of light into his eyes.

"Anybody in here?" Blue bellowed. His massive silhouette filled the doorway, largely eclipsing the diplomats behind him.

Shit. David blanked both screens and sat back. "What's up?"

"Our guests would appreciate a tour."

"Can it wait a few minutes?"

The First Secretary shoved past Blue. "His *Excellency* requests it."

David swallowed hard. "Then now would be fine." What the hell else could he say? As he switched on the main lights, the tape drive clicked and started turning. The first pass had begun. He balled his hands to keep them from shaking. Only ten minutes before the pilots changed course.

Stepping aside to let the Ambassador in, Blue flipped his palms in a gesture that said, *Sorry, mate. I tried.*

Ambassador Porky, subtle as drool, made a beeline for Rika. He stationed himself at her side and laid a pudgy hand on her shoulder.

Rika showed no overt sign of objecting to the contact, but David could feel her disgust.

"Why is this running?" The First Secretary stabbed an accusatory finger at the tape drive.

"It's part of the memory system," Rika told him. "We're using it to test that everything is working properly."

Good girl. Just the right degree of authority to make the bullshit believable but not condescending.

"You are most impressive," the Ambassador said in a sticky-sweet tone that made David want to barf.

The First Secretary glanced derisively at his boss, then folded his arms across his chest. "Explain these instruments."

Jesus, the navigational displays showed less than six minutes to go. David recited the "quickie version" he had given to dozens of VIPs before, ending with, "So that's about the size of it. Perhaps you gentlemen would like to return to your seats while we finish our—"

The Ambassador lost his balance.

Blue caught the man's arm. "Careful, sir."

Damn! The jet was banking. So gently David could hardly feel it, but the Sudanese were standing. "Just some light turbulence," he said as calmly as he could manage.

The First Secretary's hand slipped inside his suit coat. "The plane is turning."

For a second, grisly visions of roasting to death in an iron box paralyzed David. The unspeakable pain of being scraped out with shovels, absurd since he'd be dead. And Rika? He couldn't even think about that.

"I'll check," he said too forcefully. Safety was the only excuse David could think of. He snatched up the intercom headset, feigned switching it on, and spoke into the dead microphone. "What's happening? ... What sort of problem? ... Can you fix it? ... Okay, but it's very important that we arrive in Khartoum tonight."

Pulling off the headset, he said, "Malfunction in the navigation system. Nothing dangerous. Probably just a fuse, but the pilot says he has to turn back while he fixes it."

The Ambassador scowled. "We are returning to Cairo?"

"We're changing course for Cairo, but only to adhere to international regulations while the pilots repair the system." There was no such regulation, but David hoped to hell these guys didn't know that.

"By now, we are in Sudanese airspace," the First Secretary declared. "We make the laws here."

Rika stood from her seat and faced the Ambassador. "Your Excellency, our pilots must comply with the highest safety standards. For your own protection. I'm sure you and your government expect nothing less."

David saw the man's eyes drop to her chest, and only then realized Rika had undone two buttons of her blouse.

Adjusting his jacket, the Ambassador asked her, "They are confident they can repair it?"

"I will see to it personally," she murmured.

With another glance at her chest, Ambassador Porky licked his fat lips and cooed, "Then I shall await your confirmation."

The First Secretary's jaw muscles flexed so vigorously it looked like hornet larvae writhed under the skin. Abruptly he turned on his heel.

Blue followed the Sudanese back to their cabin.

When the door closed, David slumped in his chair, his limbs buzzing with the same sense of reprieve that came from beating a jail-time speeding ticket.

Rika buttoned her blouse and resumed her seat beside him. "I want to scrub my skin with sandpaper."

"I'm sorry you had to do that. But it probably saved our lives."

For a moment, she said nothing. Then she straightened her posture. "At least, now we know how to control the First Secretary. How much longer before I have to tell them everything's okay?"

"You won't. I will."

She eyed him askance. "You think your breasts will appeal?"

"If you go, it might encourage that pig to pay you another visit up here. And his goon will come with him. We can't afford that in the middle of interpretation."

He had to think of a way to keep her up here and the Sudanese back there. "I've got it." The idea disgusted him, but when he told her, the relief on her face was all the incentive he needed.

A minute later, the plane banked again, and David sprang to his feet. "Back in a flash."

He headed aft, reaching the door just as it flew open to reveal the glowering countenance of the First Secretary. David pushed past him. "Your Excellency, the repairs have been made. We're changing course back to Khartoum. The delay will cost us only twenty minutes."

"Splendid." The Ambassador, holding an empty glass Blue was poised to refill, had removed his suit coat and loosened his tie. "But where is the young lady?"

The First Secretary cocked his head toward the open door. "In there. Sitting in the dark."

"She's still working on the memory system," David said to the Ambassador. "Then we have to calibrate the sensors. It could take us the rest of the flight, but she really wants to impress you."

Something approximating a post-coital smile spread over Porky's face. "Perhaps she would be free for dinner tomorrow."

There it was, the kind of opening David needed but feared he might have to insinuate himself. With the bitter taste of pimping his own girlfriend, he said, "She might be. But I'd wait until we land before asking her. She's really busy right now, and she'll be in a foul mood for days if we don't finish our preparations tonight. You know how engineers are. They hate to be interrupted."

"Quite so," Porky murmured, his eyes dreamy.

Having gone as far as he dared, David dug out a fresh bottle of champagne from the refrigerator, popped the cork, and poured for everyone, including himself.

"Your hand is shaking, Mr. Chamberlain." The First Secretary eyed him like a father appraising a leather-jacketed thug who'd arrived to take his daughter to the drive-in.

"Lack of sleep." In three gulps that fizzed painfully down his throat, David polished off his drink. He suppressed a burp, then excused himself to help finish the preparations. On his way out, he mouthed silently to Blue, "Keep them here."

"What happened?" Rika asked, as he resumed his place at the console.

"Lard-ass is going to invite you to dinner." The tape drive clicked off. "That's it. We have forty minutes to find the tomb." David pulled out his aeronautical chart and showed her the overlapping ground swaths covered by the three passes.

"This one." She drew her finger down the second run. "It covers the west bank of the Nile and Seddenga itself."

Wishing he could lock the cabin door, David rewound the tape to the start of pass two, the south-to-north run. He superimposed the infrared and photographic surveys on Rika's screen and the GPR and resistivity surveys on his. "Look for patterns that appear man-made, like rectangles or grids. Also straight lines leading from the river, or radiating out from some point."

He ran the tape at double-speed. For a minute or so, it tracked barren land. Then the Nile appeared on both screens.

"I see something," she said.

He stopped and zoomed in. It looked like a small village, but closer examination showed only foundations and a few walls.

She took a map from her book bag. "It's Sulb, another temple built by Tiye's husband. Seddenga should be about twelve kilometers north."

The scene progressed for another thirty seconds before he stopped it again. "There."

She leaned closer to her screen as he zoomed in on another set of ruins. "Yes, I think so. But we're not looking for Seddenga. We're trying to find a tomb that isn't on our maps."

"Which is what we're going to do now." He zoomed all the way out and engaged the Automatic Lineament Analyzer. The screens blanked, then started filling up with dozens of straight lines in various colors, some short, some long, going in all directions.

"What's this?" Rika asked.

"It's called an ALA. It scans an image and picks out straight features. Its 'eye' is super-sensitive compared to ours."

"But it's too confusing. There are lines everywhere."

"So let's get rid of some." With a joystick, he moved a cursor down the length of the Nile. Pushing two keys made all the lines east of the river disappear. "We're only interested in the west bank, right?"

She arched her eyebrows as if he'd just performed an impressive sleight of hand.

"Now, since supplies for the tomb-builders had to come in from the Nile, we can expect evidence of roads perpendicular to the river." He typed in some compass directions, and all but the approximately east-west lines disappeared. What remained was less than a tenth of the original number.

"Now we're getting somewhere." He scrutinized the screen. "Here. See this white line about six kilometers north of Seddenga? The lines are all color-coded to the images they come from. This one's white because it appears on several images."

He typed again, and the east-west lines on the other side of the river reappeared. "Our line doesn't cross the Nile. So it's probably not a natural feature, like a fault or geologic boundary. And it ends on this side at a flat-topped hill."

Rika gripped his arm.

"Now," he said, "let's see what data sets it appears on." He placed the cursor on the line, pushed a button, and a list of numbers popped up. "GPR, resistivity, and high-res gravity. It's a trench that's been filled in."

"Or canal?" she asked, her voice hushed with excitement.

He grinned. "Or a canal."

Zooming in so the length of the line nearly filled the width of his screen, he ran through each data type separately. Sure enough, ground-penetrating radar was best. In fact, the GPR line extended partway under the flat-topped hill, although very faintly. He swung the Polaroid camera into place and shot each data set, individually and in combination with the aerial photography.

The cabin door burst open. "Mr. Chamberlain."

David froze.

"His Excellency wants to know—" The First Secretary stopped in mid-sentence, advanced a few paces, and halted. "What are those photographs?"

The damn things lay all over the console. Immersed in data, David had totally forgotten the deadly threat just twenty feet away. To stall while he came up with an excuse, he said, "Close that door. You're ruining our dark vision."

The First Secretary drew his pistol. "Give them to me."

Heart pounding, David said, "We're testing the cameras. It's not my fault that you insisted on flying before we were ready."

"Knock it off," Blue barked from the doorway. "And put that fucking gun away."

The First Secretary whirled on him. "Stay out of this."

On wobbly feet that suggested he was several sheets to the wind, the Ambassador plowed his way past Blue.

"Your Excellency," David pleaded, his throat so tight he could barely get the words out. "If that gun goes off, the plane will depressurize. The air will be sucked out, and we'll all die."

The first Secretary aimed his pistol at David's chest. "Not if the bullet is in you. Now give me those photographs."

Squinting into the darkness, the Ambassador said something in a language David didn't understand.

"Spies," the First Secretary spat, his eyes never leaving David.

Behind the man, Blue raised his arms, hands gripped together for a hammer blow to the neck.

David snatched one of the zoomed-out Polaroids, stood, and held it up for the Ambassador. "We're just calibrating the cameras, sir." The photo's newly dried emulsion stuck to his sweaty fingers. With a silent curse, he peeled it free and gave it to the man. "As you can see, sir, this is a test shot of the Nile. If we're going to find groundwater, it'll be close to the river. These show us the background response."

The First Secretary reached for the photo, but the Ambassador yanked it away with what sounded like an angry expletive.

"It's just desert," David said, throwing up his hands in a sign of disbelief that anyone could be suspicious of that.

"Shut up!" the First Secretary shouted with a spray of spittle.

David recoiled, but didn't wipe his face. No way would he show the fear twisting his gut, or go down without a fight. "I will not shut up. Not when you stand there and threaten us with baseless accusations."

Rika leapt to her feet. "Excellency, this is very distressing. We are not spies. We are here to offer our services to you and your government." More softly, she added, "I was hoping for ... a warmer welcome."

Unsteady but managing to stay upright, the Ambassador handed her the photo. "You shall have a very warm welcome, my dear." A leer twisted his lips. "I shall see to it personally."

The First Secretary went livid. Snarling in a tone of protest, he trailed his boss back to the cabin. Blue shook his head and followed them.

When the door finally shut, Rika fell into her seat like a dropped marionette. Leaning her forehead on the console, she blew out a breath.

The intercom buzzed.

David switched on the headset. "What?"

"Time to buckle up," Chris said.

Oh, no. They'd just started. "Give me ten more minutes."

"He wants ten, Jim. ... Okay, David, we'll circle the pattern."

Switching off, David told Rika, "We have to hurry."

"We aren't finished?"

"All we have so far is a canal." In rapid succession, he scrolled through all the data sets on her screen. On the UV image, the hill at the end of the line was yellow. "Look at this. The yellow is limestone. It's brighter at the front of the hill because the limestone is freshly exposed."

"Freshly exposed?"

"In this arid climate, 'freshly' could be three thousand years ago."

Her fingernails dug into his arm. "The tomb?"

"Could be. Or maybe a quarry. I can't tell yet."

The buzzer sounded again.

He grabbed the headset. "Give me five more minutes."

"Can't do it," Chris said. "We're turning onto downwind."

David dropped the headset and shot two Polaroids of the UV image. As the whine of the jet's engines fell an octave, he scanned back and took several more shots over Seddenga. He heard the wing flaps extending. No more time. To Rika, he said, "Go back and tell them we're about to land. I'll be there as soon as I shut down."

Chapter 17

Eighteenth Dynasty

From the plans she had approved nearly a decade earlier, Tiye knew her tomb was unique. Into a traditional design of entry passage, burial chamber, and treasury, the architect had incorporated mechanisms of his own invention to ensure her safety and reemergence. But peering now at the threshold, she felt seized by doubt. For here stood proof, if any be needed, that her fate lay in his hands and in the perfect functioning of arcane devices tested only as workshop models.

With a full moon behind her, Baketaten and Ay at her sides, she listened intently as he described how the torchlit structure before them would conceal the tomb itself.

A wide section of the mesa had been deeply undercut, forming a massive rock overhang like a broad nose above the mouth of the tomb's entry. The overhang was buttressed by rows of tall timbers that were actually whole tree trunks brought from forests far up the Nile.

The architect, Kap, a thin man with rock dust in the creases of his face, pointed to the work area behind her where an enormous stone block rested on logs laid across two wooden rails that sloped down to the canal.

"Ropes will be tied," he said, "from that block to the bottoms of the timbers. When the block is released, it will roll down the rails into the canal. The block pulls the ropes, the ropes pull the timbers. As they fall, the entire overhang, up to the very top of the mesa, will collapse. Then the canal is filled in, and no trace of any construction remains. It appears only that there has been a landslide."

To Tiye, the overhang looked huge and unyieldingly strong. "How can you be sure it will collapse?"

"Divine Mother, I have had a deep notch cut in the underside of the overhang along its breadth at the back. If you look closely, you can see it, just there. On top of the mesa, another notch has been cut directly above this one. As such cracks would cause a longbow to break when drawn, so these weaken the rock and assure its failure."

She looked at Ay, who nodded agreement. Reassured, she said, "An ingenious contrivance, Master Architect. Let us go inside."

The walls of the entry passage were carved in low relief and painted, their scenes depicting major events in Tiye's long life. Her heart swelled at how beautifully the original drawings had been reproduced. And at the memories.

Here, she as a young girl gamboling with her brothers in their parents' garden. How the boys had loved capturing her and pitching her into the lotus pond. And what sweet, giggling revenge the night she filled their beds with toads.

Her wedding to Amenhotep in the first year of his reign. Stylized here, as she could remember so little save her fear that she might neither please him nor be able to bear the pain of conjugal union. Yet he had been as gentle as a calf. *Most beloved, you remain within me as the very beating of my heart.*

And here, enthroned beside him, receiving their first foreign dignitaries. How she had trembled that sweltering afternoon. How tiny she had felt, a commoner, barely adolescent, now suddenly Queen. And pregnant.

Dhutmose, dark-skinned and rakish, his captain's whip in his hand, their first-born who had died of a fall from his chariot. As hard as his birth had been, midwives whispering she was too small, his loss left a more painful void. A void she could only fill by believing Aten had willed it, that their second son might succeed to the throne.

Akhenaten. Tiye's heart soared, lifted on the wings of her most brilliant child. At first a disappointment to his father, for he shunned sports and the company of other boys, he in later years became the pride of the court. Breathlessly, tutors proclaimed his genius, Ay foremost among them. Tiye could still see the fervor in his youthful eyes as he sat at her feet receiving the revelation like a baby bird receiving food from its mother's mouth. She could hear his cogent questions in that high-pitched voice he never lost. His enlightened reign fulfilled her destiny.

Akhenaten again, here with her third son, Smenkhkare, during the co-regency she had arranged. A lump rose in Tiye's throat. Poor Smenkhkare, always sickly. Even the wet nurses claimed he suckled weakly. She had tried to nurture him, but though he matured in body, he seemed rarely to comprehend the import of being a pharaoh's son. Dull-eyed and heavy-browed, he succumbed to a fever in the same year Akhenaten died.

Tiye wrapped her arms around herself but could not help shivering at the memory of those losses. It was bad enough watching the coffin close on her husband, stealing him forever, so rending her heart that she could feel it still. But the deaths of Akhenaten and Smenkhkare had cast her into a pit of even bleaker despondency. Save one, all of her sons had died. Was her womb cursed? Was she doomed to betray her husband's love, to be the poison that killed his seed and exterminated his dynasty? Had Aten abandoned her?

Ay cleared his throat.

She realized he was reading her thoughts and trying to dispel them. Blessed Ay. Unwrapping her arms, she moved to the next painting.

Tutankhaten, her most beautiful boy, looking manly at age nine on his coronation throne. Tiye's spirits rose. "Image of Aten," and Aten's reward for the cruel trials she had suffered. The perfect child, beaming at her in the water garden as he recited the revelation, running to her with each new success in the scribe's art Ay was teaching him, proudly bringing her ducks he had shot with his own bow, knowing their meat was her favorite.

Now eighteen, he had become an adept regent, placating the mutinous priests while subtly undermining them with his gradual restoration of the true faith. In him lay her hopes, until she, herself, was restored.

Looking back along the passageway, Tiye felt struck at how

much her life appeared to be defined by the men in it. Her daughters, while depicted, held no place of prominence in this long gallery. That would change in her burial chamber.

As they proceeded toward it, she fixed again on the architect's skills. Concealing the tomb's entrance was a far less exacting feat than constructing a hidden exit.

The chamber was a square room, its walls carved and painted like the passageway. In the center, her red granite sarcophagus rested on a low stone platform. At the corners, facing the sarcophagus, stood four golden statues, their arms spread protectively. Each statue bore on its head a golden Sun Globe, and each had the face and cartouche of one of Tiye's daughters.

"This is me," Baketaten exclaimed.

Tiye smiled, for it had been a surprise. "Who more faithful and abiding to watch over me than you and your sisters?"

Baketaten knelt, head bowed. "I do not deserve such honor."

With a pang of grief, Tiye lifted her daughter's chin. "Rise, my beloved. I would see your face in these final days." She drifted her fingertips up Baketaten's cheek, then turned away. It would not do for her daughter to witness any hint of sorrow.

But Ay must have noticed. He stared at her grimly.

Tiye shifted attention to the lid of her sarcophagus. As she had specified, it was painted and varnished to look like granite but was actually made of lightweight wood, that it might be raised from the inside.

Her coffin, crafted traditionally of wood overlain with thin gold sheeting, lay on the floor, its own lid propped on edge beside it. She examined her effigy on the coffin's lid, then walked around to inspect the lid's inner surface, which depicted Aten with his loving arms spread over her resting place. Already she could feel His embrace.

But it would only happen if the architect had executed his responsibilities precisely. She turned to him. "You have much to show me here. I would hear every detail."

Stepping onto the platform, he said, "Divine Mother, in the bottom of your sarcophagus, a receptacle has been carved which will be covered by your coffin. In this receptacle lies the first key to your tomb's mysteries."

Tiye stepped up beside him and saw a cylindrical well, two hand spans across, containing a golden ball the size of a man's fist.

"The globe is affixed to a long rod which extends through the bottom of your sarcophagus into a small cavern below this room. There it plugs a hole which leads to yet another cavern below the first. Sand in the upper cavern will support that large stone you see lying against the wall. It fits perfectly into the opening in the floor, there, which is the stairway down to your treasury. Once the stone is in place, the only way to enter the treasury is to pull up on the globe. When the Sun Globe rises, the sand is released and the stone slides down an incline into the space vacated by the sand. In this way, a single person who knows the secret can easily move the stone which a hundred ignorant men could never budge."

"And to raise the Sun Globe if my coffin is on top?"

With a conjurer's glint in his eye, he pointed to two metal latches inside the foot of the sarcophagus. "Lift these latches, and the end will fall away. Your coffin, which will rest upon these dowels on a small incline inside, will roll out, and the Sun Globe will be revealed."

She glanced at Ay, again seeking concurrence that the mechanism would work.

"We would see this sand-filled cavern," Ay told the architect.

"Of course, Master. We may view it during our descent to the treasury." He guided them down to a landing where the stairs turned right. There, he held his torch through an opening in the wall.

By the dancing light of the torch's flame, Tiye saw a chamber filled with sand from which a thin, black pole rose into the ceiling.

Next to her, Ay stuck his head into the opening, looked all around, and withdrew. "We are satisfied."

Tiye smiled her gratitude, but Ay did not smile back.

They proceeded down to the foot of the stairs and turned left into her treasury, a large chamber filled with all the articles she would need until her rebirth. Chests of sandalwood and cedar infused the air with heavenly fragrance. Gold, silver, alabaster, and ivory glittered in torchlight like the trappings of a great festival, a jubilee attended by her family, whose life-sized statues flanked the doorway in the wall through which they had entered.

The likenesses of her husband and children, arrayed together in one place, buoyed Tiye's heart. All of them, the departed as well as those still living, would accompany her in spirit on the grandest of voyages.

In the center of the room stood her own statue. Carved of blackest basalt, it portrayed her striding toward a vestibule in the far wall above which hung a hemisphere of gold. The sight sent chills through her body—Aten welcoming her back to the surface world, His glorious light reflected in the gilding of her eyes.

For several moments she gazed in rapture. Here, at the very threshold of her reemergence, there could be no greater bliss, save the reemergence itself.

And as with all other passages in her tomb, the way was hidden. "Master Architect, I believe you have one final thing to show me."

Clasping his hands like a proud new father, he led her up two steps into the vestibule. "Divine Mother, this is the culmination of my meager talents." He pointed to the back of the vestibule. "Beyond this wall is a cylindrical shaft rising to the surface. Around its sides, a stairway is cut which leads from where we are standing to the top. The shaft is now completely filled with sand."

He gestured to the side walls of the vestibule. In each wall, there was a small niche containing a miniature alabaster column no taller than two hand spans. One column was in the lotus style representing Upper Egypt, the other in the papyrus style of Lower Egypt.

"The way is opened by breaking these columns. Break the lotiform column, and the sand will drain from the stairwell into a cavern below. Break the papyriform column, and the wall in front of us will descend."

The architect paused, then warned, "It is crucial that the lotiform column be broken first. If the papyriform column is first broken, then the wall before us will descend while the shaft is still full. The sand will fill this room, and the way out will be blocked forever."

The man was a genius. As she had been told, he built mountains and destroyed them with only pieces of wood and piles of sand. Yet a detail bothered her. "How shall one know when it is safe to break the papyriform column?"

"The shaft will drain quickly, and the sound will be as thunder. When it ceases, the way is clear."

"And to break the columns?"

"The alabaster is delicate, for the columns themselves are hollow and contain only sand. Thus any implement will suffice." He then produced a small mallet from the sheath hanging on his belt. "However, I would be honored if this were the instrument used. I fashioned it myself."

Ay accepted the mallet on Tiye's behalf and held it for her to see. It had a head of gold and a handle of ebony, both rubbed to a high polish.

The final key to the end of her journey. "Place it at the foot of my statue, at the beginning of my path into Aten's light."

#

As she emerged into the cool night air, Tiye looked back at the tomb's entrance and saw another alabaster column set into a niche in the outer wall.

"That," the architect told her, "works like the two below. When the column is broken, a stone within the wall will descend and close the entry."

"Master Architect," she announced in her most formal voice, "I am pleased by your work. Your reward shall be threefold."

He dropped to his knees.

"First, I shall recommend you to Pharaoh, to be the architect and builder of his tomb."

The man gasped. To build the tomb of a reigning king was the supreme honor of his profession.

"Second, I grant you deed to land in the sacred valley west of Waset, where you may build your own tomb amidst those of the kingdom's noblest courtiers."

He prostrated himself.

"And third, I shall answer the question I have seen in your eyes, but which you have dared not ask. The stairway from darkness into light is necessary because I, unlike others before me, shall return to the face of this land."

He gazed up at her, as at a comet, his mouth open in awe.

"Now rise, Master Architect. Dawn approaches, and your work here is not yet concluded."

#

In her cabin aboard the royal barge, Tiye watched the eastern horizon slowly brighten. The air was still, but a storm brewed within her. "The architect is a clever man. Do you suppose he is too clever?"

"I have considered it," Ay replied behind her. "But I think not. His ambitions lie in his profession, and you have brought his dreams within his reach."

"I did tonight. But what about before?" She turned to face her brother. "He has had years to construct my tomb and to ponder his possibilities. The devices he has built are well-concealed. Might there be others?"

"Your personal overseer should have guarded against such treachery. He reports nothing of that nature."

"The overseer is an intelligent man who served my husband well. But I wonder whether his intellect is a match for the architect's."

"Your concerns are wise," Ay agreed. "I shall find out."

"Be careful, Ay. You are old. And greed does terrible things to men."

For the first time that night, Ay smiled, a roguish grin that took her back to their youth. "Divine Mother, what I have lost in physical prowess over the years has been returned to me a hundredfold in cunning."

Chapter 18

Although she'd never been to Khartoum before, and could see little of it beyond the few functioning streetlamps, Rika found the city depressingly familiar. From her contorted position on David's lap in the front seat of the coughing Fiat, she saw an idyllic location—the confluence of the Blue and White Niles—scabbed with concrete and shanties, rutted with teeth-cracking chuckholes, and reeking of the acrid stench that only comes from burning thoroughly picked-over rubbish. An African paradise turned to pox.

At least, she didn't have to endure the hypocrisy of touring this dilapidation in the blithe company of the city's privileged. She'd accepted the Ambassador's invitation to dinner next evening, with no intention of being there. But she had declined, on grounds of not alienating her colleagues, his offer to ride into town in the shiny Toyota that awaited him and the First Secretary. Instead, she, David, Blue, and the pilots had crammed themselves into the second car on the tarmac, a dented Fiat with a chain-smoking driver and only one working headlight.

The long drive to town finally ended at their hotel, a two-story, Elizabethan-style structure with pitched roofs and multi-paned windows. Once a grand Britannic oasis, it now resembled more closely one of those haunted houses in American horror films. To Rika, it was shamefully emblematic of all that had gone wrong in post-colonial Africa. Granted, colonialism had been a blight on the face of the continent, but at least the Europeans left beautiful cities, viable economies, and competent bureaucracies. All of which their African successors had neglected, squandered, or abused for personal benefit, shackling their own countries into the slavery of total dependence on foreign aid.

As she climbed splintered steps to the hotel's front doors, she pledged all her influence, as future Minister of Culture, to preventing Eritrea from making the same mistakes.

The reception area smelled of stale curry. While David handled check-in formalities, Rika scanned the lobby. A few tables and chairs surrounded zebra-skin rugs. Old hunting photos hung on wood-paneled walls. A suited man sat in the corner reading a newspaper. At one in the morning?

So the Sudanese had assigned them a minder, a watchdog to make sure they neither got into nor caused any trouble. Not very subtle. A page rustled as the man turned it, revealing a jackal-faced fellow with—

Rika's breath caught. His face disappeared again behind the newspaper, but the Hitler moustache remained burned in her retina. Had the First Secretary assigned one of his personal bootlickers to spy on them? It didn't seem like he could have had time. More likely, the moustache was a badge of the intelligence service, a filial bow to the father of all fascists.

"We're set," David announced. He handed out five keys, then led the way up a flight of stairs. Outside their doors, he told the pilots, "We'll probably fly the demo in the afternoon."

"Chris and I will pre-flight in the morning," Jim Mitchell said, "then stay put 'til you show up." He patted his overnight bag. "You folks care for a night cap?"

David shook his head. When the pilots' doors closed behind them, he turned to her and Blue. "Let's meet in my room as soon as you're settled."

Suspicious of listening devices in a hotel where, despite its dilapidation, only foreigners would stay, Rika tapped her ear, then the wall. "I'd rather go for a walk in that park across the street."

David peered at her, as if assessing whether her caution were paranoid or rational. "Yeah, okay. I feel like stretching my legs."

"Bring your valuables," Rika added, sticking her key in the lock.

Her room was stifling. The turpentine stink of overheated

varnish stung her nose. A ceiling fan might have helped, but there was only a circular hole where one had once hung. She wrenched open the window. The "garden" below was an expanse of weeds surrounding two stagnant ponds, a rusted aviary, and the crippled remains of an old gazebo. Turning back, she noticed a brown blotch on the thin chenille bedspread, as if a wounded rat had crawled up there and bled out. The dark wooden floor creaked as she walked to the bathroom. In the sink, tiny ants swarmed over a dead cockroach.

Well, she'd slept in worse places.

Downstairs she found David with his attaché case and Blue rubbing what smelled like insect repellant on his arms.

"Definitely first class accommodation," David said.

"I especially like the lovely brown color of the water." Blue offered her the small plastic bottle of repellant. "Hundred percent DEET."

"I don't need it." Darting her eyes around the lobby, she saw no evidence of their minder. Maybe he'd gone to use the toilet. She shifted her book bag to the other shoulder. "Let's get some air."

The park across the street was another English leftover. Acacias, the shade trees of Africa, filtered moonlight through their flat canopies, as they must have done in colonial times. But native scrub now choked the former lawns and flowerbeds. In places, white-painted stones still edged the pathways of gray, hard-packed dirt. Occasional wrought-iron benches brought to Rika's mind scenes of prim courtship promenades among white couples in a land that wasn't theirs.

Part way down one of the paths, David said, "Did you see that fellow with the newspaper?"

Rika nodded. "Compliments of the intelligence service."

"Listeners, watchers." Blue glanced behind him. "This place gives me the creeps. If you folks got what we want, I vote for getting the hell outta here, quick as bunnies."

"You brought the photographs?" she asked David.

He held up his attaché case, then quickly recounted for Blue the gist of what they'd found.

"Tomb or quarry, huh? Shouldn't be too hard." Blue pulled a penlight from his shirt pocket. "Let's see the pictures."

At the next park bench, they all sat while Blue studied one of the photos. "Looks like a small mesa, sticking out from the back wall of a T-shaped valley. Probably a fault block, dropped off that plateau behind." Balancing the photo on his knees, Blue hunched over with a small lens in one hand and his penlight in the other. After a minute, he sat upright. "Sorry, folks, but that 'freshly exposed' rock at the front of the mesa is a landslide."

"Landslide? It can't be." Rika grabbed the photo. "Let me look." Juggling photo, lens, and light, she finally got the area illuminated and in focus.

"See the fan shape of the debris slope?" Blue touched the spot with the tip of a mechanical pencil. "And the boulder field filled in with finer sediment? And especially the scarp near the top. It's a queer-looking landslide, but that's what it is."

Her heart sank. It was all there, just as Blue described. Not only had they failed to find the tomb, but what they did find wasn't even man-made.

"But the UV image shows it's limestone." David handed another photo to Blue. "See? When I think of landslides, I think of poorly consolidated clastic sediments. Hell, limestone's so tough it'll shred your boots."

"Indurated limestone," Blue allowed. "But maybe this is more friable." He gave the picture to Rika.

She had no idea what indurated meant, or friable. But if David thought a landslide was the wrong interpretation, then there was still hope.

"And the sides of the mesa," David continued, "they don't look steep enough to be susceptible to landslides. The valley walls around it are steeper, and there're no landslides there."

"It's hard to tell how steep something is from one photo. You'd need a stereo pair."

"Wait a minute." David looked through his attaché case and retrieved another photo. "Here's a previous scene showing the same place, but from six kilometers south. The two of them should make a stereo pair." Then his shoulders sagged. "The only stereoscope I have is in the plane."

"Never fear, mate. I can do it without one. But not in this light. We'll have to go back to the hotel."

They'd lost her again with their stereo this and stereo that. "What will it tell you?"

"She's got a point there, sport. So the sides are steep or gentle. So what?"

"I don't know," David said tiredly. "I guess I'm grasping at straws."

Rika lowered her head, the fatigue of defeat descending over her like a heavy fog. Her eyes fell on the picture in her lap, the one David called the UV image. She noticed a round, black dot on top of the mesa. "Is this anything?"

David took the photo and studied it with Blue's lens. "Weird. Could be the foundation of some sort of tower or lookout post. It's black because it isn't limestone. Maybe they built it out of cobbles from the river."

"Why use river stones," she wondered aloud, "if they had all this other rock right below them?"

"Who knows? Maybe it's not even man-made. Nature can play tricks on us when we view her from twenty thousand—"

"Do not move," someone behind her barked in Arabic.

Rika spun around to see a soldier jabbing the barrel of an Enfield rifle into Blue's neck. With an instant flashback to the Ethiopian ambush that almost cost her life, she clamped the hand holding the barrel and yanked it forward between herself and Blue. In a wheeling motion, she pulled down on the hand, drove her forearm upward under the man's armpit, and rolled him over the bench top. As he flipped onto the ground in front of them, she chopped him in the throat. Survival instinct raised her hand for another chop, but David grabbed her arm.

"Rika!"

She wrenched it from his grasp, the heat of combat still firing her veins. Only the soldier's obvious incapacity kept her from delivering the deathblow. She scoped the foliage for other movements, strained to catch the slightest sound that might betray the approach of more men. Nothing.

Dropping to his knees beside her, Blue opened one of the soldier's eyelids and shone his light into the pupil. "We'd better find a doctor. This guy's not getting up any time soon."

Damn! Now she'd done it. If this fellow died ... She bent to give mouth-to-mouth resuscitation. Thank God she hadn't struck that second, larynx-crushing blow.

Running footsteps.

She cut her eyes to the path and saw a man sprinting toward them with a pistol. Adrenalin braced her muscles. There was no defense against a firearm until he got to within arm's reach.

"It's the bloke from the hotel," Blue said.

The man charged up to them. "Stop! What is happen here?"

David stepped between her and the man. "She's trying to save his life."

"Move away!"

"Get a doctor," David told him. "Fast."

Spotting a hint of uncertainty on their minder's face, Rika uncoiled just a fraction. If shouting staved off physical violence, they might get out of this with a severe reprimand. Provided the soldier didn't die. With renewed urgency, she huffed air into her victim's lungs. Raising her head between breaths, she saw the security man look from David to the limp figure and back again.

"Go on, dammit," David yelled. "You want your boss to find out you stood here and let a soldier die?"

The security man shook his pistol in David's face. "Stay here." Then he dashed back the way he'd come.

The soldier convulsed.

Rika turned him over just as he vomited in the dirt. Good sign. "Blue, help me get him up on this bench."

While she and Blue wrestled the fellow onto the bench, David gathered up the photos, then tossed some papers from his attaché case onto the ground.

"What are you doing?" Blue asked him.

"If the Sudanese confiscate these images, they could question us for days. Or worse." David pulled out his shirt, shoved the photos down the back of his trousers, and left the shirt out to cover them.

Propped upright, the soldier moaned something. His eyelids fluttered open, then closed again.

Rika felt the pulse in his wrist. Stronger. He'd come through, probably with nothing worse than a hellish sore throat and a few weeks of impaired speech.

"Okay, here's the story," David said. "I did this. Not Rika. It's dark, and it happened too fast for our security guy to have seen anything clearly. I thought this fellow was a thief, so I hit him. All Rika did was save his life. Got it?"

"Why you?" Rika asked.

"Because I'm a man, and women don't do this kinda shit in Muslim countries." He gave her a crooked smile. "Which, by the way, was damned impressive."

Their minder returned with a scrawny, bespectacled youth in shirtsleeves and carrying a medic's black leather bag.

"He's gonna be okay," Blue announced.

As the medic lifted the soldier's wrist, the security man turned on Blue. "You—"

"You," David snapped, "should teach these guys not to sneak up on people in the dark and stick a rifle in their backs. How the hell are we supposed to know he's not a thief? Or a murderer?"

"What you are doing here?" the man demanded.

"Sitting in the park. Talking."

"Why you are not in hotel?"

Rika was about to chime in about the stifling heat in their rooms when David exploded.

"We're guests of your goddamned government. We're out for a breath of fresh air, and this sonofabitch creeps up and shoves a gun in our ribs. What the hell kind of welcome is that?"

"What you are reading with little torchlight?"

"Papers." David scooped up a handful from the ground and thrust them at him. "Read 'em yourself, if you want to."

The man took one, shined his own light on it, and dropped it. "Go back to your room. Go asleep. Do not come to here at night."

David bent to gather the rest of the pages. "I'm going to report this tomorrow. Come on, folks, let's go."

As they emerged from the park, Rika took David's hand. "You think very fast."

"You're the fast one. That poor soldier never had a chance."

"Ah," Blue intoned, "the lovebirds find common ground."

"You were good, too," she told Blue. But David was the one who had rescued them from arrest and interrogation. He and she were like teammates in battle, with different but complementary skills. And as sometimes happened after a close call in battle, the subsiding rush settled between her legs, igniting an urge for carnal celebration. She glanced at David, wondering if he felt the same.

When they reached the hotel steps, Blue said, "By the way, squire, there's a bottle of your company's Scotch in my room. What say we all go drink it while I have a gander at your stereo pair?"

"I'll have a double."

With more disappointment than she cared to admit, Rika dragged her mind back to their luckless efforts to find Tiye's tomb. The smoldering inside her flickered out.

Blue's room was a carbon copy of her own, down to the missing ceiling fan, although his bedspread was unstained. While he filled three glasses, David pulled out his photos. The top one showed the white line that had gotten him so excited. A trench or canal. But why would anyone dig a trench or canal to a landslide? Then something David had said came back to her. "That's it!"

"What?" David asked.

"What you said about nature playing tricks on us." She snatched up her book bag, extracted a sheaf of notes, and shuffled through them. "Here. Listen to this."

Then she caught herself. If the room was bugged ... She tapped her ear. "We have to go outside again."

"Hang on," Blue told her. He produced a small portable radio from his overnight bag and tuned it to the only station broadcasting at that hour. "I shoulda thought of this before."

Perfect. Accompanied by a high-pitched female singer, Rika read from her translation. " 'Shun the architects of your immortal father and brothers. Your tomb must be built in the manner of my own, relying not on false passages for the security of your worldly body, but on artifices of nature, aided by stonecutters and the clever mind of the architect, Kap, whom I shall send to serve you. He, too, will design the pathway of your reemergence into the glorious light of Aten, for he knows well the properties of weights and balances, stone and sand, slope and cavern.' "

She looked up at David. "Doesn't that sound familiar? In the park you talked about a trick of nature, and here it is in the papyrus. 'Artifices of nature.' And her architect, Kap, who's more clever than the others at hiding a tomb—not with false passages, but by tricks of nature, carried out by stone cutters. And you," she said to Blue, "say the landslide is queer."

"Jesus Christ," David breathed.

Blue hoisted her in his arms. "Sweetheart, you're a right bloody genius."

"Give me the hand lens." David laid his images on the edge of the bed. With Blue's lens, he knelt on the floor to reexamine them. "Blue, come here. Look at the top of the landslide. At each side. What do you see?"

Blue took David's place and bent over with the lens. "Naw, I don't believe it. The edges are straight as a cue stick."

"Here," David said, pulling out another photo. "These two make the stereo pair."

Blue lowered his head over them, his eyes becoming trance-like as he slid the two photos back and forth.

"He's focusing one eye on each image," David explained to her. "When he gets it just right, it'll pop into 3-D."

"Got it. And you were right. The slope near the fall is too gentle for a landslide. But there's way too much debris to be a simple quarry failure, either. Unless …"

"Unless what?" she prompted.

"Unless they were undercutting."

"Undercutting a quarry would be suicidal," David said.

Suddenly it all clicked in Rika's mind. "The architect made an artificial landslide to bury the tomb's entrance."

For a second, David just looked at her. Then his lips curled into a smile. "I think you nailed it."

#

On the bed that she'd stripped to bottom sheet only, Rika lay naked in the dark. Mosquitoes whined but never landed on her. Something about her sweat had always kept them away. Something they could smell, although the only thing she could smell was her own sex.

The thrill of finding the tomb had rekindled the burning inside her. Fanned it to flames she could barely stand. She slid her fingers down her thighs, then pulled them away with a shudder. No, this was not what she wanted. What she wanted was David.

And he was right next door.

She sat up and slipped on her blouse, fastening only a middle button. Forget the panties. She felt too vital to suffer through preliminaries. She pulled on her jeans, but left them unzipped.

Barefoot, she padded down the darkened hallway to David's door and knocked softly.

"Who is it?"

"Me."

When he unlocked the door, she stepped inside, undid the last button of her blouse, and stood there, letting him drink in the sight of her.

Chapter 19

Five minutes after the museum opened, Abdul Imbabi, wearing Saudi robes and headgear, purchased admission for one adult and one child. At his side, freshly scrubbed and combed, Imbabi's "son" wore the blazer, tie, and shorts of one of Cairo's elite boys' schools.

Inside, they climbed the Grand Staircase and stopped near the row of offices along the front of the building while Imbabi got the feel of the place. His impression was of an outsized mausoleum, cold, dark, and silent, filled with smells of dust and stone and, if his imagination wasn't conning him, the parchment smell of the desiccated dead. He almost felt at home.

Satisfied they were alone and knowing the first tourist buses would not arrive for another twenty minutes, he said, "Second office from the corner. If it is locked, pick it. The papyrus should be in a cedar wood cabinet left of the desk. Rack number eight. Confirm this, then get out. If anyone walks in on you, you got lost looking for a lavatory."

The boy, narrow-eyed and dark-skinned, glided to the door, his nimble pace at odds with the overfed impression conveyed by his blazer's girth. He knocked, waited, then tried the doorknob and slipped inside.

Footfalls on the stairs.

Imbabi moved to a defensive position near the office door, where the boy could see him before coming out. Cursing himself for not purchasing a guidebook he could pretend to consult, he feigned checking his watch.

An old fellow in a wool suit and thick glasses crested the stairs, a sheaf of papers under his arm. Taking little notice of Imbabi, he turned left along the row of office doors and disappeared into one of them about halfway down.

Just briefly, Imbabi relished the thrill of almost being caught, the electric tingling in his thighs, the feeling of extra strength afterwards. It was years since he had operated. He told himself he didn't miss it. But once in a while …

The door beside him opened. "Master."

"Come quickly." Imbabi walked away, down the corridor with the alcoves on the museum's west side. He heard the office door close behind him, then the boy catching up.

"It's just as you said, Master."

Imbabi hadn't doubted it. Hassam's legendary attention to detail would be heightened tenfold in this case, for the major was gambling his life if found out. Imbabi savored his own advantage in possessing this knowledge. Still, he would never undertake such a dangerous heist without confirming every particular.

Picturing Hassam's sketch, Imbabi glanced into each alcove they passed. "Here."

They stepped in to admire the wooden bust of an "Unknown man from the 12th Dynasty," piece number 32888. Imbabi pointed to the metal grate in the wall, then stood watch in front of the sarcophagus at the alcove's entrance. Displayed on a thick stone slab, the lidless sarcophagus rose to the level of Imbabi's nose. A good hiding place, open on top but too high to see into unless a person stood on tiptoes.

The boy knelt before the grate, pulled a screwdriver from his blazer pocket, and removed the four screws. They'd been painted over, and he wiped up the small paint chips on the floor and put them in his pocket. After removing the grate, he unbuttoned his blazer.

"Wait." Before they went any further, Imbabi wanted to check the air vent himself. After another scan of the corridor and display areas to confirm they were alone, he moved into the alcove, got down on his hands and knees, and peered inside the hole. A square tunnel, eighteen inches on a side and about five feet long, ran horizontally through the massive stone wall and opened directly to the outside. Piles of pigeon shit fouled the far end but posed no obstacle to passage.

Imbabi heaved himself to his feet, blessing the British who'd built this place and must have assumed an air duct was secure merely because it opened thirty feet above the street. "Proceed."

The boy took off his blazer and drew two coils of rope, one thick and the other thin, up over his head. He stashed these inside the wall, then replaced the grate by finger-tightening the screws.

"We are finished here," Imbabi told him. But the best was yet to come.

With his "son" now looking skinny, instead of overweight, he strolled toward the Tutankhamun collection at the back of the museum. On their way, they passed a guard, a stubble-faced man sitting on a stone bench, leaning back against the corridor wall and already dozing at this early hour. "They are here day and night," Imbabi cautioned.

"I understand, Master."

The boy had nerve. Known as "Spider" for his ability to squeeze into tiny spaces and his skill with ropes, he'd gained a reputation for daring before Imbabi recruited him from the streets two years ago. Now, at only twelve years of age, he was the best second-story man Imbabi had.

Most of the Tutankhamun collection stood in three large rooms at the rear of the museum. Although Imbabi could detect no alarm systems, each room had only one entrance, protected by an iron gate with a heavy chain and fist-sized padlock. The locks would be no problem, but the treasures they guarded were too large to be secreted out and too famous for even him to dare possessing.

On the other hand, the open area in front of these rooms held row upon row of horizontal cases with tilted glass tops displaying hundreds of lesser artifacts from the boy-king's tomb. Finger rings, toe rings, sandals, daggers, necklaces, arm bands in the form of cobras, ceremonial fly-whisks, walking sticks.

Imbabi stopped. There, among a collection of walking sticks, was a staff that fired his blood. Made of ebony wrapped in three places with wide bands of gold, its head was the head of Anubis, the dog-god who weighed men's hearts in the underworld. The insides of the dog's erect ears were gilded. Its collar featured a cartouche of green stone delicately carved with what Imbabi had come to recognize as Tutankhamun's name. A flanged holding piece, made of ivory, joined head to shaft and had four inset scarabs carved from the same green stone as the cartouche. Slight wear on the bottom of the shaft showed the young pharaoh had used it.

"That one," Imbabi breathed. "The black-and-gold one with the dog's head."

The boy knelt, as if tying his shoelace, and inspected the simple lock by which the lid of the case was secured.

"When you take the stick," Imbabi said, "shift the others so it looks like nothing is missing. And be sure to bring me that card with the label and number on it."

Spider stood and smirked.

In a flash of anger, Imbabi snarled, "Get rid of that attitude. If you fail, or if you damage the stick, I will personally strip the skin from your body with a dull blade."

The boy's smile vanished.

They walked downstairs and out into blazing sun. Two streets away, Imbabi gave his final instructions. "Take this money and buy a small lock cutter and a new lock like the one we saw on the case. Do not steal them. Also, buy some fruit and eat it. But drink nothing. I do not want you having to piss. Discard the blazer and tie. Go back to the museum and wait outside until you see a large group of people entering. Join them. After you are inside, conceal yourself in the sarcophagus at the front of that alcove and wait there. Do not move until after midnight. Then be swift and silent. And be sure you get the grate back in its place. Tomorrow morning someone else will replace the screws so it appears nothing is amiss. Do you understand?"

"Yes, Master."

"Repeat it to me."

As the boy did, Imbabi's Mercedes pulled up beside them. Eyes still fixed on the boy, Imbabi opened the rear door. "Follow my words exactly, and a garden of delights shall be yours."

#

In a concrete room on the third floor of a concrete building in central Khartoum, Rika listened with half an ear as David spoke of sensors, data quality, and groundwater resources to six Sudanese men seated around a long table. It was a sham. David had no desire for a contract, and neither the Ambassador nor the Agriculture Minister was even present. Which was why she let her mind drift back to David's room last night. If someone really was eavesdropping, he'd gotten an earful.

The first time was pure animal savagery. She'd even bitten his shoulder. In the panting aftermath, they fell asleep still coupled. Then some time before dawn, he'd kissed her awake and made love to her so tenderly she almost cried, his mouth and his fingers suspending her over the abyss for an eternity before letting her fall. After that, she couldn't sleep. Propped on an elbow, she watched him, listening to his gentle breathing. As daylight broke, she molded herself to his body, nuzzled him to consciousness, and took the lead this time, doing her best to suspend him as he'd done her. They crashed together in a mind-shattering impact that left her breathless. As they lay in each other's arms, she knew their relationship had changed forever. But it had cost her, for she was now more vulnerable.

Scraping chairs jolted her from reverie as men rose from the table. Her watch showed 12:45. They'd been here three hours, after getting a late start because she and David had lost track of time in the shower.

General M'botou, the only one of the Sudanese who'd bothered to introduce himself, strode around the table from his position at the far end, where a poster-sized photo` of President Nimieri frowned at them from the wall. M'botou, a stout, short-haired man with tribal scars on his cheeks and the countenance of a Cape Buffalo, wore starched camouflage fatigues and a red beret. "Mr. Chamberlain, two of us will accept your offer of a demonstration flight. I suggest two-thirty."

"That will be fine, sir."

Damn. Rika had hoped M'botou wouldn't be interested, and she, David, and Blue could fly out of here without delay. It was bad enough that she didn't trust the general, worse that his few glances at her brimmed with contempt. *Sharia*. A woman's place was in the kitchen, the bedroom, or the nursery. Even foreign women should cover their heads with a scarf and isolate themselves from the men.

Screw him.

At least no one with a Hitler moustache had shown up at the meeting. And their minder had sat sullenly in their car during the ride from the hotel, suggesting there'd be no repercussions from her almost killing the soldier in the park.

"Umar." M'botou beckoned the bespectacled fellow who'd asked most of the questions during the meeting and scribbled notes furiously as David answered. When the young man trotted up, notebook in hand, M'botou said to him, "Tell them what you need."

Umar, who blinked almost constantly and carried three pens and a small slide rule in his shirt pocket, said, "Every instrument, we must see how it's work. You will show us?"

David knitted his brow. "All of them?"

"Yes, all."

With a shrug, David said, "Okay."

"And instrument maintenance records. You will show us, also?"

David's eyes narrowed slightly. "They're on file in Denver. Why would you want to see them?"

M'botou answered. "Reliability is an important factor in determining whether to accept your offer."

The request sounded reasonable. But David's guarded tone suggested otherwise. And Blue, who'd stood aside when M'botou first approached them, was pulling his beard the way he did when in doubt. Recalling their ruse with the Ambassador on the trip down here, Rika tried to satisfy the general with, "We confirm reliability before every flight."

"Mr. Chamberlain," M'botou said, "we are addressing you. Not this woman."

Rika clenched her fists. What she wouldn't give to be alone with this pig for two minutes.

"General, Miss Teferi is a highly trained engineer." David moved closer to her, shoulder to shoulder.

Arctic silence, except for the honking of traffic on the street below and a periodic squeak in the ceiling fan overhead.

Finally, M'botou turned to Umar, who was blinking even more rapidly than before. "Continue."

"Service manuals," Umar said to David. "Is most important we inspect the service manuals."

Suddenly goose bumps prickled Rika's chest. She knew next to nothing about remote sensing, but she knew plenty about equipment upkeep. If these guys wanted service manuals, it could only mean they planned to maintain the equipment themselves. And that could only happen if they confiscated David's airplane.

#

Struggling to keep a poker face, David waited for the Sudanese to file out, then whispered, "We're in deep shit."

"You know what they want," Rika said.

"I sure as hell do." His watch read 1:15. "We've got barely an hour to get out of this country."

"Shit." Blue grimaced. "I was hoping you two had a different take on this than I did."

Outside, the dented old Fiat stood at the curb, their surly driver and the hotel security guy both leaning against the front fender.

"Airport," David told them. "And hurry. General M'botou will be angry if he has to wait for us."

Scrunched with Rika and Blue in the back seat, David held her hand as the three of them braced against the constant bottoming out. The driver, using both sides of the two-lane road, seemed never to miss a pothole. The security man, apparently unfazed, slouched in the front passenger seat, smoking cigarettes that smelled like a blend of seaweed and raw sewage.

At the airport, they drove past a row of Quonset huts, then turned onto the aircraft parking apron where David spotted his jet—in the company of six Sudanese soldiers and an open-bed truck fitted with a big machine gun.

"Soviet," Rika said. "Fifty-one caliber."

At least it was pointed away from the plane.

A kid with lieutenant's insignia ambled up to confer with the hotel security guy.

In no mind to wait for anyone's permission, David rushed Blue and Rika up the stairs into the aircraft. "Jim? Chris?"

"Back here," Jim called. The pilots sat in the rear cabin playing gin rummy.

"Jim, the Sudanese want to steal our plane."

"Are you shitting me?"

"Dead serious. They'll be here in thirty minutes, expecting a demo. My guess is they'll wait 'til we're on the ground again because they want to see how the instruments work. But we can't count on that."

"Fuck." Jim threw his cards on the floor. "We're rolling."

Chapter 20

In the cockpit, David stood with Rika and Blue behind the seated pilots while Jim hurriedly consulted a thick black binder and Chris listened to air traffic control through his headset. Thirty yards away on the tarmac below, the soldiers watched, their big machinegun glinting in the sun.

"Can't use the runway," Chris said. "They have two inbound commercials."

Jim, who'd flown thirty-one missions in Vietnam and could have been the model for GI Joe, held up his binder, opened to a diagram of Khartoum airport. "There's no civil taxiway we might have used for take-off and the military taxiway shows abandoned." He glanced over his shoulder at David. "That means unusable."

David felt Rika nudge in closer behind him, presumably to look at the diagram. "So where does that leave us?" he asked Jim.

"It's hairy, but the only option I can see is the civil apron we're parked on. We taxi to the north end, then turn and take off to the south."

From the diagram, David estimated the apron to be only a third the length of the runway. "It looks too short. And the terminal's at the south end. What about congestion around that?"

"Apron's thirty-two hundred feet. Below our minimum, but we can make it. And there're no aircraft at the terminal. Yet."

"First commercial is on final approach," Chris said, brushing a lock of blond hair off his suntanned forehead.

Jim fired up the engines. "Close the door and cross your fingers. The north end of the apron is next to the military sector.

When we roll in that direction, our gunners out there are liable to get hinky."

"Wait a minute. I have an idea." David pushed past Rika to the head of the stairway and hollered down to the hotel security man, "General M'botou just radioed a message. We're supposed to meet him in the military sector." Without waiting for a reply, he pushed up the lever that raised the stairs. "Clear!"

"Good job." Jim wiggled the throttles forward. As the plane started rolling, he told Rika and Blue, "You two go back to the cabin and strap yourselves in. I want David up here."

"I'll put 'em in the operators' chairs." David wanted everyone as close together as possible. He unlocked the first chair, slid it all the way forward, and locked it again. "Rika, sit here. Blue, slide the other one in behind her. This lever locks it."

"Glad my life insurance is paid up," Blue muttered.

Although the cabin was cooling rapidly now that the engines were on, a light sheen of perspiration glistened on Rika's forehead. David gave her a reassuring smile, then buckled into the jump seat behind the pilots.

Jim accelerated, using the knob by his left arm to steer. As they taxied northward, Chris ran through the pre-liftoff checklist, leaving the transponders switched off, David noticed, to help avoid detection. At the exit to the military sector, Jim turned the plane around.

The Fiat stopped near their wingtip, followed by the truckload of soldiers with their machinegun.

"Here comes the first commercial," Chris said.

"And the general!" David pointed at a black Toyota racing toward them, a small red flag flapping furiously from the short staff mounted on its front fender.

"Fuck him," Jim snarled. "I haven't lost an airplane yet. And no way are a bunch of Third-World dipshits getting this one."

David tore his eyes from M'botou's car and looked up to see the jetliner in nose-high landing attitude, flaps and slats fully extended. "The inbound's coming toward us. Doesn't that mean we'll have a tail wind?"

"Five gusting to ten," Jim said. "Okay, I'm gonna hit it as soon as he touches down. And I want everyone looking out for ground traffic. Cars, trucks, anything. If you see something, shout it out."

The jetliner flared to land.

Jim set the brakes and jammed the throttles forward. The engines roared. The plane trembled, straining like a drag racer at the starting lights. "Flaps twenty?"

"Twenty degrees," Chris confirmed.

The general's Toyota skidded to a stop behind the Fiat. M'botou leapt out waving his arms. The soldier manning the machinegun swung it around.

Jim released the brakes. Their plane surged into maximum acceleration, throwing David back against his seat.

"Sixty knots," Chris said, as the airspeed indicator rotated on the dial. "Eighty."

A fuel truck pulled onto the apron and slammed to a halt.

"Ninety knots," Chris called.

"I've got the yoke." Jim let go of the steering knob and put both hands on the yoke, steering now with the rudder.

They screamed down the apron as the commercial liner, an Alitalia, zoomed by in the opposite direction.

Then a single-engine Cessna emerged from a Quonset hut six hundred feet ahead of them.

"Airplane!" David yelled. "On the right."

The Cessna, a high-wing, turned onto the apron, facing them.

Jim's knuckles went white. At this speed on the ground, their jet couldn't turn, or even swerve. They were bearing down on the little aircraft at a hundred and twenty knots, two hundred feet per second, and still accelerating.

Now David could see the terror-stricken face of the Cessna's pilot. Instinctively David braced for impact.

"V-one," Chris called. "Rotate."

Jim hauled back on the yoke. With a gut-sinking wrench, they leapt into the air, missing the Cessna by mere feet. Although it was impossible to see behind, David could picture the tiny two-seater spun around—maybe flipped over—by the blast of two jet engines at maximum thrust.

"Speed safe," Chris said.

Jim rose to three hundred feet and turned right. "Gear up."

Chris raised the landing-gear lever. Four seconds later, three green lights on the instrument panel signified all three wheels had fully retracted.

"Flaps up," Jim ordered, still banking right.

From his private-pilot days, David recognized their maneuver as a short-field take-off. To clear trees or power lines at the end of a short runway, you lifted off before you had climb speed, then leveled out above obstacle height until you had the speed to climb. But he'd never done it in a jet or out of real necessity.

He pried his fingers off the backs of the pilots' seats. "I thought we'd bought it."

"Yeah, that one had a high pucker factor," Jim said.

Twisting in his seat, David saw Rika and Blue both wide-eyed. "We're okay," he shouted over the roar of the engines. Sudden movements were harder to take when you couldn't see them coming, but he was glad they hadn't witnessed this one.

Jim dipped the nose slightly. "Tree tops are low. I'm going down to two hundred AGL." At two hundred feet above ground level, he came around to a compass bearing of forty-five degrees.

From the aeronautical chart in Chris's lap, David saw this put them on a direct, northeasterly course for Port Sudan on the Red Sea coast.

"Uh-oh," Chris said. "Chart shows a Soviet base just south of Port Sudan, about one o'clock from our current heading."

"Then I'll drop another fifty feet. Last thing we need is the Russians scrambling to find out who's headed their way."

Still studying the chart, Chris said, "Should be a valley just north of us and parallel to our present course." He looked out and pointed to the left. "There. Other side of those hills, about twenty miles. Could cover us from Russian radar."

"Is it clear?"

"Only one town of any size, a place called Musmar."

"Okay, hang on." Jim pulled up steeply into a climbing left turn, crossed the hills, and dropped down into the valley. Two hundred feet above the ground he banked sharply right again to regain his course. "If they got us on radar, they saw us heading north."

David groaned, swallowing against the rising contents of his stomach.

Chris reached into his flight case, pulled out a small bottle, and passed it back. "Take two of these."

David squinted at the label.

"I wouldn't wait if I were you," Chris said. "We could be in for more of this."

David popped two tablets and turned around to Rika. "Want some air sickness pills? The ride could be rough."

Lips pressed together, she shook her head.

"You sure?" She looked like she'd just come off her first-ever rollercoaster.

Rika nodded stubbornly. "I don't like to take medicine."

Behind her, ashen, Blue held up his hand. David tossed him the bottle.

"Traffic at eight o'clock," Chris called. "Northbound at twelve thousand feet."

"If he's behind us, he must be Sudanese." Jim dropped the plane to one hundred feet, firing it down the valley at four hundred miles per hour. Dead ahead, the town of Musmar came into view. They thundered over it just above the top of the mosque's minaret.

"Traffic's now nine o'clock. Eleven thousand and descending. He's spotted us, Jim."

Three minutes later, a Sudanese fighter streaked over their heads.

Jim turned hard left to escape the wash, then climbed to four thousand feet and pointed the nose toward Port Sudan. "Our escape route's blown. We're heading for the nearest international border."

David could see the fighter several miles out. As he watched, it looped high, turned, and dropped to their altitude, coming straight on.

"He's trying to scare us," Jim said. "He has orders to bring us down in one piece."

"And if we don't comply?" David asked.

Jim's tone dropped a notch. "Keep your eyes open for a flash under his wings."

"We've got magnesium flares." Old fashioned technology for night operations in the visible spectrum, but David knew they were still on board.

"No time."

The fighter came at eye level, growing in a matter of seconds from a speck to a fearsome killer. Jim dove hard left, then pulled up the nose and rocketed skyward in a right-climbing turn. At nine thousand feet, he leveled out.

David gulped a breath. "I'm glad you gave me those pills."

"Yeah," Chris said, his own face slightly gray. "I think we exceeded our G-rating on that one."

Seconds later, as if they were standing still, a shadow rolled slowly over the cockpit and materialized on their left side in the form of a warplane with two rockets under its swept-back wings, two long-range drop tanks, and a huge air intake for a "nose" that give it the appearance of an open-mouthed shark.

"Shenyang F-six," Jim said. "Chinese copy of the MiG-nineteen. I splashed one in Cambodia."

Matching their speed, it crept menacingly closer until it was barely twenty feet off their wing tip. The pilot, in helmet and oxygen mask, looked like a praying mantis eyeing its meal. He flashed his navigation lights and rocked his wings, the universal "follow me" signal.

Jim pointed a finger forward and down.

The pilot nodded. His fighter eased away from them about a hundred yards.

"He's agreed to us landing at Port Sudan."

"You can't do that," David insisted.

"I'm not. But I want him to think I am. Chris, show me the chart. Yeah, that's what I thought. Look, we're here, about twenty-five miles southwest of Port Sudan. If we follow this course across the Red Sea—"

"Mecca?" No, David realized. "Jiddah." Then it dawned on him that the Saudi border was even nearer than that. He reached around Chris and touched the map on the dashed line running down the middle of the Red Sea. "Saudi airspace starts here."

"You got it," Jim said. "At nine thousand feet, it's only fourteen minutes away. And I've got eight thousand feet of dive height to play with. Remember, the border's at sea level."

The fighter moved in from the left, flashed its navigation lights again, and rocked its wings.

"He wants us to start our descent. Chris, call Port Sudan and give 'em our position."

As soon as radio contact was established, the fighter rose slowly upward and slid back.

"Now that he's heard us talking with Port Sudan," Jim said, "he thinks we're gonna behave. But he'll sit above and behind us to make sure."

David leaned forward. "What if we ask for an over-water approach from the east? That'd get us closer to the border."

A second of silence, then Jim said, "Do it, Chris. Tell 'em we have engine trouble and don't want to endanger the city. David, those flares. I don't think it'll happen, but just in case, go back and lash about ten of them together. Wire the timers for two seconds. Then get back up here. I want us all together on this."

David unbuckled and went immediately to Rika. Her seatbelt looked tighter than a tourniquet. "We're almost out of it." *Or in it so deep it wouldn't matter.*

Seeing Blue had regained some color, David slapped him on the shoulder, then knelt beside the flare locker on the opposite wall to the console. The locker hadn't been opened in months, and God only knew if the flares were still good. He pressed a red button beside the chute's port and heard a short whoosh. At least the chute worked. After readying the flare bundle, he loaded it and set the selector switch to "Cockpit."

He made it back to his jump seat in time to hear Chris tell Jim, "Port Sudan refuses permission to land from the east."

"Apologize," Jim said, "but say we have to. Tell 'em we'll report to flight control to give a full explanation as soon as we're on the ground."

David strapped himself in. "Flares are ready." *I hope.*

Suddenly the fighter was on their wing tip again, signaling them to descend. They were over-flying Port Sudan and still at nine thousand feet.

Jim pointed forward and looped his finger back, indicating he'd land from the east.

The fighter pilot turned a gloved hand thumbs-down.

"Hold tight, folks." With a jerk, Jim rolled hard left, directly into the fighter's path.

The fighter leapt upward.

They were over the Red Sea when it appeared again, standing off a hundred yards and rocking its wings furiously.

"Chris," Jim said, "you ever do a slip and cut?"

"Not in combat conditions."

"Well, you're about to do one now. Squawk seventy-seven hundred."

The highjacked code. David realized it would be the perfect excuse to enter Saudi airspace.

As Chris switched on the transponders and dialed in the international distress frequency, David visualized a flashing red blip lighting up on every air-tracking radar screen within two thousand miles.

A stream of bright dots arced across their path. "Tracers," Chris shouted.

Jim cut throttles, turned the yoke hard right, and kicked the rudder hard left. The plane wrenched into a "slip," an aerial skid that he accentuated by pulling the speed brake. The airspeed indicator plummeted as their plane practically fell out of the sky.

The fighter roared past overhead.

"Here goes the cut." Jim dropped the nose and applied full throttles. The airplane lurched into an accelerating dive.

David gripped his seat. Ahead and to their right, the fighter banked into a long turn.

"He's pissed off now," Jim said. "David, we might need those flares."

On the back of the console between the pilots was a yellow switch protector. David flipped it up to expose two buttons. "Ready."

"Airspeed four hundred and twenty knots," Chris called. The clacker went off, warning that they were exceeding red line velocity.

As Jim leveled out, the fighter dropped to their altitude on a collision course. "He's gonna fire," Jim said.

David pressed the left button, opening the flare chute.

"Wing flash," Chris shouted.

"Drop the flares. Now, now, now!"

David stabbed the right button. "They're away."

Jim held steady, facing the fighter head-on. "Never turn your ass to a heat-seeking missile."

David saw the rocket weaving toward them, trailing a string of white exhaust.

At the last instant, Jim barrel-rolled into a sharp left dive. A concussion rocked them. Jim let the plane roll again, making a wild target for the wing canon of the closing fighter. Tracers seemed to fly in all directions as the fighter screamed past overhead. Jim pulled out of the roll barely a thousand feet above the choppy surface of the Red Sea. "Do you see him?"

"Not yet," Chris answered.

"How far to the border?"

"Gimme a minute."

"We've crossed it." David pointed excitedly out the cockpit at an oil tanker steaming southward. "He's flying the Saudi flag. No reason for a Saudi ship to sail in Sudanese waters when he can sail in his own."

Chris looked at him over his shoulder. "You've got better eyes than I do."

"You did it, guys." David wanted to jump out of his seat.

"All of us did." Jim angled the nose into a gentle climb, then glanced back at David. "Without your flares, we'd be air pollution right now."

"Hold on." Chris adjusted the volume knob on one of the radios. "Someone's answering our seventy-seven hundred. It's Jiddah control."

"I'll take it." Jim switched on the overhead speaker and gave the plane's call sign. He said he was being pursued by a hostile aircraft, now departed, and asked permission to transit Saudi airspace en route to Cairo. Jiddah requested details of the aggression. Jim told them he was in Khartoum at Sudanese request and, on departure for Cairo, was intercepted by an aircraft of unknown origin, possibly rebel, which fired on him. Jiddah asked the nature of his visit to Khartoum. Jim gave them the company's name and business.

Jiddah came back with, "Zero niner Papa, stand by one."

Jim crossed his fingers.

"Zero niner Papa, Jiddah control. Do you need assistance?"

"Negative, Jiddah. The bandit has departed. But to be safe, I request permission to fly inside Saudi airspace until we reach the Egyptian border."

"Permission granted. You are ordered to maintain contact on this frequency."

"Roger that, Jiddah. And thank you."

With a bolt of energy, David unbuckled and dashed back to Rika. "We're safe."

"Truly?" She gave a forced smile, her dark eyes doubtful.

"We're in Saudi airspace and heading for Egypt." For a moment, the strain on her face, her glistening black curls, reminded him of their lovemaking. He had an impulse to take her into the VIP cabin, but settled for taking her hand. "Come on up to the flight deck."

As she undid her seat belt, Blue, a self-professed "recovering Catholic," lowered his head and crossed himself.

David flipped up the jump seat so the three of them could stand behind the pilots. Outside Chris's window, the grayish-brown mountains of coastal Saudi Arabia cruised past beneath a thin haze. Sanctuary.

"Bad news." Chris sat back from punching buttons on the instrument panel. "We don't have enough fuel to make Cairo."

Chapter 21

Spider lay on his back in the cold, lidless sarcophagus, using his shoes and socks for a pillow. For at least an hour now, it had been quiet as a crypt inside the ghostly halls of the museum.

After closing, the guards had walked their rounds, making jokes, complaining about their wives, arguing about a bunch of American soldiers killed at the airport in Beirut.

Sometime well after dark, Spider had smelled food cooking, a lamb stew that roused churnings of hunger in his belly. Then the guards made another round. After that, he'd heard occasional laughter in the distance. Then silence.

He didn't like silence. He liked to hear where people were when he was working.

Spider raised his eyes to the edge of the coffin. Only a few lights burned, but he could see well enough. No one in sight.

Quiet as a dribble of honey, he slipped his arms and legs over the edge and slid to the floor in a crouch.

The display case with the dog-headed stick stood in a dark area of the hall to his left. Barefoot and stooping low, he crossed the corridor and scuttled between other cases to reach it. There, he hunkered down to listen again. No sounds.

The small padlock on the side of the case hung at eye level. He took the cutters from his hip pocket, clamped their jaws over the lock, and wrapped a handkerchief around them. *Snap!*

He cringed. The noise was loud. Or maybe his ears were just too close. Darting his eyes in all directions, he saw no movement.

Still, he waited until the thumping in his chest settled down.

Very slowly he stood. Looking all around first, he raised the hinged lid and lifted out the heavy stick. He laid it on the floor then balanced the lid against his forehead and rearranged the other sticks in the case. When he was satisfied that it looked like nothing was missing, he snatched the stick's card, lowered the lid, and clicked the new lock in place.

With a rush of warmth, he saw himself presenting the prize to Imbabi. The great man would hug him to his side, praise him, favor him above all other thieves.

Someone snorted.

Spider dropped to the floor.

The snort came again. Then again. Snoring.

This was bad, a complication he hadn't planned on. But he had worked around sleeping people before.

He listened harder, turning his head slightly with each new snort until his ears homed in on their direction. It came from the same side of the hall as his alcove, but a little closer.

He put the lock cutters in one pocket, the severed lock in another, and crawled with the stick to the open corridor that separated the display-case area from the alcoves.

A guard lay curled on a stone bench against the corridor wall, two alcoves before his own.

Allah preserve him, he should have noticed the man before.

With the stealth of his namesake, Spider tiptoed toward the sleeping man. Staff in hand, pockets weighted with hardware, he crept past the guard, then crabbed the remaining thirty paces so he could keep one eye on the guard and the other on his alcove. It took all his control not to run the last few steps.

Inside the alcove at last, he leaned against the cold wall, taking deep breaths silently through his mouth. Surely, Allah had blessed him.

His eyes fell on the grate in the wall, the only barrier between him and the five-foot tunnel to freedom. Kneeling, he removed the loosened screws and pulled out the grate. The sight of his ropes inside reassured him. Now was the time to get them ready.

Spider secured the heavy rope to the inside center of the grate, using a release knot to which he tied the thinner rope. He wrapped his lock cutter and the broken lock in the handkerchief and tied this around the thick rope in a slipknot. Then he pushed the remaining coils back into the wall and laid the staff inside next to them, its dog-headed end projecting out into the midnight air so he wouldn't accidentally scrape it when he slid out.

He was good with ropes, which must have been one of the reasons the great Imbabi picked him for this important job. With a satisfied smile, he replaced the grate. He would not disappoint the Master.

He was about to reinsert the screws when he saw that the grate stayed in place by itself. Another blessing, for it would save him time later.

Peeking around the corner, he saw the guard still asleep. The rest of the hall looked empty. Once more he stepped into the corridor, keeping to the side this time as he worked his way to the front of the building. The office door was still unlocked. He opened it noiselessly and slipped inside.

City lights lit the room through the big window in front. He wished it were darker, but at least he wouldn't have to feel his way around the layout he'd memorized that morning.

He unlatched the cabinet and removed rack number eight. The papyrus, sandwiched between two cedar lattices, slid out easily. But it was too stiff to roll up.

Spider searched the desk for some string. Finding nothing, he stripped off his shirt. After coiling the papyrus as tightly as he dared, he held it between his knees and tied the shirt around it.

Pleased with his ingenuity, he put everything back in place, then listened at the door for several seconds before opening it a crack. Still nobody in sight. This was easy. He'd done houses that were harder.

With the papyrus under one arm, he stepped outside and closed the door. At the first alcove, he darted inside to reconnoiter. Still quiet.

Cautiously he continued along the corridor, moving from alcove to alcove until he was just one away from his own. When he peeked out from that one, his heart stopped.

The bench where the guard had been sleeping was empty.

Spider dropped to a crouch, muscles taut, eyes probing the vast hall. No one.

He backed into the alcove next to his and waited. Probably the guard had gone for a piss. Which direction would that be? Spider lowered his chin to the floor to look under the legs of the display cases. Terror seized his throat.

There was the guard. Squatting, just visible beneath the cases. And directly opposite his alcove.

Choked with fear, Spider searched the entire hall at floor level, looking for other guards this one might already have alerted. He saw no one else. But could somebody be waiting in his alcove? Allah protect him, it was a chance he had to take.

Suddenly the lights came on, all the lights, as if the sun had flown in through a window. Yelling rang out from the big staircase behind him.

Spider dashed into the corridor.

"There he is! Get him!"

Scrambling into his alcove, Spider slipped making the turn and slid into the side wall. The papyrus cracked in his arm. He didn't care. He had to get to the grate.

The grate! It was on the floor, where it must have fallen and wakened the guard while Spider was in the front office.

He leapt for the opening, but a shout too close behind made him wrench around. The guard who'd been crouching dashed into the alcove.

Grabbing the grate, Spider swung it with all his strength. It caught the man square in the head, knocking him sideways and dropping him to the floor in a heap.

But the other guards were almost there, howling like a horde of blood-crazed devils.

Frantically Spider yanked up the grate, snatched the papyrus, and wriggled backwards on his stomach and forearms into the ventilation tunnel. If he could just get the grate in place—

Too late! One of the guards, a bull of a man, rounded the sarcophagus and lunged headlong into the alcove.

In panic, Spider grabbed the pointed end of Tutankhamun's stick and thrust it outward. The impact jarred his whole body as the guard, driven by his own momentum, impaled himself through the mouth. The man's astonished eyes stared in helpless shock.

For a second, Spider stared back, horrified at the skewered

head, its mouth opening and closing like a speared fish around the shaft between its teeth.

The screams of the other guards broke his trance. He jerked the stick from the dead man's head and pulled the grate into place, the anchor for his descent. Holding it there with constant tension on the heavy rope, he scuttled feet-first to the outside of the building and dropped over the edge.

With the stick in one hand and the heavy rope in his other, he clenched the shirt-bound papyrus in his teeth and glided to the ground.

Almost immediately a car halted behind him, its rear door open.

Spider pulled on the thin rope and stood back as both ropes plummeted to his feet. He grabbed up everything, threw it into the car, and dived in behind.

Tires squealed. The car swerved right, then left, hurling him around the back seat like dice in a cup. He covered his head.

Finally the car slowed, made a few more turns, and halted.

Raising his head, Spider saw they were in an alley beside the Master's Mercedes. Through the open rear window, Imbabi himself beckoned.

Praise Allah. With the papyrus and stick, Spider climbed out of the escape car and into Imbabi's.

Safe, at last.

#

At a second floor window of Imbabi's villa in the City of the Dead, Major Hassam watched the Lord of Thieves balloon out of his Mercedes, empty-handed.

"*Khara.*" Shit. He stabbed out his tenth or twelfth cigarette on the window ledge.

Then bare arms reached from the sedan's back seat, passing to Imbabi a long pole and a small bundle. Eyes on the bundle, Hassam gripped the sill, the old pain lifting from his shoulder as if by magic. When the car drove away, lights off, he seated himself on the big Persian carpet and tried to look composed.

Imbabi pushed open the heavy door, waddled across the

room, and dropped a shirt-bound parcel at Hassam's knees.

With anxious fingers, Hassam untied the sleeves. The scroll fell apart in two pieces. "It's crushed!"

"It can still be read." Imbabi settled into his pile of cushions, then clapped twice. "If you wish, I will tell you a man who can do it."

"Imbecile!" Hassam leapt to his feet. "Now it can't be returned."

Imbabi recoiled as if an electric wire had been shoved up his ass. "You never told me you wanted to return it."

"My intentions are not your concern." Assuming the writing could be viewed by some nondestructive procedure, like the ones used to detect forged documents, Hassam had planned to replace the papyrus surreptitiously. Now that was impossible. When the lab finished, he'd have to destroy the papyrus and plead ignorance if Ragheb ever confronted him about its absence. Ragheb wouldn't believe him but would be powerless to prove anything.

The same boy as before brought whiskey and glasses on a silver tray.

Hassam wanted to hurl him down the stairs for interrupting. Instead, he lit a cigarette and inhaled deeply. When the boy was gone, he said, "How did this happen?"

"There were complications."

Icy fingers crept up Hassam's back. "What complications?"

"A small matter." Imbabi filled the glasses, leaving one on the tray for Hassam. "The thief was discovered at the last moment. A guard caught him in the process of climbing out through the wall. There was a fight, and the guard died."

"What?" Hassam threw his cigarette at the wall. "That son-of-a-whore killed a guard?"

"Major, please. If you will let me speak."

When Imbabi finished, Hassam had him repeat the whole thing, but this time he interrupted the narrative with questions. At the end, he lit another cigarette and tried to assess the consequences of this monumental screw-up. Top priority was disposing of the thief. "Where is the boy now?"

Imbabi cast his eyes heavenward.

"You are certain?"

"Quite certain."

Hassam pictured a naked body with a slit throat, roasting to blackness on one of the smoldering garbage dumps outside the city. "At least you did something right."

Imbabi's face reddened in anger. "I have done everything according to your instructions. I have no control over the sleeping habits of museum personnel. You should thank me for choosing a boy so capable that, even in the face of overwhelming adversity, he was able to secure exactly what you wanted."

"In pieces. And leaving such a mess that there will now be a huge investigation."

"Major," Imbabi said calmly, "there is no possibility that tonight's events could be tied to either of us. The guard was an unfortunate casualty, but life is full of unfortunate casualties. We cannot grieve for them all." He spread his arms wide. "Tonight was a success."

Tonight was a fiasco. And it *could* be traced to him, through Imbabi. Hassam needed a trump card. "What did this worthless turd take for you?"

Imbabi clapped once and told the man who appeared to "Bring the stick." When it was placed before him, he held it out to Hassam. "It is from a case of many such sticks. The others were rearranged so that this one will not be missed."

Smart. A beautiful piece of unquestionable authenticity, but only one of many. Worth a lifetime's salary, if not more.

Then Hassam noticed blood on the pointed end. *Perfect.* Even if the staff were cleaned, there would be microscopic traces sufficient for the laboratory to type it to the guard. So he could pin everything on Imbabi if that ever became necessary. Provided Imbabi kept the staff.

"You would be well-advised," Hassam said, "not to dispose of it until this affair has died down."

"Why do you persist, Major, in regarding me as a fool?"

Hassam gathered the pieces of papyrus, rewrapped them in the shirt, and stalked out.

Half way to his car, he halted. With all of Headquarters focused on the museum, he could not possibly submit an ancient papyrus for laboratory analysis. Connections would be made, questions raised. Suspicions even he might not be able to manage.

A sudden wind kicked up dust around his ankles. It whistled through the derelict crypts, as if beckoning him to join the deceased.

But maybe ... He regarded the bundled papyrus. Teferi had removed some of the surface characters. Either she'd scraped them off, or washed them off. And if she could do it, so could he. If it meant ruining the damned thing, so what? He was going to destroy it, anyway.

The wind whistled again. He turned his face to it. *"Anikak."* Fuck you.

In his car, Hassam removed the cap of his fountain pen and scraped its edge over the hieroglyphs. No luck. He moistened his fingertip with spit and rubbed. Was that a smear? In the overhead light, it was hard to tell. With more spit, he tried again. Yes. And there were finer lines, another character, beneath the one he'd partly wiped off.

Thirty minutes later, he roused the phlegmy antiquities dealer and told him to fetch a glass of water. As the man stumbled off, Hassam unwrapped the scroll and laid its pieces on the back-room table. Under the bright bulb hanging from the ceiling, he saw the finer lines he'd revealed were red. A different kind of ink. Something resistant to water, or at least to spit.

When the dealer came back, he set down the glass, took one look at what Hassam had brought him, and broke out in a coughing fit. With hands braced on the table, he bent lower. *"Abu,* this is a royal papyrus. Authentic. From the Eighteenth Dynasty."

Betting everything dear to him, Hassam poured some water from the glass onto one of the pieces.

"No!" The dealer grabbed Hassam's wrist.

Hassam pulled him back, pinning the man's thin arms as the water soaked in. "Compose yourself. I know what I'm doing."

The wheezing body trembled in his hands. Hassam released him, then wadded up the thief's shirt and scrubbed it gently over the dampened hieroglyphs.

"Abu, no!"

Hassam examined the cloth, now blackened, and wanted to cry out with joy. More red characters. Not where Teferi had covered them with new ink, but every place else he had rubbed. With a flourish, he pointed at the revealed text. "There."

The dealer gaped. "What is this?"

Hassam couldn't stand still. He jigged from one foot to the other like a fighter who'd just knocked out his opponent. "It's the same writing you translated in those photographs. But now you have the complete text."

"By the beard of the Prophet, this is a miracle."

Better than a miracle if the text shed any light on Teferi's cause. Thumbing away some spittle that had run out of his mouth, Hassam adopted his most official voice. "This writing is crucial evidence in a very important case. By translating it, you will help me prevent a most serious crime against our country. But you must work in absolute secrecy. Not a whisper can reach another soul."

"As you command."

"Clean all of the black ink from these pieces and do not rest until you have finished your translation. I want it by seven o'clock in the morning."

"But *Abu*." The dealer looked at his watch.

"Seven o'clock!"

Hassam left the shop with a belated case of the shakes. He turned up his collar, hunched his shoulders, and tried to rub the chill from his hands. But the chill was within him. Now two people, Imbabi and the dealer, possessed knowledge that could land him in front of a firing squad.

He whipped around, peering into the moon shadows along the passageway behind him. No one. Shops dark. No lights behind the shuttered windows above them. Fine feast he'd prepared for himself. Waiting for betrayal, real or imagined, would eat him alive from the inside out.

So why suffer through the wait? Imbabi's usefulness was already finished. And later today, the dealer's would be, also.

Hassam slipped a hand over the reassuring pistol at his hip. An extreme solution, one he'd rarely resorted to and never for cold-blooded murder. But this wouldn't be murder. It was self-defense. National defense.

He picked up his pace. An extreme solution maybe. But these were extreme times.

Chapter 22

Eighteenth Dynasty

By late afternoon, the treasury had been sealed. It was done in Ay's presence, and during the proceedings he had made particular comments to the architect—comments a potential grave robber would react to reflexively but which an honest man would misconstrue as idle conversation. The architect had misconstrued.

Ay also made a point of casually encountering the overseer and both of the funerary priests, each man individually and at a private moment. All seemed totally loyal.

When he returned to the royal barge that evening, he found Tiye pacing, holding a sprig of lemon blossoms to her nose.

At the end of his report, she laid the flowers aside and sat. "Thank you, old friend. You place my mind at ease. I am now ready to conclude the message to my son."

Ay unrolled the papyrus and prepared his ink.

After extolling the virtues of the architect, Kap, Tiye gave her final advice to the young king, a short list of principles for governing a land only tenuously united. She ended with, "You must guard against the priests but forgive them their beliefs, for while Aten shines upon all of us, some cannot yet see His light. In time they will."

Ay weighted the papyrus to hold it flat while the ink dried. Then he bowed and spoke in the formal language of the court. "Divine Mother, as your message is now completed, I beg leave to offer a gift with which to protect your words during their journey to our king."

She leaned forward. "What is your gift?"

Ay laid at her feet a gleaming cylindrical tube made of electrum, an alloy of gold and silver much favored for its strength and workability. It was the length of a man's forearm and as large around, the golden metal intricately incised with scenes of wildlife along the Nile and images of Tiye and Tutankhaten. "One of the closed ends is removable, allowing your papyrus to be secured inside."

Tiye looked deeply into his eyes. "Beloved Ay, truly I shall miss you. Throughout the years, you have been faithful, beyond the fidelity of kinship. Steadfastly you have championed the true religion. You gave your beautiful daughter, Nefertiti, to my immortal son, Akhenaten, to be his wife and queen. Since those days we have grown old together, and always your companionship has brought me joy."

She swallowed, then straightened her posture in the chair. "Now, as you have given a final gift to me, so I have a gift for you. As of this day, I grant you all of my lands between the City of the Globe and Maru-Aten, and all of the servants who till those lands. May they enrich you and your seed throughout their generations. Further, I grant you a fifth part of my household staff and a fifth part of my treasury in the City of the Globe, that you shall not want for any worldly thing in your remaining years."

Ay felt overwhelmed but could not find his tongue to speak. Nor could he find the heart to tell her that he would gladly exchange his earthly wealth for beggar's rags if she would reconsider her decision to depart this world prematurely.

"There is one more thing," she said. "I wish only you and the funerary priests to be present during the final moments in my burial chamber. At the end, I want you …" Her voice cracked, and she swallowed again. "I want you to be the last to leave. I also desire that you should be the one who strikes the ultimate blow that seals my tomb."

Only by force of will could he withhold his tears.

She settled back in her chair. "Please leave me now. I wish to be alone until Aten rises again."

#

Unable to sleep, Ay was praying for his sister when a voice outside begged leave to speak with him. The intrusion nettled, but duty outweighed grieving. "Enter."

With a bow, the flotilla's pilot stepped inside. He had with him his son, Khu, the young lookout who had spent most of the long journey squatting on the prow of the royal barge to warn of any obstacles that might appear in the river.

"What is it?" Ay said.

"Great Keeper of the Queen's House, my son, in these past idle days, has befriended the son of the overseer, Senuset. In the course of their gaming together, the overseer's son boasted of a great adventure he is to undertake in the employ of his father. Master, it is a grievous crime of the highest magnitude. A crime against our Divine Mother and all who love her."

Ay stared at the man in disbelief, then set his eyes upon the boy whose sidelock of youth—the braided ponytail on the left side of his otherwise shaven head—showed he was not yet adolescent. "Is this true?"

Khu trembled. "Yes, Master."

"Speak up," Ay told him. "What did Senuset's son tell you?"

"He said there is a way to enter Our Mother's tomb after it has been sealed. But the passage can only be opened from inside. He is to open it."

A claw raked Ay's heart. His fury soared, tethered only by unbreakable self-discipline. "How?"

"The overseer will present a gift to be placed in the tomb. It is a chest filled with gold and precious stones from the south. It is of such great value that the priests will not dare to refuse it. But the chest will be only half-filled with treasure. There is a false bottom, and Met will be hidden inside it."

"Met?"

"The son of the overseer. And a store of food and water will be hidden there also. And oil lamps. And when the tomb has been sealed, he is to remove himself from the chest and wait until he has defecated ten times."

Ay winced.

"That is how he will mark the days."

"What then?"

"After the tenth day, when everyone has left, Met is to open the tomb. He said his family will then be rich."

With a leaden heart, Ay wondered if he had lost his cunning, as well as his physical prowess, for he had failed to detect any sign of deceit in the fat overseer. Yet he felt in his bones that Khu spoke the truth. "Who else knows of this?"

"No one, Master."

Ay fixed the boy with a glare that had brought generals to their knees. "Are you certain?"

"Yes, Master." Khu did not flinch. "When Met told me, I said my head was hurting and came immediately to tell my father."

Ay turned to the pilot. "Who now is aboard this vessel?"

"Only ourselves, our Divine Mother, Princess Baketaten, and three servant girls."

"The princess, how is she disposed?"

"She ..." The pilot lowered his head. "She weeps in her cabin."

"Look at me," Ay commanded. "Listen and obey. No one is to leave or board this barge. Under any circumstances. Both of you remain here. Act as if nothing has happened."

He returned his attention to the boy. "You have done well, Khu. I shall see that you and your father are rewarded. But you must speak no word of this to anyone. Not a breath. Your silence now is the most precious gift you can give our queen."

#

Ay peered out from the doorway of a mud-brick house on the edge of the workers' camp. The smell of wood smoke signaled approaching dawn, but no one yet stirred outside.

He turned back to the headman of Sadjedju, who had journeyed through the night to meet with him. "Then it is set?"

"Master, it shall be as I described."

From around his neck, Ay lifted his most cherished possession, a pendant depicting the Sun Globe above a scarab flanked by two sacred cobras. Each cobra bore a cartouche on its head, one with Tiye's name, the other with his. The pendant was one of a pair given by her husband to the two siblings in recognition of their devotion to one another. Solemnly, Ay placed its chain around the headman's neck.

The man gaped, for such a treasure was as the moon, visible but untouchable by mortals. To possess it was beyond imagining.

"Protect her," Ay commanded. "Now and through all your generations."

#

When Ay arrived back at the royal barge, he found two servant girls huddled on the deck, weeping. He pulled his own girl to her feet and demanded to know what the trouble was.

"Our Mother," she sobbed. "A horrible affliction has come over her."

Ay released her and rushed to the queen's cabin. The royal physician was bent over Tiye's bed, Baketaten and a servant girl kneeling beside him. The scene chilled Ay to his bones.

He moved slowly forward and saw Tiye's fragile body drenched in sweat, her face contorted in an awful grimace. The servant girl held a white linen cloth to the queen's ear. On the floor lay a pile of similar cloths, all stained red. As he watched, Tiye's body went into spasms, convulsing violently while the physician and Baketaten tried vainly to hold her still. In a few moments, the seizure passed.

Ay jerked the physician to his feet.

"I know not, Master." Trembling, he stammered, "Perhaps a vapor of these marshes. I have not seen it before."

"When did it begin?"

"In the middle of the night, I am told. But I was not summoned immediately. Perhaps if I—"

"You were not summoned?" Ay shouted.

Baketaten grasped Ay's arm. "The pilot would allow none of us to leave the barge. I pleaded with him until he finally agreed to go, himself, to fetch the physician. When he was gone, I called for the guards to execute him instantly upon his return. But he told them you had given the order."

Ay's heart shriveled in his chest.

"I know you are wise," Baketaten said, "and Our Mother's most trusted servant. For that reason only, I spared the pilot's life until you could give your counsel. He is being held on one of the guard boats."

As the full impact of her words crushed down on him, Ay buried his face in his hands. Then he whirled on her. "The island. What happened there?"

Her eyes lowered. "I cannot say."

"Tell me!"

"Please, Ay, I am commanded to say nothing."

His shoulders slumped. She did not have to tell him. Tiye also had been silent upon her return, had seemed for some hours afterwards uncommonly morose and withdrawn.

He turned aside, gazing out the window as the sun crested the horizon. Vividly he recalled their childhood flight, the whispered conversations between their parents and grandfather.

"Master," the physician cried. "Behold!"

A beam of sunlight slanted across Tiye's face. Her hand reached up to touch it. A weak smile came to her lips. As though Aten's rays were effecting a cure, her eyes fluttered and opened.

Chapter 23

Fit to be tied over the worthless translation in his sport-coat pocket, Major Hassam stomped into Headquarters shortly before eight o'clock. The normally somber building buzzed with gossip about the killing at the museum. Knots of people in the hallway to his office stopped talking when he approached. As he passed, he felt their eyes following him and knew what was in their minds—a bleak day for Domestic Branch.

Outside Hassam's office door, Samir, his aide, intercepted him. Lanky and prematurely balding, Samir looked uncommonly flustered for a ranking chess master. "The Head's been screaming for you."

Let him scream, Hassam wanted to say. Instead, he affected the stoical face of a camel trader. "I'm on my way up."

He'd anticipated the summons and prepared. Driving in, he'd cruised past the museum, noting the logjam of official cars and the policemen scurrying about like ants after a boy pokes a stick in their nest. That picture, plus knowing what the investigators would find, gave him enough information to claim he was already on the case.

"We're looking for a boy in his teens," he told Samir, recalling the thin arms of the youth in Imbabi's Mercedes. "Skinny, on foot, possibly wounded. Round up all our informants and any beggars who sleep in the area. Check the hospitals. Question the night clerks of every hotel within five streets of the museum. Ask them about employees and guests who came in after midnight, then find those people and see if they noticed anything unusual last night."

Make-work, but Hassam had to keep up his image as the bulldog.

He waited for Samir to scuttle off, then unlocked his office door, closed it behind him, and slapped a stack of files off his desk. As papers flew, he cursed the cause of this whole fiasco. "That damned papyrus."

Rubbing the ache in his shoulder, he walked to the window and pulled the full translation from his pocket. It contained nothing new except the town where the tomb builders lived, a place the antiquities dealer couldn't find on his maps. Hassam had gleaned not a single piece of information relatable to any sort of plot.

And he now had a pointless investigation to misdirect and a scapegoat to find for the murder rap. Not to mention Imbabi and the dealer to dispose of. He felt like a beetle staring up at the butt hole of an outhouse from the dung pile at the bottom.

His phone rang. It would be the Head, about to squeeze out another deposit on top of the pile.

Hassam let it ring. He gave the translation one last glance, then spit on it and threw it in the trash.

#

Feigning contrition, David followed Blue across the Arab carpets in Harold Carson's office and out into the reception area. Carson's Egyptian secretary kept her eyes lowered as they passed.

They'd thanked the SEECO VP for getting them off the hook with the Secret Police, who had met the plane at Cairo airport that morning and grilled them about the skyjacking attempt. But despite David's altering the story to a simple misunderstanding, Carson was pissed and had even threatened Blue with dismissal if he ever again ran off to "help a mate" without prior approval.

"At least everyone else will be out of Egypt in an hour," David said as he and Blue descended the stairs from the executive floor. By eleven o'clock, the jet, with Paul Rackowski and the ground-station equipment, would be on its way to Ireland, two days early for a recon job that Paul could handle. "And, thank God, Carson never realized there was a woman with us."

"Carson can go stuff himself. Last month, I had two offers to jump ship."

They turned into Blue's office where Rika sat on the tall stool at the drafting table, poring over a map of northeast Africa that Blue had dug out of SEECO's files when they first arrived.

"How was your meeting?" she asked.

"Ugly," David said. "but we'll survive."

"Carson's a wanker." Blue plopped onto his chair and lit a cigar. "Only thing that soothed his feathers was your boyfriend saying he'd stay on a few days to help our morons interpret the survey. No extra charge."

David stepped up behind her and kissed her neck. A faint smell of saltwater still clung to her skin from their sunrise swim in the Red Sea. Unable to reach Cairo, the pilots had identified several alternative landing sites and enthusiastically chosen Hurghada when Blue said it had a Club Med, Egypt's only topless resort.

What a glorious night. An idyllic setting, a three-quarters moon, a cabaña on the beach.

Rika looked up at him. "How long will it take you to help the 'morons'?"

With a quick shift of mental gears, he said, "This afternoon should be enough." Then something in the way she'd oriented the map caught his eye—or rather, the shape of the Nile caught his eye.

"Look at this." He picked up a green pencil from the drafting table and sketched some lines along the river's course. "In northern Sudan, the Nile runs in two preferred directions, northeast and northwest. And the directions are about sixty degrees apart."

"Sixty degrees?" Blue hoisted himself from his chair and came to stand beside them. "Bloody hell. Gotta be stress fractures from a north-south regional compression. How come I never noticed that?"

"What does it mean?" Rika asked, squinting through Blue's cigar smoke.

Blue switched the cigar to his other hand. "When you compress something brittle, like the earth's crust, it cracks in an X-pattern. In the direction of compression, the angles between the cracks are sixty degrees, roughly."

"The cracks are geologic fault zones," David added. "In this case, fault zones big enough to influence the river's course." He put his finger on the map. "And two of them intersect at Seddenga."

Rika furrowed her brow. "Is that good or bad?"

"Could be good." David dug out his aerial photos from their flight to Khartoum. When he oriented them in the same direction as the map, he saw immediately what he'd hoped for. With the green pencil, he started highlighting linear features. "Look here. We've got splinter faults from both fracture sets running right through the canyon with the tomb. In fact, right through the mesa itself."

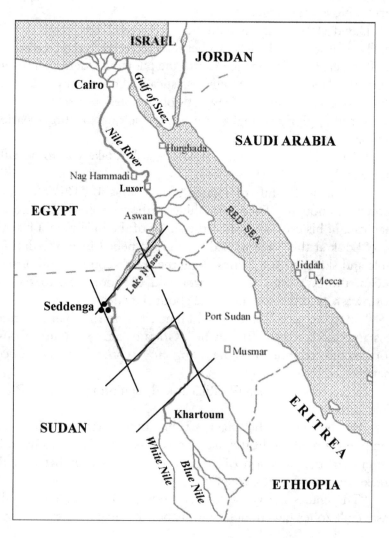

Rika let out a groan. "Does that mean the tomb is damaged?"

"No," David said. "It means the limestone will be full of fractures. And we might be able to exploit them to blast our way in."

"Blast?" She pushed back from the drafting table. "We can't blast. It would destroy the tomb."

"We'd just do it to tunnel part way in. Until we got close enough to dig." Then David saw Blue shaking his head.

"Nice try, sport. But you can't get explosives here. The government's scared shitless they might fall into the hands of fundamentalists."

"What about dynamite or gelignite for onshore seismic?"

"All controlled. Army checks our inventory every— Hang on." Blue tugged at his beard and mumbled, "Landmines."

Suddenly David remembered their conversation in the bar with Kai, the Norwegian new-hire. "Perfect."

"You have landmines?" Rika asked.

Blue winked at her. "For you, milady, there's a dozen of 'em, all stacked up and waiting. At an abandoned seismic camp about four hours south of here." Then he squinched his face. "And come to think of it, we've got an old Mini-Sosie."

"Can you speak English?" she said.

But David knew instantly what Blue was thinking, and he loved it. "A Mini-Sosie is basically a jackhammer with a base plate instead of a spike. They're used sometimes to send shockwaves into the ground for shallow seismic surveys. Blue, can we jerry-rig a spike?"

"I believe it came with one, plus compressor and hoses."

"Fantastic." David turned to Rika. "With that, we can break out loose rock a lot faster than using picks and sledge hammers."

She looked pensive. "I don't think we'll need a jackhammer. Or explosives. Not if Efrem can bring some heavy equipment."

"Who?" David asked.

"My brother. I told you he could help us."

Now David remembered. She'd mentioned him, but not his name, at Blue's house after the escape from her hotel. What was it, three nights ago? Well, a lot had happened since then, none of it involving this brother of hers. And the thought of letting him horn in at the end and grab the glory of opening the tomb stuck in David's throat like a fishbone.

"In fact," Rika said, "I need to go to the museum and leave a signal for him. Can Hagazy take me?"

Warning bells rang in David's brain. On the drive in from the airport, Hagazy had shown them the newspaper, its headline blaring, "Murder in the Museum." According to the story, a thief was caught trying to break in through a grate in the second floor wall. He had a knife and a club and put up a ferocious fight, no doubt crazed on western drugs. The guards, unarmed, fought him heroically, hand to hand. But the thief stabbed one of them and clubbed another one senseless.

Reason told David it had to be a coincidence, nothing to do with them. The papyrus was back in place, and Rika hadn't been there for two days. But his gut said stay away. "The museum will be crawling with cops."

She unhooked her heels from the foot ring of the stool and stood. "I have to go. It's the only way I can contact him and tell him we've found the tomb."

"I don't think we need him," David said. "The fewer people down there, the better. And a bunch of earthmoving equipment is bound to attract attention."

Rika eyed him as though he'd just farted in church. "Of course we need him. Three people can't do it."

David thought they could. But pressing the issue would only set off her temper. He opted for reason. "What if Dr. Ragheb sees you?"

Rika walked to the door of Blue's office. "I'll be careful."

#

Wrung out after three hours in the upstairs conference room—grilling from the Head, good but useless advice from the Chief of Foreign Branch, false sympathy from the simpering weasel who ran Diplomatic Branch—Major Hassam sank into his chair and lit a cigarette. He noticed his ashtray was clean and realized Amina had tidied up in his absence. A grandmotherly secretary, she'd also re-stacked the files he'd knocked to the floor.

Out of habit, he leafed through the sealed envelopes containing the day's confidential memos. His anger had withered, along with his enthusiasm for this dog-sucking job.

He should sell his apartment and buy a date farm in the delta. Find a boarding school for the kids, put his wife to work slave-driving the pickers, and get a mistress. Maybe two.

His head ached. His shoulder ached. Despite his closed window, the stink of hot tar from a repair crew on the road below stung his nostrils.

He was entertaining a temptation to use the crew for target practice when he noticed a green dot in the corner of one envelope. It was the mark of one of his two moles in Diplomatic Branch. Hassam tore open the envelope, but urgent knocking interrupted him.

"Come."

Samir, his aide, entered with some papers in his hand and closed the door behind him. "Sir, if you're interested in the American, David Chamberlain, I think you should see this."

Hassam crushed the memo in his fist, instantly on guard. Only he and Corporal Malik were supposed to know about Chamberlain. "Who said I was interested in someone by that name?"

"Sir, that corporal you sent to pull the rental car records? Well of course he didn't have the authority. If you'd asked me instead ..." He left the rest of the sentence unspoken.

Hassam steadied his fingers on the desktop, trying to conceal the dread freezing his veins. The chain, Chamberlain-Teferi-museum-papyrus-theft-Imbabi, led directly to his own destruction.

Facts. He needed to find out what Samir knew.

In the calmest tone he could muster, Hassam said, "What about the records?"

"The car and driver are still assigned to Mr. Chamberlain."

The man's face betrayed nothing. But a guileless countenance was standard equipment for a chess master. Hassam needed more information. Pointing his chin toward Samir's hand, he said, "What's that?"

Samir laid the papers on Hassam's desk and stepped back. "The report of an interview conducted this morning by one of our men and two investigators from Foreign Branch."

Hassam scanned the header information on who, where, and why. He saw Chamberlain's name, then stiffened. "Teferi?"

"A French woman, sir. According to Immigration records."

Hassam searched Samir's eyes for any sign that Teferi meant more to him than "a French woman." He found none. The chain was broken at its first link. Or so it seemed.

Relaxing a little, he forced himself to read slowly. Chamberlain had been flying around Egypt in a private jet loaded with surveillance equipment, then had flown with Teferi to Sudan on business. A patrol plane that challenged him was called off when Sudanese authorities told its pilot Chamberlain's visit was friendly.

Teferi and Chamberlain in the Sudan on "friendly business." Three of his original threads now definitely twined. Hassam pinched his lips, the old fire rekindled. He still couldn't see the pattern, but he was more certain than ever that a malevolent plot lay encrypted within it. And he did have a new thread.

"Impound this airplane."

Samir gaped at him. "On what charge, sir?"

"On my orders, dammit!"

As Samir scurried out, Hassam regretted his outburst. The last thing he needed was for his closest assistant to become leery of his motives. The stench of tar seemed to intensify. He reached for his cigarettes and noticed the mole's memo wadded up on his blotter. With only half his mind engaged, he uncrumpled it, scanned rapidly, then almost choked.

Sitting bolt upright, he read it again.

When Chamberlain and Teferi flew to Khartoum, the Sudanese Ambassador and resident intelligence chief had secretly flown with them. The Ambassador's car had been found at the airport, and the checkpoint guard identified photos of the two diplomats, who he said had passed themselves off as Egyptian officials.

Hassam slammed his hand on the desktop. *All* the threads now wove into place.

Too agitated to sit still, he stood and paced, his rubber heels squeaking on the wooden floor as he rehashed the facts and their now-obvious connections.

Chamberlain had flown a high-tech spying mission in Egypt

and, when he finished, he, Teferi, and the two top Sudanese envoys had taken their findings to Khartoum. Why Khartoum? Because that goatherd Gaddafi had recruited the Sudanese. With Egypt keeping a constant eye on Libya, it made diabolical sense for Gaddafi to run his operation through the newly fundamentalist regime on Egypt's southern border.

Hassam pictured Gaddafi's smug face and what he could do to it with a pair of pliers.

Gaddafi's goal, of course, was conquest. But Egypt was far too strong for invasion to succeed. So the plot was to foment a revolution from within—exploiting weaknesses identified by Chamberlain, arms supplies located by the black terrorist, and the same fundamentalist underground that had murdered Sadat.

God, he'd love to round up those pigs, bulldoze a giant hole in the ground, and bury the lot of them alive.

Hassam heard knocking and realized it had been going on for several seconds. "Come."

"Sir," Samir said, "the aircraft has already departed."

"*Khara!*"

"But it had only one passenger, a Paul Rackowski."

"Chamberlain and Teferi are still here?"

"Chamberlain hasn't checked out of the Hilton, sir."

Maybe Allah existed, after all. Maybe He saw the upstairs office, not a date farm, in Hassam's future. Among the citations decorating his wall, Hassam now visualized a presidential commendation.

Instead of tar, he smelled blood.

"Send Corporal Malik to arrest him the instant he shows up at the Hilton. Alert security at all airports, shipping terminals, and border crossings. Send Chamberlain's and Teferi's passport photos and a notice declaring them armed and dangerous."

"Sir, what charges shall I—"

"Do you understand a direct order?"

Samir shrank back, then blanched as Hassam pulled his pistol.

But Hassam was only checking to be sure it was fully loaded. If Chamberlain came home to roost, maybe Teferi would also. "I'm going to the museum."

#

Filled with optimism, Rika rode in the front passenger seat as Hagazy sped her toward the museum. Soon she'd make a huge contribution to Eritrea's independence, a contribution worthy of a future minister in the government. At the same time, she'd learn more than she'd ever imagined possible about the queen whose philosophy so closely mirrored her own. A philosophy similar to Marxism, but one that had actually achieved the ideals Marxist nations seemed never to attain. A template for the new Eritrea.

Hagazy hit the brakes, swerving to miss a young man who'd dashed in front of them to leap onto the rear bumper of a moving bus.

Jolted back to the present, Rika focused on her immediate dilemma—she had no idea whether it would take hours or days for Efrem to respond to her signal. He might even have left Cairo, in which case she'd have to contact him through their mother's network in Oslo. Hard as she tried, she saw no better solution than to post the signal and wait.

In front of the museum, bumper-to-bumper traffic edged around a police car and an unmarked car, both angled halfway up on the broad sidewalk. The building itself, fronted by a sparsely treed garden of monolithic sculptures, gave her an unexpected queasy feeling. Last time she was here, Dr. Ragheb had almost caught her returning the papyrus, and the time before that, she'd helped to steal it. In either case, she could have been jailed or, at best, deported.

Although she had no choice but to revisit the scene of her crimes, she could at least distance Hagazy. Without explanation, she asked him to park in the short alley behind the Hotel Princess Cleopatra and stay there until she came out.

Striding toward the museum, she saw that only one of its two iron gates was open. Outside it a policeman stopped her. "Closed," he said.

"I work here." She was conjuring replies to an "I don't care" when she saw the museum's chief guard leaning against the ticket counter inside. With her friendliest smile, she beckoned him. "I need to pick up some papers in my office. It will take only five minutes."

"She's okay," the guard said.

Looking dubious, the policeman withdrew a notepad from his shirt pocket. "Name?"

Rika told him.

"Where were you last night around midnight?"

"I was out of town. I only read about the murder this morning." Affecting an appalled expression, she added, "It sounds just awful."

The chief guard confirmed that he hadn't seen her for two days.

Closing his notebook, the policeman said, "Five minutes."

Relieved that he hadn't insisted on accompanying her, Rika climbed the staircase. Two steps from the top, she halted. Another policeman sat on a bench by one of the alcoves, about ten meters to her right. He appeared to be dozing.

No one else in sight. Only the stink of old cigarette smoke hinted at the throng of officials who must have swarmed over this place earlier in the morning.

On tiptoes, she entered her office. She pulled a twelve-by-fifteen-inch Egyptian flag from her hip pocket and had just finished taping it on her window when someone in Ragheb's office next door spoke her name.

Why would anyone be talking about her?

Then the same voice growled, "black bitch."

Astounded, Rika put her ear to the connecting door.

"Major Hassam, you are out of your mind," Ragheb was saying. "It is inconceivable that Rika would be involved in anything that could possibly interest the Secret Police."

Secret Police? Had they discovered her repairs to the papyrus? She cut her eyes to its cabinet. Closed. Her office looked the same as she had left it. And if they thought she had anything to do with the museum guard's murder, the policeman at the entrance would have seized her.

"You love-blind cretin." The growl turned rabid, as if the speaker were spitting foam with each word. "She and Chamberlain are part of the worst threat this country has faced since Sadat's assassination."

Rika couldn't believe it. What in hell was this madman talking about?

"I've sealed all the borders. There's no way those terrorists can escape. I'll catch Chamberlain when he returns to his hotel. And if *you* don't help me find Teferi, I'll snap Chamberlain's teeth off, one by one, until he tells me where she is."

Raw terror paralyzed Rika's body.

"Hosni, stop talking that way," Ragheb pleaded.

"And after I've broken them, I'm going to personally blow their brains out."

Chapter 24

Forcing a "Thank you" to the policeman at the front gate, Rika fought the urge to run. Honking traffic made it impossible to hear if footsteps were pursuing her through the sculpture garden in front of the museum. The uncertainty twisted her stomach, but she didn't dare look back.

She had to warn David. And Hagazy and Blue, who could both be in danger by association with David. Thanks ultimately to her. Somehow, something she'd done had backfired horribly.

At the sidewalk, she turned left toward the Princess Cleopatra and stole a glance over her shoulder. No one following. Slowly her stomach unwound.

Halfway to the corner, she realized she'd better put a face to this Major Hassam. She'd been hunted before, but only by Ethiopians chasing anonymous Eritrean ambushers. Never by someone who'd sworn to kill her specifically. Despite the midday heat, goose bumps rose on her skin.

In the square to her right, three buses stood in a queue facing her, the front two taking on passengers. The third hadn't yet opened its doors. A crowd of people milled around, waiting to board. Good camouflage for observation.

Dodging traffic, Rika crossed to the square. She threaded her way to the third bus and joined the crowd, women with small children in hand, young men in shirts and slacks, soldiers in various degrees of uniform.

The first two buses growled away. The engine of the third one cranked to life, belching an acrid cloud of diesel exhaust. The people around her jostled for position, but Rika stayed put, her eyes riveted to the museum.

Suddenly the policeman at the front gate snapped a salute.

A man smoking a cigarette came out. About five-foot-seven, close-cropped hair, sport coat and slacks. Built like a bag of cement. For a moment, he talked to the policeman, who stood at attention. Then he appeared to yell something. The policeman recoiled, fumbled with his shirt pocket, and pulled out his notepad. The man snatched it. The policeman pointed in the direction Rika had gone. The man threw an uppercut that dropped the policeman to the ground.

This had to be Hassam. His violence matched the brutality of the words she'd heard through the door to Ragheb's office.

As the policeman struggled to his knees, spitting blood, Hassam jogged to the sidewalk. He turned toward the Princess Cleopatra and halted, his eyes seeming to lock on hers.

In that instant, she realized the bus's doors had closed. She stood alone, exposed, beside its grumbling rear engine.

Rika bolted. Using the bus for cover, she dashed across the street, sidestepping trucks, cars, motor scooters. On the far sidewalk, she turned at the first intersection, then stopped to peer back around the corner building. Pedestrians everywhere. No one running her direction. But if Hassam were holding himself to a fast walk and keeping close to the buildings on this side, she wouldn't spot him until it was too late.

She took off again, sprinting to the next intersection, where she plunged into the warren of narrow streets behind the office of Trans World Airlines. To track her in this maze, Hassam would have to stop and ask questions. Every stop would put him farther behind her. And he wouldn't suspect her destination.

Slowing to rush-hour stride, she ducked between stalls, around hawkers vending fruit from pushcarts, workmen sawing lumber, until she came full-circle to the short alley behind the Princess Cleopatra.

Hagazy paced among the rubbish bins, chewing his fingernails.

"Get in the car," she said. "Go to SEECO. Get David and take him to Blue's house. He must not go to the Hilton. I don't care what he's doing. Get him to Blue's house. Now."

"You are not coming?"

"I'll take a taxi. Go!" Rika didn't wait. With a quick check up and down the thoroughfare at the mouth of the alley, she slipped out and headed for a tailor's shop she'd passed once before.

After four turns, she found it, a place catering to the clothing needs of women who, out of tradition or forced obligation, adhered to strict Muslim custom.

Thirty minutes later she shuffled out, covered head-to-toe in black *chador*, only her eyes and hands exposed. She hated the way it muffled her hearing and restricted her peripheral vision. These poor women. But no disguise suited better the vigil that lay ahead. For however long it took, she had to watch the Princess Cleopatra, the only rendezvous point she'd ever established with Efrem.

On her way back to the square, she stopped in a bookstore and purchased a Michelin map of northeast Africa and Arabia. Efrem would need it, if he agreed to help them.

As she crossed to the square where she'd observed Hassam, she noticed that the unmarked car previously parked in front of the museum, presumably his car, was gone. Still, for the next three hours she kept an eye out for Hassam as she alternated between sitting on a bench near the buses and walking a circuit from one end of the square to the other.

Despite being black, the *chador* was surprisingly cool, especially when she walked. Like heavy Bedouin robes, it kept the sun off her skin but let air circulate underneath. Even though she wore it over jeans and blouse, the temperature against her body felt like a balmy evening.

Perched again on the bench, she thought of David. He must be fuming, cooped up at Blue's house with no other explanation than "She said so."

A man sat down next to her. "Where have you been?"

Rika almost jumped off the seat. "Efrem!" Still dressed in the same Arab garb, he looked even more haggard than before. "How did you recognize me?"

"You do not carry yourself with Islamic modesty."

A flaw in her subterfuge. But it did get his attention. "I'm so glad you're still here."

"Why are you no longer registered in your hotel? I have been worried about you. I come past here every day, checking for that flag up there."

She glanced at her office window. "We have to talk. There's a teashop ten minutes from here."

Walking two dutiful paces behind him, she spoke in Tigrinya, their native language, mixing directions to the teashop with a full account of what she'd just heard and seen at the museum. "Which is why I'm dressed this way. Here we are."

Aromas of Orange Pekoe and Darjeeling wafted from the shop's open door to the sidewalk, where men with glasses of brew sat at tiny metal tables. Inside the air was sweltering.

Efrem ordered hibiscus tea from a fat, headscarfed woman who tended six brass urns and two hissing kettles behind the counter. He carried their glasses to a wooden table in the rear corner of the shop, where they sat with their backs to the walls.

"The Secret Police pursued me twice," he said, still speaking Tigrinya. "They must have connected us and somehow imagine you are involved in my efforts to find arms."

Rika gripped the table edge. "Why didn't you tell me they chased you?"

"What would you have done?"

The implied answer stung. There was nothing she could do. She was no longer useful as a fighter, let alone a tactician. She'd traded her military value for the role of a mere scholar. Well, the tomb would change her brother's opinion.

"In any case," he said, "we have to extract you."

"I can extract myself." While waiting for Efrem and pondering Hassam's disclosure of the sealed borders, she'd come up with a way to kill two goats with one chop.

Efrem arched his eyebrows skeptically.

"Your little sister is still a soldier." She was sweating now inside the *chador*, wanted to rip it off her body, free herself from this black straitjacket. Only fierce determination to make an impact on the war effort kept her in her seat. Swallowing some pride, she said, "But I need your help for something else."

Rika told her brother the whole story, from spilling tea on the papyrus to locating Tiye's tomb, leaving out nothing except her involvement with David. She ended with, "I know a man in

England who could sell the treasure for cash. We wouldn't have to beg anymore. We could buy all the Stinger rockets we need and anything else you want. All I need from you is men. And some earthmoving equipment."

In a tone of withering sarcasm, he said, "You want me to truck bulldozers and backhoes a thousand kilometers across the Sudan?"

An unrealistic request, perhaps, but worth a try. "We can do it with men only. It'll just take longer."

Efrem's response was a dubious frown.

Deflated and angered at the same time, she lashed out. "How successful have *you* been, Commander? Have you found the replacements for our 'weary Kalashnikovs?' "

If looks could freeze, Efrem's eyes would have iced her solid.

Fed up with his cynicism, she leaned back in her chair. "I won't beg you. I'm going to do it. Either you help or you don't."

The woman who had poured their tea waddled up to them. "You don't like it?" she asked, pointing to the two untouched glasses.

"We prefer it cold," Rika said. When Efrem scowled, she realized a strict Muslim woman would have deferred to her male companion. Quickly she added, "My husband wished me to tell you."

When the woman left, Efrem muttered, "Your 'husband' needs time to think about this."

Rika retrieved the Michelin map from beneath her *chador*, dipped her finger in her tea, and stabbed the tomb's location. Pointing to the red stain, she said, "This is the place. I'm leaving tonight."

#

In an alley that stank of urine, Rika ditched the *chador* and, to her surprise, felt strangely exposed. Perhaps women who wore it appreciated the anonymity it afforded. She could have used the concealment as she walked back toward the square to find a taxi. Hassam or his men might be anywhere and no doubt knew exactly what she looked like. But the garment was too confining and would draw unwanted attention in Blue's neighborhood.

Tensed to run, she darted her eyes in all directions, silently reciting the infiltrator's dictum, "Anticipate and avoid." Just before the square, she spotted a cab and flagged it down. "Semiramis Hotel, please."

The Semiramis was less than half a kilometer from the museum but was a big tourist hotel where she wouldn't stand out and where she could check that she wasn't being tailed. On the way, she looked back twice, trying to memorize the cars behind them. Too many. Biting her lip, she slumped lower in the seat.

At the Semiramis, she paid off her driver and walked into the lobby, all honey-colored wood and blue upholstery. For ten minutes, she peered out through the big glass doors, looking for new arrivals "on a mission." No one fit the bill. With growing confidence, she went back outside and chose the second taxi in line. "Maadi," she said, naming the suburb where Blue lived.

The driver used one of those wood-beaded seat covers. He also chain-smoked Gauloises cigarettes, whose rank odor took her back to cafes near the Sorbonne, innocent days that now seemed like a childhood memory, instead of five weeks ago.

When they reached Maadi, she had the driver drop her off three blocks from Blue's house. From there, she strode the remaining distance, glancing back frequently. The streets were empty. Tall trees cooled the air and filled it with scents of cedar and eucalyptus. An oasis she would have enjoyed much more if a madman weren't hunting her.

At Blue's house, she saw his Land Cruiser in the driveway but no white Peugeot. With a final check in both directions, she walked around to the back door and let herself in. A bottle of Scotch stood on the kitchen counter. "Hello."

David came out of the living room, glass in hand, with Blue right behind. "What's going on? We've been waiting here for hours. Hagazy said there was some kind of trouble."

"Where is he?" she asked.

Blue cocked a thumb over his shoulder. "Sent him out for more beer. And food."

"What happened?" David demanded.

"We have to get out of Egypt." She took the glass from his hand, and swallowed a gulp of icy whiskey that turned to fire in her throat. "Someone in the Secret Police wants to kill us."

"Secret Police?" Blue stepped back.

As he did, a movement caught her attention. She spun around to see Hagazy's Peugeot stopping behind the Land Cruiser. "Blue, you may be in danger, also. And possibly Hagazy."

David eyed her as if she'd just cheated him at cards. "I hope to hell you've misinterpreted something."

"I haven't." She heard the Peugeot's door slam. "We have to talk. Privately, where Hagazy can't hear. They'll surely question him, so the less he knows, the better."

Hagazy butted open the back door, carrying four plastic bags of groceries. "Miss Rika! You are okay?"

"Fine," she said as cheerily as she could manage.

Blue took two of the bags from Hagazy's hands and set them on the counter. "Look, son, be a mate, would you? Put this stuff away for us, then go bring in the beer. You got two cases, right?"

"Yes, two cases."

"Good lad. Stack the beer bottles on the bottom shelf of the fridge. When you've unloaded them all, pop a bottle for yourself. We'll join you in two ticks."

While Hagazy went to work stacking canned goods in cupboards, Rika led David and Blue to a front corner of the living room and told them exactly what had happened.

As she spoke, David's expression changed from incredulous to irate to defiant. "This guy must be insane."

"He is. And he has all the tactical advantages. We have to leave immediately."

"Fuck," Blue grunted. "Not even Abdi Asir, SEECO's president, has enough stroke to stop a Major in the Secret Police. That rank means he's top dog in one of the three operational directorates."

Rika had suspected as much. Anyone who could close borders and assault policemen possessed fearsome power. "Blue, he didn't mention your name or Hagazy's. But you were with us at the airport this morning when the Secret Police questioned us. And Hagazy is David's driver."

"Yeah, I already figured that." Blue tugged on his beard. "Well, it's not your fault this drongo's got his head up his ass. But we're definitely in deep shit."

"Rika's right," David said. "We've got to get out of here. At least find some place to lay low until this Hassam character comes to his senses."

"That won't happen." The deranged hatred in Hassam's voice was something Rika couldn't convey. "The man is a fanatic. I see only one solution. We go to Seddenga."

"Seddenga?" Blue blurted. "We can't do that now. You said the borders are sealed."

"The border with Sudan is hundreds of kilometers long. All desert. We can cross it anywhere. In your Land Cruiser." When she got no response, Rika added, "We were going to do it, anyhow."

David shook his head slowly. "There must be another way out of this."

None that she could think of. "Your airplane has left. They will be looking for us at every airport and harbor. Hotels will have our passport pictures. Blue told them this morning that he works for SEECO. We have no place to hide, and only one way to run."

Despite a tan, David's face looked pale. His brown eyes flitted between her and Blue, obviously searching for some alternative. Then he rolled his lips into his mouth like a commander accepting his losses. "How soon?"

"Now." Every minute they delayed made her more fidgety. Hassam could knock on the door any time. "And we'll need those landmines and the jackhammer. We can't count on Efrem."

David ran a hand through his hair. "I have to warn Hagazy. I don't want him getting the third degree because of us."

"He hasn't broken any laws." Rika had retraced in her mind everything they'd done involving Hagazy. "So if they do question him, all he has to do is tell the truth. The only exception was when we took the Sudanese diplomats through airport security. And if Hassam even knows about that, Hagazy can simply say we told him they were Egyptian."

"No worries," Blue said. "You've seen Hagazy in action. He could talk his way out of a whorehouse without paying."

"I do not go to whorehouse."

Rika whipped her eyes to the kitchen doorway and felt her fingers go cold. How long had Hagazy been standing there?

Chapter 25

Had Hagazy overheard too much for his own good? David found it hard to tell from his face, shadowed in the kitchen doorway. Scrambling for a way to level with him without revealing details that could endanger them all, David walked up and put a hand on his shoulder. "There've been some developments we need to talk about."

"You go to Sudan." Hagazy's tone was accusatory.

Shit. If he knew about Sudan, then he'd probably heard "Seddenga." But he wouldn't know where it was. And in any case, they were only going to be near there.

Hagazy inflated his chest. "I go with you."

Would it be better if he did? No. They were being hunted, a definite threat that outweighed any potential ones. Besides, Hagazy hadn't done anything illegal, but if he went with them and they got caught, he'd have broken enough laws to land him in prison for the rest of his life. David shuddered at the memory of an Angolan prison he'd once seen, so overcrowded that half the inmates were simply left in the exercise yard, perpetually chained to cement-filled tires.

"You can't," David said. Hagazy's shoulder felt bony through the white cotton of his shirt. "There's a man who thinks Rika and I did something terrible against Egypt. I don't know why he thinks that, but he wants to kill us. If you came with us, he could try to kill you, also."

"David's right," Rika told him.

As she and Blue came to join them, Hagazy backed up a pace,

apparently construing the gathering as a show of force. His dark eyes flicked from one to the other, then settled on David. "Who is such bad man?"

"His name is Hassam. He's a major in the Secret Police and he might want to question you."

Hagazy's jaw dropped. "He knows me?"

"He knows about *me*. So he'll find out about you." The truth of that statement pierced David with a pang of guilt. If it weren't for him, the Secret Police would have no interest in the boy. Maybe it was true that Hagazy could handle himself and had nothing to fear, but David would rather not subject him to the test. "Is there someplace you can go and disappear for a while? Say, a week or two?"

"Good idea." Rika touched Hagazy's arm. "Perhaps a friend you could stay with."

"How 'bout Sophie?" Blue suggested.

"I do not see Sophie. Now I see Gina." Hagazy broke a smile. "She is very nice."

"Another Italian, huh? Well, ring her up, lad."

Hagazy hesitated. "She is not such good girlfriend." Then his eyes brightened. "But maybe soon."

David ground his teeth in frustration. This was getting nowhere. He caught a whiff of fresh bread and glanced past Hagazy at the loaf on the kitchen counter, below shelves newly stocked with canned goods. "Can he stay here?"

"Hell, why didn't I think of that?" Blue clapped a hand on Hagazy's shoulder. "This is the perfect place, son. You know that grocery store you just went to? They also deliver. Just call 'em and tell 'em what you want and pay them when they get here." Blue turned to David. "That way, he won't have to go out and risk being seen."

"I also think he should turn in the car," Rika said. "Then no one will see it, either."

Hagazy jutted out his chin. "I am driver. I must have car."

David sided with Hagazy but for a tactical reason. "As long as he's got the car, they'll think he's still working for me and won't wonder where he is." To Hagazy, he said, "But don't drive it anywhere unless you absolutely have to."

Finally, things were coming together. If Hassam hadn't given up searching for them in a week or so, he might at least have some leads that would take his mind off Hagazy. Until then, Hagazy would be safe if he simply laid low.

Blue went into the kitchen and came back with the phone number of the grocery store. Then he and David pooled their Egyptian, British, and American currency, and David handed the roll to Hagazy, some eight hundred dollars' worth.

Hagazy's eyes bugged out. "I can have party. Bring Gina."

"No." Blue scowled at him. "Just lock the bloody doors and keep your head down."

Under the pretext of shaking hands with Hagazy, David leaned in close and whispered, "No loud parties. But bring Gina if you want."

#

As they rolled away from Blue's house, Rika squinted into the setting sun and estimated they'd need a full day to reach the Sudanese border. Assuming they drove without stopping and didn't break down.

Certainly Blue's Land Cruiser seemed solid and well-equipped. A long-wheelbase model, it had an electric winch on the front, two spare tires on the back, a fire extinguisher next to her knee in the front-passenger foot well, and ... "What's that?" She pointed to a clear plastic cylinder, about eighteen inches wide and six inches high, between the axe and spade clamped on top of the bonnet.

"That, milady, is a Donaldson centrifugal air filter. Fitted it myself." Blue curved south onto the Corniche el Nil. "Spins out the dust before letting the air into the regular air filter."

Too bad they didn't have those in Eritrea. Rika couldn't count the number of vehicles whose engines had seized up from grit in the cylinders.

In the rear seat, David rapped on something that sounded like a steel drum. "Is this a water tank?"

"Forty-gallons. Also fitted by yours truly, with help from a local welder."

Rika craned her head around to see a narrow tank, about the

size and shape of an air mattress turned on edge, spanning the backs of the two front seats.

"And there's two saddle tanks for extra diesel," Blue said. "We'll fill 'em all at the storehouse."

Rika couldn't help smiling at Blue's pride. The Land Cruiser was obviously his baby, fathered by him and reared in its father's self-image as a rugged adventurer. It also fared well on the Corniche, plowing through evening traffic like a rhino among wildebeest.

A few kilometers south of Cairo, Blue turned off into a warehouse district of dusty roads and widely spaced buildings, lit here and there by flood lamps atop concrete telephone poles. He stopped at a group of three metal buildings set in a dirt yard surrounded by a chain-link fence with a guard shack at the gate and a large white sign lettered "SEECO" in red.

The guard, a man in his forties wearing a starched khaki uniform with a plastic nametag that read "Mohammed," stepped up to Blue's window. "Mister Blue."

"Evenin', Mo. Gotta kit out for a field trip."

Mo unchained the gate and swung it back, shielding his eyes as the freshening breeze raised a swirl of dust from the yard behind him.

Blue inched forward to where the man stood, then reached out and handed him a cigar. "Thanks, mate."

Mo snapped a salute.

At the building on the right, Blue unlocked a sliding steel door, switched on some lights, then drove inside and slid the door closed.

Rika gazed through the windscreen at what looked like Ali Baba's cave for mobile infantry. Beyond half a dozen vehicles of various types, a floor-to-ceiling chain-link fence caged off ten rows of metal shelving stacked with radios, tires, shovels, camp stoves, tarpaulins.

Opening Rika's door, David said, "If we can't find it here, I bet we don't need it."

She inhaled the familiar smells of canvas, axle grease, and burlap. The metal roof squeaked in the wind.

After unlatching a gate in the cage, the first thing Blue selected was a case of motor oil. "Caltex Sixteen Hundred," he said. "Only oil that can handle the high sulfur content of Egyptian diesel."

Nothing but the best for Baby. But Rika was drawn to the field radios. She picked up one of the walkie-talkie handsets. Motorola. Evidently SEECO didn't cut corners on quality.

"No use to us without repeater stations," David said. "Besides, we have no one to call."

Unfortunately he was right. If they got into trouble, they were on their own.

Blue joined them, carrying a plastic bucket. "For odds and sods."

"Are you sure we can take these things?" she asked him.

"SEECO's rich as God. And our inventory system is run by Egyptians who believe pilfering is a birthright. What we're taking is nothing by comparison. Besides, we'll return what we don't use."

Stealing from someone because they could afford it was no excuse in Rika's mind. But she tempered her reservations with the Marxist dictum: To each according to his needs.

Moving down the aisles, they chose two medical kits, a large fire extinguisher, a cooking kit, two Coleman lanterns, and three bed rolls, all of which they stacked on the floor as they went.

"Grab three of those camp cots, also," Blue said to David. "No sense offering ourselves to the scorpions and camel spiders."

David cast him a wary look. "What's a camel spider?"

"Voracious bastards, about the size of your hand and so light they can blow in the wind."

"They don't blow in the wind," Rika corrected. "But they are very fast."

David grimaced. "Are they poisonous?"

"No. But Blue's right, they'll eat until they can't move. At night, you can sometimes hear them crunching beetles or lizards."

"Then we're definitely taking cots." David pulled down three of them. "How much room have we got?"

"I've a luggage rack on top, but I figure that's where we'll put the landmines."

On top of their heads? Suddenly, Rika had second thoughts. But even if they towed the mines in a trailer behind them, an accident would be fatal. "Is there a mattress we could use to cushion them?"

"I don't think so." Blue stroked his beard. "How 'bout some blankets?"

"Not as good but they'll do." Then it occurred to her. "What kind of mines are these? We need to know so we can decide how to detonate them."

Blue squinted at David. "Kai said Soviet, didn't he?"

"Yeah. He said the clearance crew cut the trip wires and taped the electrical contacts."

"If they have electrical detonators, we could use a car battery." Rika turned to Blue. "Do you have wire here?"

"Miles of it, love." He took them to another aisle where two shelves held 1000-foot spools in various gauges.

The gauge labeled "18-2" looked and felt like lamp wire. Rika chose three spools of it. "What about the Mini ..." She couldn't remember the name. "The jackhammer?"

"Back corner, I think." Blue led them to the rear of the building where they found the jackhammer propped against a metal wall, with a field compressor, four coils of high-pressure hose, and a wooden box of assorted parts.

David inspected the various components. "Looks like it's all here, including the spike."

After loading the jackhammer equipment, they jammed in the other items they'd collected, plus rope, a bundle of burlap bags, a spare car battery, and three pails of "odds and sods." Although Rika saw no use for the ropes or bags, she didn't argue. When Blue had locked up the building, they drove around to three elevated cylindrical tanks stenciled: "Gasoline," "Diesel," and "Potable Water."

While Blue and David topped up their fuel and drinking water, Rika stepped away into the darkness. They were minutes from commencing the greatest, most heartfelt mission of her life. Facing the breeze, she could almost hear Tiye's voice, a whisper on the wind, as the sleeping prince may have heard when the Sphinx spoke to him from beneath the sand. In her mind, Rika whispered back, "I will unearth your glory. Grant me the possessions you no longer need, that I may free my people as you freed yours."

#

Just before midnight, Hosni Hassam woke with a start. Beside him, his wife snored like a well pump sucking air. But what had wakened him was a dream. Rubbing his eyes, he tried to recall. "Rupert Ross." He could see it now, the interrogation report that had swum in and out of his sleeping vision. Ross, the third passenger on Chamberlain's airplane when it returned from Sudan. Hassam swung his feet to the floor, and sat up. How in hell had he missed that?

Rupert Ross, employed by SEECO. When investigators followed up on that, after their interviews at the airport, all three passengers had been vouched for by an "H. C. Carson, vice president, SEECO."

Knowing he'd throttle any subordinate who overlooked such a lead, Hassam cursed himself, threw open the shuttered window, and lit a cigarette.

Rupert Ross and H. C. Carson would receive personal visits in the morning. But before then, there were files to pull, backgrounds to check, indiscretions to identify. All foreigners were guilty of some transgression, and by God, he'd twist that knife until they spilled everything they knew.

With this thought sparking his nerves, Hassam dressed and rushed down to his car. He rousted Ishmael from slumber in the front seat, told him to go home, then got in, cranked the engine, and floored the accelerator.

Chapter 26

Feeling like he'd just beaten a lame donkey, Major Hassam walked out of the air-conditioned quiet of SEECO's building into glaring sunlight and the growl and jangle of morning traffic. Barely nine o'clock and already the day was going to hell.

On the sidewalk, he paused and lit a cigarette. Mr. H. C. Carson knew nothing, except that Chamberlain and Ross had flown to Sudan on some business of Chamberlain's. Hassam could spot a liar before he spoke, and Carson wasn't lying. Perplexed at first, irritated later, he'd nevertheless been forthright throughout Hassam's questioning. Which was fortunate, since Hassam had found nothing in the man's dossier to use as leverage. He was either a walking saint or a eunuch. And the latest dead end.

Earlier, on Hassam's orders, Samir had discovered that Chamberlain's driver still hadn't shown up, Chamberlain hadn't returned to his hotel, and the Sudanese diplomats hadn't returned to Cairo. With the Teferi bitch having slipped through his own fingers, that left Hassam exactly zero suspects to interrogate. Unless the last item on his list panned out.

Rupert Ross. "Blue," as Carson called him, hadn't come in to work yet and didn't answer his home phone when Carson called. But he lived in Maadi, only a few miles from here. Hassam checked the address Carson had scrawled, then waded between the honking vehicles that were trying to get around his double-parked car. A fellow rolled down his window, shook his fist, and yelled. Hassam flicked his cigarette, hitting the asshole in the forehead. Then he flashed his ID. " *'S'emo.*" Your mother's cunt.

As the fellow fumbled around his seats to find the burning cigarette butt, Hassam drove away.

Ten minutes later, he cruised slowly past the Maadi Tennis Club. Through the tall, wrought iron fence he saw a dozen or so expatriate women darting around the courts in white skirts that barely covered their asses. If fundamentalists ever got control of the government, there'd be a rampage of stoning against these "harlots." Preceded, of course, by rape.

Fucking hypocrites. Illiterate murderers, invoking the name of Allah to justify pillage, slaughter, and a return to the Twelfth Century. He pictured Leila, his precious little girl, veiled and wed at age thirteen to some bearded old bastard with three other wives—*if* Egypt fell to the "soldiers of God."

He hawked up some phlegm and spat it out the window.

Turning onto Ross's street, he noted two Egyptian women chatting, string sacks in their hands, presumably on their way to pick up groceries for their foreign employers. In front of one house, a gardener clipped hedges while another pushed a lawn mower, filling the air with the smell of cut grass.

Then he saw it, there on the right. Ross's house. And ... *What!* At the back of the driveway a white Peugeot. *Allah be praised.*

Hassam parked at the far end of the street where he could watch the house in his rear-vision mirror. He radioed headquarters and told them to patch him through to Samir. In the mirror he saw a black BMW pull into a driveway. Too damn much activity for a potentially messy daylight arrest. Foreigners coming and going, their tattletale servants milling about.

It killed him to be this close but have to wait until nighttime.

When Samir came on, Hassam gave him the Peugeot's license number and Ross's address. "Find out if this is Chamberlain's car. Have Corporal Malik meet me across the road from the Maadi Tennis Club. Now. And I want you in the radio room at eight o'clock tonight. Understood?"

"Yes, sir."

"If you breathe a word of this to anyone but Malik, I'll personally extract your fingernails."

#

Rika leaned forward in the back seat. "Are you sure you don't want me to drive?" Since leaving Cairo fifteen hours ago, she'd had little more to do than catch up on sleep as David and Blue took turns at the wheel. The inactivity both irked and numbed her.

"No need, love." Blue chomped on one of the carrots they'd bought while refueling in Luxor twenty kilometers back. "I'm fine."

Fine, maybe. But also a chauvinist, at least where his baby was concerned. It made no difference that Rika had driven trucks much larger than this, even half-tracks and armored personnel carriers. Only male fingers, it seemed, steered Baby.

David looked at her over his shoulder and shrugged.

With a roll of her eyes, Rika settled back.

They hit a bump in the road, which made her glance at the ceiling for the thousandth time. On the roof, tied down and covered with a tarp, they carried enough high explosive to demolish a small town. Nine MON-100 fragmentation mines, packed with shrapnel, effective against lightly armored vehicles, and devastating against people. Plus two big anti-tank mines. The Ethiopians used both types in Eritrea.

Rika had judged the twelfth mine at the abandoned seismic camp to be too corroded to trust. Working by flashlight in the rock-strewn desert, she'd checked to confirm that the mine-clearance crew had secured the mechanical fuses with tiny cotter pins. That was enough for the tank killers, which were activated by trip wires. But the MON-100s also had electrical detonators, which the crew had simply taped over, not removed. She'd unscrewed the detonators, wrapped them separately in newsprint, and stuffed wads of paper into the recessed sockets they came from.

Theoretically the mines were now disarmed. Still, every pothole in the highway gave her jitters. If she were driving, they would damn-sure hit fewer of them. And they wouldn't ride so close behind the stake-bed trucks hauling produce, livestock, and people. Half of Egypt must have picked today to transport something along this single artery linking north to south.

The other half chose the river. Never had Rika seen so many feluccas plying the Nile, a forest of triangular sails, bleached by the blistering sun and straining to catch the faint breath of a stingy wind god. Her window, opened just a centimeter, admitted the flinty smell of baked earth, and for once she was glad to have air conditioning.

Three hours later, when they reached Aswan, Rika felt she was standing on the doorstep to home. At least half the inhabitants were Nubian, more black Africans than she'd seen in one place since leaving Eritrea six years ago. On top of that, these were Tiye's people.

"Let's take a break," Rika said.

Blue unsnapped the leather cover over his watch. "It's almost two. I'd like to hit the desert before dark."

"Let's take a break anyway," she insisted.

David sided with her. "I need to stretch my legs."

Outvoted, Blue found a place to park in the market district of an old section of town. "You two go ahead."

While he stayed to guard Baby, Rika and David wandered off among the shops and stalls and open-air restaurants.

Rika inhaled deeply. "Smell the difference?"

"What difference?"

"The cooking. Fewer spices, roasted goat instead of mutton, grilled yams. It's the African influence." And it whisked her back to her grandmother's cooking pot, steaming over an open fire on cool evenings filled with birdsong in the days before they had to live in caves.

"Whatever it is," David said, "it makes me hungry."

Rika stopped at a street vendor, bought two skewers of charcoal-grilled goat, and handed one to David. "Careful, the meat still has bones. They just chop up the carcass and throw it on the fire."

"Mmmm." David picked a piece of bone from his mouth. "Delicious. But a little tough."

She smiled. "The gristle stays in, too."

They passed a few more shops, then David said, "Sorry about Blue not letting you drive. He's kind of quirky about some things. Superstitious."

"Never mind." The walk, the hints of Africa, being alone with David—all seemed to refresh her, to perk her up like a dose of elixir. A few feet from a fruit stand, she pointed. "Watermelons."

"You want one?"

"Let's get two." She rapped her knuckles on a fruit twice the size of a rugby football. "The Prophet Mohammed once said watermelons come from Paradise. You'll believe it when we're hot and thirsty."

They lugged two back to the Land Cruiser, where Blue squatted amid a crowd of giggling kids from whose ears he was magically plucking coins. When he stood, they cried out in protest, arms reaching up to him, brown and black hands tugging on his shirt.

Rika couldn't help smiling.

As they drove away, the kids trailed after them, pleading for one more coin.

After refueling for the last time, they crossed the Aswan High Dam, the two-edged sword that tamed the Nile on their right, but flooded millions of acres beneath Lake Nasser on their left.

An hour southwest of Aswan airport, the road narrowed to two lanes of sun-grayed blacktop covered in places by sand drifts. Parched desert surrounded them, spotted here and there with thorny scrub. Traffic all but evaporated. Aside from a family of gazelle, the only wildlife she saw was a mother warthog and three offspring trotting along with tails straight up.

In the distance, a sand hill ran roughly parallel to their route. It continued for miles, whitish tan against the rocky hardground this side of it. Eventually it petered out, leaving only an occasional wadi, a dry streambed, to break the monotony.

As though mesmerized by boredom, no one spoke. The Land Cruiser jounced along. Blue smoked a cigar, but had the courtesy to crack his window while he did. David alternated between dozing and studying his aerial photos. Rika watched the shimmering asphalt reeling them southward like an endless fishing line.

Finally, with a red sun balanced on the horizon, Blue pulled to a stop. "We're about ten miles from the turnoff to Abu Simbel. There's supposed to be a checkpoint right after that. So I reckon somewhere around here is where we go bush-bashing."

David held up an aerial photo. "There's a big wadi about a mile farther south. It trends southwesterly, toward the Sudanese border."

When they reached the wadi, Rika scanned the road in both directions. "We're clear."

After shifting into four-wheel drive, Blue angled down the embankment, drove about a hundred meters, and stopped. "Call me paranoid, but I'd feel a lot safer if we wiped our tracks. We can use those burlap bags."

"Good idea." David opened his door. "Why don't you keep going to that bend up there while Rika and I do the sweeping."

With two bags each, she and David climbed up to the road, then backtracked, erasing tread marks and footprints as they went. "It feels good," she told him, "to be doing something physical for a change."

"Car," David said.

Now she saw it, way in the distance, coming from the north. She grabbed his hand and pulled him behind a small boulder. "Lie flat."

It seemed like ages before the sputtering engine rattled past. When the noise faded, she raised herself on an elbow. "You have good eyes."

"You have gorgeous breasts." Twisting onto his back, David rolled her on top of him. "Let's make love."

Rika almost laughed. "What you Americans call a quickie?"

"I mean it."

"We can't." She kissed him but didn't slide off. Instead, she pressed herself into him, briefly savoring this stolen moment.

"Blue can wait," he persisted.

She saw the urgency in his eyes, felt it against her pubic bone. She was tempted to relent. Sundown in the desert. What could be more romantic? But until they were out of Egypt, her giving and receiving would both be distracted. She got to her feet. "Later."

David blew out a resigned breath, stood, and dusted himself off. Then his lips curled into a smile, and he started brushing the dirt from her. His hands lingered on her buttocks.

She shuddered as he squeezed them. Already he knew her too well. "You're evil."

"Look who's talking." He gave her a quick kiss, then picked up the four burlap bags and handed her two. "Time to go."

"I'll get you for that."

"I can't wait."

After sweeping another thirty meters, they walked the remaining distance hand-in-hand.

"What took you?" Blue asked.

"A car came by. We had to hide." Then Rika noticed the tires were almost flat. "What happened?"

"I let out half the air. Have you not noticed how deep our ruts are in this sand? Drop the pressure from thirty-five to eighteen, and we get a footprint fifteen inches wide."

It made sense. Wider footprint, less chance of sinking up to the axles. "Clever."

With a grin, Blue said, "You ain't seen nuthin' yet. These are Firestone nine-hundred-by-sixteens. When the sand gets really soft, I'll drop 'em to eight pounds. Then you'll see wide."

"How the hell can you steer like that?" David asked.

Blue kissed his fingertips and touched the Land Cruiser's tailgate. "Built to UAE specs. United Arab Emirates. Specialized for the desert, including wider wheel wells for just that purpose."

No wonder he loved this vehicle. And no wonder that, according to David, Blue had no serious girlfriends. How could any woman compete? Rika was glad the big the Australian was part of their team, he *and* his sweetheart.

"How 'bout you drive for a while?" Blue said to her.

"Me?" After all this time?

"Keys are in the ignition, love. Davey can navigate, and I'll get some shut-eye."

Rika got in behind the wheel, moved the seat forward, and started the engine. She was reaching for the headlight switch when she realized headlights would be visible for miles. Until the moon rose, she'd have to wind her way through unknown terrain in darkness. Was Blue testing her?

"One other thing, love." Standing at the open driver's door, Blue pointed across her lap to a khaki-colored plastic case between the front seats. "Hand me that, would you?"

As Rika gave it to him, she noticed Hebrew writing on the case.

Blue extracted a pair of goggles and a black disk that looked like a big lens filter. After screwing in the disk over the front of the searchlight mounted next to the driver's side mirror, he said, "Infrared."

Amazing. What didn't this fellow have? Rika switched on the searchlight, fitted the goggles over her head, and saw the wadi illuminated in bright lime green. "Wonderful!"

"Thought you'd like it." Blue climbed into the back seat. "Ready when you are."

#

The dark street in front of Rupert Ross's house showed no sign of activity. Two lights burned inside the house, one in the living room and one on the side in what Hassam supposed was a bedroom. The white Peugeot remained parked in the driveway. Corporal Malik, who'd watched the house all day, now sat beside him, cracking his knuckles and smelling ripe in the gray suit he'd obviously not cleaned with the money Hassam had given him. Samir waited in the radio room at headquarters.

Hassam cleared his throat, snatched the radio microphone off his dashboard, and said, "Make the call."

A moment later, he heard, "It's ringing, sir." Then, "No answer."

"Let it ring."

"Still no answer, sir."

"Hang up and try again." Hassam shook a cigarette out of his packet and lit up.

"He answered," Samir said. "I apologized and said it was a wrong number. Sir, he's not a foreigner."

It had to be Chamberlain's driver, which meant no holds barred. Hassam flicked his cigarette out the window. "Come on," he told Malik.

At the front door, Hassam knocked. No reply. He tried the handle. Locked. "Break it down."

Malik stepped back, turned sideways, and hurled himself at the door. It cracked down the middle. He lunged again and smashed through, almost stumbling to the floor.

Hassam yelled at him, "Go around the side."

As Malik took off, Hassam drew his gun. At the end of a short hallway, light shone beneath a closed door. Hassam kicked it in.

Empty. The window over the bed gaped open. He heard a scream outside, and a grunt.

Then Malik's sinister grin appeared in the window.

Chapter 27

In a basement interrogation cell at Headquarters, Major Hassam stood triumphantly over the naked, unconscious figure of Hagazy Masud.

The boy, his wrists and ankles bound with yellow plastic lock bands, lay next to the floor drain beneath the glare of a 500-watt ceiling bulb. He would waken to white concrete walls, splotched brown from the various fluids of previous occupants, and to a nauseating abattoir smell that buckets of disinfectant couldn't purge. For some guests, that was enough to induce cooperation.

If it weren't enough, Corporal Malik would present additional incentives.

Hassam turned to the Service medic standing next to Malik. "Wake him."

The medic, a wiry young man four years out of the army, stooped to administer the injection, then followed Hassam and Malik out of the cell. Malik clanged the door closed.

"I'll call you if I need you," Hassam told the medic. Then he slid open the door's observation slit. Best to let the newly conscious take stock of their circumstances alone.

The boy stirred. He struggled with his bonds, frowning drowsily at first. Then his eyes opened wide. He thrashed on the floor like a landed fish, his face distorted with growing panic as the unyielding lock bands cut into his flesh. "Help! Anybody. Help me!"

Classic reaction of the untrained. Hassam bet himself the kid would break in less than an hour. Done by midnight. And it might not even be necessary to have the place hosed out.

Hagazy Masud screamed. Twisting into wild contortions, he wailed at the top of his lungs. His voice grew hoarse. Soon nothing came out but croaking sounds. He curled into a ball and sobbed.

Hassam let him blubber and quake for several minutes. Then he stood back from the observation port, buttoned his sport coat, and said, "He's ready."

Malik slammed back the bolt and followed Hassam inside.

"I didn't do it," the boy screeched, eyes huge and suddenly defiant as he uncoiled from his fetal position. "I'm innocent. I swear by Allah I didn't do it!"

"Do what?" Hassam asked in a tone of concern.

"Anything! I didn't do anything. I'm a driver. A Budget driver. All I do is drive people around."

"Oh, I know exactly who you are. And exactly what you do. That's why you're here." Hassam stepped closer, smiling down at the cringing mongrel. "I wish to ask you some questions. If you answer quickly and honestly, you may be released. If you take a long time or I don't like your answers, then it will be very unpleasant for you."

The boy screwed up his face in obvious confusion.

Everyone was guilty of something. Hassam let Hagazy Masud reflect for a few seconds on his own sins before coming to the point. "I want to know the whereabouts of David Chamberlain, Frederika Teferi, and Rupert Ross, also known as 'Blue.' I want to know what they have been doing for the past week. And—"

"I don't know anything."

"Do not," Hassam growled, "ever interrupt me."

The boy shrank instantly.

"Speak only when I tell you to. And speak only the truth." For a moment, Hassam savored the boy's fear. Then he lit a cigarette. "Before we begin, I will tell you that, when the Soviets were advisors in Egypt, they taught us many interrogation methods." He motioned Malik forward. "This gentleman is expert in all of them. They leave no marks on the body. But they can reduce a man to a permanently mindless piece of meat."

Hagazy Masud tried to scoot away but gave up after a few feet. Teeth chattering, he fixed his stare on Malik whose cloudy eye no doubt added menace to the threat.

Hassam tapped an ash onto the floor. "Nevertheless, despite learning the Soviet methods, he has always retained a fondness for the old ways. And I've agreed to let him use whatever means he chooses. *If* you do not answer quickly and truthfully."

Desperate eyes darted back and forth between the two men.

Hassam felt the beginnings of an erection. Did God enjoy his power this much? "Tonight, for your pleasure, the gentleman has brought his favorite form of encouragement."

Malik reached under his suit coat and withdrew a pair of castrating pliers, the kind used on horses.

"No!" The boy coiled into a ball, obviously recognizing the instrument. Tucked tight, he shook like an epileptic, piss pouring down his legs. "I'll tell you anything you want. Anything."

Hassam smiled. "I know you will."

#

Money. It was as simple as that.

Climbing the stairs just before midnight, Hassam shook his head at how he could have missed something so obvious. A revolution needed financial backing. Sudan was bankrupt. Gaddafi was rich but capricious, promising money one day and withdrawing it the next. What better solution than to sell a royal treasure? With Egypt's ban on the sale of antiquities, a starving market would leap on the chance to buy from Sudan.

So the papyrus had been the key all along. An Egyptian tomb in Sudan. And now he knew where.

Hagazy Masud had disclosed the name with only minor coaxing, his one bout of resistance shriveling the moment Corporal Malik flexed the castrator's jaws and asked, "Now?" After that, the boy was entirely cooperative. As the Soviets had taught: Properly frightened beforehand, it was seldom necessary to damage an amateur.

Although Headquarters was nearly deserted at this late hour, Hassam closed his office door before consulting the big map on his wall. In less than a minute, he found Seddenga.

He checked his wastebasket for the translation he'd thrown

out that morning. Empty, already dumped by the cleaners. But it
didn't matter. He remembered that the tomb builders lived in a
place that began with an S. And Teferi, Chamberlain, and Ross
were, at this very moment, driving to Seddenga.

A hunter's thrill surged through him. With a company of
airborne commandos, he could land in Seddenga before dawn.
Bursting with anticipation, he called the Head of Service at his
residence, requested an urgent meeting, and assured him it could
not wait until morning.

Thirty minutes later, the Head received him, wearing a silvery
white, pinstriped galabeyah that shimmered from silk threads
woven into the cotton. With the rolling gait of the grossly overfed,
he steered Hassam through a high-ceilinged reception room and
out to a flagstone patio where a lighted swimming pool glowed blue
in the night. Groupings of white, wrought-iron furniture
surrounded the pool. At one of the tables, the Head motioned
Hassam to sit before taking a chair opposite him.

Stately palms towered overhead, their fronds rustling in a cool
breeze. The smell of wet grass in the manicured lawn mingled with
scents of lemon trees and chrysanthemums. Hassam pictured
himself reclining on one of the chaise lounges, eating grapes off the
back of a Nubian girl on all fours beside him.

Soon. But first …

Disdaining to use the word "sir," Hassam came straight out
with, "I have uncovered a fundamentalist plot to overthrow our
country."

His boss stiffened, eyes wide, as if he'd pulled back the bed
sheets to find a scorpion.

Pleased with the effect of his shock tactic, Hassam went on to
lay out his evidence. He had just reached the tomb connection in
his narrative when a man in white livery appeared with tea and a
tray of fresh fruit. The Head leaned forward, selected a date from
the tray, and placed it pensively in his mouth. Light from the
swimming pool danced over his jowls.

When the servant was gone, Hassam said, "It is imperative that
we prevent these conspirators from opening the tomb and selling
the treasure. Without that money, the plot will fail."

The date pit squeezed out between the Head's lips and was

placed carefully back on the tray by manicured fingers.

Sensing skepticism, Hassam rushed to conclude. "Fortunately, this tomb is in a remote desert area just south of our border. With helicopters, a contingent of commandos could fly in below radar, capture or kill the conspirators, and return before Khartoum had any idea what was happening. But we must act quickly. Within the hour."

"Hosni, I have received no other evidence of threatening activities, from either outside Egypt or within. While I do not deny the facts you have accumulated, I am forced to question your conclusions. Could there not be some other interpretation?"

"None." Hassam dug his fingernails into his palms. "They left last night. They might already have crossed the border."

"But what's the rush? It could take weeks, perhaps months, to open the tomb."

Are you deaf? "Not with the Sudanese helping them. They could be inside in a day or two. We have to act now."

"My point, Hosni, is that commandos could be there in a matter of hours. So time is on our side. That is supremely important." He leaned forward, rested his forearms on the table, and lowered his voice to a confidential tone. "While I would like to keep such an operation within the Service, it must ultimately become known to the Minister. Perhaps even the President. So you can see, we must be absolutely certain before we proceed. For that, I need concrete evidence of an impending revolution. And that can best be acquired through discussions with the heads of the other intelligence services."

"Sir—"

"Hosni! I will speak with them tomorrow. If I receive any positive indications, then we will proceed with your plan."

Hassam felt kicked in the balls. "And if not?"

"Then we shall reconsider our options."

"But, sir—"

"Major. We have time. Let us use it wisely." He stood from his chair. "Good night."

As his boss waddled away, Hassam studied the bald spot on the man's head, wishing he had a hammer. He could hear the sound, like stabbing your thumb through the shell of a fresh egg.

For a moment he sat there, swallowing against the sting of bile in his throat. Then he grabbed the fruit tray, hurled it into the pool, and stormed out. With a squeal of burning rubber, he shot toward the front gates. A guard managed to open them just in time. Hassam fishtailed onto the main road.

Head of Service. Asshole of Service was more like it, that spineless pile of pig shit. The other intelligence chiefs would know nothing. His Assholeness would then "reconsider our options." Meaning he'd stall, go through the motions of demanding "concrete evidence," play with his penis until Cairo erupted in flames.

Foot to the floor, Hassam swerved around midnight traffic. He veered onto a bridge, spun momentarily out of control, and almost broadsided a horse-drawn cart. The horse reared.

"Out of the way," Hassam yelled. He pulled straight and sped off. On the bridge, he threw his cigarette out the window. Wind whipped his face. His shoulder felt like someone had it in a death grip.

In front of Headquarters, he parked, lit another cigarette, and inhaled so deeply it made him cough. *"Khara."* He'd built his case, woven all the threads, seen the design emerge as perfectly as on the finest carpet. "I've done it all."

But had he?

In truth, he'd only uncovered the plot. He hadn't stopped it.

Teferi, Chamberlain, and Ross. Three civilians, one of them a girl. If he caught them before they connected with the Sudanese, he wouldn't need commandos. He had men of his own. He even had a captive who knew the targets well and, if necessary, could be used as a decoy.

He'd be disobeying a direct order, but he was done taking orders. From now on, he answered to no one. On the other hand, if the Head found out, it would cost him his job, maybe land him in prison. With a shudder, he saw the inmates he'd put there, a faceless mob, cornering him with broken bottles and makeshift knives.

Hassam shook off the vision. A man who saved his country would not go to prison. He'd get presidential gratitude, the top-floor office, maybe even the whole ministry. Spurred by a bolt of new energy, he got out of his car, slammed the door, and bounded up the steps.

#

For five hours now, ever since moonrise turned the arid landscape silvery white, Rika hadn't needed the night-vision goggles. The cool desert air was so clear she could have read a newspaper by the stars alone. But fatigue was becoming a problem. Twice she'd caught herself bearing too far west, disoriented by the shifting angle of illumination as the moon arced across the sky. The compass fixed to the windscreen would be more help if it stopped bobbing and turning in its water-filled bulb.

Cresting a sandy rise, she wrenched the steering wheel left to avoid a boulder, then right to regain her southward heading. From her waist up, every muscle ached. Much more of this obstacle-course maneuvering on nearly flat tires and she'd have to wake David or Blue to take over.

Their ability to sleep through all the wrenching and jarring reminded her of exhausted soldiers returning from a firefight. Or maybe that was just the way men were.

A straight line, left to right, appeared in the distance. In this trackless wilderness, it could only be one thing. A road.

Rika halted.

"What's happening?" David mumbled, sitting upright in the seat beside her.

"We may have crossed the border. There's a road down there." She checked the compass, which had stopped wobbling. "It runs east-west."

"Where are the goggles?"

"Can't you see it?" She pointed dead ahead. "Less than half a kilometer."

"Yeah, okay, I've got it." David pulled out his aerial photos and switched on one of the two map lights on the dashboard.

Blue leaned forward between them, his breath rank with stale cigar smoke. "Three o'clock. The timing's about right."

"We're in the Sudan." David gave a thumbs-up.

Sitting back, Rika rubbed her eyes. They'd escaped Egypt and that rabid maniac, Major Hassam.

"How're you feeling?" David asked her.

"Like a lorry ran over me. Someone else can drive when we reach the road."

"This'll help. Blue took three bottles of beer from the ice chest, opened them, and handed them out. "Ahh, that's better. My mouth was beginning to taste like something you squat over."

And smell that way. After a swallow of beer, Rika drove down the rise. At the road—two ruts, really—she got out to stretch her legs while David and Blue took turns with a hand pump to re-inflate the tires. The engine made clicking sounds as it cooled.

She wandered along the road about twenty meters. A nearly-full moon hung halfway to the horizon amid millions of glittering stars. A soft breeze caressed her face. In all directions, endless rocky desert, unspoiled. Like standing at the beginning of time.

What a perfect place to make love. Primordial man and woman consecrating primordial earth.

She looked back at David. He'd disconnected the pump and was wiping his hands on his jeans. Time to go, unfortunately. As she walked to the Land Cruiser, she pictured them lying behind that boulder at sunset and wished she hadn't said "Later."

After an hour of traveling due east, Blue halted at a fork in the road. "Turn right?"

"Yes." Seated beside him, Rika pointed to the junction on her map. "Straight ahead goes to a ferry landing for Wadi Haifa on the other side of Lake Nasser."

Twenty kilometers south, they crossed a barren bluff and the lake came into view, silky black beyond the dappled silhouettes of low plants hugging the shore.

"Beautiful," David said, leaning forward from the rear seat.

In a way, it was. But if her map were correct, the infamous rapids of the Second Cataract—since earliest times a barrier to all but the most determined invaders of Nubia—now lay drowned and impotent beneath those waters.

The road, still a rough track, ran southwesterly, sometimes alongside the lake, more often parallel to it but inland. They'd bounced and rolled about forty kilometers when the sun finally topped the horizon. Seeing it made Rika think of baboons. Ancient

Egyptians interpreted the dawn frenzy of baboons as a joyous response to their first sight of the sun god. In this belief, pharaohs had had a row of baboons carved into the topmost friezes of their monuments, where the sun's rays struck first.

She, too, felt an ingrained joy at sunrise. Since childhood, daybreak had meant an end to the dangers of the night, the movement of supplies, the raids on Ethiopian outposts. Dawn heralded a return to the safety of their underground shelters, to family and friends, and hope.

An hour and a half farther south, the road wound up a low hill, and Rika saw below them the ruined tops of two stone towers poking above the lake's surface like the heads of shipwreck victims. "Stop."

David craned his neck between her and Blue. "What are those?"

She knew without checking her map. "The twin fortresses of Semna. Ancient Nubia's northernmost border with Egypt. From here on, we're in the land of Tiye."

Chapter 28

Eighteenth Dynasty

At midday, with the glorious face of Aten smiling directly overhead, Tiye halted her funeral procession to perform her last official act. In a voice buoyed by gratitude, she blessed the multitude kneeling before her tomb, the builders and their families and all those who had voyaged with her up the Nile. As she spoke, women in the throng wailed and pulled their hair. When she finished, her personal guards rose and saluted.

Tiye inclined her head in acknowledgment, then faced the tomb's entrance, anxious to embark on her journey before another seizure struck. That Aten had allowed her to contract the disease could only signify how eagerly He awaited her.

Dressed in a simple white gown, leather sandals, and the tiny ring her future husband had given her upon their first meeting, Tiye walked behind the two funerary priests, who carried torches and chanted a hymn to Aten. Behind her on the swept path came the measured footfalls of Ay and Baketaten, followed by the shuffling of two servant girls.

As she approached the entry, the footsteps and chanting seemed to recede. Her heart danced with excitement.

In the passageway, she gazed not at the paintings of her life but at a vision of the ecstasy to come. Of rising as effortlessly as wood smoke above a fire, ever upward toward a blinding light that did not blind, the purest of breezes washing her upturned face, a chorus of voices singing sounds so beautiful she almost wanted to cry. Sweet fragrances came to her, numberless scents of flowers and exotic vines, rare woods, aromatic roots. A familiar bouquet.

Of her own creation.

Tiye stopped, her eyes focusing on the bouquet's source. In front of her, nested inside the granite sarcophagus, her coffin brimmed with the fragrant mixture of oils and extracts, waiting to receive her. Green urns in which she had transported the precious liquid lined the back wall of the chamber. One urn stood near the head of the sarcophagus.

Still chanting, the priests extinguished their torches and stepped onto the stone platform. The chamber now shimmered in the flickering light of oil lamps perched on tripods. All was in readiness.

Unexpectedly, Baketaten knelt before her and kissed her feet.

Tiye smiled. "Blessed child, rejoice."

When Baketaten had withdrawn, the servant girls removed Tiye's sandals and gown. Taking turns, they tipped out oil from the final urn and with soft hands anointed her body.

Suddenly daggers of pain stabbed into her ears. Tiye clutched her head. Her body shook uncontrollably. The daggers ignited.

Ay sprang to her side, his eyes urgent. But she waved him away. Aten's impatience would not be denied. Through clenched teeth, she uttered, "Quickly now."

The priests assisted her into the coffin. As she lay back, the searing pain subsided. Her body relaxed. Her breath came again in normal rhythm. She saw Ay peering down at her and extended her hand.

He clasped it so tightly she feared he might not let go.

"Beloved Ay, He awaits."

#

Ay stepped back. Turning to Baketaten, he nodded.

With tears in her own eyes, she led the crying servant girls away.

When they were gone, one of the priests handed Tiye a cup of pale liquid. She drank it without hesitation. In a moment, her eyes closed.

As the priests chanted, Ay watched her closely. Before the

chant was finished, he knew she was in a deep sleep. "Proceed."

Gently the priests submerged her head.

Half expecting her to snap awake gasping, he felt a wave of relief when she did not. Followed by a wave of grief.

The priests lowered the coffin's lid into place, then the wooden lid of the sarcophagus.

That completed the service. Except for one act of cleansing.

Ay pointed to a large chest near the sealed stairway to the treasury. Fortunately Tiye had seemed not to notice it. "Is that the gift of the overseer?"

"Yes, Master. It arrived too late to be placed in the treasury."

"Remove it. Place it outside beneath the overhang."

"But Master, it is—"

"Remove it."

With grunts and much straining, the priests dragged the chest out of the room.

Alone at last, Ay laid his palms upon the sarcophagus. His heart ached, but he had no tears to shed. He saw her laughing face, heard her childhood squeals as she tried to escape dunking in their parents' garden. He saw her fear when she learned she was first pregnant, her exhaustion when she had borne the child. The rapture during her long prayers to Aten, more like conversations than prayers.

He could still feel her hand, clutching his from the coffin as her last seizure abated. By sheer strength, she had subdued it. But she would not have survived another. And in that knowledge, he found peace. Whether she would rise again or not, his beloved sister now rested safely.

"Farewell," he whispered. Then he left her in the many hands of God.

#

Striding down the long passageway, Ay heard a commotion near the tomb's entrance. He emerged to find the overseer and priests arguing violently over the chest between them, while Tiye's guards looked on nervously. As he had instructed, the chest sat on the ground just outside the entry.

When the overseer saw Ay, he fell to his knees. "Master, I implore you. Stop these vile priests from denying Our Mother this gift from my humble family."

"Seize him," Ay commanded.

Instantly two guards yanked the man to his feet and pinned his arms behind him.

"But, Master, I don't understand."

"Silence!"

The overseer cringed, his blubbery face pouring sweat.

Only the dignity of this sacred day stayed Ay's hand from meting out its own justice. Bile burning his throat, he growled, "Withdraw."

As the whimpering swine was dragged away, Ay turned to face the entry, the bitterness on his tongue now gone. A workman's hammer lay against the tomb's front wall, below the niche containing the small alabaster column. *I also desire that you should be the one who strikes the ultimate blow.*

When all, save him, were assembled by the canal, Ay picked up the hammer and smashed the column. With the grating crunch of rock grinding upon rock, a stone slab two steps within the passageway descended. In ten heartbeats it was down, the entrance sealed.

With the hammer still in hand, Ay walked out from under the overhang into dazzling sunlight. A hundred paces away, poised on its incline, stood the great stone block from which ropes as thick as a man's thigh snaked across the ground to the timbers supporting the overhang. As Ay approached, the crowd of hundreds drew tighter. Tiye's servant girls huddled behind Baketaten. The architect clasped his hands to his heart.

A single pin secured the block. Ay raised the hammer high. He glanced back at the chest, in deep shadow beside the entry, then bored his eyes into the overseer and struck the pin.

With a creaking of wooden rails, the stone began rolling toward the canal. As it gained speed, Ay backed up instinctively. The ropes straightened, then the one closest to him snapped taut. Suddenly the bottoms of the timbers jerked forward. The overhang cracked.

In a thunderous roar, like stampeding beasts, the face of the mountain broke apart and collapsed. The blast of wind and dirt was as a storm. All but Ay fell to their knees.

Ay stood fast, awed at the magnitude of the destruction. Through roiling dust, he watched boulders the size of hippos skid down the slope and halt, piling up smaller rocks behind them as rivers of dirt flowed past.

Truly no man could penetrate this barrier. Satisfied, he dropped the hammer and walked away.

#

That evening, as the royal entourage prepared to depart, Ay received a message from the headman of Sadjedju. "He dies slowly," it read.

Ay lay back on his bed, picturing the scene as the headman had said it would be. He saw the fat overseer wrapped like a mummy, save his hands and feet, and laid in a shallow open grave. He saw the four exposed extremities scored with a coarse blade and smeared with sour milk. By morning, maggots would arise, filling the wounds like grains of spilled rice. The traitor would survive perhaps eight or ten days—days of unspeakable agony—until the maggots reached his liver.

Chapter 29

On Friday morning, ten minutes after Motor Pool opened, Major Hassam climbed out of a nearly new 1983 Ford van. He cast a quick eye over the other vehicles penned within the chain-link fence, then slapped the van's roof. "This one. Have it ready by seven thirty."

The chief mechanic, a tall, square-jawed man in his fifties, pulled a pocket watch from his coveralls. "That's only twenty minutes, sir. The coolant hoses need to be changed, and I'm short-staffed on weekends."

"Then do it yourself." Hassam stalked off, passing through the service and repair garage, immaculate as always, then through the steel door connecting to the ground floor of Headquarters.

He stopped at Quartermaster and requisitioned three AK-47s, three nine-millimeter Ruger pistols, ammunition for both, and a case of rocket-propelled grenades plus launcher tube. "Deliver them to Motor Pool in the next fifteen minutes."

Three doors down the hall, at Dispatch, he told the clerk to record that Corporal Malik and Samir were on assignment in Suez City helping Hassam check out information on a drug-smuggling ring. Samir should have done all this, but he hadn't come in yet.

Climbing the stairs, Hassam questioned the wisdom of bringing Samir along. Although qualified in small arms, he had never been a field operative. Analysis and strategy were his strengths. Four years ago, Hassam had plucked him from the ranks precisely for his ability to detect patterns. On his own initiative, while still just a corporal, Samir had constructed a diagram of the entire Cairo underworld, revealing two inter-clan relationships even Hassam had been unaware of. It was unlikely that this operation would require such skills. But Hassam needed two men he could trust, and Samir was the only person, besides Malik, who knew about Teferi and Chamberlain.

On the third floor, he found Malik hulking in the hallway. The man's gray suit had dark crescents under the arms and wafted an odor like day-old fish. Opening his office door, Hassam said, "Is Samir here yet?"

Malik shook his head and followed his boss inside.

Hassam kicked the door closed. They should be leaving in five minutes, and Hagazy Masud was still in the infirmary. Hassam wanted Samir to collect him, since the kid was scared brainless of Malik. Too late now.

"Take the prisoner to Motor Pool," he told Malik. "And be kind to him, or you'll wreck Psych Department's work."

As an unwitting pawn who'd ultimately cooperated, the boy had been given a sedative and transferred to a comfortable bed. On Hassam's orders, a Service psychiatrist had wakened him at five this morning, explained to him that he'd played a heroic role in averting national disaster, and asked what he wanted for breakfast. If the mind-bender had done his job well, Hagazy Masud would be willing, if not exactly anxious, to continue serving his country.

A few minutes after Malik left, Samir charged in, smelling of new cotton. "I'm sorry, sir. But when you rang last night, the shops were already closed. I had to wait until seven to buy clothes suitable for the desert."

More suitable for a British colonial dandy. "Epaulets and knee sox?"

"Rather dashing, don't you think?" Samir looked down admiringly at his khaki shirt, matching shorts, and suede boots.

Hassam balled his fists, wanting to dash the man's teeth down his throat. But time was at a premium. With a slow, steadying breath, he unclenched his fists. "If you're quite ready now, and it's not an inconvenience, I suggest we leave."

The van, tan with brown stripes on the side, was parked in front of Motor Pool's garage. In the rear seat, Hagazy Masud sat white-faced, his arms clutched around him. Malik stood beside the driver's door, taking a piss on the asphalt.

"Zip it. We're late." Hassam climbed into the front passenger seat, gestured Samir to the back, and told Malik to drive.

Outside the perimeter fence, they turned right. As they approached the main street in front of Headquarters, Hassam looked up at the Head's corner office on the fourth floor. It had occurred to him this morning and he wondered again now: Was he playing right into his boss's hands? Had that dog-sucker manipulated him into doing precisely this? It would make sense, covering the risk while preserving what the Americans called "plausible deniability."

As the Head's office faded in the distance, Hassam imagined the wily bastard turning from his window with a smirk.

#

By ten in the morning, they'd passed Sai Island, and Rika felt they were finally in countryside Tiye would have recognized. Lake Nasser had tailed off. Here the Nile was untamed, fast-flowing, laden with a healthy burden of entrained sediment that gave it the color of milk-tea. Its floodplain, half a kilometer wide and strewn with boulders, extended to a line of brick-red cliffs on their right. Somewhere in those cliffs lay the valley Tiye had chosen for her final resting place.

The dirt track followed a low rise beside the river. Tire-churned silt coated the Land Cruiser's windows, except for pie-wedge "eyes" Blue cleared by periodically running the windscreen wipers. Fortunately the silt didn't adhere too thickly to the side windows. With a favorable mid-morning sun angle, Rika and David peered out, searching for a gap in the line of cliffs.

"Stop," David said. When Blue tromped on the brakes, David leaned forward from the rear seat and pointed. "See that V-shaped notch in the ridgeline? About two o'clock."

Rika saw it, but she'd been looking for a break in the cliffs, not just a dip.

"We know the gap is vertical," David said, "and the cliff tops are horizontal. That makes right-angle corners, which nature has eroded to create that notch. I'll bet you anything."

"One way to find out." Blue let out the clutch.

They'd gone about a kilometer when she saw a wide slit in the cliffs, just where David predicted. "There!"

Blue slowed to a crawl and lowered his head to look out her window. "Ain't science grand?"

When they came abreast of it, her heart leapt. "A pyramid."

"What? It's not on my images," David said.

A rush of warm air told her he'd rolled down his window. "Not a real pyramid. Look at the top, in the background." Visible beyond the gap, the back wall of the canyon rose even higher than the cliffs in front. Atop the wall stood a triangular pinnacle of rock. "Pyramids are ancient symbols of resurrection. When they became too expensive to build, Egyptians dug their tombs near natural ones."

Tiye could not have chosen a better site. And as Rika's eyes drifted downward, she saw through the gap's walls a sliver of the low mesa and of the landslide created by Tiye's architect.

Blue shifted into four-wheel drive and bounced over the dirt berm flanking the road. After thirty meters, he halted. "Let's erase our tracks."

Rika started to protest, then thought better of it. She was eager to get into the valley, and Blue's caution seemed unwarranted. The nearest town on this side of the Nile lay almost two hundred kilometers away. But even the slightest chance of being noticed was a chance they didn't need. She hopped out and helped David with the sweeping while Blue rebuilt the berm. Finally they set off again.

As Blue jounced and jolted around the larger boulders, the Land Cruiser rattled like a toolbox being shaken. Dislodged dust cascaded down their windows.

"Remember we have landmines," Rika cautioned.

Blue slowed down. Still, they rocked in their seats. Forward, backward, sideways, like riding a camel.

Around the entrance to the gap, car-sized chunks of red-and-gray rock littered the ground. Obviously shed from the cliffs, some had fallen into the gap itself, but not enough to block their passage. Blue wound an easy path between the sheer walls. "Ground in here's awfully smooth."

"Man-made," David said. "We're right on top of the canal the tomb builders dug then filled in."

Rika listened to their chatter but couldn't take her eyes off the mesa, glowing in bright sunlight beyond the shadowy confines of the gap.

When they emerged into the red-walled canyon, Blue pulled to a stop. "Pretty damned impressive."

To Rika, it felt like a giant throne room. The ground was as flat as a marble floor. Long vertical cracks in the canyon walls gave the impression of stately columns, and centered against the back wall stood the "throne"—the mesa bearing Tiye's tomb.

David started to get out, but Blue said, "Hang on, squire. First rule of the bush is don't walk anywhere you can drive."

"Then go around to the right. That's where the clearest fractures are." As they rounded the mesa's northern side, David leaned forward again between the seats. "See that wedge-shaped rock? That's where we want to go."

It was the size of a railway carriage, wide end angled downward toward them, as if the carriage had rolled up the debris slope and embedded itself in the mesa's side. When Blue halted, they climbed out into heat that could have baked bread. Radiating off the steep walls, it assaulted her from all sides, unrelieved by even a whisper of breeze. To labor under such conditions, Tiye's tomb builders must truly have loved her.

With her blouse sticking to her chest, Rika followed David and Blue up the slope. A shadow flitted past. She looked up to see a vulture circling. Nekhbet, patron goddess of Upper Egypt, protector of mothers and children. And eater of those who die in the desert.

When she looked back, David was on top of the wedge and had already reached its uphill end. By the time she and Blue got there, David was coming out of a crevice in the side of the mesa. He scrambled along the rock face like a mountain goat, disappeared into another crevice, and popped out with a huge smile. "This is the place. Two mines here and two in that other fracture, and we can probably gain twenty feet."

"How 'bout we eat first?" Blue grunted.

Rika agreed, not because she was hungry but because she wanted time to just look around and digest the fact that she was actually here. "Let's unload the mines, and find a place to camp."

David looked disappointed.

"We're all tired from traveling," she told him. "Tired people make mistakes. A break for lunch will revive us."

After they'd stored the landmines, spare battery, electrical wire, and jackhammer equipment under the overhang of a large, trapezoidal rock, Blue wiped his face with his canvas hat and asked, "Where you wanna pitch camp?"

"Up there." Rika pointed to the top of the mesa. Training told her to take the high ground. But even if it hadn't, she felt that was the closest place to Tiye. "Can the Land Cruiser make it?"

Blue broke a grin. "Is that a challenge?"

They drove a quick recon around the mesa's perimeter. On the south side, which was more cobble-strewn and less precipitous than the north, Blue lined up for a low-angle ascent.

It didn't look possible. "Are you sure?" Rika asked.

"There's the sissy bar." Gunning the engine, he pointed to a horizontal handle on the dashboard in front of her. "Hang on."

They hit the slope at frightening speed. Rika grasped the bar with both hands as their tires spun, grabbed, spun again, throwing up dust all around them. Rocks thunked the undercarriage. The Land Cruiser rocked, lurched higher up the slope, and started to tip sideways. Blue increased the angle. The engine screamed like a bull in agony. The ground disappeared. White sky filled the windscreen. Then the front wheels left the ground, and they vaulted over the edge onto the top.

"Holy shit," David breathed, as they came to a rocking halt.

Rika pried her hands from the bar, grateful to be alive.

With a satisfied smile, Blue patted Baby's dashboard. "Welcome to camp."

"Camp" reminded her of a dirt football field in Africa, flat, unvegetated, grayish white like the scars on the cliffs where chunks of wall had broken off. The air, surrounded by so much limestone, smelled like hot cement. But at least up here a gentle breeze cooled the dampness of her blouse.

While Blue and David moved the Land Cruiser to a more central spot where it couldn't be seen from the road, Rika walked to the front edge and looked out through the gap. Straight as a gun barrel, it aimed her vision directly at the Nile. She could picture the canal, its line extending with Egyptian precision to the tomb's entrance—right below her feet.

She wanted to laugh and cry at the same time. Dance to her own heartbeat. Cast her arms wide and soar like the vulture, goddess of all she surveyed.

"Beautiful, isn't it?" David said behind her.

She turned to face him. Dark smudges on either side of his nose gave him the look of a cheetah, her favorite cat. "More than I ever imagined."

He slid his arms around her waist. "Reminds me of standing on top of El Capitan, a big rock I once climbed in one of the most picturesque valleys you've ever seen. One day, I'll take you there."

Could that ever happen? Could they go together to scenic places, share experiences beyond this one, plan a future not darkened by war? They could if she succeeded in funding victory for Eritrea. With victory would come the freedom, at last, to be normal.

It all depended on what lay inside this mesa.

"By the way, have you noticed the chisel marks?" David got down on his hands and knees at the very edge. "I saw them when we first entered the canyon."

Kneeling beside him, she stretched her neck over the precipice. Sure enough, long, vertical gouges scored the rock face.

David rubbed a hand over them, leaning forward far enough that she could see his chest through the open neck of his white dress shirt, the shirt he'd put on two days ago in Hurghada after they'd made love in the Red Sea. The shirt was now stained with sweat, his hair disheveled and dusty. Two days' growth of beard matched the feral tang rising from his body.

Rika moistened her lips, regretting again their missed opportunity behind the rock.

"How 'bout a hand here?" Blue shouted.

In their absence, he had unloaded the camping gear. Now, together, they arranged the cots as three sides of a square, the Land Cruiser forming the fourth. David and Blue set up the stove and lanterns. Rika cut in half the two watermelons they'd bought in Aswan and propped them in the shade under her cot, for later.

After a lunch of canned beef, oranges, and Egyptian bread that had gone hard, they drove down the way they'd come up, a less harrowing experience now that the tires had grooved a route in the talus.

When they climbed out at the trapezoidal rock where they'd left the landmines, Blue said, "We've only got eleven of these things. You sure you wanna use four of 'em right off the bat?"

"The small ones. We'll save the two big ones for later." David turned to Rika. "How powerful are the small ones?"

She thought back to disarmament training. The MON-100, about ten inches in diameter and three inches thick, contained four hundred pieces of chopped steel rod propelled by ... "Two kilograms of TNT. Effective to one hundred meters."

"Two kilos." David rubbed his jaw, his fingers rasping over the stubble. "So two mines would be about nine pounds of TNT. I guess we could try that."

"Let's get the wire ready first," she said. To guard against the possibility of a static spark, she wanted to be sure the ends nearest the Land Cruiser were well-splayed before she attached the other ends to the fuses.

They spooled out and cut off two lengths running from the top of the wedge to the Land Cruiser, then trekked back up the slope, David and Blue each cradling a mine while Rika brought the fuses. No one spoke. The muted clomp of boots on rock reminded her of midnight forays into enemy territory. As they climbed, she tried to reassure herself that landmines were rugged, simple, designed to be set by frightened soldiers under fire.

They were not, however, foolproof.

At the mouth of the first crevice, Blue laid his mine gently on the rocks and stepped back. "Am I the only one who's spooked by this shit?"

"I think we all are." Now that the moment to arm them was at hand, Rika's stomach knotted. Crucial factors lay beyond her control. A careless worker on the Soviet assembly line, internal corrosion she couldn't see. "You two wait for me at the Land Cruiser."

"Like hell," David said.

"This is no time for bravado." She knew too many people who

hobbled around dangling half a thigh. One man, about to be married, had been carried back without his leg and with nothing but gore where his genitals had been. Others might as well have been buried in cigar boxes, for all the pieces anyone found. "There's nothing for you to do here. *I'm* the one who knows how to set them."

"I'm not leaving you," David insisted.

Stubborn bastard. But if their roles were reversed, she'd want to stay, too—undercover nearby, so she could get to him quickly in case of an accident. She pointed to the wedge. "Get down behind that."

David's jaw muscles pulsed like blood vessels. Finally, he edged past her, said "Come on" to Blue, and took a position where only his head showed above the wedge.

Once Blue had joined him, Rika knelt beside the first mine and wiped her hands on her jeans. Sweat was salt water, and salt water was electrically conductive. With narrowed vision, as if sighting through a sniper scope, she screwed a fuse into the concave "front" face of the mine, then twisted together the bared ends of the two black-coated wires running down the slope and attached the twisted ends to the fuse.

After wiping her hands again, she carried the mine into the crevice, pushed it as far as it would go into the darkest recess, and backed out, careful not to step on the wires.

So far, so good.

She picked her way across scree to the second mine. This one looked almost new, its olive-drab paint still shiny in the sun. With slightly more confidence now that she'd done it before, she screwed in the fuse, attached the wires, and again set the mine as deeply as she could into the crevice.

Fifteen minutes later, they all stood behind the Land Cruiser where the spare car battery lay on the ground. Rika wound the two pairs of wires into one pair and wrapped one of these around the battery's negative pole. Holding the other in her hand, she turned to David and Blue. "Ready?"

David held up a hand, his fingers crossed.

With a final glance at the black strands snaking twenty meters up the slope, Rika touched the wire to the positive pole.

A concussion shook the ground. Flying debris shot out of the rock face.

"Get down," she shouted. Bits of rock pelted her back. She heard tit-tatting on the Land Cruiser like rain on a corrugated-iron roof. Then it was quiet. Rika raised her head to see dust still swirling in the air.

David leapt to his feet and charged up the slope. But when she and Blue caught up with him, he was sitting slump-shouldered on a boulder.

"What's wrong?" she asked.

"We only made ten feet. If that."

Chapter 30

In the front passenger seat, Major Hassam swore he'd never requisition another American-made vehicle. Only nine hours on the highway running south along the Nile, and already they'd had to stop twice to slake the van's thirst for petrol. Its sloppy suspension threatened to roll them on every curve. And about an hour ago, the air conditioning had wheezed its last. Since then, late afternoon sun had been frying him through his open window.

Fortunately, at Nag Hammadi the highway turned east over a bridge spanning the river. With the sun now behind them, Hassam relaxed a little. At least the seat was comfortable.

Even better, Samir had concluded his latest professorial monologue, something about a bunch of old books found in the white cliffs flanking Nag Hammadi. So what if the books said Jesus had a mistress and a twin brother? If Christians wanted to kill each other over that sort of thing, let them.

Thankfully, Hagazy Masud and Corporal Malik kept their erudite thoughts to themselves. The boy seesawed in and out of sleep as his system processed last night's sedative and this morning's antidote. Malik, in that suit coat he never took off, kept both hands on the wheel and stared dead ahead with his one good eye.

The highway, crowded with trucks, cars, and buses, wound east along a lightly populated stretch of the Nile. A few farm shacks of plastered brick sat back from the road among fields of cotton, beans, and sweet-scented cantaloupe. Ahead in the distance, brown smoke hung low over sugarcane fields set alight before harvest.

Bounty of the Nile, Egypt's ancient but everlasting heart.

He felt a sudden longing to stroll again along the paths of the village where he'd grown up. Smell the cooking fires, bathe in the river, watch his father at the loom.

But his father was dead. As lifeless and skeletal as Egypt would be if Teferi's fundamentalist masters ever gained control.

Hassam probed a finger into his packet of Marlboros. Empty. He crumpled the pack and threw it out the window. "Samir, reach into my—"

Pop! Hiss. Steam shot up in front of them, turning dirt on the windshield into yellow mud.

Malik jammed the brakes. Behind them, tires screeched. A horn blared.

"Pull over," Hassam yelled. As the van halted on the verge, he threw open his door and got out. White steam billowed from the engine compartment. It stank of rubber. Fucking radiator. "Malik, open the hood. Samir, find the toolbox."

How far had they traveled from Nag Hammadi? Had to be at least ten kilometers. Hassam got back into his seat and opened the glove box, looking for a map. Owner's manual, registration, a folded piece of pink paper. Hassam unfolded the paper. Recall notice? He scanned down to the summary.

> EXTREME OPERATING CONDITIONS COULD CAUSE PREMATURE DETERIORATION OF HEATER HOSES OR ENGINE BYPASS HOSES. ENGINE COOLANT COULD DISCHARGE ONTO ENGINE AND ITS EXHAUST MANIFOLD CREATING POTENTIAL FOR A FIRE DUE TO HIGH EXHAUST MANIFOLD TEMPERATURES.

Hassam leaned out the door. "Malik, close that hood!"

As it slammed down, Hassam crushed the paper in his hand. That pig-fucker in Motor Pool. When he got back to Cairo, he'd put a bullet in the bastard's forehead. "Good morning, Chief Mechanic. Thank you for replacing the hoses." Boom!

"Sir," Samir called through the open back doors, "there's no toolbox."

#

To make herself useful, Rika spooled out and cut lengths of wire while David and Blue took turns with the jackhammer.

Although the first two mines hadn't excavated as deeply as David hoped, Blue had pointed out that they did fracture a lot of rock in place. The plan then became to dig out the broken material, detonate another mine, and repeat the process of alternating explosions with jackhammering. To conserve mines, they would work their way in through the larger crevice only.

Their work area sounded like a construction site, compressor roaring, jackhammer rattling. Limy dust hung in a haze. At its source within the larger crevice, David's back muscles rippled as he braced the hammer horizontally and leaned into it. Rock chips spewed out around him. A boot-sized chunk thudded to the ground. Blue shoveled it out, along with smaller bits of dislodged stone.

The rattling stopped, leaving an abrupt silence that made Rika's ears hum.

David lugged the jackhammer out of the crevice and let it drop from his hands. Sunglasses and a protective towel wrapped around his head gave him the appearance of a Palestinian gunman. With exhausted slowness, he pulled them off. "That's enough."

She handed him a canteen.

"I'll have another go," Blue said.

"I don't think you need to." David gulped from the canteen, then wiped his mouth with the back of his wrist. "We've made about five feet. Let's set another mine."

"You two rest," Rika said. "I'll set the mine." Then she noticed a bloodstain on the grimy chest of David's shirt, and a small hole just above it. "Let me see that."

He undid the buttons, revealing a fingernail-sized rock chip embedded in the skin below his collarbone.

"Hold still." With moves gained from extracting shrapnel on the battlefield, she pinched up the skin and plucked out the fragment.

"Ouch." David wiped away the blood.

"Go down to the Land Cruiser and clean this before it gets infected."

"Virgin rock is clean."

Probably. And so was desert air. But only a fool took unneeded risks. "Do it anyway. Blue, you go with him. It's getting late."

When they were gone, Rika dragged the jackhammer and compressor to a sheltered spot off to the side. The sun had dropped below the canyon's rim, leaving only a rosy glow of reflected light from the red cliffs surrounding her. It might be better to wait until morning, but David's and Blue's efforts deserved a payoff.

She screwed in the fuse, connected the wires, and picked up the mine. Weighing only five kilos, it was less burdensome than the problem of making her way into the crevice. She shuffled to keep from tripping. At the back, amid the flinty smell of broken rock, she found a narrow ledge, rough and raw from the jackhammer's chisel, and pushed the landmine as far as it would go into the space above the ledge. Then she followed the wires back down the slope.

At the Land Cruiser, she found David and Blue lounging against the front fender, sharing a beer. David sported a small, white bandage above chest muscles that gleamed in the fading light. For a second, she was embarrassed that her bite mark on his right shoulder was also visible, but if Blue had noticed it, he gave her no outward sign.

"Time to take cover," she announced.

They moved to the far side of the vehicle, where she wrapped one wire around the negative pole of the battery and touched the other wire to the positive.

Nothing.

She touched the wire again. A spark popped.

"What's wrong?" David asked.

She yanked the wires off and hurled them to the ground. "It's defective." What was the word? "A dud."

David tried the wires himself. "Shit."

"This is not good." Blue pulled on his beard, frowning. "Assuming the wire's okay, we've got either a crap fuse or explosive that's deteriorated with age. My bet's on the fuse."

"So we change it out," David said.

"Guess again, Wonderboy. If it's a faulty capacitor, just

touching the fuse could set it off." He turned to her. "Sorry, love, but nothing is worth blowing our own asses to smithereens. I think the party's over."

#

"Make a hose," Hassam shouted. He was not about to be put off by the only car-repair shop still open in Nag Hammadi. Especially after standing on the highway for almost an hour, eating dust and exhaust in hundred-degree heat, until he and Malik finally flagged down a ride. "Take one from another vehicle. I don't care. Just give me a replacement."

"As you can see, I have no vehicles to take one from." The scrawny simian who owned this one-bay grease pit held up the crudely severed hose Hassam had brought him. "And I have nothing this size. Perhaps, if I put in a request tomorrow morn—"

Hassam clamped his hand around the man's esophagus. "You will get me a new hose tonight. You will call everyone you know until you find one. Then you will drive us out there and fit it. If you fail, this gentleman with me ..." He cocked a thumb at Malik. "...will remove your eyes with the same knife that cut that hose. Do you understand?"

The garage owner fainted.

#

In camp that night, Rika forked the last of her tuna fish out of the tin. Wiping her mouth, she glanced at David, sitting next to her on one of the cots. He'd changed into a navy blue T-shirt. Blue, in the same khakis he'd worn since leaving Cairo, sat facing them on another cot across the circle of light cast by a Coleman lantern.

"That settles it. First thing in the morning, we'll set another mine." Rika wanted no further argument.

They'd been at it for hours, sometimes logically, sometimes heatedly. Shoot the mine with Blue's pistol. No clear shot. Use a rope to lower another mine from above. The first one was too far back in the crevice. Place a second mine close to the first. That was Rika's preference, but Blue had argued that a capacitor could discharge at any time. They'd wrapped an identical fuse in a rag, smashed it with a rock hammer, and found no capacitor, thus eliminating his fear. Still, Blue didn't trust the handiwork of their "East Bloc brethren." While Rika shared his misgivings, the alternative—walking away—was not open to discussion.

"Let's bag up our mess. A clean camp is a happy camp." Blue took a burlap sack from the back of the Land Cruiser and dropped in his beer bottles.

As he and David gathered other refuse, she retrieved the halved watermelons she'd placed under one of the cots. "Dessert."

David pulled a face. "Looks like they've spoiled."

"Oh, ye of little faith," Blue intoned. "This is a favorite Down Under. Cut away, fair lady."

She sliced off the upper few centimeters, removing the dried-out part of the fruit, then sectioned the remainder lengthwise and handed out the pieces.

When David took a bite, his eyes widened. "Christ, this is cold."

Blue winked at her and said to David. "Evaporative cooling, Mister Scientist."

"Makes my teeth ache."

"Eat it slowly," she said. "Remember, it comes from Paradise."

The frigid sweetness cleansed her mouth of the tuna's oily aftertaste and re-energized her batteries. When they'd dropped the rinds into Blue's burlap sack, she touched David's arm. "Let's go for a stroll."

Blue tossed the sack in his Land Cruiser. "You'll understand if I don't wait up."

She smiled at him and got a knowing smile in return.

Hand-in-hand, she and David walked toward the back of the mesa. The farther they got from camp, the more her senses seemed to sharpen. Away from the lantern, their path was lit by a three-quarter moon perched above the canyon rim behind them. Overhead, the Milky Way wrapped a gauzy belt across infinite blackness. Heat from the cliffs tempered the desert's chill and bore the crystalline scent of rocks ancient beyond fathoming. She could almost taste the purity of the air.

David drew her to a stop. Gently he cradled her face in his

palms and kissed her, a long kiss that melted away everything but just the two of them.

Still kissing him, she slid her hands under his T-shirt and up his back. She dug her nails in and felt his muscles tighten.

With a low moan, he clutched her hair and kissed her harder.

She raised his T-shirt. When he lifted his arms, she pulled the shirt over his head and off. Then she stood back and unbuttoned her blouse.

David slipped it from her shoulders. "You're so beautiful," he breathed. His fingertips brushed over her, circling her breasts, raising goose bumps as they closed in on her nipples.

God, she wanted him. But not this close to camp. She pointed toward the rear of the mesa. "Back there."

He grabbed her hand and hurried her across the pebbly surface.

She thought they'd gone far enough when something strange caught her eye. A large circle on the ground, ten meters ahead of them. "What's that?"

"Who cares." David steered her to the left.

"Wait." There was something familiar about it.

"Rika."

"I've got it." The black dot she'd found on David's photos in Khartoum, the dot Blue had said was a pit. She pulled her hand from David's. A dozen quick strides took her to the circle, a shallow hole really, about five meters across. Filled with …

Kneeling at its edge, she leaned over and scooped up a handful of sand. Sand? Up here?

She felt David's body heat close behind her. "This is the circular pit," she said. "The one we saw on your photos."

"It can wait." He took her elbows and raised her to her feet.

He was right. Distractions were the last thing she wanted. The warmth of his arms wrapping her made the pit fade away. Only the two of them remained, about to make love. She closed her eyes and leaned back against him, skin on hot skin.

Nuzzling her neck, he cupped one of her breasts and slid his other hand slowly down her stomach, inside her jeans, under the waistband of her panties, and—

A gunshot shattered the silence.

Chapter 31

Rika yanked David to the ground. From the sound of the shot, she judged large bore, short barrel. Blue's black-powder .44. Could he have fired at an animal? Loosening her grip on David's wrist, she craned her neck.

"To the right of the Land Cruiser," he whispered.

She saw them, dark shapes, barely visible outside the lantern's corona. Blue holding his pistol, facing several cloaked figures. There'd been no return fire, so the intruders probably weren't armed, at least with guns.

David rose to one knee. "Come on. He may need help."

"Wait." So far it was a standoff. The intruders held numerical advantage, but Blue had the pistol. "Let's circle around to their flank. Keep the element of surprise. If Blue can't handle them, we'll rush them from the side."

"There's no cover for a stealthy approach." He looked around. "Unless we can get to the edge and crawl along there."

Her thought precisely. "Put your shirt on. The dark blue will help camouflage your skin."

"What about you? Your blouse is white."

She wadded it up and shoved it down the back of her jeans.

"That'll drop 'em to their knees," he said.

This was no time for a joke. But then it occurred to her that he might not be joking. If the intruders were Muslim and she had to confront them, the shock value of a half-naked woman would buy precious seconds of distraction.

Crouching low, she and David made a wide arc around the

south side of the mesa. Erosion had carved small gullies in the edge, some of which had eaten back into the top, scoring the ground with shallow furrows like marks from a dull claw. She slipped into one of these and flattened herself, the hard grit rasping her bare breasts.

David stretched out beside her.

She heard a high-pitched voice, followed by rattling like beads in a wooden box.

"Take your fucking voodoo," Blue snarled, "and shove it up your ass."

David held up six fingers.

The same number of intruders she had counted. Black men wearing black robes. One held a staff with a gourd tied to the top, probably the rattle she'd heard. The other five carried longbows. She zeroed in on the bows. A chest from Tutankhamun's tomb showed the young king on a chariot shooting a bow of the exact same design.

She whispered, "We have to get closer."

They crawled to the next depression and crabbed to a position behind the intruders and to their left.

Blue's eyes flicked toward them for an instant. Almost imperceptibly, he raised an index finger, apparently signaling he could deal with this.

If he could, it was wisest to stay concealed and not unbalance the situation. If he couldn't, she and David were less than twenty meters away.

In a sweeping gesture, the man with the staff waved it over the mesa. "Sacred place."

At least that's what he'd said if he was speaking Bedouin. Rika knew only the basics of the language and couldn't be sure. She tuned her ears as the man raised his arms to the heavens and intoned something that might have been a prayer or a curse. Yes, bits of Bedouin and bits of Arabic. But mostly something else. The "something else" had a vaguely familiar ring, like disconnected notes from an old song. Then a string of syllables jolted her. She couldn't believe it. Was that ancient Egyptian?

No one knew precisely how to pronounce it. But scholars related it to the Semitic family, which included Tigrinya, her native tongue. She listened harder. It had to be. In less than a minute she picked out "guardians" and "goddess" and "all generations."

"… Sadjedju …"

Her breath caught. Never had she heard that word spoken, except by herself. And the only place she'd ever seen it written was in Tiye's papyrus. Suddenly the fragments of Rika's understanding came together. "These are descendents of the people who built Tiye's tomb."

David stared at her with the same shock she felt. "After three thousand years?"

The man with the staff drew something shiny from the neck of his robe. He held it up to Blue like a priest brandishing a crucifix at the devil.

Gold. No mistaking the luster. A rectangular pendant, larger than Blue's hand, on a thick gold chain. Moonlight glinted off finely worked surfaces and inlaid stones. Although she couldn't be positive from this angle, she could almost swear it was Egyptian.

"I'll give you one last chance." Blue leveled his pistol. "Haul your asses outta here, right now, or I'll blow you to hell."

Rika tensed.

"He won't do it," David whispered.

There was no predicting what armed adversaries facing each other might do. Especially if neither understood what the other was saying. She braced to spring.

The man with the staff raised it, and she almost leapt. But he only shook the staff, as if the rattling gourd would cast a spell. Then he whirled around and stalked off. The other five followed him over the rim of the mesa.

Rika lay there, too relieved to move, the words of the papyrus sounding in her ears. *Faithful men of Sadjedju.* Incredible. Generation upon generation devotedly protecting their goddess. A duty passed down for thousands of years. And with it, surely, stories of the great queen born of their own Nubian blood. Narratives, anecdotes. An oral tradition rooted in the eyewitness accounts of their distant forebears.

A unique trove of priceless knowledge. Rika had to have it. She sprang to her feet and called out, "Wait!"

David grabbed her from behind. "What're you doing?"

"I have to talk to them." She twisted to free herself, but he held her tightly.

"Rika, we just averted bloodshed. If you go after them now, there's no telling what might happen."

"Let go of me!" She was about to stomp his instep when David lifted her off her feet.

Arms still around her, he spun to face the opposite direction, then set her down. "You can't do this."

The instant his grip slackened, she tore herself free and sprinted to the edge of the mesa. No sign of them. She ran to the front of the mesa. Nothing. The men from Sadjedju had vanished.

"Come back," she yelled in Tigrinya. But there was no response, no movement she could detect in the moonlit canyon. She'd lost them. And with them, something else she couldn't quite identify, something that made her heart ache with longing. More than just a link to history, a link to part of herself.

On the precipice above the landslide, she peered into the night. A faint breeze ruffled her hair, like the passing of ghosts.

#

David woke to the sound of an engine starting. *What the hell?* He fought his way out of the sleeping bag into freezing air. In pre-dawn twilight, he saw the Land Cruiser rolling out of camp, with Rika at the wheel.

"Blue, get up." David pulled on his boots. No time for shirt or trousers.

"What's wrong? Is it the blackrobes?"

David charged after the Land Cruiser, his boots clomping, their untied laces whipping his calves. He caught up as Rika was easing the front wheels over the edge of the mesa. With both hands, he latched onto the open windowsill, sidestepping to stay with her. "Where are you going?"

She jerked the wheel right, throwing him off.

David stumbled to a halt, helpless to stop her as the Land Cruiser angled down the mesa, its brake lights flashing sporadically like angry eyes. On the valley floor, she accelerated, upshifted, and disappeared in a rooster tail of dust.

Blue trotted up to him in boxer shorts and flip-flops. "Who's in my truck?" he panted, fury bulging his eyes.

"Rika."

"Rika?" He rubbed his face, apparently relieved. "I thought it was bandits. Where the hell is she going?"

David could think of only one possibility. "Probably to look for the blackrobes, as you call them."

"I hope you're wrong." Blue turned toward the gap, the break in the cliffs, where the distant revving engine sounded Rika's impatience with maneuvering around the boulders. "Those blokes are crazy in the eyes. We're lucky they bought my bluff."

"That's what I tried to tell her last night." She'd stormed into camp, blouse on but misbuttoned. When he intercepted her, she snapped, "Don't touch me," then snatched up her cot and carried it to the back of the mesa. After he and Blue decided they should sleep in shifts, so someone always stood guard with the pistol, he ventured back to tell her and received a look of interest that he thought signaled truce. But she'd dashed that hope with, "I'll take the three-to-six watch. Now leave."

In retrospect, he was sure her look of interest actually came from realizing he'd unwittingly given her a chance to sneak out of camp while he and Blue slept. It hurt to think she'd felt compelled to do it on the sly.

"You did the right thing, stopping her last night." Blue scratched his cheeks through his beard. "I suggest we break camp and be ready to leave as soon as she gets back."

"Like hell. We're just getting started."

"No point. The dingoes have already feasted."

David rubbed his arms to ward off the morning chill. "What are you talking about?"

"Didn't you notice that bauble our witchdoctor flashed? Egyptian, and old as Moses. You suppose he found it fossicking around in the dirt?"

Oh, no. "You think the blackrobes found a way into the tomb?"

"The penny drops."

But if there was an entrance somewhere, a fissure in the side they hadn't noticed during their scouting drive, he and Blue could find it on foot. "Come on. We have to do a better reconnaissance."

"You're daft. The tomb's empty."

Possibly. But Rika could still study the wall paintings. And he'd get the proof he needed that ground-penetrating radar had practical applications. Dramatic proof he could parlay into commercial contracts, R and D money, and a resurgent career. "Humor me."

By nine o'clock, they'd tramped the entire perimeter of the mesa, Blue playing sentinel with his pistol while David slogged up the scree and scaled near-vertical rock faces to check shadows that never panned out. Lots of cracks and crevices, but not one of them deeper than six or eight feet.

Now, with three hours wasted, David had grit in his boots and down the back of his pants. Sweat had caked a layer of grime to his body. And physical exertion had done nothing to alleviate the low-grade queasiness he'd been trying to swallow away since Rika left camp. He glanced at the gap in the brick-red cliffs. Still no sign of her. "We're going back to Plan A."

"Excuse me, cowboy, have you forgotten the blackrobes?"

"You scared them off once. We can do it again."

Blue pulled on his beard. "I don't know. There could be more where those came from. And even if not, three of us can't hold 'em at bay forever without somebody getting hurt."

"That's why we've gotta work fast."

When they reached the slope at the base of their worksite, David hefted one of their two big mines, the ones Rika called tank killers. "Grab a small one," he told Blue.

"Whoa. Two mines?"

"We need more explosive. And since the big mines don't have electrical fuses, we'll use a small mine to set off this one. Kind of like the atomic bomb used to detonate a hydrogen bomb." Too much was at stake to keep pussyfooting around. "We're gonna blow the shit out of that fissure."

#

The frontier checkpoint, a tiny cinderblock building above which the Egyptian flag hung limply, stood in a wasteland of rocky desert that was already sweltering in midmorning sun. Hassam eyed the two soldiers outside the driver's door, then leaned across Malik, extending his State Security identification card.

The nearer one gaped. "Secret Police." Both soldiers snapped to attention.

Gratified, Hassam slipped the card back in his wallet. "We're on a classified mission. So far as you're concerned, we have not been here. Do you understand?"

"Yes, sir," they barked in unison.

Their disheveled uniforms gave Hassam an idea to ensure silence. He narrowed his eyes. "Have you two been buggering each other?"

Terror twisted the men's faces. "N-no, sir."

"That's a hanging offense." Hassam let them sweat for few a seconds. "I'm going to check on you when I come back. Malik, drive on."

Ten minutes later, they came to a rusted signpost marking Egypt's otherwise invisible border with the Sudan. Beyond it, the tarmac deteriorated into an obstacle course of potholes.

Hassam couldn't help smiling. Here, he was one hundred percent illegal but totally in command. He could smell his quarry, feel the plush carpet of the corner office under his feet, taste the dates served on silver trays by naked girls at his poolside.

Only one more hurdle, and he knew exactly how to clear it.

"Stop," he told Malik. He twisted around to address Samir and Hagazy Masud. "When we reach the Sudanese outpost, you will keep your hands open and in plain sight. You will say nothing."

The boy cowered back next to the door, his chin quivering.

"Sir," Samir bleated, "I forgot my passport."

And I tapped you for your brains. Hassam laid his pistol in his lap and covered it with his jacket. "Lucky for you, we won't need it."

Two miles farther south, a tan-colored tent, bleached almost white, appeared like a wart on the scabby landscape. The road narrowed to one rutted lane blocked by a pair of battered oil drums. In front of the tent, a black soldier waved them down.

As Malik slowed to a stop, a second soldier emerged from the tent, his shirt unbuttoned, an old Enfield rifle slung carelessly over his shoulder. Unshaven, he shambled around to Hassam's side.

The first one scowled at them through Malik's open window. "Egyptian?"

"Diplomats," Hassam said, reaching under his jacket. "Here are our documents."

He pulled out his pistol, shot the man in the face, then turned and shot the one by his door at point-blank range.

Hagazy Masud screamed hysterically. Samir gaped, eyes bulging, palms pressed to the sides of his head. Malik arched his eyebrows as though he'd just learned an astonishing bit of news.

Good. Let them all understand that the constraints of civilization no longer applied. He got out of the van and fired another round into each soldier's forehead. "Malik, drag them into the tent. Samir, roll back those barrels."

Inside the tent, Hassam found two canvas cots, a single-burner camp stove, blackened pots encrusted with something brown, old newspapers, a German girlie magazine, and a field radio. He pumped two rounds into the radio.

Raising the barrel to his nose, he inhaled the gun smoke. For a moment, he closed his eyes, relishing the sulfurous sting in his nostrils and the metallic taste the odor produced on his tongue. He felt a heady sense of supremacy, like the time he'd tried opium. Only better.

#

At nine-thirty in the morning, Rika ploughed through the roadside berm, still as dejected as she'd been when she finally gave up on Seddenga. Nothing but ruins, and poor at that. One standing column, some mounds of rubble, a few palm trees where there'd probably been a ceremonial lake in Tiye's time. Worse, she'd neither seen nor smelled any smoke from dawn cooking fires. She'd run the Land Cruiser up every gully and wash along the whole six-kilometer stretch of cliffs between Seddenga and here. All dead ends.

As she bounced toward the gap, she scanned the red cliffs on either side but saw no place a man could even squeeze through. That left only one possible explanation for the rapid disappearance of the Seddengans—they lived somewhere behind the cliffs, perhaps in another valley, with a connecting pathway hidden in the craggy walls of the tomb's canyon. David's photos might show the valley, maybe even the pathway.

But then what? During her search this morning, she'd suddenly realized that her anger at David last night, her thirst for the Seddengans' knowledge, had blinded her to the fact that these people still worshipped Tiye. What could she possibly say to them when she was about to "desecrate" their deity's tomb? She'd sought solace in the dictum of the greater good, that the few must sacrifice for the many. But try telling that to the few, especially when guilt stuck in your throat like unchewed meat.

In the shadowed confines of the gap, cooler air came in through her window, soothing her slightly. Much as she hated to miss such an opportunity, maybe it was best, after all, to avoid further contact with the Seddengans.

At the end of the gap, she halted to survey the mesa. David and Blue were probably waiting for her at the work area, where setting up for the next blast was going to be tricky with a dud wedged in that crevice. Easing around to the right, she saw them crouched behind the big trapezoidal rock.

A shockwave walloped the Land Cruiser. Rika hit the brakes as the hill face in front of her erupted like a broadside of cannon. Rocks fired out in fanning arcs through a roiling cloud of dust and debris. The cloud tumbled down the slope, showering dirt and sand in all directions.

She sat there, unable to tear her eyes away. The site was so thoroughly demolished it was difficult to recognize. Then a second rumble. Not like rock falling. More like the whoosh of retreating surf.

When David and Blue stood, she accelerated toward them, skidded to a stop, and jumped out of the Land Cruiser.

David jogged up to her.

"What have you done?" she demanded.

He beamed. "You're just in time to find out."

"Mornin', love." Blue cocked a thumb over his shoulder. "Welcome to the big bang."

"We set two new mines," David said, "one of them a tank killer."

"Three altogether?" Rika shuddered. "That much explosive could destroy an office building."

"Or get us half way into the tomb. Come on, let's see." He took off up the slope.

Nerves taut as bowstrings, Rika dashed after him, skirting the mishmash of sharp-edged, unstable rocks that now littered the route they'd established yesterday. As she neared their worksite, Blue's boots thumping behind her, the cordite smell of spent explosive filled her nose. Dust hung heavily in the air, but through the haze she could make out a mound of rubble.

Rika's fingers went cold. Near as she could tell, David had blown out about five meters of rock, which had filled in with four meters of rock from above. Some of the fallen boulders would take a crane to move. Her spirit drained out of her, like blood from a mortal wound. Eritrea, Tiye, everything that mattered had been blasted to hell. She sat down and put her head in her hands.

"God dammit." David's voice came to her through a tunnel with no light at the end.

At a loss for what to do now, she stood and trudged down the slope. A few minutes later, as she leaned against the far side of the Land Cruiser staring at the dirt, she heard the driver's door open.

"We're gonna go up and make breakfast," Blue said, his tone despondent.

David's boots intruded into her peripheral vision. She got in the rear seat and shut the door.

When they reached camp, she climbed out and plodded toward the back of the mesa where she'd left her cot beside that sand-filled ring. Late morning sun burned down on her. Her head ached as if someone pinched it in iron tongs.

High above, a vulture circled against the colorless sky. Nekhbet, the guardian. With little effort, Rika could imagine the goddess laughing at her.

When she dropped her eyes to the ground again, Rika halted. The circular pit looked deeper. She walked over to the edge, and her breath caught. The sand was gone. In its place was a vertical shaft ringed by stone steps.

Hundreds of steps, spiraling down into darkness.

Chapter 32

Eighteenth Dynasty

The returning flotilla had just docked at Semna when Ay received the terrible news. Tutankhamun was dead.

Embalming procedures, which took seventy days, were already in progress. Hurried efforts were underway to prepare a tomb in the sacred valley west of the Amunite capital. It would have to be small, for there was no time to construct a more princely resting place. But work progressed rapidly.

Ay sent messengers ahead to postpone the tomb's sealing until Baketaten arrived. He doubled the men on the flotilla's oars and gave orders to cast off immediately. With a heavy heart, he then announced himself at Baketaten's door, stepped inside, and informed the princess in his gentlest voice.

She collapsed on her bed. "It cannot be," she wailed. "Not Tutankhaten."

Ay tried to console her but knew it was useless. As much as Tiye, Baketaten had mothered the boy, barely three years her junior. She had tickled him to stop his crying, held his hands as he wobbled his first steps, clapped joyfully when he managed to pronounce her name.

But much more was lost than a brother. Ay clamped his jaw as he rubbed Baketaten's back. Tiye's last great hope was gone at the age of eighteen, only nine years into what should have been a long and splendid reign. Worse, no successor from Tiye's line remained to replace him. The end of a glorious empire loomed, just when it had been poised to soar.

#

Within the tiny burial chamber, crowded with Amun priests, Ay stood at Baketaten's side, hoping his strength shielded her from the loathsome incantations. For the priests, insisting the king was of their fold, had demanded that the funeral be conducted in the traditional manner.

At the end of the ritual, the assembly withdrew to the treasury. There, Baketaten placed the electrum cylinder, containing Tiye's last message to her last son, on a table of other offerings. Next to it she laid a small wooden coffin inscribed with Tiye's name. "May mother and son rest together until the next life."

Then she wept, for there had been no time to commission a finer gift.

Ay wrapped an arm around her shoulders. "May I suggest that a lock of your own hair might be more fondly appreciated than a golden statue or an alabaster boat?"

Baketaten looked up at him, gladness sparkling behind her tears. "It is no wonder Our Mother cherished you."

Touched by her words, Ay offered his dagger.

She accepted it, cut a lock from her head, and laid the gift inside the small wooden coffin bearing Tiye's name. "That the bond among brother, sister, and mother shall remain unbroken through all eternity."

Chapter 33

Barely able to contain herself, Rika stood shoulder-to-shoulder with David and Blue at the mouth of the stairwell. "The papyrus says Tiye will return physically. This must be the way."

"You say the explosion opened it, but nothing looks damaged." David prowled part way around the rim. "The whole thing's cut from limestone. And the only fractures I see are natural."

"Remember, her architect was a 'master of stone and sand.' I think he built some mechanism she could operate from inside. It would have to be delicate because she was an old woman. And the mines tripped it. Did you hear that second rumble?"

"I did." Blue spoke in an unusually soft voice. "A sort of sucking sound. I thought it was a back draft from the explosion."

"It had to be the sand rushing out."

David leaned over the edge. "Some kind of trapdoor with a cavern underneath. A damned big cavern."

Big was right. With the sun not yet overhead, Rika couldn't see to the bottom. But the stairs she *could* see went down the equivalent of at least three stories.

Backing away from the edge, Blue said, "Remember what happened to Carnarvon and his mates when they dug up Tut."

She recalled David's mentioning that Blue was superstitious. "The mummy's curse is tabloid rubbish. But if you're afraid of it, you can wait up here."

Blue eyed her as if she'd offended his manhood. "Just thought I'd remind you. This is, after all, Tut's mother."

Rika needed no reminding. She felt drawn to the unseen depths of the stairwell and the woman beyond like iron to the invisible force of a magnet. And she wasn't waiting any longer. "We need lights."

"And your camera," David said. "I want pictures of this."

As they strode back toward camp, Blue mumbled, "Pictures may be all you get."

Rika halted. "What do you mean?"

"He thinks the pendant the headman was wearing had to come from the tomb." David recounted their morning of scouring the mesa for a hidden entrance.

She thought of how quickly the Seddengans had disappeared into the night and her conclusion that it could only have been through some hidden crevice in the canyon's cliffs. Had they also found an "invisible" crack into the tomb? Visions of plundered remains, rubble and shards, eddied through her mind.

"Look," David said, taking her arm, "it's senseless debating this. We're about to find out for ourselves."

After topping up the fuel in one of the lanterns and grabbing two flashlights and her camera, they returned to the stairwell.

David handed her a flashlight. "I think you should have the honor of going first."

She'd intended to, but was still touched by his thoughtfulness. She shoved the flashlight into her hip pocket and slung the camera around her neck. Then for a silent moment, she gazed into the shaft. Whatever else lay below, this was undoubtedly Tiye's final resting place. A frisson of excitement rippled through her. With a fortifying breath, she stepped over the edge.

David followed with the other flashlight, then Blue, carrying the lantern.

Rounded ridges carved in the stairs gave grip to her feet. But Tiye's architect had not wasted effort on non-essentials, for the cylindrical wall was roughly hewn. Sand fell occasionally from its undressed surface as Rika wound her way down in an anticlockwise spiral.

Behind and above her, the men's boots crunched. Glancing up, she noticed the stairs had wedged-shaped undersides that allowed passage beneath them, and it suddenly occurred to her that spiral staircases were unknown in ancient Egyptian construction. They were treading an engineering innovation.

As they descended below the sun's direct reach, the air grew cooler, more thickly suffused with the concrete smell of limestone. Like the caves in Eritrea. Like home. And as if she were going home, her palms dampened with the uncertainty of what awaited.

David switched on his flashlight.

"Save it," Blue said. Above her on the opposite side of the shaft, a match flared. Gas hissed, and in a few seconds Blue had the twin mantles of the lantern glowing.

Overhead, the stairwell looked like the inside of an artillery barrel. Below, it disappeared into a black, gaping maw.

"Bottomless pit," Blue mumbled.

Rika reached out a hand to keep contact with the wall and started down again. Five minutes later—or maybe it was ten—she wasn't so sure that using the lantern was a good idea. Its cylinder of light encapsulated them, moved with them, creating a hypnotic sense of no progress. Endless stairs. Ceaseless circling. The constant cadence of crunching footfalls.

Her knee buckled. She caught herself as a hand grasped her collar.

"Steady," David said, his voice alarmed.

Regaining her footing, she realized she'd robotically stepped down where there was no step. The stairs had ended. She now stood on a small landing. Three meters below it, at the farthest reach of light from Blue's lantern, lay a broad cone of sand, the top of the column that once filled the shaft.

Rika switched on her flashlight and saw an alcove to her right. About a meter deep and twice as wide as her arm span, it ended at a stone wall that rose above eye level but not quite to the ceiling. On tiptoes, she shone her light through the opening. The ceiling inside was painted with the Sun Globe. "Oh, my God."

David let out a low whistle, his height advantage obviously affording him a view without needing to stretch. He laced his fingers into a stirrup. "Want a lift?"

Still holding the flashlight, she got an awkward grip on the top of the wall, stepped into his hands, and hoisted herself up onto her stomach. She was half-in and half-out of the opening, squirming for a stable position, when the wall shifted downward.

Panic seized her. She twisted around, trying to scramble off. But it kept dropping from under her, grinding rapidly down into the floor. David grabbed her waist, but she was falling so fast her descending weight must have pulled him off balance. She hit the bottom with him sprawled beside her, right where the wall had been.

"What happened?" Blue hollered from the stairwell.

David rolled onto his side and faced her. "Are you okay?"

Panting, she pushed herself up to hands and knees and pointed her flashlight down. The top of the wall lay flush with the floor. She aimed the beam through the opening and saw a black woman staring back at her.

Rika almost fainted. Then her senses returned, and with them, her breath. "A statue."

"What the ... ?" Blue's voice came from right behind her now.

She got to her feet and took his lantern. They stood at the entrance to a vestibule about three meters long. A spill of sand, presumably from the stairwell, spread over half the floor. Brilliant paintings covered the walls. On the two side walls, the paintings showed Tiye receiving gifts from a joyful populace. The principal gift on each side was represented by a shoebox-sized niche containing a squat replica of a temple column, one papyriform the other lotiform.

At the far end of the vestibule, a short flight of steps led down to the statue. Beyond the statue lay darkness.

She gazed at the lifelike image of Tiye, so real it sent shivers through her. This was her place, a sacred place. Although she felt foolish, Rika found herself silently asking Tiye's permission to enter. It was then she noticed that the queen's visage had been rendered in an expression of serene happiness.

Taking this as a welcome, Rika walked slowly to the end of the vestibule, raised the lantern, and gasped. Before her, reflecting light for the first time in three thousand years, stood the treasury of Queen Tiye. On all sides, in every direction, her possessions filled it. By lantern light, the room glittered like a star field.

"Holy God," David whispered.

"We must be bloody dreaming," Blue said.

Rika's hands trembled. "It's just as she left it."

Stacks of chests in all sizes, carved and gilded, inlaid with colored glass paste. Tables, chairs, footstools, all of ebony detailed in gold. A bed frame with twin stylized lions forming the posts and rails. Figurines in painted alabaster. Oil lamps of bronze and silver.

To the right lay a wooden model of a working farm and two large models of royal barges.

Along the back wall stood a phalanx of statues. Even at this distance, Rika recognized the likenesses of Tiye, her husband, and their children. Her heart swelled at the sight of so many family members.

In a corner by the statues, two royal thrones sparkled with gold and colored stones. She recalled Tiye's words to Tutankhamun: *You and I shall reign together.*

Rika felt tiny. Insignificant. Unworthy even to set eyes on this hallowed place.

"Come on," David said. "Let's see what we've got."

"Wait." His words had burst her reverie and brought to surface the academic within her. "I have to photograph it first, before we disturb anything."

She gave him the lantern and descended two steps to the floor of the treasury. The room smelled of dust and wood and stale air, like her office at the museum. Fine grit scraped underfoot as she approached the central statue of Tiye.

Michelangelo could not have sculpted a more realistic face. Yet it had an unearthly quality. The eyes. The whites of Tiye's eyes were rendered in gold. A creepy feeling slithered up Rika's back, a feeling that in spite of her imagined invitation from the queen, she really shouldn't be here.

Nonsense. If anyone deserved the right, she did.

She unslung her camera and was removing the lens cap when she noticed a hammer at the foot of the statue. Curious. She stooped to examine it. Shaped like a rubber mallet, it had an ebony handle and a head made of gold, obviously not a workman's tool. Possibly something ceremonial, a harbinger of other wonderfully unique things they would find.

With a tingle of anticipation, she raised her camera and photographed the statue. The flash set off sparklers in her eyes. She waited for her vision to clear. Then, with her back to the statue, she moved around it two steps at a time and took pictures of the room, closing her eyes before pressing the shutter button.

She'd come full circle and was framing her last shot, looking back at the vestibule, when she saw Aten. Stunned, she lowered her camera and stared.

"What's wrong?" David called.

Above the entry to the vestibule, affixed to the section of wall between there and the treasury's ceiling, hung a hemisphere of polished gold. She looked back at the golden whites of Tiye's eyes and felt a flush of pride at the perfect symbolism.

"Come in here," she said, "and look up behind you."

David and Blue descended the steps and turned around.

"Mother of Christ." Blue wiped a hand over his mouth. "That's gold."

"It's Aten, the Sun Globe," she told them. "And look at Tiye's eyes. They're lighted by Aten's radiance. And her posture. She's striding toward him as he lights her path and welcomes her return."

David reached up, rapped the hemisphere with a knuckle, and got a metallic thunk, as from an oil drum filled with fuel. "It's gotta weigh hundreds of pounds. We'll never get it out of here."

Rika cringed inside. That he would even entertain such an idea sickened her. Granted, all gods were bogus, but Aten—or Tiye's concept of Aten—lay at the very heart of everything the queen stood for. Separating them now was unthinkable.

Wasn't it?

She bit her lip. That much gold could equip several operating theaters, or buy an arsenal of Stinger rockets. But removing Aten would feel like ripping out her own heart.

She tasted blood and realized she'd chewed her lip too hard. Had she been wrong to believe her love of Eritrea and her devotion to Tiye could both be satisfied, or would loyalty to one mean betrayal of the other?

David pointed to the stacked chests. "Let's see what's in those."

Glad for a reprieve from her quandary, she chose a chest the size of a footlocker. Made of reddish wood and inlaid with ivory images of waterfowl, it stood on four short legs with silver caps.

The lid was stuck but yielded to light force with a cracking sound that made Rika wince until she realized it had only been stuck by age.

The scent of cedar wafted up to her. Inside, a garland of now-desiccated flowers lay atop two stacks of white cotton gowns. Rika slipped her hand under one of the necklines and could see her fingers through the sheer fabric. Though worn in everyday life, it would have looked and felt like a negligee.

Blue bent over her. "Think she hid anything underneath?"

"Of course not," Rika snapped. "Why would she? Everything here is hers."

"Don't bite my head off. I was just asking."

Surprised at her outburst, Rika softened her tone. "Tiye's belongings will be organized into groups of similar things. Clothing with clothing, jewelry with jewelry, and so on."

"Let's try this one." David patted the dusty top of an unadorned wooden box only a hand span high but at least a meter long.

Rika opened it and found six rows of *ushebti*, figurines glazed with blue-green faience. Handmaidens, scribes, musicians, dwarfs, beekeepers, and others she didn't immediately recognize. "These depict the servants who will attend Tiye in her next life."

She started to photograph them, but stopped. With only two rolls of film, she had to be selective.

"Food implements," David said.

She turned to see him fishing out platters and skewers from another chest. Her fists clenched, but she held her tongue. They'd been through this together, and he had as much right to open a chest as she did. Almost. So, why did she feel that his hands defiled while hers did not?

He held up two metal sieves.

"Drink strainers," she told him, forcing calm into her voice. "The copper one is a beer filter. Would you put them back?"

He narrowed his eyes. "Is something wrong?"

More weird than wrong. But how could she tell him? "We have more chests to look in."

"Too right," Blue said. "Let's get after it."

The one below the utensils was twice as large and carved with scenes of planting, irrigating, and harvest. Appropriately, it held food. Preserved meats, a mummified duck, triangular loaves of bread, small reed baskets of nuts, seeds, and dried fruits. Plus the carcasses of tiny, reddish-brown insects that must have hatched from eggs unknowingly entombed with the food.

Blue picked up the duck, grimaced, and dropped it back.

Bristling at his reaction, Rika said, "To Tiye, preserved food was just as important—"

"Jesus Christ." David waved a hand. "Bring that lantern here."

She saw he'd opened another box, ebony with a gold-painted column at each corner. On a tray inside lay two magnificent diadems, ceremonial headbands crafted from gold and inlaid with lapis lazuli and deep-red carnelian. One portrayed the vulture and cobra of Upper and Lower Egypt, the other a sun globe flanked by scarabs.

"Now we're talking." Blue, who'd apparently overcome his fears of a curse, set the lantern on a chest behind the jewelry case and bent down, hands on knees.

As Rika struggled to restrain herself, David lifted the tray, revealing beneath it a collar necklace made of long, thin strips of gold. Each strip ended in a tiny hand, and each hand held an *ankh*, the cross of life, carved from amethyst.

"The radiating hands of Aten." Rika had never seen a more exquisite piece of jewelry, not even in the Place Vendôme in Paris. She reached for it, but David got there first. Her fingers curled into talons.

Then he held it up in front of her. "Allow me." He hooked it around her neck.

Taken aback, she looked down at her chest. The golden arms fanned out like spokes in a perfect semicircle that ran from shoulder to shoulder. Absolutely stunning. "I don't do it justice."

"It's made for you." David reached for her camera and snapped her picture. "You look gorgeous."

She suppressed a temptation to take off her shirt and see the gold against her dark skin, as it must have looked on Tiye. To feel the metal on her flesh as Tiye had felt it.

"If you're laying claim to that one," Blue said, "then I'll have the vulture and cobra."

Rika's temper flashed. "Try it, and I'll break your arm."

Blue recoiled as if stung by a hornet. "Whoa, sweetheart. What's this about? You said ten percent for us."

Damn. Her mind must have blanked that out. Into the divided loyalties churning inside her she now had to mix the impulsive promise that got her here. But on this issue she would not bend. "No one is taking anything, until and unless I say so."

Blue rose to full height. "I don't recall that being part of our bargain."

Chapter 34

Lit from below by the lantern, Blue's ruddy countenance gave Rika the impression of a bearded ogre demanding toll. Well, he could demand all he wanted. "What happens to Tiye's possessions is my decision."

David stepped between them, facing Blue. "Calm down, will you?"

"Tell *her* that. I'm not the one welshing on our agreement."

"Look," David said, "there's tons of stuff here. Just give her a chance to sort through it all. We owe her that."

"If we're calling in debts, Romeo, you two owe *me* for getting your asses out of Egypt. Especially when *my* ass wasn't in a bind." Blue shot her a barbed glare over David's shoulder. "Besides, if we're going to sell it all anyway, what difference does it make if we take our shares in kind, instead of cash?"

Embarrassed that she couldn't answer that question logically, Rika turned away. To disperse what Tiye had accumulated, what Tiye valued most, seemed more morally corrupt than just taking it all. A hard lump rose in her throat. She couldn't help feeling this whole experience would leave scars.

She replaced the Aten-armed necklace, then blew dust off the next box and opened it. It brimmed with smaller pieces of jewelry arranged on partitioned trays. Earrings, toe rings, bracelets. Nailets that fit over the ends of the fingers. Beneath the lowest tray lay a pectoral pendant on a thick gold chain. When she lifted it out, she heard a sharp intake of breath behind her.

Wide-eyed, Blue said, "That's what I saw on the witchdoctor."

"Impossible." The pendant, as large as a man's hand and heavy as the lantern, was unlike anything she'd seen or heard of before. A garnet scarab supported not the traditional red sun, but the golden Sun Globe of Aten. Aten's hand-tipped rays, holding the *ankh* of life, reached down to touch two cartouches, each borne on the head of a turquoise cobra. "This shows a unique mixture of ancient symbolism and Tiye's faith. There's nothing else like it."

"I damn well know what I saw. Either this thing has a twin, or the blackrobes come in here to borrow stuff whenever it suits their fancy." Blue glanced warily around the room, his head turning in short, jerky motions. "Wish I hadn't left my gun up top."

David touched one of the cartouches. "These are names, right? Can you read them?"

Shining her flashlight on the pendant, Rika immediately identified the cartouche on the left. "This is Tiye." The other took her a couple of seconds. "This one's Ay, Tiye's brother. He became pharaoh after Tutankhamun."

"Maybe he had a duplicate pendant," David offered. "Maybe he's also buried around here, and the blackrobes found *his* tomb."

"Ay's tomb is in the Valley of the Kings." She paused to let the finality of this fact sink in, then drilled her eyes into Blue's. "You're mistaken."

"No, sister. You are." He stalked off toward the front of the treasury, stopped in front of Tiye's statue, and picked up the golden hammer, hefting it as if gauging its utility as a weapon.

In a lowered voice, David said, "You're being a little rough on him."

"He's wrong."

"We're not Egyptologists, dammit. If there's something we don't understand, just take a minute to explain it."

"I did."

He took a slow breath. "Look, we're all in this together. We need to get along."

"If he doesn't get over it in a few minutes, I'll go talk to him."

David looked in Blue's direction. "We'll both go."

Thankful to have that settled, Rika laid the pendant back in its tray and pointed to three trunk-sized chests covered in gold sheeting embossed with court scenes. Stacked one on top of the other, they rose nearly to eye level.

She and David gripped the top chest and lifted.

"Feels empty," David said. When they'd set it on the floor, he raised the lid. "Wigs?"

"Oh, my god." The one in conventional style was rare enough, but the other was quite possibly the only example in existence.

"This is the traditional kind," she said, lifting it from its ball-topped pedestal, "like you see in the monumental statue of her and her husband in the museum." A lavish cascade of straight, black hair hung down to cover chest and shoulders from a concealed wicker frame. Unfortunately, oils that would have given it luster had now hardened, making the hair feel coarse and stiff.

She put it back and reverently picked up the other, an oversized helmet of tight curls. "This one imitates Tiye's hair. The style became fashionable during her husband's reign. I can't believe I'm actually holding it."

"I bet it fits on this." David shoved the other two trunks out of the way and brushed dust off an ebony statue of a bald-headed, naked woman, about five feet tall, with ivory eyes.

"A dressing dummy." What a wonderful stroke of luck, for it would have been crafted as realistically as possible so Tiye could choose what to wear and know exactly how she would look. Rika broke into a smile. Now *she* could know, also. Eagerly she positioned the wig on the statue's head.

"Jesus." David's eyes flicked several times between her and the mannequin. "She looks like you."

A little, Rika supposed. The high cheekbones and narrow nose. And maybe the chin line and almond-shaped eyes. But she hoped their mouths were different. Tiye's was unflattering, its corners turned down in an aspect of melancholy that Rika found discomforting. She'd always pictured the woman as fiery, indomitable. Perhaps Tiye somehow knew that her revolution was doomed without her.

On the verge of extrapolating that thought too far, Rika removed the wig from the dummy's head. As she knelt to replace it in the chest, an eerie feeling came over her. Would this have been made from Tiye's hair? She pressed her nose to the soft curls and inhaled a faint, tallow scent of soap made from animal fat. Like the homemade shampoo she'd used in Eritrea. Her fingers tingled. That's what was eerie—a ghostly sense that the hair in her hands was not Tiye's, but her own. With a shudder, she shut the lid.

Turning to the two similar trunks that this one had rested on, she said, "These should also have ceremonial items."

In one, they found a woolen robe the color of pomegranates and pleated gowns of white linen threaded with gold. Atop the garments lay a gold-handled flywhisk and an ivory-handled fan set with ostrich down.

The other held cotton gowns, red sash-belts, and six pairs of leather sandals decorated with iridescent mother-of-pearl and tiny faience beads. Rika turned over a pair of sandals. Judging from the soles, Tiye had never worn them. They were meant for a future that never came. With a twinge of sorrow, she put them back.

"It's overwhelming," David said. "And there's so much left to open. Blue, come on and help us."

"Sod off." He sat on the steps to the vestibule, his elbows on his thighs.

To her, David said, "You've gotta go sort this out. Just give him a break, okay?"

"You sort him out. He's your friend."

"Rika, he's been a damn good friend to both of us."

"He's acting like a child."

"What the hell's wrong with you? Oh, screw it. I'll go."

As David walked away, Rika felt unleashed, free now to explore without pausing to explain.

One by one, she unveiled the queen's belongings, feasting her eyes on the things Tiye held dear. Frankincense, probably from northeastern Somalia, the biblical land of Punt. More jewelry. Decorative jars of polished onyx, calcite bowls as thin as paper.

She heard David say, "Look, man," and immediately tuned him out.

In a wooden box pin-pricked with insect holes, she found a library of rolled papyruses. Her heart leapt. Here was the real treasure. Partly nibbled-on but reparable by a competent restorer, these scrolls would contain the writings that were most important to Tiye. Possibly records of her philosophy and how it developed, proclamations by which it was conveyed to the people, the means by which Tiye countered protests from the priests and other naysayers. Carefully she replaced the lid.

Another box held cuneiform tablets, probably correspondence from Egypt's allies. The Louvre would swoon over such an archive. Perhaps she could trade it to them for an agreement to help build a national museum in Eritrea. Her mother would like that.

For Tiye's own scribes, there were two sets of writing implements—jars of soot and red ochre, sea reeds for writing, scrapers of fine-grained sandstone for erasing mistakes, and ivory smoothers for restoring the roughened surface to a non-absorbent finish.

For the musicians who would entertain her, she had lyres, sistra, trumpets, and castanets.

There were stores of powders, herbs, and what had once been pastes. Some, like the silvery powdered antimony, were medicines. Others Rika recognized as aphrodisiacs, such as persea, which Egyptians considered the fruit of love. Had Tiye needed such stimulants or just enjoyed them once in a while? Perhaps giving birth to at least eight children had taken a toll. In any case, that she possessed them after her husband's death suggested her love life hadn't perished with him. Rika was glad.

Blue's voice intruded on her consciousness with something about the "blackrobes" and "bad-ass motherfuckers." Some people had one-track minds.

Turning back to Tiye's possessions, Rika opened a small ebony box and did a double-take. It held two honey-colored cones of perfumed fat so exceedingly rare that she'd only read about them. Worn on the head by nobility during festive occasions, the wax would slowly melt from body heat and cover the person with a scent that masked the odor of perspiration. Rika scraped off a tiny bit with her fingernail and held it to her nose. Sandalwood. Like the wig that imitated Tiye's hair, these cones belonged in a museum.

Rika closed the lid, swept her flashlight's beam over the other boxes, and stopped at an ivory case beautifully engraved with scenes of waterfowl and bathing women. Tiye's toiletries. The centerpiece on the top tray was a hand mirror of polished silver, its ebony handle inlaid with red jasper and pink feldspar. Despite the tarnish, Rika could see her likeness. In the reflected light, her eyes seemed to take on a golden hue, like those in the big statue facing Aten. Probably just a combination of coloring from the tarnish and the fact that her eyes did have tiny, goldish flecks. But it gave the fascinating illusion that the face staring back at her was Tiye's.

"Are you okay?" David asked.

Rika took a breath. "Of course."

"You looked like you were in a trance."

"Her things affect me."

"So I've noticed." He touched her shoulder. "I didn't make much headway with Blue. You need to try."

"Later." Rika replaced the mirror and removed that tray. Beneath it she found alabaster jars with the desiccated remains of unguents and creams, a chalcedony dish of black kohl for darkening the eyelids, calcite perfume phials that still smelled of juniper, cinnamon, and civet. The deepest compartment held obsidian rouge dishes, combs made of seashell, silver tweezers, and a cleaver-shaped iron razor with a handle of carved antler.

Rika lifted the pieces lovingly, knowing somehow that, unlike the sandals, these were things Tiye had actually used. She was about to replace them when she noticed a plain wooden box in the bottom corner. She opened it and could hardly believe her eyes.

"Looks like little round sponges," David said over her shoulder. "For applying makeup?"

"No." She picked out one. "They're for contraception."

David squinted skeptically. "I thought she was in her sixties. Isn't that a bit optimistic?"

"Not if you expect to be rejuvenated, as well as reborn." Rika held up the sponge. "This is the most powerful statement Tiye could possibly make to affirm her belief. She expected to be capable of childbearing."

Rika laid the sponge in its box and put everything back in place. What she wouldn't give to spend just an hour speaking with this incredible woman. Then a realization kicked her. She'd opened dozens of chests, found hundreds of the queen's things, but where was Tiye?

Using her flashlight, Rika scanned the walls of the treasury. In most tombs she knew of, the burial chamber was concealed behind a bricked-up doorway plastered over to look like a wall. Would Tiye's architect have resorted to this ineffectual technique?

The walls looked solid until she ran the beam along the statues in the back. It disappeared between two of them. "There!"

"There what?"

"The burial chamber." With David close behind, she slipped through the stone phalanx of Tiye's family members to find a flight of stairs ascending to the right. She climbed about twenty steps and stopped. On a landing, just before the stairs turned left, there was a window-like hole at chest height in the left wall. It opened into a rough-hewn room about three meters square and half-filled with sand. Even stranger, a black rod rose out of the sand and disappeared into the room's ceiling.

David held the lantern through the opening, furrowed his brow, then withdrew the lantern and edged past her to where the stairs turned. "Blocked."

"It can't be." Crowding in next to him, Rika saw a wall of rock five steps up the passage. No, not a solid wall, a stone block set in place. While its top fit flush to the ceiling, its bottom slanted downward to the left, and under its tilted base on the right-hand side more stairs were visible.

"Hang on." David's eyes flashed in the lantern light. Then he grinned. "Clever."

"Clever?"

"It's like a sliding bolt lock. That block's on an incline and goes through the wall into the room next door. The sand is what's holding it in place." He stepped back and pointed through the window. "See the sand pushed up by the leading edge?"

How could she have missed it? The sand held the stone and, "The rod holds the sand. Like the little boy in Holland with his finger in the dam."

David shook his head. "This place is more like a machine than a tomb."

A machine Tiye would have had to operate. How? Rika hoisted herself onto the ledge.

David grabbed her elbow. "What are you doing?"

"I'm going to pull out the rod."

"You're not thinking. If that rod releases the sand—"

"I'm going." She climbed through the opening, tested her weight on the sand, and duck-walked to the rod in the center. Planting her feet on either side, she pulled with both hands. It wouldn't budge. Something must be holding it in the chamber above them. Something Tiye could have moved or unlatched to come down. But she and David were going up, the opposite direction to what the architect had planned.

So, what now?

On her rump, Rika scooted around to the back wall. Bracing her hands against the wall, she put both feet on the rod, and pushed. It bowed slightly, then snapped.

The top part of the rod now dangled from the ceiling. The stump projected just enough above the sand to get a grip. This time when Rika pulled, it moved easily. She drew it hand-over-hand until it came free, revealing a plug at the end the size and shape of an American football.

She stood, but before she could take a step, her feet slid from under her, and she toppled backwards. The sand was funneling out.

"Rika," David yelled.

A low, crunching noise made her look up. The block was moving.

"Blue, help us!" David vaulted over the ledge and dived.

Frantically she rolled onto her stomach and belly-crawled against the flow. But it was like pushing on water. She kept sinking. Kicking desperately, she stretched out to David. His hands clamped her wrists. But now they were both sinking.

With a sound like grating millstones, the block picked up speed. She spit sand from her mouth. They'd drown in it if the block didn't crush them first.

David slid closer to her down the rushing funnel. Their eyes locked. His face would be the last thing she saw. She clutched his wrists as tightly as she could.

A massive force drove into her. The relentless block, ramming them down. Then she felt herself move upward, plowing against the flow.

Blue had hold of David's ankles. Bellowing like a wounded buffalo, he hauled backwards, dragging David and her on their stomachs.

The block drove them sideways. Like a giant ram, it was closing the window and would shear off anything on the ledge.

Which right now was David.

Then he was out. But she was still in.

With panic in his eyes, he let go of her hands.

"No," she cried, petrified he was abandoning her.

But he leaned in and grabbed the waist of her jeans. He pulled her onto the ledge and, with a final heave, tumbled her out, into his lap.

She looked back as the huge stone ground past the window. Then she buried her face in David's neck.

"What the hell were you doing?" Blue said.

She twisted to see him hitching up his trousers, an ogre who'd sprouted angel's wings. "Blue, if you hadn't—"

"You dipsticks deserve each other." He wrinkled his nose, then tilted his head back and sniffed the air. "Do you smell that?"

Now she did. A waxy, floral scent like those candles the English burned at Christmas. Snatching the lantern, she rushed to the end of the landing. The stairs were clear. They led to a rectangular opening in the ceiling of the passage. The odor, now stronger, seemed to spill from the opening like an invisible fog. "It's coming from up there."

She took the stairs two at a time, but halted short of the top. This was the most sacred part of the whole tomb. She smoothed her shirt, straightened her posture, then raised the lantern. Pulse thudding in her ears, she climbed a few more steps, and poked her head through the opening ...

... into a sight so stunning she felt paralyzed.

The burial chamber was pristine. Tiye's sarcophagus rested on a low, stone platform in the center. At the corners of the platform, four golden statues spread their arms out protectively. Six bronze tripods for oil lamps ringed the platform, well back from it. Beyond them, in the light from her lantern, the walls fairly shimmered with murals so dazzling they could have been painted yesterday.

"What do you see?" David called from below.

She climbed the remaining steps to let him and Blue come in.

"Holy Christ." David came up next to her. "This is fabulous."

Slack-jawed, Blue just gaped.

The ceiling, painted in the traditional sky motif with gold stars on a deep blue background, reflected a cobalt hue over the whole room, a hue that accentuated the red granite sarcophagus and its golden guardians.

Blue crossed himself. "It's like a chapel."

More like the holy of holies in an Egyptian temple, the innermost sanctum where the god itself resided.

David touched her shoulder. "You're crying."

She blinked and realized she was.

He turned to Blue. "Why don't you and I go check on that stone block."

"Huh? Oh. Yeah, okay."

As the scuffing of their boots receded down the stairs, Rika placed the lantern on the floor and squatted against the near wall, arms around her knees. She felt overwhelmed, as though gods she'd denied had forgiven her faithlessness and showered her with blessing.

A dark corner of her psyche had always feared that, if she found this room, something would be wrong. The sarcophagus would have been opened, the roof would have collapsed, it would be a fake burial chamber, the real one hidden elsewhere. Yet it was all here, more perfect than she'd ever dreamed.

Under her gaze, the sarcophagus seemed to dissolve. She saw Tiye lying peacefully within, beautiful, majestic, graceful even in repose. *I have found you.*

Rika shut her eyes. When she opened them, the sarcophagus was once again impenetrable granite. She pushed herself up and walked to a corner of the stone platform on which it rested. The statue next to her, like the other three, was child-sized. She touched one of the arms and felt the coolness of solid gold. The cartouche atop its head ... Rika squinted at the name. Sitaten?

Sitaten, or Sitamun as people called her now, was Tiye's first daughter, the one Tiye's husband had married as the third of his six known wives.

Then it dawned on Rika. She checked the statue at the next corner. Baketaten. Yes. For her burial, Tiye had replaced the four traditional protective goddesses—Nephthys, Neith, Isis, and Serket—with four of her own daughters. Rika couldn't help smiling. How characteristic of the woman, the child-queen who dedicated her life to revolution.

As I have dedicated mine. Rika stepped up to the sarcophagus and laid a hand on its lid. "I wish I could see your face."

With a start, she pulled away. The lid wasn't cold. She ran her palms over it. Nowhere was it cold. But the side of the sarcophagus was cold as stone. Could it be?

She scratched at a corner of the lid and felt her nail catch. Wood.

"David!" She dashed to the head of the stairs. "David, Blue, come up here."

"What's wrong?" David hollered.

"The sarcophagus," she said as he and Blue clomped up the steps behind bobbing light beams. She led them onto the platform. "The lid is painted to look like granite. But it's wood. I think two people can lift it."

David felt around the top, then peered at the edge. When he pushed sideways on the lid, it budged just a hair. "I'll be damned. Blue, you take that end, I'll take this one."

Blue looked at her as if she were about to dive off a cliff. "You sure you wanna do this?"

"Positive."

"Come on," David told him. When Blue was in place, David bent his knees and dug the heels of his hands under the lid's edge. "Ready? Lift."

With a creak, the lid came up, unleashing an intense dose of the same flowery odor they'd smelled before.

Blue sneezed.

"Set the lid over there." David cocked his head toward a row of green faience urns lined against the back wall.

She hadn't noticed the urns before. They resembled Greek amphorae without the handles. As David and Blue lowered the lid to the floor, Rika stepped up to the sarcophagus.

Nested inside, radiant against the dark red stone, lay a golden coffin. It depicted Tiye in high relief, lying peacefully with her arms crossed over her chest. She was clad in full court regalia, rendered in gold cloisonné with glass paste and colored stones. She gazed up with eyes of painted ivory so realistic Rika found them unsettling.

Blue clutched the lip of the sarcophagus, his knuckles white. "It's just like Tut's."

Rika barely heard him. "Would you raise the coffin lid?"

"How?" David asked. "We'd need a crane to lift that much gold."

"No. If it's like Tutankhamun's, it's gold sheet over wood."

David arched his eyebrows, then turned to Blue. "Let's give it a try."

"I'd rather not." Blue fidgeted. "There'll be nothing but a body wrapped in bandages. Why don't we just leave the dead in peace?"

"I have to see her." Reaching into the sarcophagus, Rika grasped Tiye's effigy under the elbows. "David, help me."

"Ah, hell." Blue shouldered her aside, his lips tightened in reluctant resignation.

With David gripping the feet, the two men lifted.

A cracking sound told her the lid had budged, although she saw no movement.

"It's coming," David said. Tendons stood out in his neck.

A longer cracking sound, like plywood ripping, and the foot end rose. Then the head end.

David edged sideways. "Set it over there next to the first one."

As the lid cleared the sarcophagus, Rika moved in with the lantern and stared in shock.

Chapter 35

Something reddish brown filled the coffin. It looked like solidified blood. As Rika bent closer, her heart faltered. Protruding from the dull, flat substance were the skeletal remains of two small hands. No linen wrapping. Just bones.

The hands curled downward, as if crossed over the chest, exposing the backs and knuckles, while the fingertips and wrists remained hidden below the opaque surface.

"Looks like two friggin' tarantulas," Blue said.

David leaned over the coffin's lip. "What the hell did they do to her?"

In a flash, Rika knew. "Hold this." She gave Blue the lantern, then reached into the coffin and touched the surface. It felt like beeswax. She tapped the surface and got a hollow sound. The wax wasn't completely solid. She pressed on it, felt some give, and pressed harder. With an ease that startled her, the surface broke. When she held up her hand, thimbles of pale, honey-colored liquid coated her fingers. A droplet fell back in the coffin. "A bath of oils, just like the papyrus said."

"Of course." David beamed at her. "Now it's obvious what happened. Evaporation solidified the surface and formed a wax seal that prevented further evaporation. But it also reduced the volume, which is why her knuckles are exposed. Look here." He pointed to a band of reddish stain that rimmed the inside of the coffin just above the wax. "That's the original level."

"You think her knuckles are bones because of exposure?" Blue asked. "That maybe the rest of her is … you know."

Please, yes. With trembling hands, Rika pressed again on the wax. It broke like a thin layer of ice over water. She pushed the shards aside, moving carefully upward from the chest area until she reached the head of the coffin. There she paused, took a breath, and spread the shards wide.

Her jaw dropped.

Just below the surface lay a face so bloated with blisters she could hardly tell it was a woman. The nose had split open. The lips had drawn back, exposing yellowed teeth in a hideous grin. The bulbous ears appeared to have bled, leaving dark brown clouds in the amber liquid. Worst of all, one eye was open, an uncannily lucid eye that seemed to look up at Rika in pleading recognition.

"Don't touch her!" David pulled Rika away from the coffin, tore off his T-shirt, and used it to rub her hands. "Blue, pour some of that lantern fuel on my shirt!"

"Fuck." Blue unscrewed the lantern's filler cap and sloshed some fuel onto David's shirt. "Is it leprosy?"

"Not unless lepers bleed from the ears."

What had happened to Tiye? Rika couldn't take her eyes off the poor woman's face. What horrible thing had— With a start, she realized something was rubbing her hand. She blinked David into focus. "What are you doing?"

"Getting the oil off your hands."

She jerked them free. "Why?"

"Can't you see? She had a disease. A bad one. And you've just exposed yourself to it." He tossed his shirt aside and grabbed her arm. "Come on. You need antiseptic and antibiotics. Fast."

No, there had to be another explanation. "They're just blisters. Maybe she was in a fire."

"Look at her!"

Shocked at the harshness of his tone, she glanced again at the ghastly face in the coffin. "I didn't touch her." At least she didn't think she had.

"It doesn't matter." David grasped her shoulders. "Don't you get it? If the oil preserved her flesh, then it's probably preserved the pathogen. So the oil, itself, is now infected."

Oh, no. She looked at her palms and felt suddenly woozy. Were the germs already inside her?

#

Quiet as a thief, Major Hassam crept down the last few stairs, stepped onto a landing, and peeked around the corner. Pitch dark. He wanted to switch his flashlight back on, but that would make him an easy target if the terrorists were armed and had heard him coming down that damned endless stairway. He withdrew and turned to the nearly invisible figures on the steps behind him— Samir, followed by Hagazy Masud with bound wrists and a gagged mouth, followed by Malik who cupped the head of his flashlight in one hand to reduce the beam.

"Stay here," Hassam whispered. "If you hear gunshots, push the boy over the side and return fire. I'll be on the floor, so don't shoot below waist level." Hassam's faith was in Malik, who carried an AK-47 as well as a pistol in a belt holster. Samir, unqualified in automatic weapons, had a pistol stuffed in the front pocket of his khaki shorts where it was more likely to blow his balls off than be of any real help. But at least it would make noise.

Ready to drop at the first hint of ambush, Hassam stole around the corner and stepped in sand. *Sand?* His grip tightened on his pistol. Could it be a trap? Cautiously he shuffled forward, feeling his way along the right-hand wall and plowing sand with his shoes to stay on solid footing. The sand thinned out, and in another few steps the floor ended. More stairs down or a deadly drop-off? He felt the edge with his foot but couldn't tell. He ran his hand along the wall. It ended, also. *Khara.* No choice but to use his light.

Crouching, he leveled his pistol into the darkness. With his left hand, he held the flashlight far out from his body and toggled it on.

Merciful Allah. Gold, jewels. Everywhere he looked, he saw treasure heaped upon treasure. His mouth went dry. His hand shook, making the light beam jiggle as he swept it over the room. The wealth of sultans.

All for the taking.

But where were the terrorists? Maybe hiding behind the chests. Lying in wait.

Keeping his eyes on the room and his pistol at the ready, he backtracked to the landing. "Malik, come with me. Samir, there're some steps at the end of this passage. Take the boy there, put a gun to his head, and wait. If I tell you to shoot him, do it."

"But, sir—"

"Do it, or I'll shoot *you*."

Samir looked miserable, the gutless pussy. He drew his pistol, leaving his balls intact, and pushed Hagazy Masud ahead of him until they reached the short flight of stairs at the end of the passage.

Hassam beckoned Malik to his side. "Either the terrorists are hiding in this room or there's another room they've gone to. The first thing you and I do is split up and search for them behind all these chests and statues. Assume they're armed."

Malik nodded.

"Do it quietly," Hassam cautioned. "If we don't find them here, I want to surprise them wherever they've gone."

It took only five minutes to confirm the terrorists weren't hiding in this room and to discover the stairway between the statues leading up to where they must be. During those minutes, Hassam's plan crystallized like a vision from heaven. Take the terrorists alive. Put them to work carrying up treasure. Fill the Land Cruiser—fuck that American van. When the Land Cruiser was full, have Malik shoot the others. Then shoot Malik.

Like an infusion of young blood, new vigor swelled Hassam's muscles. Screw the top-floor office. Screw the whole damned Egyptian bureaucracy and their spineless efforts to placate the fundamentalists. Let them wallow in their own dithering, bow their own heads to the Islamic sword. He was moving to France, to the Riviera. He would take his son and precious daughter, but his wife could stay and snore in someone else's ear. He'd live like a king, have a harem of doting concubines, and never look back.

All for the price of the bullet he would put in Malik's head.

Distant voices broke into his musing. The terrorists were coming down the stairs. In a flash of inspiration, he conceived a theatrical touch. It would never have occurred to him in his old life, but it suited perfectly the panache of the new Hosni Hassam. He motioned Malik to turn off his light, then doused his own and slipped behind one of the statues flanking the terrorists' route down. This would be fun.

#

Petrified that what happened to Tiye would happen to her, Rika descended the stairs two at a time, her way lit by the nearly-empty lantern Blue carried as he brought up the rear behind David and herself. Her hands felt desiccated and smelled of lantern fuel from David's scrubbing. But even though he'd acted fast, some of the oil had probably soaked into her skin. Could modern antibiotics kill germs so ancient, germs they weren't designed for? How much time did she have to get treatment?

At the bottom of the steps, she turned into the treasury and waited anxiously between the flanking statues for David and Blue. When the lantern's glow appeared around her feet, she headed for the stairwell. Suddenly, a light beam lit up two men in the vestibule. One held a pistol to—

Rika's mouth fell open. "Hagazy?"

"At last we meet," said a man's voice from behind her to the left.

She whipped around but saw no one.

"Get back!" David grabbed for her, but a gunshot kicked up sparks between his feet and hers.

A low chuckle then, "Come in slowly. All of you. Stand in the center of the room."

Raw terror iced her bones. She knew that voice. "Major Hassam."

In an amused tone, Hassam said, "You have two choices. Obey my orders, or die."

Rika's mind raced back to hostage training: cooperate meekly, assess the situation, and create an opportunity. She walked obediently to the monumental statue of Tiye and beckoned David and Blue to follow. The situation was grim. Confined space. Nowhere to run. Hagazy was bound and gagged, which meant he wasn't on Hassam's side, but he was neutralized as a potential ally. That left them facing two armed men. Rika swallowed to wet her throat. Bad odds but not entirely insurmountable.

Hassam stepped from behind a statue. "Malik."

To Rika's left, another flashlight switched on. A gorilla of a man, almost the size of Blue, came out of the shadows with a cruel grin and an AK-47. Her heart sank. Their odds—her odds—had shrunk to near zero.

David, shirtless, moved in front of her. "Look, Major, I don't know what you think we've done—"

Malik backhanded him with his rifle barrel, striking David in the jaw and knocking him to his knees.

Rika lunged instinctively for the barrel, but Malik's flashlight crashed down on her head in a staggering burst of stars.

Blue caught her elbow.

She gritted her teeth against the brain-jarring pain in her skull.

"That bastard's mine," Blue whispered.

Holding his chin, David looked up at Blue. "I want him."

"Malik," Hassam snapped, "you broke the damn light."

Malik shook his flashlight. Glass tinkled to the floor. He peered into the dark lens, tossed the light aside, and picked up David's.

Big and dumb, Rika concluded. Possibly the weak link. Then she recognized him. The burglar her brother had knocked out in her hotel room. Same gray slacks and brown shoes, only now the suit coat was gone and he stank like a boar in rut. Something she hadn't noticed when he was unconscious was that his right eye was opaque. Her spirits lifted slightly. When an opportunity came—if it came—she'd attack from his right.

Her head throbbed, but Rika refused to grant Hassam the satisfaction of seeing her rub the bump she felt rising. For the same reason, she let David struggle to his feet unassisted. She turned baleful eyes on Hassam, then stopped herself. *Be meek.* Forcing her shoulders to droop, she asked, "What do you want?"

"That's better." Hassam came closer, his pistol pointed at her chest. "Cooperate and you might live. Samir, untie the boy."

Rika twisted around to appraise the man called Samir. Thin, balding, with a bookish face more befitting a scholar than a thug. He untied Hagazy, then stood squirming as though his safari shirt itched from too much starch. Possibly a weaker link than Malik. She let her hopes rise another notch.

"Miss Rika." Hagazy rushed up to her. "I do not tell them. But they come to here."

He must have told them. Hassam wouldn't be here otherwise. But Hagazy had only heard "Seddenga." They were six kilometers from Seddenga. She looked at Hassam. "How did you find us?"

His lips curled derisively. "Your wheel marks, of course."

They'd covered their wheel marks. Blue had insisted on— *Oh, no.* The memory struck her like a punch in the stomach. Her return from Seddenga, when she was so frustrated she'd barreled right through the berm and hadn't even thought about sweeping her tracks.

Hassam's sneer changed to a satisfied grin, as if he read the guilt on her face. "Criminals always make mistakes."

"We're not criminals," Blue said.

"Silence!" Hassam brought up his pistol in both hands. He aimed it at each of them in turn, ending with the black hole of its barrel staring directly at her. "There is one rule here. I speak, you obey. The penalty for not obeying is death. Do you understand?"

Rika tore her eyes from his trigger finger and exhaled slowly. A reprieve, no matter how temporary, was still a reprieve. She looked at David, who rubbed the ugly red abrasion on his jawbone as he glared at Hassam. Blue, the lantern still in one hand, had wrapped his other arm around Hagazy's trembling shoulders. She nodded compliantly to Hassam. "We understand."

In Arabic Hassam addressed his henchmen. "We can't take all of this stuff. We have to consolidate the best things. I'll choose. Samir, you direct the repacking. The terrorists will do the work. Malik, you stand back and keep them covered."

Samir wrung his hands. "We're taking it to the museum, right?"

For a moment, Hassam shut his eyes, as if he couldn't believe the man's idiocy. "On second thought, Samir, go up to the top and lower the winch cable on that Land Cruiser. And find some rope we can use for slings on the heavy stuff."

"But I thought you wanted—"

"Do as I tell you!"

Seeming to wilt, Samir tramped into the vestibule and out to the stairwell.

Hassam turned his attention back to her. "Open all of the boxes."

Rika strained to think rationally. With manpower now four-to-two, maybe they could increase their odds by frustrating Hassam into dropping his guard. Hoping his English was more limited than hers, she turned to David and Blue. "Humdrum appurtenances. Informal attire, culinary paraphernalia."

David squinted at her. Then comprehension gleamed in his eyes. To Blue, he said, "You twig?"

"Shut up!" Hassam waved his pistol. "Open the boxes."

Moving slowly to bait his impatience, Rika lifted the lid of a gold-covered chest containing woolen robes and cotton gowns. From a nearby chest, David pulled out two dinner platters. Next to him, Blue held up the mummified duck.

"You think you are clever?" Apparently deciding to choose for himself, Hassam pointed to one of the two chests of *ushebti*. When she and David opened it, their captor snarled like a rabid dog. He kicked another chest. "This one."

Safe again. It was the library of papyruses.

Hassam's face went livid. He stomped his foot inside the chest.

"No," Rika screamed. All that knowledge, trampled to confetti.

He whirled on her. "Open one more box without gold, and I give you to Malik." In Arabic, he said, "Malik, you want this bitch?"

The ape's leer oozed down her like pus from a boil. He rubbed his crotch.

Bile stung Rika's throat. Had all her efforts come to this? To be raped, or worse, and then die of a blistering disease that exploded her ear drums?

"Here." David yanked open a jewelry case. "Here's your gold."

Hassam lifted his foot from the chest of trampled papyruses and sidestepped to where David stood with the open jewelry case. "Now we make progress." He stabbed his index finger at her. "Carry this box to the stairs and wait there. Malik will go with you." Then he swept his pistol over David, Blue, and Hagazy. "You three, show me more gold." In Arabic he told Malik, "Cover the black bitch. I'll handle these turds."

Trailed closely by Malik's goatish breathing, Rika lugged the jewelry case into the vestibule and set it just inside the landing. Hassam was no dummy. By separating her from David and Blue, he'd severed their ability to communicate, cut the heart out of their power to resist. Bereft of options, she hunkered down in the sand, her back to the wall.

Malik leaned against the opposite wall and pulled out a knife. Something crusty scabbed its blade, like dried entrails from the last creature he'd gutted. "Me and you," he said, "will have a good time."

She shuddered at memories of the atrocities Ethiopians had inflicted on Eritrean females. Accounts circulating in the caves said the women endured bravely. She doubted she could. The best she might do was gouge out his eyes, pop them like grapes with her thumbs. Make him kill her quickly. At least she wouldn't suffer the horrible death that had befallen Tiye.

Hagazy brought another chest. Bending to set it next to her, he said in English, "From Mister David. Look under."

"*Inchev*," Malik snorted, Arabic for "shut up."

Hagazy mouthed, "*Kol khara*," Eat shit. He repeated, "under," and returned to the treasury.

As Malik glared after him, his foggy eye toward Rika, she nudged the chest with her hand. It slid relatively easily on the sand, revealing something that looked like a handle made from antler. *Antler?* Adrenalin surged through her. David had sent her Tiye's razor.

Quickly, Rika covered the handle with sand. The key was silence. If she could slice through Malik's esophagus, he wouldn't be able to yell. Then she'd grab his AK and take out Hassam. But to make this work she had to get Malik into arm's reach.

Digging her fingers into the sand around the razor's handle, she summoned her filthiest gutter Arabic. "Only ball-less eunuchs have to get their thrills with a knife. Is that your problem, fish-eye? Can't get it up, so you've got to use a knife?"

Malik pushed himself off the wall. "*Sharmoota*." Whore.

"Oooh. Such a big man—when the girl's helpless and you've got a knife for a cock. I can just see you, lying there at night, jerking off the blade."

With a low growl, Malik propped his AK against the wall. He came slowly toward her, the knife in one hand, his other flexing like a crab claw.

Her grip tightened on the razor's handle. "A thousand cocks in your ass."

Malik reached for her hair.

In a single motion, she whipped out the razor and slashed.

He howled, his head snapping back, his cheek sliced open to the teeth.

Rika launched herself, caught his knife hand at the wrist, and ploughed him onto his back. He arched upward to toss her off, but she held onto his wrist and slashed again. Blood spurted from his neck. Not enough. She hacked with the razor. *Die, you loathsome—*

Gunfire exploded in the treasury. A bullet zinged past her ear.

Jolted away from finishing off Malik, Rika rolled to the side, snatched his AK, and rolled back to use his writhing body for cover.

Hassam charged toward her, teeth bared, pistol leveled.

She took aim, but dark figures were rushing behind him. David and Blue. No clear shot. Damn, this was going to hell.

Hassam fired again.

She ducked and heard the meaty sound of bullets slapping into Malik's body. He jerked twice, then wheezed and went limp. She rolled back to the wall, hoping for a better angle on Hassam.

He bounded into the vestibule. But as she leveled the AK, David tackled him at the knees. Blue leapt over David and ripped away the pistol.

From behind, David threw his arms around Hassam's throat and gripped the collar of his shirt in both hands. He yanked down in a choke hold, tightening the collar as he dug the inside edges of his forearms into the sides of Hassam's neck. Hassam groped for David's hands, but David held firm.

Hagazy ran up and kicked Hassam in the ribs. "Bastard!"

"Hagazy, stop it. I've got him." David wrenched tighter. Hassam's eyes rolled up in his head.

Rika recognized it as a judo hold that cut off blood flow in the carotid arteries. A moment later, Hassam passed out. They were safe.

But as she got to her feet, distant shouting broke out in the stairwell.

"What's that?" David dropped Hassam's unconscious head.

Rika dashed to the entry.

With a thud, Samir hit the landing, an arrow through his neck.

"Oh, God. The Seddengans." She peered up the long stairwell. "A horde of them!" Still fairly high up but spiraling down like a long, black centipede.

"Holy shit," David breathed behind her.

As Blue joined them on the landing, an arrow ricocheted off the far wall.

"Get back," she said, pushing both men into the vestibule. Her hand came away sticky from David's chest, and she noticed bloody scrapes he must have gotten tackling Hassam onto the stone floor.

Blue wiped his face with the crook of his arm. "How many?"

"Too many." The AK-47 was notoriously inaccurate. But even if she could make every shot count, its banana clip held only thirty rounds, assuming it was fully loaded. Hassam's pistol, less accurate than the AK, had maybe three or four rounds left. "We don't have enough bullets."

"Is bad?" Hagazy asked. He stood white-faced next to Hassam's limp form, apparently on guard to deliver another kick if the man regained consciousness.

"Throw up a roadblock." David pointed into the treasury. "We take some of that furniture and start a fire on the landing. It slows them down, and we pick 'em off as they try to get past. That should scare away the others."

"Yeah," Blue said. "They don't know how many bullets we have. We could be armed to the teeth."

She closed her eyes for a second at the futility. "You don't understand. They're on a holy mission, to protect their goddess. No matter how many die, the others won't give up." She could almost feel the arrows, piercing her thighs, her chest, her hands as she tried to cover her face.

In the treasury, the lantern's light dimmed, flared once, and went out.

"Fuck," Blue muttered.

He and the others were now barely visible, shades against the crisscrossed beams of flashlights dropped haphazardly on the floor.

In the murky gloom, Hagazy whispered a prayer begging Allah to forgive his sins.

As his words trailed off, the last of Rika's strength drained out of her.

Chapter 36

*P*rotect *their goddess*. Rika glanced at the blackness of the stairwell. Was it possible? "The Seddengans are coming to protect Tiye. You said I look like her."

David squinted at her, his mouth slightly open. "Are they that primitive?"

"They're deeply devoted. They'll see what they want to see." *I hope.* "If I wear her clothes and put on one of her wigs—"

"Hang on," Blue interjected. "Are you talking about getting yourself up in fancy dress and trying to con them into thinking you're the queen?"

"Do you have a better idea?" She didn't.

"What about us palefaces? And my red beard?"

Blue had it wrong. "The rest of you have to stay out of sight. There should be no one in Tiye's tomb except Tiye."

"Can you conceal the pistol on you?" David asked.

"I don't think so."

He rolled his lips inward in apparent resignation, then took the AK from her hand. "I'll have you completely covered."

With a moan, Hassam tried to raise himself. Hagazy kicked him in the head, and Hassam went down again.

"Dammit!" David yanked Hagazy's arm. "You'll kill him."

"Fine by me," Blue said.

Rika had a better idea for what to do with Hassam, but she was too antsy to explain it now. "We're running out of time. David, Blue, we need light so they can see me. Go up to the burial chamber and bring down two of those tripods with the oil lamps.

Fill the lamps with some oil from her coffin."

"The coffin?" David said, his voice incredulous.

She felt guilty asking him. It would be better for her to get it, since she was already infected, but she had too much to do down here. "Just be careful."

Blue cocked a thumb over his shoulder. "Why not prop up a couple of those flashlights and aim them at you?"

"It has to look like the Eighteenth Dynasty. Now go, will you? We only have a few minutes." Rika's heart hammered. She couldn't afford a mistake. As David and Blue hurried away, she said to Hagazy in Arabic, "Tie Hassam's hands behind his back and gag him. Use the same rope and cloth he used on you."

Instead of flashing the grin she expected, Hagazy looked at her with the desolated eyes of a man condemned to the gallows. "Are we going to die?"

"Not if I can help it."

He glared at Hassam. "If we die, I kill him first."

"Just tie him up. But before you do, help me dump these bodies."

When they'd heaved Malik and Samir over the side, onto the sand at the bottom of the stairwell, she looked up. The Seddengans were already halfway here.

Hagazy made a whimpering sound. "So many. What if—"

She jerked him into the vestibule. "After you've secured Hassam, bring these two chests back inside and stack them with the others. And get the razor and Malik's knife. Go!"

Rika dashed into the treasury, grabbed the flashlight David and Blue hadn't taken, and started opening boxes. She pulled out a pleated linen gown, the pomegranate-colored robe, and a pair of ornate sandals. But when she unfolded the gown, it split apart in her hands. Damn. Had all of Tiye's clothes become brittle? With forced care, she laid out the woolen robe. It didn't split, but the creases where it had been folded were so deeply ingrained that the garment would never hang properly. Rising panic stuck in her throat.

Cotton. It was the softest of Egyptian fabrics. Rika opened the first trunk they'd looked in, brushed aside the garland of dry flowers, and lifted a cotton gown. Not perfect, but at least it held together and didn't show the wrinkles too badly. She tore off her boots and socks, stripped out of her shirt and jeans, then realized the gown was nearly transparent—something she'd noticed previously but forgotten. Since Egyptian women didn't wear panties, she pulled down hers and kicked them away. After stepping into the sandals, she slipped the gown over her head.

"Where do you want these?" David edged sideways into the treasury, followed by Blue, each of them carrying a tall, bronze tripod in one hand and an oil lamp in the other.

She pointed to Tiye's statue. "One on each side, about a meter in front. Put Hassam at the foot of the steps to the vestibule. Hagazy, what did you do with those chests?"

"Just here." He stood beside the two thrones near the back of the treasury, Tiye's razor in one hand, Malik's knife in his belt. As she hurried up to him, his eyes fixed on her chest which the gown did little to conceal. "If they touch you," he declared, brandishing the razor, "I cut their hands off."

She gave him a brief smile, opened a jewelry case, and found the Aten-armed necklace.

"You wanna throw those buggers for a loop," Blue said, "use the big one like the witchdoctor had."

She thought a moment. Almost certainly it wasn't the same, but if it were even close, it could have a psychological impact. She found the big pectoral pendant and hung it around her neck. "David, help me with a wig. Blue, light those lamps. Hagazy, make sure the knots on Hassam's wrists are tight."

As the oil lamps flickered to life, David placed the wig of Tiye's hair on Rika's head.

"You were careful with the oil?" she asked.

"Didn't have to be. We found some unused oil in one of those urns along the wall." He adjusted her wig, nodded approvingly, and picked up the AK. "Swear to me, if anything goes wrong, if you get even a hint that something might go wrong, you'll dive for cover."

She reached for his hand, but heard scuffing footsteps, an army of them. "Everybody, out of sight. Now!"

While David directed the others to strategic locations, she smoothed the front of her gown and stationed herself in front of Tiye's statue.

Hassam groaned. He strained against the rope binding his wrists but stopped when he saw her. His eyes widened with confusion, then narrowed in hatred.

Putting him out of her mind, Rika did her best to strike a pharonic pose, left foot slightly forward, arms straight down at her sides, chin up. The tomb seemed unbearably cold. Goose bumps prickled her arms and chest.

The shuffling footsteps grew louder, accompanied now by anxious whispers.

David would cover her, she was confident of that. But if this failed, they would all die anyway. If it succeeded, at least the others would live.

For her there was little hope. While she stood here freezing, voracious germs gnawed at her cells, multiplying, spreading their poison throughout her body. If she ever reached the medical kit, it could be too late.

Never again would she see her mother. Or the mountains of Eritrea. Never again would she lie in David's arms, except to be cradled by him in her final moments. No. She couldn't risk infecting him, or bear the thought that he might see her looking like Tiye. She would die alone.

Tears welled, but she quickly rubbed them away and resumed her rigid posture.

By the quivering light of the oil lamps, she saw the hem of a black robe above sandaled feet moving cautiously around the far side of the stairwell. She took a deep breath, but it failed to calm her. Could she cobble together enough Bedou and ancient Egyptian, salted with Tigrinya and bits of Arabic, to be understood? As the crunch of footfalls halted, she cleared her throat.

A face appeared, its dark eyes peering cautiously around the entryway wall.

Rika waited a regal moment. Then in ancient Egyptian, she said, *"Tiwy."* Come.

Chapter 37

Rika thought it was the headman but couldn't be sure. She'd seen him only obliquely, in the low light of their camp, and this fellow wasn't carrying a staff. Instead, he held the kind of double-edged gutting knife camel herders used. Still, as he stood up from a guarded crouch, his bearing suggested authority.

He moved a few tentative steps into the vestibule. Behind him, other robed figures with bows and arrows crowded onto the landing like bats in a cave. Their menacing eyes glittered in the lamp light.

Rika swallowed to moisten her throat. "Faithful men of Sadjedju, welcome."

The man's mouth fell open. He crept forward another two paces, then his hand seized his chest, his eyes wide as if he were having a heart attack. He dropped the knife, reached slowly inside the neck of his robe, and withdrew the pectoral pendant.

From this distance, it did look like a duplicate. How that was possible she had no idea. But the critical thing now was to cement this fragile connection. Imagining how Tiye would have responded, Rika nodded once.

He dropped to his knees and prostrated himself. "Divine Mother."

Relief crashed over her like tropical surf. Without moving, she fought to steady herself against the warm, dizzying sensation. "Divine Mother" said it all. She was their god.

Behind their headman, the other Seddengans jostled to prostrate themselves. "It is Tiye," murmured up the stairwell, fading from her ears as it rose.

"Listen well," she commanded. "Through all generations, you have protected me. I am pleased." She felt the words coming more easily. "Today you have prevented infidels from defiling my resting place. Only their leader survives. He lies at your feet." She paused. "He is my gift to you, for your fidelity."

The headman rose to his knees, glared at Hassam, then turned his eyes to her. "Divine Mother, a traitor threatened you once before. On the day you entered your tomb. Our ancestors dealt with him. This dog shall suffer the same fate. We ask only your blessing."

"My blessing is in the glorious light of Aten. It shines upon you always."

He bowed his head.

"Now hear my will," she told him. "Remove this man. Return to Sadjedju. Continue your holy duty, for my time is not yet come. Soon I shall cause a great thunder. It will again seal my tomb. When you hear its sound, rejoice. For then it shall be as it was before. And you shall remain the blessed of my heart."

The headman looked up at her, tears streaming from his eyes. "Divine Mother, our joy is boundless."

Rika shifted her attention to Hassam, who seemed spellbound. In Arabic, she said, "You are leaving now, major."

Hassam twisted around, dawning horror in his eyes. He rubbed his face against the stone floor in a frantic effort to work the gag out of his mouth.

"Take him," she told the headman.

He barked at the men behind him, and two Seddengans came forward. They wrenched Hassam to his feet.

Hassam struggled against them to no avail as they dragged him across the vestibule. On the landing, he looked back.

Rika gazed at him serenely. "Good-bye."

#

With a slow exhalation, David slid his finger from the trigger. He hadn't understood a word of it, but the blackrobes were gone, their footsteps receding up the stairwell. Rika still stood there, partially obscured by Tiye's statue. He wanted to rush to her. But something in her bearing told him not to move until she did.

Still bent over behind two stacked chests, he held up a hand to Blue and Hagazy, signaling them to wait. They had to give the blackrobes time to clear off, anyway, before he could get Rika up to the medical kit. God, he hoped it wouldn't be too late. He pictured that horrible face in the coffin, and raw fear crowded out his relief at being alive. Could their strongest antibiotics be any match for a pathogen that had survived for three thousand years?

Hang on. That didn't make sense. David stood. With three thousand years to feed on Tiye, why hadn't the pathogen consumed her whole body? The stains in the oil around her ears showed she still had blood in her when the progress of the disease—halted.

"Rika!" David leapt up, dashed to her, and grabbed hold of her shoulders. "I don't think you're sick. I think the pathogen's dead."

She blinked at him, as though coming out of a trance. "What?"

"I should have realized it before. The germs have to have died off thousands of years ago, or there'd be nothing left of Tiye. You're not infected."

#

Rika came back to the present with a muddled sense that David had said something momentous. Her mind replayed his words. *Not infected.*

Almost faint with relief, she closed her eyes, then slowly re-opened them. Dirt smeared David's face and his scraped chest. The bandage was missing from the wound where she'd removed the rock chip. He had several days of stubble and the most radiant smile she'd ever seen.

"You saved us," he said.

His mention of "us" untunneled her vision. There they were, Blue and Hagazy, smiling at her in the flicker of the oil lamps.

A sense of peace enveloped, and for a luxurious moment she just enjoyed it. She felt reborn. Not only reprieved from the death sentence of the oil but, even more than that, resurrected onto some higher plane of existence. The Seddengans had recognized her as their immortal god. Their faith was in *her*. And her responsibility was to them. The sacred responsibility of a goddess to her people, of the Divine Mother to all who perceived her divinity.

Rika squared her shoulders. It had come to her out of nowhere, the "great thunder." But now she knew. "We will use our remaining landmines to reseal this tomb. We will take nothing."

To her amazement, not even Blue objected. She smoothed the diaphanous gown over her body, glancing at Hagazy who seemed no longer to notice her underlying nakedness. In fact, all of the men looked at her with something approaching awe.

Among them, only David spoke. "You've changed."

Chapter 38

While he and Blue replaced the coffin's lid, David watched Rika perusing the wall paintings in the long corridor of the tomb's original entrance. Carrying one of the oil lamps and still wearing the white gown, she reminded him of a wraith gazing upon ancestral portraits in the dark hallway of a Gothic mansion.

"You with us, mate?"

David refocused on positioning the lid. But he couldn't escape an uneasy feeling that, if he tried to embrace Rika at that moment, his arms would pass right through, as though she were mist.

#

All of the scenes in this corridor depicted Tiye with her family, Tiye in her earthly life, blessed by Aten but not of his rank. She was a woman, perhaps saintly enough to stand in Aten's presence and receive the gift of rebirth, but a woman nonetheless. What made her a god—what made any god a god—were the believers.

Rika still felt that spark of divinity and, with it, a sort of mental clarity, as if years of accumulated rubbish had been swept from her mind. She'd always believed that Tiye's greatness, her legacy, lay in the enlightened society she created. But Rika now saw something equally marvelous that had been hiding in plain sight. Tiye had accomplished her revolution, one of the most radical in history, without violence.

Like Mahatma Gandhi, Tiye achieved her reforms through strength of character, force of reason, and appeal to basic instincts of human dignity and equality. She even advocated forgiving her enemies, the priests of Amun, which did border on godliness. No wonder the people loved her.

Could a similar approach work in Eritrea?

Nearly all her life Rika had believed that freedom could only come from the barrel of a gun. But a decade of warfare had won nothing. Violence bred only misery and the lust for revenge. Now she understood that. And feeding the violence with more weapons was not the answer.

Suddenly a burden lifted from Rika's shoulders, a burden she'd hardly been aware of until it was gone, but which she now recognized as guilt—the guilt of knowing her decision to leave Tiye's tomb intact meant abandoning her goal to supply "decisive" weapons to Eritrea. Her chest swelled with the pride of realizing she'd found a better solution.

In the burial chamber, David said, "Easy, don't bump it."

She turned to see him helping Blue place the wooden lid on top of the sarcophagus. He'd put his T-shirt back on, its front darkened by the oil he'd rubbed from her hands. Now that she thought about it, he, too, shunned violence. Unless it was forced upon him. His answers to conflict were rational discourse, finding common ground, and giving a little to gain a lot. Even with Hassam, who'd fully intended to kill them, David had stopped Hagazy from kicking the man.

That's what Eritrea needed: to replace the failed tactics of the past with tactics more like those employed by Tiye, and by David. It needed a leadership strong enough to admit mistakes and courageous enough to strike out in a new direction. A leadership that took the long view of life after war and saw the wisdom of adopting a strategy that could lead to peaceful coexistence, perhaps even an alliance.

"We're done in here," David called.

She looked back at the burial chamber and saw him watching her, his brow creased with worry lines in the flickering light of the oil lamps. *My love, there is nothing to worry about.*

Her love. With a rush of joy, she realized it was true. She loved him.

Blue pointed to his watch. "It's just gone four o'clock. If you wanna set those mines before dark, we'd better get a move on."

Yes, they needed to get out of here, not only to set the mines, but also to escape this confinement. She longed for the open air, for sunlight and sky. Never again would she enter a tomb.

Or live in a cave.

But before she left, she had to tell David. She walked into the burial chamber and kissed him softly.

He touched her cheek. "Thank God, you're back."

"Back?"

"I was afraid you'd passed into some other world, through a one-way gate."

She smiled. "The gate works both ways."

"Uh," Blue said behind her, "I think I'll take Hagazy up top and start collecting the mines. You folks don't be too long."

As Blue's footsteps retreated on the stairs, David looked at her guardedly.

She slid her hands around his waist. "I love you."

His eyes flickered in surprise, then searched deeply into hers, and the tension drained visibly out of him. With a soft exhalation, he wrapped her in his arms.

Rika melted into his embrace. The warmth of his body filled her with peace. She pressed her cheek to the hard pillow of his chest and heard his heart beating in rhythm with her own. The heady smell of his skin through the T-shirt both comforted and stirred her. In all of her life, nothing had ever felt so right as this perfect, precious moment.

His grip loosened, his hands rising to cradle her face. "You mean everything to me."

She looked into his eyes. When the tomb was sealed, they'd steal away and spend the whole night together. Under the stars. Just the two of them.

#

Racing against the sun, they managed to set the landmines with an hour to spare before nightfall. Rika had accepted David's recommendation that the most effective placement would be in a ring about ten meters below the top. The explosion should collapse a cone of rock from above, demolishing the upper steps and filling at least the lower third of the shaft.

Well back from the stairwell's mouth, with David, Blue, and Hagazy standing around her, she took up the two wires into which the other wires fed and prepared to touch them to the Land Cruiser's battery. It felt good to be out of that hole, to smell the hot desert air and see the brick-red glow of the canyon walls as the sun descended. It felt even better to know she had preserved the faith of the Seddengans.

"Someone's coming." David took off toward the front of the mesa.

When Rika reached his side, he was already crouched. She squatted next to him as two big trucks came rumbling through the gap. Rika's stomach tightened. They were Soviet-built Zils, the six-wheeled, stake-bed vehicles designed to transport weapons and infantry. Olive-drab canvas concealed their cargoes, and the insignia had been painted over. Sudanese army?

Then she noticed the mirrors were folded in, an Eritrean habit. *Efrem!* She sprang to her feet and waved her arms.

"What are you doing?" David shouted.

"It's my brother!"

David stood and wiped his hands on his jeans. "Fine time for the cavalry to show up."

But for Rika, the timing couldn't have been better. She foresaw a change in Eritrean policy, from more of the same to something far superior. And Efrem, who epitomized the former, should be the first to know.

As he climbed down from the first truck and a dozen of his men piled out of the back, Blue whispered beside her, "Ready when you are, love. But I only have six shots."

She saw the pistol in his hand and said, "No. It's Efrem, my brother."

"He is not happy," Hagazy muttered.

"'s never happy." But if she were persuasive, he might at

g him hike up the side of the mesa, his men behind
ked her shirt into her trousers. She would not go
'm. He could come to her.

When he topped the mesa, he gave Blue and Hagazy a quick once-over, shot a glare at David, then pointed at the second truck and said in Tigrinya, "A backhoe is the best I could do. What have you found?"

Still the pompous bastard. "Good afternoon to you, also. And speak English. These are my friends."

With a contemptuous glance skyward, he repeated in English, "What have you found?"

"A new way to end the war."

He looked confused. "Did you find the tomb?"

"Yes," she said, gesturing toward the entrance. "But we are not taking anything out of it."

"Explain."

"It's simple. First of all, I don't think we need more weapons. And second, I will not have Tiye's possessions scattered. You probably won't understand this, but she needs them."

"Have you lost your mind? Of course we need weapons. And a dead woman does not need gold."

Rika decided to take the second point first. Perhaps an analogy would help her explain. "You know who Tutankhamun is?"

"Of course."

"You only know because the contents of his tomb were not sold off to private collectors. They have been kept together in the Cairo Museum. Together, and only together, they tell a story, provide insights, captivate interest around the world. Together, they breathe life back into the young king. A king, by the way, who was far less important than Tiye."

"What does this have to do with the war?"

"It's greater than the war. Maybe one day, if Sudan is ever blessed with a more enlightened government, I will reveal the tomb's location, and they can create for Tiye what the Cairo Museum created for Tutankhamun."

He spat on the ground. "An enlightened government in Sudan?"

"If they follow our example." She told him about the long view, about starting now to lay the groundwork for a future of peaceful coexistence with Ethiopia, about a strategy based on compromise, on giving a little to gain a lot, and ultimately ⌐

mutual forgiveness. "Just think what we could create. A society that would be a beacon to the rest of Africa. An economic alliance that would lift us out of the Third World."

He shook his head slowly, as though pitying her. "Now I do understand. Six years of the soft life in western universities have filled your head with rubbish."

"You're wrong to think I've gone soft. In actual fact, I am stronger."

"An alliance with the criminals who commit genocide against us?" His pitying look hardened to disgust. "You are worse than soft. You are insane. And totally unfit for *any* role in Eritrea."

"The Politburo will think differently."

"The Politburo will have you shot."

"How typical that you think of violence before reason," she said. "That's why you're just a soldier."

"A commander!"

"Who, unlike me, was not chosen for any position in our future government." Granted, the Politburo would be skeptical of her ideas at first. But the Professor had declared six years ago that Eritrea would not be ruled by military commanders. So why, she'd put to him, should military men lead the struggle for independence? What Eritrea needed more than courage on the battlefield was intelligence at the negotiating table. And she was more than ready to help. Even to lead. "We'll see what the Professor has to say."

With dripping sarcasm, Efrem informed her, "The Professor does not speak much anymore. He has been dead for two years."

Dead? She shut her eyes as the shock sank in. Why hadn't she heard? He'd been the revolution's philosopher, her ally in spirit, the one man who might embrace Tiye's wisdom and change course. Without him, she felt abandoned. She didn't stand a chance.

Or did she?

W⁷ better to champion Tiye's philosophy than herself? "⊤ ⅋n replace him."

ʹu are a failure. You have failed in your assignment, ʹiled—"

ʹnock it off," David said, stepping in front of

"Get out of my way, American. Or I will crush you where you stand."

Rika pulled David back, then faced off with her brother. If the only things Efrem understood were authority and force, then for now, at least, that's how she'd have to deal with him. "You will crush nobody. What you *will* do is comprehend one thing. I am in command here."

Efrem glanced around the site before turning back to her. His lips twitched in that miserable excuse he had for a smile. "You are hereby relieved of your ... 'command.' "

"I wouldn't try it, if I were you."

"You are not me. You are no longer competent even to be one of them." He inclined his head toward the soldiers, all of whom had holstered pistols and most of whom carried AK-47s slung over their shoulders. "While you dream of forgiving mass murderers, we will load our trucks with whatever I choose."

"You will not!"

As if she no longer existed, he turned to his men, barked, "Come," and led them toward the Land Cruiser and the stairwell beyond.

Jaw clamped, Rika stalked after them. He had left her no choice. Against all his armed men, she had only one weapon. And she would use it. At the Land Cruiser, she stopped and picked up the two wires. "Efrem, I am about to seal the tomb. I will do so regardless of where you are."

He looked at her over his shoulder, did a double-take, then seemed to notice for the first time the pair of black wires running along the ground.

His men broke out in nervous whispers, obviously now recognizing a danger all Eritrean soldiers were trained to spot—a booby trap.

Efrem sneered at her. "You would not."

She wrapped one wire around the battery's negative pole.

Efrem turned on his good leg and continued limping toward the stairwell. His men waited in a hushed cluster. They might not understand English, but they plainly understood that this was a life-and-death battle of wills.

"Rika." David materialized in her peripheral vision. "We can talk him out of it."

"Do not try." She poised the other wire, so close above the positive pole that David wouldn't dare grab for her hand.

David spun around and shouted, "Efrem, stop. I know this look of hers. She's not bluffing."

One of the soldiers, apparently reading her determination, unshouldered his AK and leveled it at her.

"Shit." David stepped into the line of fire. "Efrem! You can't win this."

But Efrem kept walking.

Rika pictured Tiye's golden-eyed statue striding toward Aten, then the queen lying helplessly, grotesquely in her coffin. Hope and reality.

Like the hope that her brother would see reason and the reality that he would not. He was now barely twenty meters from the stairwell. At the rate he was walking, just seconds remained before he'd be too close to survive the explosion.

An arid wind swept down from the cliffs, flapping her shirt as if urging her to action.

Rika touched the wire to the Land Cruiser's battery.

A massive blast jolted the ground. Rocks shot into the air. Efrem stumbled backwards.

She heard shouts in Tigrinya of "Duck" and "Take cover." But she did not duck. In the chaos of flying debris and rocks raining down and soldiers scattering, she stood tall and at peace.

Rest, my queen.

David pushed her against the Land Cruiser and covered her with his body.

As sand and grit pelted them, she saw again the smile on Tiye's face when the queen's statue welcomed her into the treasury. The vision filled her with the same warm glow Tiye clearly felt at the sight of Aten.

You will see Him again.

"Damn." David raised himself from covering her. "That was close."

When Rika looked back, dust roiled in great plumes above a crater where the stairwell's entrance had been. "She is safe now."

"You bitch!" Efrem yelled in Tigrinya. He struggled to his

feet, waving his men aside as though their help would diminish his manhood. "You're not my sister. I disown you. Eritrea disowns you. You're a traitor!"

His words stung. Everything she'd done, everything she wanted to do, was for Eritrea and her family. But he would never understand that.

Fists clenched, Efrem shook with more rage than she'd ever seen in him before. "You almost killed me."

"If I'd wanted to kill you, you'd be dead."

"What's he saying?" David asked.

She swallowed a lump in her throat, then shrugged. "Nothing important. He's just angry."

"Forget him." David put a gentle hand on her arm. "You did the right thing."

Blue nodded agreement. "We're on your side, love. You need us to do anything, just say it."

"Your brother is bad man." Hagazy hitched up his pants and stuck out his chest. "I will tell him you are—"

"No." She'd had enough shouting. And while she'd said Efrem's outburst meant nothing, it still stung. As he mustered his men for retreat and headed back down the mesa, she couldn't quell an ache of sorrow in her chest. Yes, she'd "done the right thing" by Tiye. But at the cost of her only remaining brother.

Family versus country. Did it have to be that way?

Halfway to the trucks Efrem hollered over his shoulder, "I still know where it is."

Bluster. It had to be. How could he even think of getting into the tomb after what he'd just witnessed?

She wanted to rush down and try once again to convince him that negotiation was the key to victory. But the sight of his back, his determined if limping step, told her it would be useless. She'd lost him.

"You okay?" David asked.

"I'll be back in a moment." What she needed now was time to think, to regroup.

She walked to the front of the mesa. At the edge, directly above the original entrance to Tiye's tomb, she gazed out through the gap at the life-giving Nile, now darkened by dusk the way her heart felt darkened by the dusk of her relationship with Efrem. He'd never listened to her. Was that always the lot of little sisters with their elder brothers? No. Tiye's elder brother had revered her. But from Efrem, all Rika had ever received—when he bothered to acknowledge her at all—was condescension. And now hatred.

Tiye had also been the target of hateful attack, from Amun priests bent on destroying her. But she had triumphed, thanks to her husband and to the faithful.

My faithful are David, Blue, and Hagazy. She looked back at them. Three men. Three different nationalities. All of them as dirty and haggard as refugees, but beautiful to her. Each had played a crucial role in bringing her to this stage of her life. She trusted them, which she could no longer say of anybody else. And she loved David every bit as much as Tiye had loved her pharaoh.

At that moment, Rika sensed another presence. Looking up, she saw Nekhbet circling beneath the evening's first stars. Head cocked, the vulture goddess peered down at her as if asking, *What now?*

It was a question Rika could not yet answer. But new strength coursed through her veins. Peering out through the gap, she looked beyond the Nile to the far horizon.

The horizon where Aten always rises.

Epilogue

With no royal successor to ascend the throne in the wake of the young pharaoh's death, the kingdom was again in danger of falling into chaos. The fragile truce between the priests of Amun and followers of Aten was breaking down. The two factions were once more at each other's throats.

As much to save the new faith as to preserve the empire, Ay gathered support from both sides and maneuvered himself onto the Eternal Throne of Horus.

For four years Ay ruled wisely. But he was now a very old man. He had little taste for military matters and came to rely upon his commander, Horemheb, to conduct foreign affairs. Horemheb was staunchly in the Amunite camp, and when the priests sensed Ay's growing weakness, they encouraged the commander to seize power and rid the land of this last vestige of the Aten heresy. He did.

Horemheb ruled for twenty-eight years. During that time, he destroyed or defaced nearly every monument created by Tiye's sons.

When he died, the Eighteenth Dynasty of Pharaohs, the pinnacle of Egyptian civilization, died with him.

\#

In 1993, ten years after the events of this story, Eritrea finally won its independence from Ethiopia. Freedom came not through conciliation, but through force of arms.

\#

Today ground-penetrating radar is used for all the applications David envisioned, and many more. It has proven especially useful in archaeology.

About the Author

John Oehler has spent much of his life overseas, beginning in 1966 with two years as a Peace Corps Volunteer in Nepal. His time in the Himalayan kingdom immersed him in a culture of Hindu gods and Buddhist monks, gave him breathtaking opportunities to trek into the high mountains, reduced him to a scrawny 150 pounds, and ignited his passion for foreign lands.

He subsequently earned a Ph.D. in Geology at UCLA and spent the next three years working in Australia where he travelled extensively through the harsh beauty of the Outback. Upon returning to the United States, he went to work for a major oil company, first in research, then in international exploration. The latter took him to about fifty countries and fueled his writing with quirky characters, exotic settings, and cultural contrasts.

All of John's novels have originated from personal experience. While living in London, he became interested in the business and culture of perfumes, an interest that blossomed during later visits to the renowned perfume school in Versailles and led to his novel APHRODESIA. While working in Egypt, he spotted a potential way to break into the Egyptian Museum in Cairo. Combining that with a longstanding attraction to Egyptology gave rise to his novel PAPURUS. His work in Venezuela, combined with his vacations there in the jungles and highlands, inspired his novel TEPUI. During a Christmas vacation in Prague, he spent an afternoon at a monastery where he learned about their collection of "forbidden books." His imagination took over and created his latest (2019) novel EX LIBRIS.

John has an abiding love of animals, strong interests in art, history, and science, and a hunger for challenging experiences. Writing gives him a chance to combine all of these into page-turners that keep readers thinking long after they finish the final chapter.

Also by John Oehler

Ex Libris
New Release (September 2019)

A chilling thriller of international deception, worldwide peril, and soul-searching choices.

Dan Lovel, a former agent with the US Diplomatic Security Service, has saved lives, taken lives, and enraged a lot of people who still wish him dead. He now lives off the grid, recovering stolen art and destroying counterfeits. Shortly before Christmas, Astrid Desmarais, a World Bank executive, asks him to steal five books from the locked collection of "Forbidden Books" in a monastery in Prague. The very existence of the books she wants has remained secret for centuries. Finally persuaded by Astrid's appeals to his ancestry, Dan reluctantly agrees. But from the moment he enters the monastery, events spiral out of control. Dan must draw on the life he tried to bury as he faces decisions that pull at every fiber of his being.

"What a terrific read! From page 1 this book is an irresistible

page turner... The plot (and sub plots) are exciting and fast paced, and the story telling is second to none. Loved, loved, loved this book! I would rate it a 10 out of 10!"

"Couldn't put this page turner down! The action pulses through vividly described locales -- Cayman Islands, Prague and Paris. The characters are well drawn and compelling."

"Fantastic book! I absolutely loved the characters and action in this tightly woven, thrilling tale. The descriptions of the various locations made me want to hop a plane and check out the places for myself. The meals and wines described made my mouth water. A plot that's imaginative and fascinating. I was hooked from the beginning and zipped right through till the end."

Tepui

In 1559, forty-nine Spaniards exploring a tributary of the Orinoco River reached a sheer-sided, cloud-capped mountain called Tepui Zupay. When they tried to climb it, all but six of them were slaughtered by Amazons. Or so claimed Friar Sylvestre, the expedition's chronicler. But Sylvestre made many bizarre claims: rivers of blood, plants that lead to gold.

Jerry Pace, a burn-scarred botanist struggling for tenure at UCLA, thinks the friar was high on mushrooms. Jerry's best friend, the historian who just acquired Sylvestre's journal, disagrees. He plans to retrace the expedition's footsteps and wants Jerry to come with him. Jerry refuses, until he spots a stain between the journal's pages—a stain that could only have been left by a plant that died out with the dinosaurs. Now he has to find that plant.

But the Venezuelan wilderness does not forgive intruders. Battered and broken, they reach a remote Catholic orphanage where the old prioress warns of death awaiting any who would venture farther. But an exotic Indian girl leads them on, through piranha-infested rivers and jungles teaming with poisonous plants, to Tepui Zupay—the forbidden mountain no outsider has set eyes on since the Spaniards met their doom.

> "This is the kind of book you are always hoping to find and read. Exciting and grabs you right from the start and carries you along on a great adventure, mystery with historical insight, characters you can relate to and become emotionally involved with and just a little love interest.".

> "Sumptuous reading. Definitely one of my new favorite authors of historical adventure. Intelligent and smooth prose--a really delightful read!"

> "If You Want to Go on a Great Adventure - This is it! I loved the story and ...it is obvious why this novel won an award".

> "Could not put it down! Very exciting story. The setting was realistic, the plot pulled you along (relentlessly!) and you really cared what happened to the characters."

Aphrodesia

Great perfumes have always had one purpose—to seduce. Today, as in the past, a true aphrodisiac is the Holy Grail of the perfumer's art.

Eric Foster, a student at the world's top perfume school, creates a scent based on the fragrance the Queen of Sheba wore to seduce King Solomon. The result is an aphrodisiac of astonishing potency. But when his creation is tied to an outbreak of passion-driven homicides, Eric becomes the NYPD's prime suspect, facing a charge of serial murder.

"I've never read anything like it, and highly doubt I'll ever find or read anything like it again. It's truly unique."

"A really kick-ass story, and you'll get the bonus of some truly masterful writing."

"I had not read and finished a book in over 10 years. Yet, I started this one and couldn't put it down until I was done."

"You will never again look at perfume in the same way."

"What a page-turner. Although I had never thought much about perfume, I found the story of the industry fascinating, especially when the perfume in question was an aphrodisiac! On top of all that, the sex scenes were extremely erotic!"

"A delicious story."

CPSIA information can be obtained
at www.ICGtesting.com
Printed in the USA
LVHW050534030822
725075LV00008B/349